BREAKING BAMBOO

Also by Tim Murgatroyd:

Taming Poison Dragons

Breaking Bamboo

Tim Murgatroyd

MYRMIDON

Myrmidon
Rotterdam House
116 Quayside
Newcastle upon Tyne
NE1 3DY

www.myrmidonbooks.com

Published by Myrmidon 2010

A catalogue record for this book is available from the British Library.

ISBN 978-1-905802-40-1 Hardback
ISBN 978-1905802-38-8 Export Trade Paperback

Set in 11.5/14.25pt Sabon by
Falcon Oast Graphic Art Limited,
East Hoathly, East Sussex

Printed and bound in the UK by
CPI Antony Rowe, Chippenham and Eastbourne

1 3 5 7 9 10 8 6 4 2

For Richard and Philip Murgatroyd

Peace

和平

懵

one

'Now I must tell you of a wonderful sight. North of Six-hundred-*li* Lake, on Han River, lie the Twin Cities of Nancheng and Fouzhou, staring at one another across wide waters. A hundred years ago Prefect Fu Mu-ei was granted a vision of joining these two cities in a dream, though three whole *li* of flowing river divided them. Many doughty posts were driven into the riverbed and boulders piled round them to form resolute islands. By this means a Floating Bridge was constructed, with a roadway of planks laid across a hundred flat-bottomed boats, chained one to another. So the name *Twin Cities* is as apt as *yin* and *yang*.'

from *Dream Pool Essays* by Shen Kua

竹子

Nancheng, Central China. Summer 1266.

Summer was seldom a pleasant time for Dr Shih. Monsoon and breathless heat encouraged all manner of disease, not least of the spirit. On humid nights the temporary oblivion of sleep often eluded him until dawn. So the persistent banging at his gate did not take him quite by surprise.

He lay awake beside his wife, Cao, who always slept well. Tiny beads of sweat prickled his forehead and upper lip. Thoughts far from the city, far from agreeable, made a midnight summons oddly welcome. Besides, he was used to night callers, generally fetching him to attend a difficult birth – or death.

He rose and hurried down a long, dark corridor to the medicine shop. From beneath a cheap woodcut print of the Yellow Emperor he took up a burning lamp and unbarred the door.

The man before him wore a high official's vermilion silk robes and was accompanied by lantern-bearing servants, as well as several soldiers leaning on tasselled halberds. Such callers were unusual in any part of town, but especially here. Dr Shih's shop stood in Water Basin Ward, one of the city's poorer districts. His wealthiest patients were artisans and their families. He bowed respectfully and waited for the official to speak.

'Are you Yun Shih?' demanded his visitor.

He sensed movement behind him and turned to see Cao entering the room, her long hair in disarray. Alarm crossed her soft, plump face as she recognised the man's uniform. Shih motioned her out of sight.

'I am Yun Shih, sir,' he said, sounding confident for Cao's sake. He could sense her apprehension and felt enough of his own.

Official eyes narrowed, looking him up and down.

'You are a doctor?'

'I believe so, sir.'

Still the official did not seem satisfied.

'You are younger than I expected.'

Indeed Shih did appear younger than three decades deserved. There was something restless and youthful in the frank gaze of his gentle brown eyes. Yet his dark, straight eyebrows suggested an unusually determined nature.

The official wiped his moist brow with a trailing silk sleeve.

'May I assume I am not in trouble?' asked Shih.

The official shook his head.

'His Excellency Wang Ting-bo requires you. Be ready soon.'

Dr Shih flinched slightly, then turned to where his wife hovered behind the tall maple counter of their shop.

'Go back to bed. I shall be home before dawn.'

He knew she would sit up all night sipping cup after cup of tea, waiting for him to return to Apricot Corner Court.

Once the apprentice, Chung, was roused and dressed, Dr Shih joined the official in the street. It was cooler out here than indoors.

'Who is sick, sir?' he asked.

Raucous singing and clapping drifted across the canal from Ping's Floating Oriole House. A group of neighbours, fanning themselves at a stall selling cordials, called out a polite greeting. The official silenced them with a haughty stare.

'Your patient is Wang Ting-bo's son,' he said, quietly. 'They say he is unlikely to outlive the dawn.'

Dr Shih was glad Cao had not heard that. It hardly boded well to be summoned to a sick dragon's bedside. Or even the only son of a dragon.

Nancheng city stewed in its own amusements. Dense crowds slowed the small party hurrying through the night. On Vermilion Bird Way a night market was reaching its climax before the City Watchmen ordered all sober citizens to bed by beating the drum eight hundred times.

Many had no intention of heeding the command. They passed stalls where the scents of fish fried with Sichuan spices pricked one's nostrils; tea stalls surrounded by chess players; taverns raucous with fragile fellowship. Beggars and quick-handed urchins melted into the crowd at the sight of the stern official and his armed escort. Chung, Dr Shih's portly apprentice, puffed along behind.

They reached the foot of Peacock Hill, an ancient palace complex long ago converted into a warren of government bureaux and mansions for high officials. As Dr Shih climbed the hill he surveyed the Han River below, a full three *li* wide. A sickle moon illuminated the water. On the far shore lay

Fouzhou, sister city to Nancheng, the two cities joined by a huge pontoon bridge constructed upon boats. Shih could see the lanterns of river-craft moving on the dark water like floating stars.

Soldiers guarded the gatehouse of the Prefectural compound. On seeing the official they saluted and stepped aside.

'Sir, what is the nature of the boy's malady?' asked Shih, trotting after his guide up a steep flight of marble steps. The official shrugged.

'That is for you to determine.'

Dr Shih wanted to ask why Wang Ting-bo had sent for him at all. He was a physician of low rank in the city, lacking even a degree from the Imperial Academy.

'Are other doctors treating His Excellency's son?' he asked.

The official seemed not to hear. They hurried through another gatehouse and a series of small courtyards. Shih had no time to admire the splendid pillars and gilt carvings, marble fountains or miniature gardens. They entered a large courtyard guarded by more soldiers leaning on their halberds. Servants scurried past with buckets of water. Moths and night-flies fluttered round lanterns.

'Quick!' beckoned the official.

He opened a pair of bright red doors to reveal a well-lit chamber decorated with hunting scenes. A dozen men wearing fine silks muttered in small groups. Women could be heard weeping in a side chamber, their grief brittle and artificial. In his plain clothes, Dr Shih made an awkward addition to such company. Chung was visibly shaking.

'Can these gentlemen really need your services, sir?' he whispered, in wonder.

Then the youth flushed, aware of the question's insolence. Dr Shih smiled and shook his head.

'His Excellency has packed the room with doctors so that if the boy dies one may say everything was done,' he murmured. 'There is the great Dr Du Mau himself. And over there his shadow, Dr Fung. Let us make the best of it and consider ourselves honoured.'

Dr Du Mau, a small gentleman in violet silks, noticed the newcomers and frowned. He inclined his head stiffly. Shih bowed quite low but evidently not low enough for Dr Du Mau, who exclaimed irritably: 'What? Is one of the servants sick as well?'

Several of his colleagues chuckled. It was well-known Dr Du Mau opposed allowing unqualified physicians into the guild as full members. Shih's polite smile stiffened. An official clapped his hands and the room fell silent.

'Gentlemen,' he said. 'You have all examined the patient, as well as the astrologer's report. His Excellency wishes to confer with you. Please accompany me.'

'Wait in the courtyard,' Dr Shih instructed his apprentice.

He thought it prudent to take a place at the very rear of the solemn group. This was a moment of high significance for the guild. Wang Ting-bo was the Pacification Commissioner for hundreds of *li* around, appointed to his noble position by the Son of Heaven himself. Moreover, if his son and heir died early, many calculations and plans for the future would be affected. So Dr Shih hardly blamed the good doctors for ignoring his existence – lowliness was infectious as foul air.

The Hall of Obedient Rectitude had once been a throne room for the Kings of Chu. Dozens of fat candles illuminated the audience chamber; shadows floated across painted ceilings and walls. The assembly of doctors fell to their knees before two elegant wooden chairs. One contained the Pacification Commissioner wearing his most auspicious uniform, as though death was an ambassador he must over-awe. In the other sat his wife, a plain woman past what little beauty she had once possessed.

The lady immediately gained Dr Shih's sympathy, for her thick white make-up was stained with tears. She had a double reason for grief: if the boy died, her status as First Wife would perish with him. Any concubine who gave the Pacification Commissioner a male heir might supplant her – and Dr Shih had heard rumours he preferred one of his concubines to his official wife.

Wang Ting-bo inspected the physicians. He seemed unsure what to say and blinked foolishly. Then he cleared his throat.

'Lift your heads. I do not care to talk to your hats.'

The doctors exchanged glances.

'You have all seen the boy. What is to be done? And who among you is to do it? Dr Du Mau, you are the most senior man present. Explain yourself!'

Shih became uncomfortably aware that the Pacification Commissioner's wife was staring at him. Certainly he was out of place, though he could hardly be censured for it. Then he wondered if she was behind his absurd summons.

'Your Excellency,' said Dr Du Mau. 'We are of one mind on the matter.'

His colleagues nodded regretfully. There was great authority in Dr Du Mau's tone.

'Your heir is beyond the help of earthly medicine. His essential breaths are putrid. *Yin* and *yang* fiercely oppose each other. His blood is a whirlpool of contagion. This is a sad report to make, Your Excellency, but only Heaven's intervention may save him now. I have prepared a list of suitable magicians and holy men well-skilled in such cases.'

Wang Ting-bo sank back in his chair.

'Beyond help,' he muttered. 'Dr Fung, surely you do not agree with Du Mau? And you, Dr Ku-ai? Surely something more may be attempted?'

However, these gentlemen sighed regretfully.

'Very well,' said Wang Ting-bo, tears glistening in his eyes.

Dr Shih rubbed his chin. The guild's certainty that all was lost surprised him. But, of course, every physician encountered intractable cases. Then the Pacification

Commissioner's wife caught his eye. Her gaze was cold and fierce.

'You at the back!' she cried, shrilly. 'You in blue robes! What do you say? You are Dr Yun Shih, are you not?'

He trembled slightly that she knew his name. There was a rustling of silks as heads turned.

'My Lady must forgive my stupidity,' he replied. 'I have not examined your son and so cannot comment.'

The plain woman leaned sideways in her chair to address her husband.

'Should not this one examine him as well?'

There was a long silence in the room. Dr Du Mau coughed delicately.

'My Lady, with the utmost respect, although this man is generous with his remedies for the poor, he can hardly be expected to affect a cure when so many distinguished colleagues have spoken. Besides, Dr Shih is used to common people and their maladies. Your son's noble blood would be quite beyond him.'

Shih lowered his gaze to the floor. Once, long ago, he had been addressed with respect as a lord's son. This barely-retained memory, tinged with loss, coloured his cheeks.

'Do not blame Dr Shih for being here, it is I who summoned him,' said the Pacification Commissioner's wife. 'Husband, my maid told me this doctor cured her little brother of the dry coughing sickness – and many, many others in Water Basin Ward. She says he has a great way with sick children. I beg you, let him examine our son.'

Dr Shih knew it was prudent to agree with Dr Du Mau but the insult he had suffered kept him silent. He was also curious what would happen next. Wang Ting-bo shifted uncomfortably.

'We will consult Dr Du Mau's list of priests and magicians,' he said in a peculiar, flat voice. 'Only a fool opposes Heaven's will.'

'Husband, let Dr Shih see our son, at least!'

Dr Du Mau coughed again.

'Any further disturbance would endanger the boy's essential breaths,' he warned. 'I'm sure Dr Shih concurs. Is that not so?'

Du Mau fixed his junior colleague with a haughty stare. Perhaps Shih was tired of snubs, perhaps the heat made him irritable. Whatever the reason, he replied: 'It never injured anyone to take their pulse.'

There were sharp intakes of breath from his colleagues. At once he realised the gravity of his mistake. The slow closing of Dr Du Mau's hooded eyelids hinted at a lifetime's enmity.

'There!' cried the Pacification Commissioner's wife. 'What injury can it do?'

His Excellency Wang Ting-bo nodded. Tears were back in his eyes. He brushed them away angrily.

'Very well. But if harm befalls my son because of this. . . let Dr Shih beware! In the meantime Dr Du Mau must consult such magicians as he sees fit.'

The great people rose and left the ancient throne room. Shih realised hostile eyes were watching him. He blinked at the flickering candles. An official touched his arm.

'I will take you to the boy.'

Shih walked through the assembled doctors and, one by one, they showed him their backs.

竹子

He was led to a splendid bedchamber where incense and heat fogged the air. A four-poster divan shrouded by silk curtains stood in the centre from which a child's plaintive coughing could be heard. In each corner of the room crouched a uniformed servant. Stray lanterns emitted a feeble light, their flames rigid in the breathless air. Tables laid with delicacies stood beside the boy's bed: roast meat and honey cakes, fruit glazed with sugar. Enough for a large household. Despite its splendour – or because of it – the chamber was a forbidding place.

Shih felt a pang of disquiet for the little boy. When he treated the sick children of the poor, goodwill usually surrounded the child's bed in the form of parents and uncles, aunts and grandparents. This boy had been abandoned to the care of servants; his silk-curtained divan was an island drifting towards eternity. Shih turned to the nearest servant.

'Your name, sir?' he asked.

The man had a long scar across his cheek and answered suspiciously: 'We heard you were coming. I am Third Tutor Hu.'

Clearly there was to be no *sir* for Dr Shih.

'What is the boy's pet name?' he asked.

Tutor Hu seemed surprised by the question.

'We call him Little Tortoise. His official title is. . .'

'Never mind it for now. Raise all the curtains, especially the southern window. Open them wide.'

'That is not what the last doctor commanded,' replied the Third Tutor. 'He told us the incense must form a dense cloud if it is to trap favourable influences.'

Shih smiled politely.

'Then it seems I must do it myself.'

He parted the southern shutters. The direction had been chosen carefully. Already he sensed an excess of *yin* in the room, whereas a south wind could only encourage much-needed *yang*.

As fresh night air cut through the sweet fog of incense, barely audible sighs of relief came from the servants. Lanterns flickered and brightened all round the long room. Dr Shih approached the bed.

A tall boy for his age, no more than seven years, Little Tortoise was curled up on a horsehair mattress, coughing as though his lungs would drown themselves. Dr Shih immediately recognised symptoms of the dry coughing sickness, a common ailment and one he had learned to counter in all its stages, for it was prevalent in Water Basin Ward where he lived. But it was not his way to rush to a diagnosis.

He sat on the bed and smoothed the lad's forehead, sticky with sweat. The perspiration on his fingers smelt of excess metal and water.

'Little Tortoise,' he said. 'Can you look at me? I've come to make you better.'

Large, anxious eyes regarded him for a moment, then stared into empty air. Shih sensed the boy often looked away from those who addressed him – whether from pride or shyness he could not say.

'How old are you, Little Tortoise?'

The boy trembled and Shih noted the extent of the shivering.

'How old you are?'

As the boy tried to speak, Shih bent forward, sniffing his breath. He caught the word 'seven'.

'What! You are the tallest boy of seven I ever met! We can make a big, tall boy like you better before you know it. Seven, eh? How remarkable.'

While he talked, Shih took his own pulse, accustoming himself to the balances of *yin* and *yang*. Then he rested a practised finger on the boy's three pulses, not thinking, heeding instinct. He immediately judged the state of the disease to be chronic. Yet the volume and strength of the pulse were not entirely hopeless. He tested both left and right wrist, breathing in time to the fluttering beneath his finger, noting how the boy gasped to inhale and exhale. A clear picture of the patient's lungs formed – a mess of rotten and putrid elements, the bargain between the two undecided. He sensed a gathering crisis. Though he always tried to be hopeful, Dr Shih's misgivings were dark.

'Bring a lamp closer,' he commanded Third Tutor Hu in a soft, distracted voice.

Under the light, Dr Shih noted white predominating in the boy's complexion, clearly indicative of *yin*. Set against that was the boy's age. Seven denoted summer and the force of *yang*. He began to sense a possible cure. It must involve heat. The relevant element must be fire. Little Tortoise's lungs were drowning in their own humidity, which stood between *yin* and *yang*, just as sweet was the central flavour or *kung*, the cardinal musical note. He must ease the lad towards *yang*, while retaining those elements of *yin* likely to strengthen him.

Dr Shih sniffed the wind. He had noted for several days that it blew from the west. This, too, must be counteracted. He suspected noxious air lay at the heart of the matter.

Glancing round, he noticed an open doorway on the western side of the chamber and indicated to Tutor Hu it should be closed.

Then Shih thought deeply, gently massaging the boy's chest to comfort him. Above all, he felt surprised. Certainly there was a high possibility of death, a grave risk, but the case was not hopeless. Yet Dr Du Mau had stated no more could be attempted. Shih frowned at the only possible explanation – that because a cure was far from certain, Du Mau wished to avoid the Pacification Commissioner's anger if the boy died. A fine strategy! Should Little Tortoise recover on his own, Dr Du Mau would be commended for advocating the intervention of holy men. Should he die, his judgement would be sadly confirmed. He could not lose either way. The only loser was Little Tortoise.

His diagnosis complete, Dr Shih stood up and adjusted the silk sheets so they covered Little Tortoise up to the chest. The child blinked up at him and his shivering subsided a little. 'The tallest boy of seven I ever met!' exclaimed Shih, and he was rewarded with the flicker of a smile.

Turning round, Shih discovered the Pacification Commissioner's wife watching from the shadows. She had approached silently and he wondered how long she had been there.

'Well?' she asked, her eyes red from crying.

Dr Shih knew he should say Dr Du Mau was right, that nothing more could be done. His whole future depended on such prudence. And he was about to say it, being no hero by nature, when his eye fell on the boy's pale face. He had seen that same look of longing for reassurance many times, as one longs for comfort from a parent. The knowledge that someone in this cruel, fickle world will nourish you, keep you safe.

'There is no certain remedy for his illness,' he said. 'The pulse has a red appearance and the cough is obstinate. Without doubt, air has gathered in the boy's heart, and he must not eat until it has been dispelled. The disease has come about through noxious air, we may be sure of that.'

'How would you cure him?' she asked, eagerly.

'With fire,' he said. 'Water will always subjugate fire. In the process of quenching, Little Tortoise's essential breaths might find a balance and then his *qi* will grow strong again.'

The Pacification Commissioner's wife abruptly swept from the room, banging the door behind her. Dr Shih looked at Third Tutor Hu in alarm.

'She's seeking Wang Ting-bo's permission to let you try,' said the man. 'And why not?' he added. 'Why not, indeed?'

Half an hour passed. Shih remained by the bedside, massaging the boy's chest because the lungs are connected with the skin and rule over the heart. He was rewarded by gobbets of mucus when the lad coughed, but noted the secretion was black with stale blood. Too much *yin*, always with Little Tortoise, too much *yin*.

He looked up as Wang Ting-bo entered the room, accompanied by his wife. The Pacification Commissioner seemed angry.

'I hear you wish to attempt a cure,' he said.

His eyes avoided his perspiring son, yet were drawn to him against his will. Dr Shih rose and, to the amazement of the servants who were on their knees, led Wang Ting-bo to one side.

'It is perhaps better if Little Tortoise did not hear us discussing him, sir,' he whispered. 'It might cause agitation. I will try my best to heal him, if that is your pleasure.'

'My pleasure!' Wang Ting-bo snorted. 'I take no pleasure in any of this.'

Dr Shih bowed respectfully.

'I must tell you, young man, that Dr Du Mau has once more advised against further intervention. I do not know what to do. My wife argues for another attempt at a cure but she is a mother and a woman. One would expect that. I do not know what to do. Is that not strange?'

As he spoke the boy coughed and wheezed.

'Let me be frank, Your Excellency,' said Shih. 'Your son may die, indeed it is likely, I cannot pretend otherwise. Yet I have had success with the dry coughing sickness. . .' He paused before adding, with a wisp of irony: 'Among humble folk with humble lungs, admittedly.'

Wang Ting-bo's gaze was cold.

'Do not fail,' he said.

'Your Excellency, I may fail,' replied Shih, patiently. 'As I have said . . .'

'Do not!' The Pacification Commissioner had turned red. 'No one makes a monkey of me, young man!'

He stalked from the room and Dr Shih remembered that the common people often referred to great officials as monkeys in high hats.

Little Tortoise's crisis was fast approaching. Under Shih's orders the incense burners and tables laden with food were carried out. He insisted the mother sit beside her son, though she was reluctant. The lady's expression indicated she considered herself very brave.

Apprentice Chung had been sent back to the shop for the ingredients of a herbal draught useful in such cases, as well as the case of needles. But as the boy's breath whooped and clutched for air, Shih knew there was little time left. They should have called him earlier; now he must resort to desperate measures.

'I am afraid we must cause your son distress,' he told the

mother. 'You will hold both his hands firmly and fix your gaze on his face, saying reassuring things all the while.'

She nodded miserably, then burst out: 'There is an evil influence in my house, doctor! *She* is the cause of all this. But I shall make that fox-fairy trouble us no more! Doctor, I have forced a promise from my husband that if our son recovers he will send her away forever!'

The Pacification Commissioner's wife subsided into sniffling. Dr Shih frowned. This was hardly the occasion to air such grievances.

'I will apply moxa to Little Tortoise's back,' he said. 'By this means *yang* shall be restored and his *qi* stimulated.'

Dr Shih rummaged in his bag and produced a wooden box decorated with fortunate spells. From this he took a cone of artemisia leaves, placing it on the exact point on the boy's spine corresponding to the lungs. Taking a glowing taper he lit the dried leaves. They smouldered slowly. As the fire touched nerves, the boy cried out and Shih ordered Third Tutor Hu to hold him steady. Finally, Little Tortoise coughed up a great gobbet of green-black phlegm.

'Good,' muttered Dr Shih.

He let the sobbing child rest for a while before applying moxa to another area of skin corresponding to the heart.

Yet the boy was still slipping, his coughs ever more violent. He had reached a point of balance. Nothing more could be done until Chung arrived. Even then it would take half an hour to prepare the medicine.

Dr Shih leapt up as his apprentice entered the room.

'The ingredients,' he said, eagerly. 'I must have them at once.'

'Yes, sir,' said the youth, fearfully watching the Pacification Commissioner's wife.

'Pay attention to me, not Her Ladyship,' commanded his master.

'Sir, Madam Cao has already prepared the mixture! She heard on the street that the Pacification Commissioner's son has the dry coughing sickness, so she knew what to do. Madam asked me to tell you that she followed your usual instructions exactly.'

Dr Shih almost laughed with relief. There was so little time! And now Cao had anticipated him, as she always did.

'Give it to me.'

He propped up the boy and made him drink the mixture of herbs in one draught by holding his nose. The medicine took effect almost immediately, Little Tortoise lolling into a drugged doze. Shih knew he would sleep in this way for some time.

After a while the boy's mother grew restless and left the bedside to report back to her husband. 'I have faith in you, Dr Shih,' she whispered. 'Save my poor boy!' Third Tutor Hu held the door open for her as she hurried out.

'Keep a close watch on Little Tortoise,' Shih told the apprentice, once she had gone. 'At the slightest change, send for me. I will be outside. I need to empty my head.'

Dr Shih stepped out into a small garden adjoining the boy's chamber and took a deep lungful of night air. Stars glittered above the Twin Cities. Dawn was only a few hours away and, with dawn, Little Tortoise would enter a more favourable time of day. Shih's thoughts circled and tumbled. Had he considered everything? How would he know until it was too late? The boy's breath was labouring frantically to fill his lungs and exhale, draw a little life into his lungs then breathe out again, lest he drown in his own mucus.

Dr Shih realised he was no longer alone and turned to discover a man wearing splendid silks in the entranceway. He was sleek and handsome, a decade or so older than Shih. Unblinking brown eyes indicated a fierce will and much irony. Yet when the stranger spoke his tone was full of concern: 'Ah, doctor! I have been sent to ascertain how the unfortunate child progresses.'

Shih shook his head.

'He is by no means safe,' he said. 'We will know soon enough.'

'*By no means safe* . . . I see.'

The strange gentleman watched him intently and Shih's discomfort grew.

'You are a brave fellow,' remarked the man with a narrow smile. 'No doubt you are wondering why I call you that? Let me explain. Dr Du Mau says you have over-stepped yourself and his displeasure is sure to have consequences. And, of course, His Excellency will hardly welcome the fact that his heir's condition has deteriorated. Probably due to your treatment. That is why, doctor, one might call you a brave fellow.'

Dr Shih felt suitably unnerved.

'Please inform His Excellency the disease is at a point of crisis,' he said. 'I shall know very soon whether my cure is effective.'

'From your expression, I fear the worst,' remarked the man. 'It seems Dr Du Mau was right.'

'I did not say that, sir,' replied Shih.

Now the strange gentleman smiled again.

'You do not recognise me, do you?' he said. 'If you did you'd be on your knees. Yet I am sure the name of Wang Bai is familiar to you. Oh, *now* you know me! And I know you. Good night, Dr Yun Shih. No, don't bother to kneel. It is rather late for that.'

The man left as suddenly as he had come. Shih realised he had been conversing with the most powerful man in Nancheng after Wang Ting-bo. The Honourable Wang Bai was the Pacification Commissioner's nephew and Second Heir. As the Prefect of the Twin Cities, Wang Bai was responsible for all civil concerns. Worse, Shih realised that neglecting to fall to his knees, as was proper before so high an official, was generally punishable by harsh strokes of the bamboo.

Dr Shih sniffed the air. The breeze, little as it was, had turned to the east, *yang*'s foremost direction.

*

Back at Little Tortoise's divan, he found Chung drooping.

'Is the breath more even?' asked Shih.

Chung yawned and shrugged.

'I cannot be sure, Master.'

'You must pay closer attention,' chided Dr Shih, still unsettled by Wang Bai's warning. 'I will attend the patient until dawn. Make sure the case of needles is to hand. We may need them at short notice.'

A gong in the palace was ringing the third hour of night when Little Tortoise awoke. At once he retched bile and phlegm into the bowl Shih held out. The doctor praised each foul-smelling globule of mucus, calling him a strong boy and making up silly rhymes about tortoises, so that the child laughed even at the height of his misery. Shih listened frequently to his little, heaving chest, afraid the draining was less than he had expected.

The hour before dawn brought the final onset. Shih had prepared his needles in readiness and applied them at once. With each inhalation he inserted, twisted, and extracted in time to the next exhalation. Little Tortoise's breathing was so uneven, a series of wild gasps, that Shih struggled to anticipate the out-breath.

Then, almost unexpectedly, it was over. The boy's breath grew more regular, chest rattle lessened. When Shih took the pulse it swelled with *yang*. As dawn brought soft light to the bedchamber Little Tortoise fell asleep and the doctor half-dozed beside him.

Third Tutor Hu snuffed out all the lanterns except one and glanced severely at the other servants, who were struggling to stay awake.

'Prepare a fine breakfast for Dr Shih and Apprentice Chung,' whispered the Third Tutor. 'A breakfast worthy of a prince.'

Day took possession of the room. Shih slept lightly, dreaming of his twin brother, Guang, in far off Wei Valley. As ever when he imagined Guang, emotions contended – just as the shadows of leaves dance in bright sunlight, alternating between dark and light. Yet this time a greater darkness seemed to swallow Guang whole, extinguishing all his brightness, and Shih cried out in fear. Then his dream turned to Cao, sipping tea in their shop at dawn, awaiting his return to Apricot Corner Court, her thoughts reaching out to embrace him so that he felt comforted and dreamed no more.

Little Tortoise curled himself into a tight ball beneath the silk sheets, his burned and punctured body gaining strength with each dear breath.

竹子

Dr Shih woke with a start. Light reached through the open windows of Little Tortoise's bedchamber. A faint breeze was still blowing from the east, trailing scents of morning. Birds twittered and flitted around the eaves of the Pacification Commissioner's mansion.

His eyes instinctively sought unwelcome signs in his patient, but Little Tortoise slept as babies sleep, small fingers clenched, breath bubbly with life. Dr Shih detected a faint rattle of lungs, nothing much, only what one might expect.

He rose and was surprised to find Third Tutor Hu still crouching in his corner, watching intently. The other servants were asleep. Even for those accustomed to dutiful waiting, it had been a long night.

'Do you have a message for His Excellency? Or Honoured First Wife?' asked Third Tutor Hu.

'Tell them their son is recovering rapidly. One should never underestimate how the young bend and spring back.'

'Like green bamboo,' added Tutor Hu, smiling faintly.

Dr Shih bowed in acknowledgement, for the words came from one of his Great-grandfather Yun Cai's most famous poems, the long one about the lotus.

The servant left and Dr Yun Shih stepped outside into the enclosed garden. He listened to the sounds of the palace – a drone of gossip as two servants passed down an adjoining corridor believing themselves unheard. A vague hum from the city surrounding Peacock Hill.

Then he was disturbed by two voices arguing in a nearby apartment. Their words were indistinct; not so the fierceness on either side. The voices belonged to the Pacification Commissioner and his wife. Shih felt an irrational, childish desire to hide and remembered his father and mother arguing bitterly one rainy, monsoon afternoon when he was Little Tortoise's age. At once he felt dejected and weary. Third Tutor Hu stepped into the garden.

'Doctor! You look faint, sir! You must eat.'

The servants were bringing in breakfast. Shih watched in amazement as dozens of delicate green bowls with an exquisitely distressed glaze were laid out: rice-balls flavoured with sesame and anise; strips of roasted pork wrapped in wafers; piquant prawns fried in batter; cups of the weak wine known in the city as *dawn-dew*, and more of the stronger brew called *dusk-dew*.

As he ate, Dr Shih's mood lifted. Still he kept an eye on the boy. Surely he had earned an absurd fee – and not just from the Pacification Commissioner! That was the least of it. Word would circulate how he had healed the great Wang Ting-bo's son. Patients would besiege his humble shop in Apricot Corner Court. With the better sort, he could double – no, triple his usual fee.

If only Cao were here now, to witness this moment! He would buy her new silks and lacquered furniture to replace all that had been scuffed and dulled by years of hardship. Oddly, the prospect of her pleasure made him restless. Soon his thoughts drifted another way.

It seemed he had also made an enemy of Dr Du Mau. The Pacification Commissioner's own nephew had said as much. As head of the guild Du Mau possessed a great capacity for mischief.

Dr Shih had laboured over many years to establish a Relief Bureau intended to assist the destitute and those without family. In return he received a pittance from the city authorities and Cao sometimes complained his work there kept them as poor as the patients. Shih's fear was that Dr Du Mau might seek to appoint someone else to manage the Relief Bureau, a prospect he could not bear.

Still he ate the delicacies set before him, making sure Chung received a share. The lad was determined to taste every dish – a banquet like this was worth a thousand boasts among the other apprentices in Water Basin Ward.

Third Tutor Hu was gone a long while. He returned with the Pacification Commissioner and his wife, accompanied by a dozen secretaries and officials. Among them was Wang Ting-bo's handsome nephew, Wang Bai.

At the sight of Little Tortoise, the couple's stern expressions melted. Husband and wife tentatively approached the bedside. Shih noticed their hands touch as they gazed down at their son.

Tears were back in Wang Ting-bo's eyes. He reached out and brushed the boy's forehead, marvelling at its coolness. The Pacification Commissioner's wife also bent over the boy and then looked up to smile at Dr Shih with fierce gratitude.

'Doctor,' said Wang Ting-bo softly, so as not to wake the boy. 'Do appearances tell lies?'

Dr Shih bowed respectfully.

'I think we might call Little Tortoise safe, Your Excellency,' he said. 'From this malady at least. Though, as the proverb says, *one step at a time is good walking*.'

Wang Ting-bo nodded stiffly.

'Perhaps I had too little faith in you. In my position one is confronted by so many incompetent and self-seeking men. . . You will receive an auspicious reward.'

'When your son wakes and eats an appropriate meal, I shall feel myself rewarded,' said Shih. 'It is crucial the boy is not stuffed with too much rich food.' He added hastily: 'Your Excellency.'

The Pacification Commissioner chuckled.

'What is your name again, doctor?'

'Yun Shih, sir.'

'Good. Carry on.'

As they left he noticed the Pacification Commissioner's wife whispering urgently to her husband, who silenced her with a curt gesture. Wang Bai was the last of the great people to leave. He stepped to the bedside and examined Little Tortoise coldly for a moment. The boy murmured anxiously in his sleep.

'Ah,' he said, looking over at Dr Shih. 'Do not forget our little conversation.'

Then he strolled out after his noble uncle.

While Shih waited for Little Tortoise to awake, Third Tutor Hu slipped from the room. An hour later he was back, looking troubled.

'Dr Shih,' he said. 'May I speak with you alone?'

Tutor Hu led him to the garden and they sat on a long bench. The sun was beyond its zenith. Shih was glad of the warmth on his face.

'I must tell you,' said Hu. 'That an embassy from the Physician's Guild has begged yet another audience with His Excellency. Dr Du Mau, in particular, is most vexed. He claims that under his instructions magicians were busy all night and that their spells are the only reason for the boy's recovery. He is concerned your meddling will undo his good work.'

'Dr Du Mau is claiming to have cured Little Tortoise?'

'His Excellency sent him away curtly. Indeed I do not think Dr Du Mau will be returning to Peacock Hill. All his fees here are at an end. I wish you to know this, so you might be prepared.'

Shih sighed.

'His anger will pass. He has many other patients.'

'Perhaps,' replied Tutor Hu. 'I must also tell you that others are displeased by the boy's recovery. You know Little Tortoise is His Excellency's heir?'

'I do.'

'If he had died, the new heir would have been Wang Bai, as His Excellency's nephew. You should know this as well. Wang Bai's wife is distantly connected to Dr Du Mau by marriage and the Du clan own much property in Fouzhou. So you see, there is more to this than meets the eye. If Wang Bai had become heir, it would have enhanced the Du clan's position inestimably.'

Dr Shih concealed his hands in his sleeves.

'I am a simple man. What has any of this to do with me?'

'Surely that is obvious,' said Tutor Hu, severely.

Weariness crept through Shih. His deepest longing was to be back home, away from Peacock Hill.

'Since we speak in confidence,' he said. 'This morning I overheard the Pacification Commissioner and his wife arguing.'

Third Tutor Hu regarded him shrewdly.

'When a man like His Excellency reaches the end of middle age, he becomes susceptible to *influences*. You see, good doctor, our household is not a happy one. And all for the sake of a mere woman!'

He nodded significantly and leaned a little closer, so that Dr Shih smelt onion on his breath.

'The Pacification Commissioner has grown too fond of his concubine, Lu Ying, and surely she is a remarkable girl. But she is foolish. Not only has Lu Ying offended His Excellency's wife, but she argued against some advice of Wang Bai, who is not a man to forgive opposition. I fear our household will never be at peace while Lu Ying holds her current station.'

'If Little Tortoise had died,' said Shih. 'This concubine might have provided the Pacification Commissioner with another heir. After all, his official wife is almost past child-bearing age.'

'I see you understand politics,' observed Third Tutor Hu. 'I have told you these things as a warning. The rest is up to you.'

It was late afternoon. Shih stood beside the sick child's divan, watching him eat wheat cakes and shreds of roast duck, dipped in a vinegary sauce, all conducive to *yang*. Shih was surprised by the boy's appetite.

'Well, Little Tortoise,' he said. 'Are you feeling stronger?'

The boy examined him coldly. There was much of the father in the son's haughty demeanour. Yet he was still a child, uncorrupted by the excesses of flattery and ambition, and his grave expression melted into a sudden giggle.

'You made up a rhyme about my name when I was sick. That was funny!'

'Yes, it was. But now I have a riddle for you.'

'What is it?'

'My back is a shield,' said Shih. 'But I walk slowly. What am I?'

'Why, a tortoise, of course,' replied the boy, scornfully.

'But you are a little tortoise! Well then, let's see if you can walk slowly.'

He helped the boy upright. The servants stirred anxiously.

'You can,' said Shih, gently.

Holding Little Tortoise's arm, they walked up and down, until the boy grew tired. Third Tutor Hu joyfully clapped his hands three times.

竹子

At dusk Dr Shih found himself on his knees before the Pacification Commissioner of Nancheng Province. He had expected Wang Ting-bo to be happy but the great man's face bore an ugly flush. As always, his nephew Wang Bai stood silently to one side.

'Ah, Dr Shih,' said Wang Ting-bo. 'I hear from Third Tutor Hu that our son is walking round his chamber.'

'He is, Your Excellency.'

'I am grateful to you,' he said, glancing at his wife. 'You have brought a painful episode to a close and now we can return to normal. I shall offer thanks at the ancestral altar and everything shall be exactly as it was before.'

Shih stayed on his knees. He sensed the great people in the room were too preoccupied by matters of their own to notice him.

The Pacification Commissioner's wife said quickly: 'Husband, may I remind you that all cannot return to its former condition. What of the girl? You promised before the tablet of your father that if our son lived, she would be sent away as a sacrifice to Heaven. Let it be done at once or the Jade Emperor will surely punish us.'

Wang Ting-bo shook his head.

'She can hardly be blamed for noxious air leading to a common disease,' he replied.

An uncomfortable silence settled. The Pacification Commissioner's nephew stepped forward.

'Honoured Uncle, hear me out,' he said. 'Examine the matter clearly, I beg you. In any case, you have already decided. All that remains is for you to tell us how she should be sent away. You have concluded Lu Ying is a source of great disquiet in your household and we all honour your judgement. That is one thing. For the sake of the girl's feelings, do not prolong her uncertainty. Send her away at once! She may then accustom herself to her changed situation all the sooner.'

Wang Ting-bo squeezed the arms of his chair.

'It is true that I spoke rash words, fearing for my son's life, but that does not mean. . .'

'Of course, Uncle!' urged Wang Bai. 'Of course your oath has no less validity. I return to the issue at hand. Where is she to be sent?'

Wang Ting-bo's eyes flicked to a side door. Dr Shih sensed the girl in question was standing behind it, listening as her fate was thrown back and forth like a wooden ball.

'You know she has no family to return to,' said the Pacification Commissioner. 'She is an orphan. Perhaps I should give her a small mansion adjoining Peacock Hill.'

Wang Ting-bo's wife and nephew exchanged hurried glances.

'I fear that might give the wrong impression,' said Wang Bai. 'Your solemn oath was to send her away forever.'

Dr Shih crouched silently on the audience chamber floor. He was not the only one in this awkward position. Third Tutor Hu knelt beside him, as did an astrologer and various intimate household officials. If only they would dismiss him to the comforts of Apricot Corner Court! He became aware Wang Bai's glance had fallen on him. A thoughtful look crossed the sleek Prefect's face.

'Honoured Uncle,' he said. 'She should be sent into the care of a kind man, a good man, who will treat her as she deserves.'

'That is one solution,' conceded Wang Ting-bo.

'I know just such a man,' said Wang Bai. 'Everyone would applaud your noble wisdom. The Twin Cities will ring with your praise!'

Wang Ting-bo shifted in his chair uncomfortably.

'I suppose that would be the best thing. But where could one find such an unfortunate fellow? In any case, is it really necessary?'

'Think of it,' continued his nephew, as though musing aloud. 'The girl is of lowly origin. It might confuse her to enter another noble household after living here. If nothing else, people would gossip that she preferred her new master to the old. That is unthinkable.'

'Someone respectable then,' said Wang Ting-bo. 'But not too high. Perhaps I will keep her here and never see her.'

He was like a fish flapping on the hook. Dr Shih kept his eyes downcast. When the powerful grow distressed they often seek relief in punishment.

'I know just the person,' said Wang Bai. 'I beg you to trust my judgement, Uncle. Heaven itself has arranged his presence here. Who better than the saviour of your son? I mean, Dr Yun Shih.'

There was a shocked silence in the room. Wang Ting-bo examined the kneeling doctor.

'You mock me,' he said, angrily. 'From *me* to *him*. That is not possible.'

'Husband,' said the Pacification Commissioner's wife, genuinely distressed. 'Dr Shih saved our son. . . If nothing else, think of the expense for him! Lu Ying's wardrobe alone would bankrupt a small town.'

Wang Bai held up a long finger. His well-proportioned mouth puckered with concern.

'I must disagree, Honoured Aunty,' he said. 'Dr Shih deserves a great reward for saving His Excellency's heir. I, for one, cannot imagine a greater honour. Besides, I have been informed by Dr Du Mau that Dr Shih's wife is barren. And he is not of high birth, so no comparison with the Pacification Commissioner is possible. Most important of all, he is assuredly kind and patient.'

Dr Shih looked in amazement between the aristocrats. What exactly were they proposing? He could barely follow their argument.

'I will not allow it.' spluttered Wang Ting-bo.

Wang Bai shook his head sadly.

'Then I tremble, sir. To have made so public an oath to Heaven . . . I know your feelings for the girl, but honour is as brittle as the petals of a frozen rose! And your enemies at the Imperial court are full of spite. They will seize on anything.'

The Pacification Commissioner stared at the floor miserably.

'I must not risk my honour,' he said.

'Whereas your inner struggle is a sign of great integrity,' added Wang Bai, smoothly. 'Everyone will know you put duty before inclination.'

All eyes were on the Pacification Commissioner. His Excellency glanced at Shih with suspicion and outrage.

'Very well,' he said, finally. 'Let it be as you advise.'

An involuntary gasp of surprise escaped from many of his servants. He turned to face the tablets on the wall depicting his ancestors, thereby indicating he had nothing further to add.

Wang Bai blinked rapidly, then looked grave and solemn. Still Dr Shih dared not speak. Did they expect him to maintain the girl as a guest? Yet they had talked about conceiving a child. Was she to be his concubine, then? In either case, who would pay for her clothes and perfumes, the other necessities of a fine lady? It was all nonsense, and he waited for his chance to refuse the great honour they offered.

'Bring us Lu Ying,' ordered Wang Bai hurriedly, before the Pacification Commissioner could change his mind. A servant returned with a slim young lady of exceptional beauty. Her silks glowed in the soft light of dusk, the corals in her hairpins caught the declining sun. Her oval face was perfect in its symmetry. Her bound feet, though a little large, were alluring enough to attract the attention of any man. Indeed, Dr Shih found himself gazing at them, then at her perfect figure. He had never seen such a woman. More striking still were her eyes of willow green, flecked with amber, copper and gold. There was something dangerous about such beauty, reminiscent of the madness for a concubine that had brought down Emperors and entire dynasties.

In that moment of astonishment Shih lost his opportunity to protest against Wang Ting-bo's reward, for His Excellency rose from his chair and rapidly left the room. Casting a mournful look of apology at the saviour of her son, his wife followed. Once they had gone, Wang Bai addressed the young woman sharply.

'Lu Ying, His Excellency has determined that you must accompany this man to his home and pleasure him in any way he requires. Your concubinage here is ended.'

The girl moaned, her hand flying to her mouth.

'I take it you agree to His Excellency's decision,' said Wang Bai. 'Of course you do. You can hardly refuse.'

Lu Ying bowed her head in assent. She seemed about to speak but thought better of it.

'By the way, Dr Shih,' said Wang Bai with a smile. 'Knowing Lu Ying as I do, I am quite certain your reward will bring nothing but joy. Rest assured, suitable financial arrangements shall be made. A small monthly stipend for food and other necessities. As for luxuries, well, you must hope Lu Ying decides all her former extravagances are at an end.'

Still smiling, Wang Bai strolled from the room. Dr Shih was

left on his knees, staring at the beautiful girl beside him. She did not notice. For her, he hardly existed. He became aware of a disturbing fragrance in the air and realised it came from her person – a musk, deep and beguiling. He quite forgot Cao waiting for his return to Apricot Corner Court. He even forgot his twin brother, Guang, facing Heaven's judgement in Wei Valley hundreds of *li* to the west – in lands occupied by the Mongol invaders.

憎
two

'All reasonable men agree Heaven has surrendered the entire world into the Great Khubilai Khan's keeping. All that is below Heaven belongs to him – and those he appoints to rule on his behalf. . .'

from *Court Memoranda* by Yeh-lu Ch'u-tso

竹子

Wei Valley, Western China. Summer 1266.

Yun Guang entered Wei as the first light of dawn filtered through the mountains. The valley was strangely deserted, no peasants about the lord's business as one might expect. Even the gibbons were quiet. He reached his hiding place, a cave on a hillside above the thatched rooftops of the village, just as the first people below began to stir.

The cave was a haunt from childhood. Here he had fled Father's moods, crawling beneath an overhanging boulder bearded with moss and lichen. Beyond lay a low-roofed, narrow space lit by cracks in the stone, reeking of damp earth and mould. Once, only ten years old, he had experimented with tinder and candles, singeing his hand to test how much pain he could endure. Then he had tried to melt the stone – his first lesson: that fire cannot consume everything.

From the cave one could spy on the village like an Immortal, seeing while safely unseen. What he saw as the light thickened brought no pleasure.

The reports were true. Wei Village and its surrounding fields, laboriously reclaimed from forest and hillside, were being transformed. The sunny side of the valley had been set aside as pasture for the enemy's herds of horses. How quickly the patient work of a dozen generations could revert to waste!

As the sun climbed he witnessed more changes. On fields of millet turned over to coarse grass, they had constructed a dozen circular tents, swarming with women and children, as well as tethered beasts – ewes, long-horned buffalo, goats, even a few camels. Guang imagined the barbarians' breakfast of rancid sheep milk and barely-cooked meat. These were creatures who despised the five virtuous grains.

Gradually men emerged bare-chested from the tents. It was rumoured that monsoon weather discomforted their kind. Let them sweat! Nevertheless, they found enough energy to gallop up and down, loosing arrows at wooden posts and cheering whenever they hit. A few villagers also applauded and this grieved the man watching from the hillside.

It was three years since the Mongols had seized Wei Valley, killing Guang's parents, occupying Three-Step-House, his ancestral home. After the death of his father, Lord Yun, a Mongol commander had been granted the Lordship of Wei Valley by the Great Khan. Yet Guang had devised a way to inspect what belonged to his family by perpetual right and, above all, to visit the shrine of his ancestors. Surely Heaven favoured such an enterprise. The constant flutter in his gut was not fear, merely a reminder he must be cautious. The Mongols would seize him if he failed, dragging him behind their horses. Then their triumph over his family would be complete.

Later that morning a fat warrior rode into the village on his shaggy pony, dragging two prisoners behind, their arms and necks bound by ropes and branches shaped into yokes. Former neighbours for all Guang knew. Certainly their clothes suggested quality.

Guang turned his attention to the village. Most of the low houses seemed intact, smoke rising from the hearths. Scores of peasants were at work in the remaining fields, tilling or tending the irrigation wheels. On the far side of the valley above the village, Three-Step-House stood as always, its elegance undiminished. This was the hardest sight, proof of right turned wrong. He examined the distant figures of servants and tried to identify them. They were too far away, in time as well as distance.

No one disturbed him in the tiny cave as the hours passed. When he awoke, he ate the last of his rice-cakes and checked his equipment. Cautiously, before darkness fell he struck flint and tinder, aware how sound travelled in strange ways through the valley. Then he lit a small fire-pot attached to his belt. Taking his monk's staff, part of an elaborate disguise that had served him well on his journey through the occupied lands, he attached an iron cylinder to the end of the bamboo pole, binding it with twisted cords of hemp.

Scents of evening entered the cave. Birdsong faded. Unexpectedly the valley's monkeys, silent all day, began to cavort and scream. He took it as a favourable omen. Sliding his pack and staff through the overhanging entrance to the cave, he wriggled out, emerging on the ridge above Wei.

Fires glowed round the cluster of tents, but the village itself was silent beneath its curfew. There had been no curfew when Father was Lord. Surely that time would come again! Guang's enterprise at the shrine could only bring it closer. Heaven loved the filial, and the scroll in his pouch was a crossbow loaded with piety. He padded into the night, a shadow moving between pine and pawlonia trees and stands of rustling bamboo.

竹子

Crossing the valley proved simple. Perhaps too simple. Were they were waiting for him to reveal himself? One could take no chances with demons. It was well-known their shamans used human bones and spells to detect enemies. Yet finding the old, familiar paths proved easy. He circled round Three-Step-House where fires flickered in the courtyard and drunken men squatted and jabbered, stealing through the darkness to a grove on the hillside above the house.

Silence of night, glow of fire-flies. Heaven's constellations lent significance to every movement. His had been a harsh, disappointed life, yet now Guang felt powerful as though destiny guided his steps.

In this mood he found the ancestral shrine built by Great-great-grandfather – a famous hero of the struggles against the Kin barbarians a century earlier – to celebrate his ennoblement. Here Great-grandfather Yun Cai also rested, a poet still honoured throughout the Empire though sixty years dead. After him little glory had been added to the Yun family name. He remembered Grandfather as a shrewd but kindly man, well-respected by the peasants.

As for Father. . . Lord Yun had been woven from a coarser yarn. For all the old man's failings, it still sickened Guang to think he did not sleep among their ancestors. No one knew where the old man's bones lay.

After the first exhilaration of arrival he examined the shrine. Grass grew high round the walls and the door hung askew on its hinges. Broad leaves from the pawlonia trees and old pine needles littered the flat roof. Something glinted in the starlight and he stooped. A sliver of carved jade, broken but recognisable: the tablet of Great-grandfather's daughter, Little Peony, who had died long ago in infancy. The Mongols had defiled her spirit's eternal resting place for a little sport. Unaccustomed tears clouded his eyes. How low his family had fallen! They had been debased. Anger confused shame and guilt. Yet he had a remedy.

Pushing aside the broken door to the shrine he bowed and entered.

The darkness was absolute. Here past and future met. He

could not bear such darkness. Fumbling in his pack, he found a candle and lit it from the fire-pot at his belt. He leant his staff against the wall, well away from the flame. The low room danced with uncertain light.

A survey of the Yun clan's mausoleum made Guang's breath hiss. The heart of all he was, all he might ever be, had been despoiled! The tablets of the dead lay in shards on the damp earth. Beside them lay dried-out human excrement.

The candle flickered. Trembling, he extracted the scroll from his pouch and unrolled it in the dim light. Here was why he had undertaken this terrible journey, the weeks of fear as he travelled on foot from town to town through lands still stricken by war. Once he had been forced to hide amidst the submerged shoots of a paddy field, only his nose and mouth above water while a Mongol patrol searched for him, prodding the water with lances and sticks.

Guang lifted the candle and closed his eyes, remembering far away Nancheng.

Four months earlier a different candle had flickered in his twin brother's medicine shop. It revealed two unusually tall men, almost identical in appearance except that one was slim and delicate, the other swollen with muscle. One possessed an officer's tufty beard and extravagant long hair while his counterpart was clean-shaven. This slim man wore a doctor's robes. The other's faded silks were cut in a military style.

It had been midnight. Empty flasks of cheap wine stood on the table between them, arranged into a neat lotus pattern by Shih. They were wild with wine, beyond all sense. At least, one of them had been.

'We should deliver a letter to our ancestors, asking for guidance!' Guang had roared at Shih. 'Everyone is doing it! Now Father is dead we have no one to intercede on our behalf with Heaven. They say such a letter should be read aloud to the tablets of one's ancestors. Ensign Liu did it last month. He was promoted within days!'

Shih sipped his wine.

'Of course that is impossible for us,' he had replied, patiently. 'Our ancestral shrine lies deep within lands held by the enemy.'

'Impossible? Nothing is impossible for a man of spirit! I'll do it myself. My present commission is ended. Why shouldn't I?'

Shih had smiled.

'Because a hundred thousand Mongols stand between you and Wei Valley.'

'By my honour, Shih, write this letter and I'll deliver it! That is my oath. I will prove to Father's ghost that I am worthy.'

'We should sleep and hope the Jade Emperor forgets your rash words.'

'No, I swear! What should such a letter say?'

Then his brother had laughed as though at a bitter joke and declared: 'Let us ask Heaven why it chose to deny Father's heir his inheritance.'

'Fetch paper!' cried Guang. 'As Eldest Son I desire my inheritance above everything. Write it down.'

'You *are* drunk.'

'Write it down, I say!'

Finally Shih had mixed ink and taken up a brush, not expecting what would follow. Guang hated to judge his only brother harshly, but as an officer he had learned it was dangerous to flinch from painful truths concerning a subordinate's character. And though he found much kindness in his twin brother, there was something irresolute about Shih, some inner weakness Guang could not name, yet distrusted.

As dawn crept through the silent streets of Nancheng, brushing closed eyelids and paper curtains, slipping through the windows of Dr Shih's surgery, the letter urging their ancestors to restore the Yun clan's lost prosperity was completed.

'This is a poor drinking game,' said Shih, laying aside his brush. 'We would have done better to compose verses.'

But the letter had been written. Even when drunk, Shih's writing was eloquent and precise.

'I will deliver this to Wei Valley personally,' Guang had vowed. 'Then they will take notice!'

'Go to bed,' urged Shih.

'I have given my oath,' he declared, half-afraid of its enormity. 'For Father's sake.'

Then Shih had shocked him.

'Our letter is addressed to empty air,' he said, so very sadly and quietly that Guang had not known how to reply. 'Father wasn't worth your oath. If you want guidance, step outside and pour a bucket of cold water over your head.'

Guang's thoughts swam with wine. How dare Shih tell him what to do? Authority from a younger brother bordered on insolence. If he chose, as family head, he could force his younger brother to kneel before him – that was the law. Yet anger swirled into quite another mood. He felt like weeping. All he wanted was that Shih, so long estranged, so stupidly a stranger, should love him and forget the folly that had kept them apart most of their lives.

So, as a joke, Guang had followed Shih's advice, pouring not one but ten buckets of water over his head until the occupants of Apricot Corner Court laughed and cheered him on. Even Cao forgave him for keeping her husband awake all night with his rumpus. Yet he had remembered his vow. A reckless desire to prove himself better than other men lent him purpose.

'Do not be so foolish!' urged Shih, over and over. 'If the Mongols capture you, they will surely execute you as a spy. Father would weep to see his favourite son killed.'

Guang had ignored the warning. He enjoyed preparing for his journey to the West, devising tools to deceive the enemy, boasting to friends in the taverns of Nancheng of the honour he would win. After so many boasts there could be no turning back.

Now, in the mausoleum of his ancestors, Guang unrolled the scroll with trembling hands. Suddenly he felt foolish. Surely Shih was right: silence would greet their message to the dead.

Yet the darkness was full of watchful eyes, he could sense them. And they were waiting. Clearing his throat, he peered at the characters on the scroll, illumined by the flickering candlelight.

'I, Yun Guang, head of our clan, bring you most respectful greetings, so that you might report our welfare to the Jade Emperor's secretary.'

Nothing stirred. No sign he was heard. He cleared his throat again.

'Although our home has fallen to the barbarians, we still strive to emulate your illustrious example. We beg forgiveness that we have no sons. Did you benefit from our sacrifices for your souls over the last year? We fear that because they took place so far from Wei, they are ineffectual. Did you come to take the offerings we made at morning and evening on the first and fifteenth days of each month? If they displeased you, we beg forgiveness.'

He paused. Listened. It occurred to him that any enemies on the prowl outside must hear his droning voice.

'Honoured ancestors, I come to the purpose of this letter. We supplicate that you assist your family still alive in the Middle Kingdom. Let me, Yun Guang, gain the promotion merited by my labours in the Emperor's service. Arrange a fresh commission for me, I beg you, by interceding with the ancestral spirits of those who promote and demote. Your other descendent, Yun Shih, asks only for sons so the family rites may continue, or failing that, a daughter. If you agree to these requests, we entreat that you show your goodwill without delay.'

He lowered the letter, rolled it tightly, and placed it solemnly in an alcove choked by cobwebs. Then he waited for a sign. His heart beat anxiously. Oh, they had heard him, he was sure of it! Why did they not speak? Had he risked his life for no reward? Moments lengthened. The look of deference he had worn while reading the letter hardened into a frown, then an ugly scowl. So this was their verdict! That he and Shih were unworthy. Well, they were wrong, a thousand times wrong!

Guang drew himself up proudly as he had before hostile superiors when opposing their decisions.

'You are fools to scorn us!' he said, haughtily. 'We are your only hope.'

Then he froze. Instinctively snuffed the candle. There were voices outside. Groping in the dark, he reached out for his thick bamboo staff and held it tight, listening to the night.

竹子

One of the voices was drunk, slurring words in a barbarous language. The other, a girl with a Wei accent, protested fearfully.

'No! Please, not here!'

So *this* was his ancestors' reply: a reminder of their wretched shame. Abruptly, his mood became cruel and cold. He restrained an urge to dash outside and set about them. It was clear from the girl's cries and the Mongol's chuckling grunts what was going on. As he waited in the dark Guang's mouth twitched like a cat's tail.

Now he could hear heavy, laboured breaths. The wall of the mausoleum received rhythmic thuds, mirrored by the girl's squeals. Dust drifted from the ceiling. Guang knew that he should wait until they went away. That was the safest thing. Instead, as the thudding reached a climax, he twisted the rope handle in the middle of his staff and there was a quiet creaking noise. Inch by inch, something sharp and smeared with black paste emerged from the very tip of the bamboo pole. He checked the metal canister and fuse lashed onto the side of the end section of the staff. Then he pulled up a scarf to cover his face, crept to the doorway and slipped out.

The Mongol had the girl pinned against the wall of the family shrine. Guang recognised her as one of the old bailiff's daughters. In the starlight he glimpsed her ravisher's hairy, muscular legs.

The man was tall for one of them, dressed in expensive silks.

He possessed the shaved tonsure and pigtails customary among their kind; the usual flat, ugly nose and cold, narrow eyes beneath heavy, brooding lids. The girl's own eyes opened wide as she saw Guang. The Mongol was chuckling again, cooing affectionate words. For a strange moment Guang felt he was somehow wrong to interrupt their love-game.

Then he cleared his throat with exaggerated delicacy. The Mongol paused, turning to see who had interrupted him. The speed of his next movement surprised Guang. The barbarian leapt straight at him. He barely had time to swing the spear and twist the poisoned blade.

When the girl stopped weeping he questioned her. She gazed up at him fearfully, glancing frequently at the dead Mongol as though afraid he might come to life. Guang resisted an urge to reassure her. Perhaps she was grieving for her lover. If so, she deserved only scorn. He shook her hard by the arm.

'Does anyone know you are here?'

'No!'

'Don't you recognise me?' he demanded, lowering the scarf that concealed his face.

She stared at him in disbelief for a moment, then began to shiver.

'They said the old lord's family were all dead! We thought you were dead!'

The questions he meant to ask faded.

'Tell the villagers,' he whispered, 'that I will return one day and Three-Step-House shall be as it was when Lord Yun was alive.'

She seemed puzzled. 'Is that why you have come, sir? Have his sufferings ended at last?'

'Of course, stupid girl! He has been dead three years. The enemy killed him when they seized our home.'

She shrank back. 'No, sir!'

He shook her hard again.

'What?'

'Lord Yun is still in Whale Rock Monastery,' she squealed. 'At least he was a few days ago. My father secretly sent him rice.'

He gripped her arm so it would hurt.

'Alive?'

'Yes, sir! Please!'

'We were told he had perished. And my mother alongside him.'

'No, sir! Khan Bayke – our new lord – let them live. He said the old man wasn't worth killing and whipped him away to the roads. The monks at Whale Rock Monastery took him in, sir, on account of Lord Yun's generosity to them over the years. Did you not know these things?'

Finally Guang understood what his ancestors wanted. How they had chosen to answer the letter. He felt dizzy with pride. They must have boundless confidence in him! He realised the girl was weeping again.

'Be silent!'

'You must go now. You have killed Khan Bayke's eldest son, Arike. Oh, what will they do to me? They will say I betrayed Arike,' she sobbed.

He barely heard her. Father, alive! *Alive!*

Then he realised the girl was staring past him in terror. They were no longer alone. Two burly Mongols stood at the entrance to the glade, fumbling with swords at their belts. Keeping hold of the girl, he gripped his bamboo spear.

In lectures at the Western Military Academy Guang had learned the Theory of War. If the enemy opens a door, storm in, clutch what he holds precious and secretly contrive a favourable encounter. The ground where simply surviving calls for a desperate fight, where we perish without a perilous fight, is called Dying Ground. He had learned the commentaries, too. That to be in Dying Ground is like clinging to a leaky boat, like curling up in a burning house. How might we find advantage in such a plight? The answer – disguise your potential and assault the enemy on both sides at once, roaring and beating the drums.

Between lectures they had conducted lengthy rites in honour of the Academy's heroes and those deities who favoured soldiers. Mostly they had drilled with sword, bow and halberd. And in all these things Guang had excelled. Now on Dying Ground, his training met instinct. He acted without thought.

First Guang pretended to panic and hid behind the girl, so that she formed an obstacle between himself and the two Mongols. Their swords were drawn, they were advancing slowly.

Then he pulled the cord of smouldering hemp from his fire-pot. The match glowed as the breeze caught it.

He thrust the girl to safety. They were almost upon him.

He lifted the bamboo staff as though about to surrender, then lit the fuse protruding from the metal canister tied onto the side of its end section. The Mongols were sure of him now, rushing in close. There was a sudden flash as the fuse lit. Guang pointed the staff and flames shot out a mixture of noxious lime, arsenic and pellets of gravel straight into the face of the nearest enemy. He wasted no more time on the wretch. In the moment of surprise he stabbed the second Mongol, who had leapt back, lowering his guard. The man fell. Then he turned to the first, who was on his knees, blinded by the fire lance's blast.

Despite the precariousness of his situation – at any moment more of the barbarians might appear – Guang circled the wounded man. He was crying pitifully, scrabbling at the place where his eyes and half his face had once been. Guang silenced him with a kick.

Then he listened. Dogs were barking furiously in the Mongol camp. The whoosh of the fire lance and sounds of fighting could not have gone undetected. He stepped round the sobbing girl and melted into the darkness, hurrying towards Whale Rock Monastery.

Was it weak of him not to kill the girl? After interrogating her, Khan Bayke would soon guess his destination. But Guang shrank from such cruel prudence. Now he must move swiftly. Dawn promised more than the certainty of a new day. They would hunt him like a deer until they dragged him down – and everyone knew how the Mongols loved a hunt.

竹子

At dawn Guang reached the narrow valley where Whale Rock Monastery nestled beside a series of waterfalls. The journey of thirty *li* along twisting mountain paths had depleted much of the nervous energy sustaining him. Yet he could afford a brief rest.

Guang slumped against a broad maple trunk and closed his eyes. When he awoke his error became obvious. A single glance at the sun told him the morning was well-advanced. Smoke rose lazily from a cooking fire in the monastery below. He could hear distant voices.

Guang leapt to his feet, senses alert. Banks of grey cloud were scudding west – there would be rain later. Birdsong all along the valley, just as he remembered from boyhood. Then came the low clanging of a gong. It was summoning him to Father.

Although impatient to descend to the monastery, Guang opened his pack and removed a thick leather bag with a narrow neck. He fashioned a crude funnel from paper and inserted it into the neck of the bag. Collecting numerous sharp pebbles cost further time. As he worked Guang cast fearful glances at the road winding in the direction of Wei Valley. If Khan Bayke had ridden out with his men at dawn, it would take at least half a day to reach the Whale Rock, even if they rode hard. The footpaths Guang had taken, though steep, were direct; horsemen would be forced to take a tedious detour before they could even join the road to the monastery.

Guang filled a third of the bag with gravel. Then he opened a hidden compartment at the bottom of his pack and gingerly ladled out black powder, using the paper funnel. When the leather sack had been sealed with hand-moulded wax, a crude thunderclap bomb was ready. Guang knew from experiments he had conducted in Nancheng that the design possessed virtue. Finally, he lit the slow-burning match in his little fire-pot and attached it to his belt.

Staff in hand, he hurried through the trees, jumping the limestone steps of waterfalls until he reached the gates of Whale Rock Monastery. The bronze-hinged doors inscribed with prayers were closed. Guang hesitated. He was well-known here, but in days like these who could guess the monks' true loyalties?

Guang had first approached these gates at the age of nine, a year after Shih's banishment from Three-Step-House to a destination no one would reveal and for reasons no one dared mention. It had been around the same time kindly Aunt Qin vanished in the middle of the night.

Shortly after her disappearance it was discovered that he, not Shih, was Eldest Son and therefore the true heir to Three-Step-House. Father never explained how such a mistake had come about, other than to mutter terse remarks about fox-fairies and confusion at birth. After all, he and Shih were mirror images of each other.

At nine years of age the separation from his twin brother formed a deep, hidden wound. A wound that bled inwardly, even to this day. Guang had not complained but spent more and more time alone. Often he sat in the tiny cave above Wei Village until hunger drove him home. At last, Father grew angry, shouting that he was ungrateful, that everyone was ungrateful, and Guang was sent away to live in Whale Rock Monastery so that he might learn to read and write.

Guang didn't care to dwell in the past. Weaklings are obsessed with what was. Bamboo feeds on the wind. But the monks had been kind – one especially, a young novice, had taken particular care of him, encouraging him to join the other children in their games. Sometimes he caught Novice Jian watching as he staged elaborate battles with stick-swords and imaginary enemies, pretending to be Great-great-grandfather saving the illustrious General Yueh Fei, or Great-grandfather Yun Cai freeing his noble friend Second Chancellor P'ei Ti and beheading a hundred rebels. One day he had grown self-conscious and asked the monk: 'Master Jian, why do you pity me?'

Jian had pursed his lips.

'Do I pity you?'

'I am the heir to Three-Step-House and will inherit property for a hundred *li* around,' Guang had declared haughtily. 'I am my Father's heir!'

Jian scratched his shaven head.

'Perhaps that is why I pity you. None of those things will earn you a favourable rebirth.'

'Father gives a present of silver to the monastery each year,' said Guang. 'To buy a good reincarnation in his next life.'

At first Jian would not reply, then he said: 'One can only purchase virtue through good deeds and meditation, otherwise there is no avoiding hell and karma. Go! Play with the other children. You spend too much time alone.'

An oriole had landed on the wall above where the monk and earnest boy sat. Guang had thought, in the strange way children imagine things, the bird was Shih visiting him. Then he had wept uncontrollably and, when pressed, dared not explain why in case Father learned of it. Later that day he picked a fight with a boy several years older and received a sound beating. It was as though he wished to bring a punishment down on himself, as though he, Guang, was in some way to blame for Shih's banishment.

Guang rapped on the doors of Whale Rock Monastery with his bamboo staff. The sound echoed briefly, drowned by the constant splash and murmur of the waterfalls. At last there came a scraping of bolts. Guang might have laughed out loud if he hadn't felt so grim, for there, as though summoned by his memory, stood Brother Jian, his face coarsened and lined by twenty years of contemplating the nothingness of this illusory world.

Guang bowed and the monk, after his initial surprise, looked round anxiously.

'You have finally come,' said Jian, in wonder. 'Quickly, enter. Before you are seen.'

Guang slipped inside and waited as the doors were barred. The monastery was silent. In the courtyard tall grass grew between paving stones where weekly markets had been held when he was a boy. An aged monk observed them from a doorway.

'What has happened here?' he asked. 'Where are my Mother and Father?'

'Come with me,' said Jian. 'We must be circumspect. It would be dangerous if Khan Bayke heard you were here.'

Guang followed, wary of mentioning what had happened in Wei Valley.

The monastery had supported twenty monks and as many servants when he was a boy, now the prayer cubicles and cells were empty. A smell of mildew and decay hung in the air.

'What has happened here?' he repeated.

Jian paused. They were by the entrance to the temple; all the prayer wheels were silent.

'I am Abbot now,' he said. 'Why did you take so long to come? Had you returned earlier you would know that Khan Bayke seized all our lands. We have no income. It is not as it was when men like your father supported us. Many of the monks have been forced onto the roads. Plague carried away most of the others.

Guang asked eagerly: 'How is Mother? And Father?'

'You will see.'

Jian led him deeper into the monastery, down corridors painted with scenes of transcendence and eternal torment.

'Last night I killed Khan Bayke's son,' said Guang, as though challenging the monk to disapprove. 'And two of his men – at least, I blinded one of them. I did not know Lord Yun was still alive until last night or I would have come sooner.'

The monk offered no reply. They arrived at a closed door.

'We have tried to bring him back,' said Abbot Jian. 'But the Beyond is so very dark. . . I fear his karma has unravelled early. Do not be distressed by what you see.'

Guang laid a hand on the Abbot's arm. His mouth tasted bitter as before a fight. He was trembling.

'Stay with me,' he begged. 'Tell him I am here . . . the shock.'

Jian sighed through his nose and turned away.

'It would change nothing.'

Guang slowly opened the door. A small room lay beyond, its single window covered by frayed paper blinds. In the gloom, he could make out a low bed and table. On the floor stood a large bowl. Cobwebs hung from the rafters. Guang understood the room's history most clearly through his nose. It stank, as though its occupant had repeatedly soiled himself. There was sweat, too, stale and acrid, like the fox-smell of foreigners.

Father squatted on the floor, gazing into a wide, flat bowl of circling goldfish. His long, straggling hair was matted and unkempt. Food stains covered his threadbare clothes. The old man did not look up as Guang entered.

'Father,' he muttered.

Was this Lord Yun, once so particular about every silk he wore? Famous for his good looks and elegant manners? Lord Yun, who had turned the ladies' heads whenever he rode through the streets of Chunming on a horse glittering with silver ornaments? Guang fell to his knees and banged his head on the floor three times, tears trickling down his unshaven cheeks. Still the old man stared at the fishes.

'Father! I have come to set you free.'

At last Lord Yun looked up, fixing Guang with a scornful, red-rimmed stare. A strange noise, half-giggle, half-sob, shook his chest.

'When I needed you,' said the old man. 'You were not there.

When Lady Yun died, she called out for you. But you were not there.'

Guang fearfully brushed at his tears.

'Forgive me, Father! Is Mother dead, then?'

'I will never forgive you! I am almost a ghost!'

Guang began to shake. Such words were a curse, they would echo forever. He became aware Abbot Jian stood beside him, wagging a reproachful finger.

'Come now, Lord Yun,' said the monk, sternly. 'The demons are speaking through you again.'

The old man glowered.

'I know what I am saying. Useless boy!'

Then, as swiftly as a cloud covers the sun, Lord Yun was sobbing.

'Poor little fishes! No one will set them free. If they could fly instead of swim they would be free! They would fly to my pond in Three-Step-House and be free forever!'

Abbot Jian touched Guang's shoulder and he rose reluctantly.

'You see how it is,' whispered the monk. 'Possessed by a minor demon. We have tried exorcism many times but without success. He refuses to wash or leave his room. His only companions are those fish.'

Outside the guest room, Guang struggled to compose himself. Unworthiness licked his soul like a cruel flame. Although Abbot Jian murmured that his mother died quite contentedly, having insisted she be removed to a chamber on the opposite side of the monastery to Lord Yun, Guang did not listen.

'I must take Father back to my brother,' he said. 'Shih will know how to cure him.'

Jian started at the name.

'Your twin is still alive? The one Lord Yun disowned?'

'Yes, he is a doctor in Nancheng.'

'I see. A healer. Nancheng is a long way to go. Is your father fit for such a journey? Especially through lands occupied by the Mongols. If I could advise you, I would suggest that Lord Yun stay here. After all, he is half in the next life already. You are young, Guang, and your future lies before you.'

They were interrupted by an old monk hurrying towards them, his stick clicking on the floor.

'Abbot Jian! Khan Bayke is at the gate with twenty men. They demand admittance. They say they have come for Lord Yun.'

At the Western Military Academy, Guang was taught the following: 'Swiftness is the soul of War. Abuse the enemy's lack of preparation; assault him when he feels safe; pursue an unexpected route.' In the decade of soldiering that followed his training to be an officer, he learned that a man prepared to die will always defeat one who values life.

Guang did not hesitate. Indeed action came as a kind of release.

'Tell them I forced you to take me to Father!' he hissed to Jian.

Recollecting the girl he had abandoned in Wei Valley, he said, 'This should convince them,' and punched the monk hard in the nose with all his force, so that there was a spurt of blood and splintering of bone. Abbot Jian fell unconscious to the floor.

Rushing into Father's room, Guang tore a strip from his own robe and brutally gagged the old man. Then he scooped him up along with his staff and pack and staggered down the corridors of the monastery. Already he could hear shouts as the barbarians searched the building, room by room. But Guang knew the ground better than Bayke. Emerging from a side-door, he followed the outer wall and deposited his father in a convenient rubbish tip. Then he peered round a corner at the front gate.

As he had expected, the enemy's horses were tethered outside the entrance. Now luck was on his side. In his eagerness for revenge, Bayke had entrusted the horses to two skinny youths. The boys were struggling to settle the steppe ponies, still excited by their mad gallop to Whale Rock Monastery.

Removing the leather bag of burning powder and stones from his pack, Guang checked the fire-pot at his belt. Its slow-burning match had gone out! Frantically, Guang retraced his steps, aware prayer candles were kept burning in a small shrine along the corridor they had just taken. His luck held. The Mongols were still searching the far side of the monastery. It took a precious moment to relight the match in his fire-pot.

When he returned to the rubbish tip where Lord Yun stood uncertainly, tugging at the gag with feeble fingers, Guang readied his weapons. Then, leaning on his staff like a crippled monk, he hobbled round the corner and approached the youths. One noticed him at once, shouting a warning. Guang kept going. Ten feet from the youth, he twisted the handle of his staff. Nothing happened. The spear-head had stuck! Undaunted, he rushed forward and smashed the iron-clad butt of his staff against the youth's forehead. The second boy screamed to Heaven, before fleeing into the monastery.

Guang ran back and dragged Lord Yun to a horse. There was no more time. Already he could hear Bayke's men returning to the gatehouse. He took a bullwhip from one of the saddles and threw his father over the seat, nimbly tying the squirming old man into place with the braided leather rope. He spent precious moments loosening the remaining horses' reins. At last he climbed onto the finest beast there: from the silver tracery on its saddle, he suspected it was Bayke's own.

But opportunity had run through his fingers. Although he and Father were now mounted, the enemy were rushing through the gatehouse. As a hammer seems to hover before it falls, all present paused. The Mongols wore lamellar armour, bows and swords in their hands. Bayke carried a heavy mace, which he pointed, roaring a command.

Snatching the match from his fire-pot, Guang lit the short fuse protruding from his makeshift thunder-clap bomb. It flared. Casting down the swollen leather bag into the midst of the Mongol horses, he dragged Lord Yun's mount forward by the reins. Shouts rose behind them. Soon they were cantering. Guang's back itched in anticipation of an arrow, even as he crouched low over the saddle. Why had they not struck him down? The Mongols were capable of shooting birds on the wing. Unless, of course, Khan Bayke had ordered that his son's killer must be taken alive.

A moment later the thunderclap bomb exploded with a roar that echoed round the valley. Birds flew screeching from the trees. Horses whinnied in pain and terror. As he glanced back, Guang saw all Bayke's horses scattering through a cloud of dust and smoke, their hooves drumming the stony ground. One limped outlandishly, fell on its side, tried to struggle up, then flopped on the road.

There would be no pursuit for a while.

竹子

As he galloped away from Whale Rock Monastery, Guang knew he had gained only an hour's lead at the very most. The Mongols would eventually gather their horses and thunder after them. He and Father were tied to a fraying rope above jagged stones.

After several *li* he halted, for the horses were too exhausted to go further. When he removed Father's gag the old man coughed and spluttered. Guang recalled that on trapped ground one should devise stratagems. As long as they stayed on the Chunming High Road they were certainly trapped. He glanced at Lord Yun who was muttering to himself, complaining about the loss of his fish.

'I have decided, Father,' he said. 'We shall not ride straight to Chunming but double back to Five Willows Ford, though it takes us deeper into enemy territory. That way, we shall be near water and you might find more little fishes to set free.'

He might have added, 'and you can wash there.' The old man's fox-smell was overwhelming. A look of obvious slyness crossed Father's face and Guang felt a stab of revulsion, followed by guilt. He resolved to never demean Father by mentioning fishes again.

'I like their fragrance, their scent,' said the old man, as though reading his thought. 'They remind me of something else.'

Then he chuckled, his face becoming a mask.

It was early afternoon when they left the road, hiding their tracks by following the course of a deep, fast-flowing stream until they reached a forest track. Sunbeams slanted between the pine trees. By dusk they had crossed two precipitous valleys and still Five Willows Ford lay several *li* distant. He heard no sound of pursuit. It seemed his stratagem had worked, yet Guang was not foolish enough to expect Khan Bayke to gallop all the way to Chunming. Sooner or later he would turn back. There would be men among Bayke's retinue skilful at reading hoof-prints.

Five Willows Ford appeared as a glow through the trees. Guang halted at the forest edge and examined the village below.

Coloured lanterns lit a few stalls and he heard drifting music. A notorious tavern stood in the village square, a haunt of outlaws and bandits. Half the goods traded at Five Willows Ford mocked the law, if only by ignoring taxes. Here the Mongols' curfew went unheeded.

'Father,' he said. 'We will tether the horses at the outskirts of the village and I will find food. You must not wander off or Bayke will seize you. Do you understand, Father? Bayke will tie you to a wooden yoke and drag you behind his horse!'

That prospect made Lord Yun cringe and mutter in alarm to someone invisible. Guang felt ashamed for them both.

In the village square, he approached an affable butcher and led him back to the horses. It took little persuasion to sell them for a tenth of their value.

'I won't ask where they came from,' said the man, winking, as well he might at such a bargain.

'Make sure they are out of the village within the hour,' said Guang, quite as pleasantly. The prospect of Bayke's splendid warhorse being sliced into strips and eaten by hungry peasants gratified him hugely.

Now they had several strings of the Great Khan's new-minted *cash*. Guang hoped it would be enough. He bought noodles and fried belly-pork. Lord Yun ate the meal in silence, dabbing his lips afterwards on his son's coat, which lay on the ground between them. Guang was pleased to see the return of his father's former dainty manners. The food seemed to make him strangely lucid: 'Guang,' he said. 'Where are you taking me?'

His son stopped chewing. After so much madness he found the transformation oddly disturbing.

'To safety, Father. You will live with. . .' He felt reluctant to utter Shih's name, so long unmentionable in their family. '. . . with your Youngest Son, should we get that far.'

The old man visibly trembled.

'Shih is dead!' he exclaimed, in a baffled tone. 'I cannot live with the dead. No, I must live with you, Guang, for you are my only son! Your pretty little wife, my pretty Daughter-in-law, will attend to my needs. She is pretty, eh?'

Though he possessed neither home nor wife, Guang knew Lord Yun must be kept calm.

'It shall be as you say, Father,' he muttered.

Yet Lord Yun remained downcast and afraid.

At the waterfront they found several small river craft bound for Chunming. One was due to leave before dawn, carrying a cargo of spruce logs. Its captain regarded him suspiciously, demanding most of their Mongol coins in exchange for passage.

'Sleep in the bottom of the boat,' said the surly waterman. 'Stay there until we leave.'

In the hour before dawn, Guang perched on the stern and gazed at the river. Father lay asleep at his feet. He struggled to make sense of their situation. It seemed he was the parent now and Father was the child. A wholly unnatural state of affairs. Of course he had heard of such things before and was sure Shih would know how to exorcise the old man's demon. Besides, Heaven must approve of his actions. Why else would the Jade Emperor have returned Father to him? If he demonstrated filial piety a greater reward from Heaven must follow – a Captain's commission at the very least, maybe even a Commander's, preferably with the Imperial Guard.

Guang considered these matters as the river reflected approaching day. The dull black stream turned glossy; ripples formed serpents of fiery sunrise; the water carried a sweet tang of summer plants. On the far shore he noticed a crane stepping gingerly through the shallows, its curved beak poised.

At daybreak they departed for Chunming, the boatmen poling their ship into the centre of the stream. Guang kept Lord Yun hidden amidst stacks of resin-scented timber. As Five Willow Ford fell behind he saw twenty horsemen gallop into the square. Their leader stood in his stirrups and gazed after the dwindling boat. Did Khan Bayke sense they were aboard? The river turned a corner and Five Willows Ford vanished from sight.

竹子

When Guang was a boy he often heard tales of how Great-grandfather Yun Cai freed his old comrade, the illustrious Second Chancellor P'ei Ti, from gaol in Chunming. Indeed, a stirring romance had been written on the subject. Guang often dreamed of adding honour to the family name, like Yun Cai, and always awoke to a sense of inadequacy. Now Heaven had granted him an opportunity.

On arrival in Chunming he abandoned his monk's disguise, trading black robes for the threadbare clothes of an itinerant labourer. No such precautions had been necessary for Father, who already wore filthy rags. Nevertheless, Guang looked too sleek and muscular for a peasant weakened by toil and meagre rations; even with his beard and long hair shaved he possessed an air of distinction. If Chunming had not been awash with refugees from the wars they would have been taken within hours. Yet a destitute old man and his son were a common sight in the city, and Guang made a point of sitting among the hordes of landless peasants.

Guang's first objective was a river passage east. The borders of the Empire were tantalisingly close – a few hundred *li* at most. But no one would carry them without a substantial payment and Guang had observed officials on the waterfront, questioning the most innocent-looking of travellers. He had even seen Khan Bayke riding through the streets with a dozen retainers, staring this way and that like a ravenous hawk.

That was two days ago. Since then Guang had grown increasingly desperate.

Notices had appeared on street corners that morning to announce a foul murder in Wei District and describe the wanted men in some detail. As usual, the authorities provided crude pictures of the felons. The hired woodcut-artist had portrayed Guang as a bushy-bearded hero of old and Father as a wise Immortal. Guang detected a hidden act of subversion behind the flattering portraits.

Certainly the authorities could hardly expect public outrage. He overheard excited whispers at one tea stall about the revenge taken upon Khan Bayke by the great poet Yun Cai's descendents. Rescuing Father had caught the imagination of a people cowed into silence, eager for weakness in their new masters.

Guang squatted beneath an awning in the East Market and watched for a sign how to proceed. Rain fell with dreary intensity – a fresh wave of the monsoon, likely to last for days. Nearly all their *cash* was gone. He examined Father suspiciously. The old man was following the progress of a gaggle of perfumed and powdered singing girls. They giggled fetchingly beneath tasselled umbrellas as they shuffled round puddles on tiny feet. Father's were not the only eyes drawn to the girls, but staring so intently might attract notice.

'Father, remember our situation,' he pleaded.

The old man puffed out wizened cheeks.

'I will buy the lot of them,' he declared, scornfully.

The girls made their way to a small stage covered by garish curtains and awnings. So they were actresses rather than singing girls. It all amounted to the same thing: quails who sell their feathers. Guang fell back to moodily watching the crowd.

'There will be a performance when the rain pauses,' he observed.

The actors were gathered round the stage, drinking tea and joking.

'We should find somewhere else to sit when the play starts. The Mongols like a play.'

Indeed, it was strange how they loved the theatre. Guang had heard that when they massacred cities honourable enough to resist them, they spared only artisans, craftsmen and actors.

The rain continued to fall. Tomorrow he and Lord Yun must risk leaving the city or starve where they crouched. Father stared hungrily at the stage where the girls could be seen moving about. Wearied beyond all reason, Guang fell into a doze.

When he opened his eyes the sky had cleared. Lord Yun was still watching the temporary theatre, now lit with candles and flickering torches, though the curtain stayed shut. Hundreds of townsfolk had gathered for the show. Guang's bowels ached and he cursed inwardly; a diet of cheap scraps was affecting him badly. Lord Yun, used to poor rations, seemed quite at ease.

'Father, wait here,' he hissed. 'I must relieve myself.'

When he returned from the nearest back alley he looked round in alarm. All the panic of a parent who has lost his child in a dense throng possessed him, for Father had vanished.

Guang pushed deep into the crowd. The audience laughed and talked while loud music prepared them for the drama – cymbals clashing, flutes trilling mournfully. He surveyed the excited people. How could they behave as if their land was not occupied? A group of Mongol officers elbowed to the front, accompanied by North Chinese interpreters. Other barbarian warriors watched from the side, perched on their horses for a good view.

Guang's forehead was damp with sweat. A few onlookers protested as he shoved past. Then he understood where the old man must be. At the front, the place he had always taken when Lord of Wei. In his confused mind he was still that Lord.

The curtain opened with a roll of drums and Guang concealed himself behind a tall merchant. He could see Father near the stage, gazing with rapt intensity, his mouth half-open. A dozen people formed a barrier between them.

An actor in splendid blue silks strode on stage. The crowd gasped and he examined the people haughtily. His face was fierce with red make-up and he wore an extravagant wig and false beard. In his hand was a huge scroll, tightly rolled.

'I am Chang Xi!' he declared. 'Sent through all corners of the land on the Emperor's orders to find a girl, a truly virtuous and beautiful girl, who appeared to my great master in a dream. See, here is her picture! Has anyone seen her?'

Despite himself, Guang bent forward with the eager crowd, as Chang Xi unrolled a huge picture of an elegant maiden. The Mongol officers were craning like entranced children. For an odd moment, Guang glimpsed something shared between conquered and conquerer, that the enemy were men, not immune to softer feelings. He blinked. Shook his head. The thought confused him. A traitor's thought.

At the appearance of the picture Father half-rose. One of the Mongols had noticed Lord Yun, and was nudging a companion to point out the ridiculous old fellow.

Once more Chang Xi declaimed, lamenting the impossibility of his quest in a land where all are debased by corruption and greed, unmindful of their filial duties. How could he find such a girl? He stamped his feet. Glared at the crowd. 'Impossible!' he cried. Knowing glances were exchanged among the audience. The actor's hidden message was clear, but not to the Mongols, who roared at the actor's eloquence.

The music resumed. Louder, wilder. Drums and clashing chimes. Flutes and strummed *pi-pa*. Dancers cart-wheeled onto the stage – the very same beauties who had captivated Lord Yun earlier on the street. Chang Xi marched up and down, pretending to assess each girl, before rejecting her as unworthy. Thunderous applause allowed Guang to slip closer to his father.

Lord Yun was on his feet now, staring at the dancers like one possessed by fox-fairies. It seemed he might rush forward, causing a scandal that could only end in arrest. Surely every eye in the crowd must be upon him! Someone might even recognise the former Lord of Wei.

Guang gently took the old man's arm. The tumult on stage was beginning to settle. Now was the time to slip away, while attention was focused on the actors. Yet he dared not manhandle Father, who would certainly protest. So he stood beside him and awaited the worst.

Yet a strange thing happened. As Chang Xi addressed the crowd once more, bewailing his failure to find a virtuous maiden, his glance fell upon Guang and the painted man blinked in surprise. The actor's hesitation was momentary, but the fugitive's stomach tightened. Had they been recognised? Perhaps the posters were more accurate than he supposed. The actor hurried into the wings.

A beautiful lady entered the stage. Her silks and make-up were perfect. The Mongol officers exchanged sly remarks, no doubt recollecting their own hairy women and itchy, yak-skin couches.

'I am Shu Qian,' she announced, in a shrill, nasal voice. 'My father is so poor he has arranged an auction of my virtue. . .'

A commotion at the edge of the crowd made Guang turn. Then he knew they were truly lost.

Khan Bayke and his retinue were pushing their horses straight into the ranks of people, examining faces in the crowd. In a moment they would cry out in recognition, riding down any who got in their way.

Someone was tugging at his arm. He turned to find a fat lady at his side. Closer inspection revealed a eunuch dressed in women's clothes.

'Quick!' he hissed. 'Follow me.'

The crowd was applauding again as the beautiful Shu Qian began to sing. Guang enveloped his Father in strong arms and carried him after the fat he-woman, who hustled them to the side of the stage, out of sight. Yet as Guang placed his hand over Lord Yun's mouth, the old man's jaws closed tight and Guang cried out in pain. When, in the safety of an alleyway crowded with actors waiting to go on stage, he pried open Lord Yun's clamped jaws, a bloody half-circle of tooth marks disfigured his hand, scars he would carry to his grave.

竹子

They were led to a room at the rear of a cheap tavern. The eunuch bowed very low.

'Wait here,' he said, examining the two fugitives curiously. 'My master will join you as soon as the performance ends.'

Before Guang could demand more information the man had gone. Father squatted on the floor, just as he had in Whale Rock Monastery, alternately weeping and staring into space. Sometimes he muttered incoherent words. Guang did not wish to know what haunted so troubled a mind. Lord Yun's lack of dignity revolted him. His instinct was to flee into the streets of Chunming but he held back. After all, the actors could have betrayed them while they stood in the crowd.

Guang furiously twisted the stubborn spear blade from the end of his bamboo pole. Taking a small pot from his bag he smeared thick black paste on the sharp tip. Whatever happened tonight, he would not meet the Infernal Judges alone. Father must not fall into Bayke's hands. If the need arose, he would protect the old man from further shame – forever.

An hour later there was a gentle tap on the door. Guang

stepped to one side of the entrance, balancing on the balls of his feet, spear ready to stab.

'Enter!' he called.

The actor playing the role of Chang Xi stepped inside, looking round eagerly. When he noticed the poisoned spear point hovering beside his throat he went very still and licked his lips.

'Close the door, my friend,' said Guang. 'But softly.'

'I recognised you, sir,' said the actor with a gulp. Thick make-up caked his plump young face. Guang moved the spear tip a fraction closer to the actor's fluttering windpipe.

'Let me introduce myself,' gasped the man.

'Please do,' said Guang.

A fanciful tale followed, throughout which the spear did not waver. The actor was a good talker. He claimed to be in the occupied lands on a delicate mission and that his real name was Chen Song.

'I am a scholar,' he said. 'But that is not why I helped you.'

Still Guang kept silent. Chen Song spoke in an eager rush: 'Many have heard the tale of how you rescued Lord Yun! And killed a dozen of Khan Bayke's men! Such filial piety! When I see Lord Yun's – how can I put it – unfortunate condition, I honour you all the more! Of course, I felt obliged to help. You see, we have met before, though you do not recognise me.'

'When was that?' demanded Guang.

Yet as he examined the fellow's face in the soft lamplight, there was certainly a likeness to one he had known.

'Do you not remember my brother, Chen Su, your comrade at the Western Military Academy, who you stood beside at the Battle of Lu Shan? He perished in the last campaign, before the Traitor's Peace. I saw you together when I was just a boy. My brother often told me how you saved his life.'

'He would have done the same for me,' said Guang.

Then he lowered his weapon and settled heavily in a chair. He was exhausted beyond further precaution.

'Father has not eaten for a whole day,' he said. 'And neither have I.'

Chen Song took the hint at once, ordering a banquet of five grains, five meats, and five wets to honour the fugitives. It seemed he could not do enough for them.

竹子

Two days passed in the small room. Chen Song visited briefly but he was busy with performances all round the city, including the Mongol governor's residence.

Guang ensured Lord Yun did not venture out even to relieve himself. No one disturbed them, except to bring large meals twice a day and replace the chamber pots. Beyond the bamboo curtain, which he dared not lift, rain murmured and splashed. Father slumped on the bed, occasionally sighing or chuckling.

Sometimes Guang tried to engage Lord Yun in conversation but every word felt strained and false. Perhaps Abbot Jian was right – Father's two souls, his *hun* and *po*, had been possessed by demons and there the matter ended. Yet one might find amulets or spells to oppose even the strongest devils. Shih would know what to do. Above all, they must keep Father's condition secret. Otherwise shame would taint the family name.

'Father,' he said. 'I must learn more about this Khan Bayke. He is our deepest enemy now. Tell me what happened when the Mongols first came to Wei. Did no one fight?'

He recognised the unspoken accusation in his voice and added more softly: 'Tell me, please.'

The old man turned to meet his eye. For once the steady wind of his madness slackened.

'I was never in good health like you,' said the old man, full of self-pity. 'My essential breaths were afflicted by the women. They drain one's life force, Guang! You must keep away from them, the temptresses!'

'What happened, Father? If only I had been there! I was on the coastal frontier, thousands of *li* away.'

The old man was mumbling: 'When I was young I was the

handsomest man in our district. No, in our province! In the whole of Chunming Province! When I rode to visit the Prefect, everyone stared and admired my fine figure. So noble on my horse! I had whatever I wanted. And then spring passed. And in autumn Bayke came.'

Guang almost wept. In all the years he had known him, Father had never spoken so frankly. He didn't like it. He preferred him mocking and distant, ineffably cold.

'Everything I wanted was mine by right!' cried the old man, growing agitated. 'Everything! How dare your mother hint otherwise? She betrayed my wishes like the others.'

He turned to face the wall and Guang attempted no further conversation. Who might these others be? It seemed better to think about plans for escape; that, at least, brought a kind of relief.

Each time Chen Song visited, Guang learned more about the actor's delicate position. His troupe consisted of a dozen performers and musicians, as well as porters to set up the stage. The company's previous owner had sold the entire business to Chen Song, who assumed the role of manager. None of the actors knew government funds had hired them. Neither did they know the true reason for their tour of the occupied lands, believing it was for mutual profit, and indeed they were making plenty of money.

On his next visit, Chen Song revealed that although the Empire and the Khanate were officially at peace, various spies had been sent into the Mongol territories. Given the free passage accorded to actors, Chen Song had been instructed to travel and observe, noting the enemy's weaknesses and strengths. He came from a family of notable scholars in Sichuan, but the ancestral estates had been seized by the enemy. His grudge was much like Guang's own.

'We shall go no further west than Chunming,' said Chen Song. 'I have learned enough for a full report.'

'What have you learned?' asked Guang.

It was their third night among the actors. Now they shared wine like old comrades.

'That the people are fickle,' said Chen Song, bitterly. 'Many place their necks under the yoke for an easy life. I tell you we must extinguish the Mongols or find our ancient ways snuffed out forever. Then we will live in darkness. When war resumes, as surely it must, I will no longer skulk as a spy but seek a good commander to serve!'

Guang nodded approvingly.

'I long to be such a commander,' he said. 'It is my fate.'

He glanced at Father, who was snoring on the bed.

'Perhaps I may help in a small way,' said Chen Song. 'When we reach Nancheng, I shall inform the authorities of your valiant conduct.'

Guang looked downcast and poured more wine.

'You would speak in vain, my friend. I lost my last commission for criticising a superior officer's timidity. In short, I have been branded a hot-head.'

His new friend snorted contemptuously.

'When the temporary peace ends we shall need bold officers. Consider the indecision of the court! The Chief Minister veers between appeasing the Mongols and arresting their ambassadors. We must be decisive! They respect only force. And Guang, consider how you have proved your courage! I have made enquiries about this Khan Bayke – who, by the way, is still scouring Chunming for you. He is only a minor commander, yet news of your revenge has been sent to the Great Khan's court.'

Guang did not like this news.

'How shall we escape if they are searching for us high and low?'

Chen Song spread his hands.

'Tomorrow we shall board a boat I have chartered to take us east, performing in cities on the way. Your filial piety will be a guarantee of divine favour!'

The young man's enthusiasm made Guang smile. It was both

pleasing and novel to be treated with such respect. After Chen Song left he paced up and down the small room, thinking himself a splendid fellow indeed.

Father, who had been supplied a bowl of goldfish, took no notice. At intervals he reached into the bowl and tried to stroke the fish as they circled.

They boarded the chartered craft without incident and sailed down the rain-choked river. Guang sensed Bayke's vengeance drawing close and glanced back uneasily. But the other boats were unremarkable, simple merchant vessels like their own.

By evening the river ahead began to roar and froth; soon they were riding rapids at night, white water churning in the starlight. The actresses screamed and the musicians begged the Immortal Lan Ts'ai-Ho for assistance, while Chen Song feverishly clutched a jade amulet. Only the boatmen seemed unconcerned, intent on steering and poling. Guang caught a glimpse of Lord Yun's terrified face and sat beside him to steady his nerves. Beyond the rapids lay narrow gorges and darkness. Another three hundred *li* of hostile lands before they reached the Empire – assuming Bayke did not trap them first.

憺

three

'The people of Fouzhou and Nancheng differ greatly in character. The explanation is simple: Fouzhou lies on the North bank of the Han River, while Nancheng occupies the South. Hence, the people of Fouzhou are naturally quiet and level headed, replete with cold *yin* and prone to sing the note *yu* in their traditional songs. The people of Nancheng, however, favour the note *chih* and prefer to laugh in a giddy manner. . .'

From *Remembrances of A Western Terrace at Twilight*

竹子

Nancheng, Central China. Late summer 1266.

Cao paused to listen before closing the door of her bedchamber. The rhythmic thud of Shih pounding herbs in a mortar vibrated through the bamboo walls of the house. His intensity suggested he would be a while yet, emerging with damp hair and pungent fingers.

Cao strained her ears for faint noises from Honoured Guest. She always referred to the girl in this way, conscious that guests eventually leave. Whenever Cao considered Lu Ying her thoughts drifted to the time before her arrival and then she grew confused, torn between the obligations of courtesy and something darker, harder to name.

As usual Wang Ting-bo's former concubine made no sound. Sometimes Madam Cao overheard a sigh or shuffle coming from her chamber and, once, sobbing. Otherwise Lu Ying might have been a proud, secretive ghost.

Satisfied she would not be disturbed, Cao opened a low wooden chest. It contained her most treasured possessions, many dating to the time when she still lived in the capital, Linan, with her father, old Dr Ou-yang. The capital lay more than two thousand *li* away, across half the Empire, and her girlhood seemed even further off though she was only thirty years old. Yet it was strange to touch a comb or ribbon worn as a girl and momentarily be that vanished person again. Perhaps the years in between were dreams.

She took a small bronze mirror from the chest, rubbing it on her sleeve until it shone. Then she examined her reflected face. As always, it did not satisfy. Her nose was inelegant, eyes too close together. Cao tried to arrange straying locks of hair, one hand balancing the heavy mirror. At last she gave up and stared deeply at her reflection.

Her mouth was all right. Shih had compared it to a flower on many occasions during their twelve years of marriage, pointing out that the mouth is associated with the spleen whose cardinal quality is trustworthiness. But she would never care for her nose. It was imperceptibly crooked, not quite aligned to the centre of her face.

Again, Cao listened to the house. More thudding. No sign the apprentice was stirring. Shih had instructed Chung to study a treatise on the pulse and the lad was probably taking a nap. Her father would have treated such a lazy apprentice harshly.

She deftly removed her clothes and stood naked, the mirror in her hands. She tilted it this way and that, examining her breasts, wondering if they were too large, angling the mirror to her black rose, which seemed unkempt. As for her thighs and arms, she needed no mirror to know they were overly broad, shaped by work like a peasant woman's.

As usual she could not help examining her feet. Such large feet, any lady would be ashamed of them. Cao particularly envied their guest's tiny feet, like perfect golden lilies, enough to drive a man wild. But her father had always scowled when she suggested binding and it was too late now, one had to start young. Shih maintained that bound feet did nothing for a woman except make her shuffle. Sometimes Cao caught his glance descending to Lu Ying's tiny feet and wondered what he really thought. He was a man like any other, after all.

Her imperfections distressed Cao, but soon her thoughts drifted back to familiar, comforting concerns: the shop and patients reluctant to pay their fees; whether to buy fish for dinner. It was absurd, gazing at herself like an unmarried girl. The bronze mirror grew burdensome in her hand and she felt a great urge to escape her reflection. Placing the mirror face down on her bed, she dressed hurriedly. Then she wiped its flawless oval face one last time before hiding it away in her special chest. She wiped her eyes, cloudy with foolish tears.

Opening the door to the central corridor running like a spine through the house, Cao listened once more. This time she imagined what could not be heard – the squeals and cries of noisy children, calling her name.

A little tea flavoured with a soothing herb made her feel better, and she stood by the kitchen door looking out. Apricot Corner Court was a rectangle of one-storey wooden buildings surrounding an earthen courtyard. In the centre stood the apricot tree, heavy with young fruit still too bitter to eat. Three families lived round the courtyard in houses of descending size.

Dr Shih's was the largest, as befitted his position. At the front stood his shop, known to passers-by through the sign of a yellow gourd and a banner reading *Health Guaranteed* in fading red characters. The family rooms lay behind, eight in number, if one counted the first storey tower room Shih used to dry herbs and prepare medicines. He claimed that the winds gained potency higher up and, ideally, he should prepare his medicines at the top of Blue Dragon Pagoda. Dr Shih had boundless faith in the Eight Winds.

Aside from the kitchen and bedchambers, their household contained two storerooms gathering dust. Every year Cao buried a sweet, ripe apricot from the courtyard tree in a corner of these rooms. Yet her prayers remained unanswered. The apricot stones had not bloomed. When they first came here they had never imagined how years might pass in waiting.

Old Hsu the fan-maker's dwelling and workshop were next in size. He and his family occupied a large corner of the courtyard, concealed from the street. The third house, and smallest, belonged to Cao's special friend, Widow Mu. Behind Mu's narrow shop lay a smaller, family room. In all, only a dozen people occupied Apricot Corner Court so that some in Water Basin Ward called it a barren place, despite its fertile name.

Cao stepped outside and yawned. The Twin Cities lolled in the last weeks of summer, the air moist from clouds blowing west. Old Hsu waved at her from his seat beneath the apricot tree. He worked less and less these days, restricting himself to criticising his Youngest Son and Son-in-law, who kept the fan business going.

'Madam Cao!' he called. 'At last, someone sensible to share my news!'

So flattering a summons could hardly be ignored. Cao went over, unconsciously shuffling a little as she had seen the stylish Lu Ying walk down the corridor. Old Hsu examined her sharply beneath bushy eyebrows.

'Something wrong with your feet, Madam?' he asked.

Before she could answer his question he announced gravely: 'Today I took a bundle of fans to the market and a proclamation was being read. It appears we are again at war.'

He regarded her significantly. Cao wasn't quite sure of the correct reply. As usual he provided it.

'The rulers want us all to become peasants or soldiers! So we can till the fields and feed their armies.'

In his youth, Hsu had met a travelling holy man who taught

him the outmoded thoughts of Mo Zi. He had grasped this wisdom fervently but imperfectly and, ever since, regaled the world with Mo Zi's odd views. Sometimes Shih and Cao wondered whether they would be punished for not reporting his opinions to the authorities.

'Madam, I am not a scholar like your honoured husband, but I know it is best to be happy. Our humble fans bring no glory to anyone, but they cool many a hot head.'

Cao tried to appear interested. An insect landed on Old Hsu's cheek and he brushed it off angrily.

'If we could but love each other, and consider ourselves one great family,' he continued, 'there would be no more strife between nations.'

'Of course, you are right,' said Cao. 'But do the barbarians share your view?'

'That I cannot say,' conceded Old Hsu. 'But I am certain the people worry about three things – hunger, cold, and rest when they are weary. Those are the only struggles we should wage. Never war, Madam Cao, never more war.'

His upset was not hard to explain. Old Hsu's eldest son, a young man of unusual goodwill and humour, had been conscripted five years ago. Nothing had been heard of him since. It was assumed he had died on the battlefield though Old Hsu insisted on setting aside a place for him at dinner each dusk, in case he returned unexpectedly.

Cao bowed and made her way to Widow Mu's dumpling shop.

She found Mu preparing a fresh stock of fried dumplings. The work was urgent as nearly all the walnut-sized dumplings on her wooden tray had been sold. Usually this was a quiet hour for gossip, the breakfast trade having passed and the brisker dinner trade still hours away. Cao wondered if she should return later, but Mu waved her inside.

After they had bowed, making enquiries concerning each other's health and the health of their families, Mu returned to work, dicing cabbage with a large knife. The blade tapped like a persistent drip. Cao took a seat nearby, fanning herself.

'Let me help you,' she said.

The widow pursed her lips. The click of her knife did not pause.

'You are my guest,' she said.

'Then you must pander to me,' replied Cao. 'I will prepare the garlic sauce.'

As Widow Mu fried a stuffing of pork and cabbage, crispy egg and ginger, Cao peeled and minced cloves of garlic.

'I have heard new things about your Honoured Guest,' remarked Widow Mu. 'Hey, Lan Tien! Come and help with the dough!'

Mu's eldest daughter, an awkward girl of fourteen almost ready for her hairpins, emerged from the room at the back of the shop. It was a tiny room. Widow Mu shared it with her two children and the family shrine. The foremost tablet belonged to her dead husband, who frequently advised her through dreams. Widow Mu said she could hardly miss him when he never went away. He had died quite suddenly of a mushroom in the brain and Dr Shih had declared the disease incurable.

Fortunately he left Mu enough money for the equipment needed to establish her business. Hard work from dawn until midnight provided the rest. But the profit on each dumpling was small and competition among food sellers was ceaseless. One might easily lose a loyal customer, who in turn might tell a friend that Widow Mu skimped on pork or ginger. She often feared the landlord's men putting them on the street.

Lan Tien sulkily began to detach balls from the melon of dough her mother had prepared earlier, rolling them out into small circles.

'What have you heard about Honoured Guest?' asked Cao, as though there had been no interruption.

'One of my regulars came by and stayed while he ate. It would be indiscreet to mention his name. Actually it was Market Clerk Chi. Anyway, he told me his cousin is a servant on Peacock Hill and that he drank wine with him last night. Hey, Lan Tien, leave a thicker centre!'

The girl rolled her eyes but continued to work silently.

'Your guest is very bold by his account,' continued Widow Mu. 'She almost supplanted His Excellency's wife. Imagine it! If Wang Ting-bo had not been afraid of offending his wife's family – they own great estates down South – he would have found an excuse to divorce her. Some say Lu Ying used sorcery to captivate him. Not that it takes magic for a man to lose his head.'

The women worked in silence. Cao digested this news.

'Servants' gossip,' she said, touched by a vague desire to defend her guest.

'Watch that one!' remarked Mu, and the doctor's wife didn't know whether she referred to the discarded concubine or was admonishing her daughter.

'Lu Ying has been no trouble to me,' said Cao. 'She seems a fine lady. Indeed, I do not know why she stays with us at all. I believe she wishes to obey her former master. So one might call her very filial.'

Widow Mu had reached the stage of filling the dumplings. The task gained importance when two longshoremen from the basin near the Water Gate of Morning Radiance cleared the last of her stock.

'Market Clerk Chi told me that, for all her beauty, this Lu Ying is of no family,' remarked Mu. 'Perhaps she has nowhere to go. The miracle of it is that the Pacification Commissioner did not have a child by her. Then again, his candle has never been good at lighting fires. For all the fine ladies he keeps, there is only one son.'

Lan Tien sniggered as she rolled out dough. Cao pretended to fuss over vinegar for the sauce; she knew her friend's insensitivity was well-meant.

'What happens in a palace may happen in an alley,' said Mu. 'And another thing. Your fine guest has a taste for the best, according to Chi's cousin. Silks that took a whole village a year to make and are worn only once. Make-up so finely ground the powder runs like water. She ended up with more elegant clothes than His Excellency's wife!'

Cao sighed. Really this was too much! Yet she wondered what would happen if Lu Ying asked Shih for extravagant make-up or perfume.

'Nevertheless, I pity her,' she said, doggedly. 'And Dr Shih is too sensible to spend more than we can afford.'

Widow Mu placed nuggets of filling on the dough circles.

'Let a beggar in your house and he'll soon have his feet on the table,' she declared.

The doctor's wife concentrated on the garlic sauce. Although Mu meant well, she lacked delicacy. Cao didn't mind when the gossip concerned someone else's troubles, but found it less diverting when applied to her own. Still, Mu was a neighbour and friend. No one prospered by quarrelling with a neighbour.

The little shop filled with the spit and scent of frying. Cao glanced out of the window while Mu used chopsticks to drop and retrieve dumplings from a pan of hot oil. Willows overhanging the canal, planted to ensure the bank did not crumble, stirred in the light breeze. Leaves shimmered like jade pendants catching the sun. And she wondered where a good wife's duty lay.

竹子

Madam Cao knew all about the duties of a doctor's wife. Her earliest memory was of a patient in her father's medicine house on Black Tortoise Street in the capital. He had been a water-carrier with a misshapen back, screaming as the smouldering moxa burned his bare skin. It made a great impression on her. Afterwards the man seemed grateful to her father rather than angry.

Mother had died when she was two years old. Of course no portraits of her had been painted for they were humble people. And Father was hopeless at describing her. So, as a little girl, Cao painted pictures in her imagination – Mother as a beautiful lady, bobbing in a gilded sedan chair down the Imperial Way, her make-up white as fresh snow, silk dress and hair-ornaments exquisite. Such ladies sometimes entered old Dr Ou-yang's shop to buy medicines they wished to keep secret from their husbands.

Black Tortoise Street adjoined the Imperial Way and the Emperor's palace could be spied in the distance. She would venture to the edge of the wide Imperial Way, gazing out at carriages and streams of people, noble fruit trees planted to form avenues, gentlemen drifting to fashionable tea-houses for cordials. She was sure Mother had joined this world of fine people, so happy as she went up and down, her ghost always hurrying somewhere pleasant. When she told Father he looked very sad and she felt guilty.

Once she found the courage to ask if Mother had been beautiful. Father had replied: 'Beauty doesn't always wear silks.' A funny reply. He was often strange. And distant. But she remembered his words. Later they would comfort her during difficult times.

There had been a cat to keep down the rats which frightened her with their scratching and scurrying, especially when she was alone in the house, Father having been called to a patient's bedside. Once she watched the muscles of its crouched back arch before it leapt. The cat brought her a fat mouse as a present. Father said that some poor people ate rats and called them household deer. She had wondered how their breath smelt.

When Cao was seven, Father summoned her to the shop. A small boy stood there, slightly older than herself. He was evidently afraid, for he could not stop gazing at his feet and trembling. A small bag lay on the floor beside him. If that was all he owned, she didn't think it much. Father talked to a man with an odd accent and bowed many times. Then the man went away, having given Father a heavy sack. Cao noticed the stranger did not even say goodbye to the little boy and seemed relieved to go. All three stood awkwardly in the shop.

'Cao,' said Dr Ou-yang. 'This is my new apprentice, Yun Shih.'

The boy started to cry and Father rebuked him severely. Shih stood shaking, biting his lower lip hard. Cao had taken pity on him, offering to show her toys, but the strange boy poked at her dolls and asked in his peculiar accent whether she ever pretended they were sick.

'Why should I?' she had asked.

'Because this is a doctor's house,' he replied. 'Doctors make people better. That is their duty.'

They both looked up to find Father watching. Cao wondered if he would be angry but instead he had smiled. A rare enough thing since Mother died.

'You might make me a good apprentice, little Yun Shih,' he said.

Then they all smiled and Father sent out for sugar-glazed buns. He seemed very happy about the bag of *cash* the man with the odd accent had given him.

When she was ten, Cao frequently discovered Shih staring hard at one or other of Father's many books and scrolls. A tutor from the neighbourhood was teaching them both to read. Shih seemed to learn his characters effortlessly, while she acquired them as one does an impossible skill, like standing on your head with one hand or making Father's tea exactly the way he liked it. Cao knew she was lucky to have these lessons, none of the neighbours' girls had lessons. Father told her that just because she was a woman, it didn't mean she must be a fool. That made her special. Whenever she struggled over a character, Shih would lift his dogged head from whatever task Father had set him and guide her brush until she could write it herself. Sometimes she pretended to struggle so he would help. She liked the gentle strength of his hand as it guided her own, their heads bent close together over the paper.

Once, during the Festival of Lanterns, she found Shih crying in his tiny room. While they talked, the family pig snuffled in its sty outside. There was a smell of fireworks and wood smoke in the night air. Father was out visiting a patient, for even during the festival people fell ill.

'Why are you crying?' she had asked. 'Everyone in the world is happy tonight.'

'Because I have no family,' he replied.

The enormity of this filled her with sadness. It was the most terrible thing. Then she sat beside him on his narrow bed and took his arm. He flinched at her touch. At once she withdrew her hands to her lap.

'You have Father and me,' she said, brightly.

That made his tears worse. Cao returned to her room and thought about him all evening, and how fortunate she was to have Father. The capital blazed with the light of a million lanterns and people capered in the streets until dawn.

When she was fifteen years old Cao received her hairpins. Father placed them solemnly in her hair and a Daoist nun specially hired for the occasion chanted a sutra to ensure her fecundity and happiness. One of her uncles attended, watching the proceedings with a critical eye. First Uncle's presence proved the ceremony was important: Dr Ou-yang's brothers didn't come often, the reason lying in the past.

Father told her his family had turned against Mother after they were married. It all happened because Mother's own family lost their wealth due to an earthquake and no one likes to be connected to beggars. But he had defied the pressure to divorce her, and so all his relatives kept away.

Once a year, during the Cold Food Festival, Cao was taken to Grandfather and Grandmother's house but they never stayed long. Then Father would be gloomy for days. Her told her it was a hard thing to be Fifth Son, and that too many children can be a great burden, not just for the parents, but for the children themselves. Cao promised herself that when she had many sons, each would be treated exactly alike. On the day she received her hairpins, First Uncle spoke for a long time with Father in private. Afterwards Dr Ou-yang could not meet her eye and she wondered how she had displeased him.

If she had lacked a friend, Cao might have been unhappy. But there was always Shih. In the role of servant, he chaperoned her to the West Lake for excursions, as Father preferred to stay at home. On one trip, he smiled shyly at her and recited a poem – a poem full of longing and romance. She learned then of his noble ancestor, Yun Cai, who had composed it to honour the beautiful singing girl, Su Lin. Everyone in the city loved that old story.

Soon afterwards Shih used his small annual allowance to buy a cheap woodcut book of Yun Cai's verses. Cao agreed the poems were very fine, very fine indeed. She even memorised his favourites and Shih seemed inordinately pleased. Father barely noticed what they did. His patients absorbed him and, when he was too sick to work, as happened more frequently, Shih took his place for the simpler cases. No one seemed to mind if they went to the West Lake together.

But when Cao was eighteen, everything changed. Dr Ou-yang took to his bed and Uncle came unexpectedly to examine the objects and furniture. Once she heard a quarrel in Father's room and felt afraid. Shih took on yet more patients, always bringing the fees straight to his master and preparing the medicines as instructed, though really he required no instruction.

One summer's day Shih and Cao slipped out to the Che River while Father slept deeply, having asked a neighbour to sit with him. They walked along the shore until they found a secluded place, away from the main paths. Paddle boats churned the water and they ate buns she had steamed earlier. He sat on a low wall by the waterside, throwing pebbles into the water. Cao finally found the courage to sit close beside him. He smelt of home, always a place of herbs and compounds, as well as an aroma unique to himself – indefinably comforting – like the scent of warm clothes.

'Your father's condition is graver than you imagine,' he said, at last. 'I can no longer conceal the truth from you. I must tell you because. . .' He blushed. 'Because I esteem you.'

'Perhaps we should go back?' she suggested, in alarm. 'I should not have left him.'

Yet she did not rise.

'I am afraid what will happen if he grows weaker,' he said. 'I have watched so many strong people fade. I am worried for you.'

He continued to flick stones into the water.

'You must realise there is a plan to marry you off to one of your cousins,' he continued. 'I believe the boy's name is Wen.'

Her hand flew to her mouth. Could Father really want that for her? Wen was the least of her cousins – in every conceivable way.

'I believe your father does not like this match,' said Shih, loyal as ever to the master who had been so kind to him. 'Dr Ou-yang desires only the best for you. When he has gone, someone must provide for you.'

His earnest face was softened by the declining sun. Her fluttering heart felt uncomfortable, yet its restlessness was oddly pleasant.

'Why can't another provide for me?' she asked, amazed at her boldness. 'Am I so unattractive that no one will have me?'

They had turned to each other, faces very close, trying to read one another's souls. She heard herself whispering, quite shamelessly, as though someone bolder than herself spoke through her mouth: 'Why should it not be you?'

Then that shameless mouth was kissing his, tentatively at first, until it came naturally and her eyelids fluttered like her heart.

Afterwards, Shih begged her forgiveness. He seemed distressed.

'I have betrayed my master,' he muttered. 'I am a despicable chaperone!'

He gasped with surprise when once more she pressed her lips against his own.

'Then we betray him together,' she said.

They returned to the shop, secretly brushing shoulders on the

Imperial Way, as though touching by accident. The neighbour keeping watch by Father's bedside told them he had not stirred.

That evening she entered Father's bedchamber and cried out in fear. Shih appeared in the doorway and hurried to the sick man's bed. Father lay flat on his back, mouth open as if about to speak, yet quite peaceful, his eyes staring into emptiness. Shih took his master's pulse then gently pulled down Dr Ou-yang's eyelids. Apart from a buzzing fly, the room was silent. Outside, two friends talked excitedly as they passed beneath the window. Cao caught the words, '*more silver than the God of Riches*', then the voice faded. Shih watched the first of a procession of tears run down her face.

'I must tell your uncle,' he said. 'He will arrange a noble funeral. Sit with your father until I return. We shall remember his many kindnesses forever.'

But the funeral had been plain rather than noble. Uncle did not even bother to inform Dr Ou-yang's fellow physicians in the guild, though Shih ensured word got around. A score of senior physicians accompanied the dead man to his pyre and Uncle seemed surprised by their presence.

After the funeral he returned to Dr Ou-yang's shop and spent hours searching the rooms for hidden valuables. Whatever he found was deposited in a lacquered chest. Then he ordered Cao to fetch tea and examined her closely.

'Niece,' he said. 'Your father made arrangements concerning your future. Did he tell you of them?'

She shook her head, eyes lowered.

'Well, that does not matter. You are to marry Fifth Cousin Wen. This house and its contents are your dowry.'

He did not ask if she was pleased. She stood trembling before him, unable to look up.

'I will collect you tomorrow and take you home. As for the apprentice, inform him he must leave the house at dawn, when I will settle any outstanding wages.'

After he had left, weighed down by the lacquer box, Cao

rushed to Shih and told him what Uncle had decided. He paced the room angrily.

'I am not distressed for myself,' he said. 'Only for you. I cannot believe your father seriously intended you to marry this man. There is a stench of greasy money behind all this. Yet it is a crime to oppose a father's will.'

Cao wrung her hands.

'I do not wish to become Fifth Cousin Wen's wife!' she cried. 'I have another love. One I can never forget.'

Shih stopped pacing and met her eyes. They had been little more than children. It would be a year before Shih reached the age of capping into manhood in his twentieth year.

'There may be another way,' he said, cautiously. 'A less than honourable way, perhaps. If we have the courage.'

'When I am with you I have the courage for anything,' she said.

She had meant it with all her hope and heart, unaware how cruel people can be, and how kind when least expected. Since that day, twelve years had passed. . .

竹子

Madam Cao walked across Nancheng to the East Market, where she was curious to read the proclamation mentioned by Old Hsu. Such notices were customarily hung on the Gate of Fragrant Increase and she joined a small crowd round the strip of paper. When her turn came, a retired clerk politely offered to read it to her.

'I can read, sir!' she said with more passion than she had intended. 'Just because I am a woman does not mean I must be a fool.'

Cao flushed with embarrassment at her rudeness. She did not know what had come over her. Afraid of causing a scandal, she added in a wheedling voice: 'But if you would help me with the more difficult characters, sir, I would be very grateful.'

The man chuckled. Cao noticed with surprise that he had taken no offence.

'What, young lady? Speak a little louder.'

The proclamation gave advanced warning of civic restrictions, should the enemy approach the city. Everything was expressed in vague terms, yet Cao could not avoid a pang of fear. She had heard rumours that those towns which fell to the Mongols perished utterly. Many people preferred to kill their entire family than suffer captivity, or worse. Surely it was impossible the enemy could reach as far as Nancheng. The Son of Heaven's armies would scatter them long before that. Cao reassured herself she was glad to have read the notice; it would provide something to tell Shih over dinner.

As she bought peppers and dried wood-ear, lily flowers and onions, to make pour-fish sauce – one of her husband's favourite dishes – unwelcome thoughts arose. Why did her guest not help with the cooking? Perhaps she did not know how, having grown used to meals served at her whim. Although Shih's fees from patients had increased since curing the Pacification Commissioner's son, to the extent that he talked about hiring a maid, Cao still prepared all their meals. Thankfully, Shih did not object to Lu Ying eating alone in her room, though it was hardly friendly.

That made Cao wonder, too. She had noticed he grew awkward whenever Honoured Guest emerged to ask for something. He glanced away, as though trying to dismiss Lu Ying from his mind. While Cao approved of such delicacy, she distrusted what lay beneath it.

'A noble fish!' declared the merchant. 'A prince of trout! A dish fit for the Pacification Commissioner's own table!'

Cao did not haggle over the price. She wished to get home soon and see what was going on in her absence.

懀

four

'Now I will explain how the cities of Nancheng and Fouzhou are defended. Water subjugates fire: in this way the wide moats and canals surrounding the Twin Cities drown the burning will of besiegers. Earth subjugates water: thus the high walls of pounded earth lined with stone channel water in ways beneficial to the Son of Heaven's subjects. One might say the defence of Nancheng and Fouzhou relies upon the five elements. . .'

From *Dream Pool Essays* by Shen Kua

竹子

Han River, Central China. Early autumn, 1266.

Guang felt stale, inaction made him restless. Being a passenger did not suit him at all.

After Wuhan, the actors' boat sailed east until it joined the great Han River, gateway to the Empire's rich heartland. There had been no pursuit, and part of him would have welcomed one to make the dull hours sat in the stern pass more quickly. Yet the trip was not entirely lacking in satisfaction.

Once safely within the Empire, Chen Song announced Guang's true position as heroic saviour of Lord Yun and single-handed slayer of a dozen Mongols. After that he was treated with awe by the troupe of actors. The prettiest of the dancers even felt obliged to share her favours. But as Guang returned from a tryst with her in the bushes when their boat paused to gather firewood, he caught Father glaring at him with such strange intensity that he avoided the old man's eye all that day.

On the Han they made swift progress. It was a merry party, despite the risk of pirates. The boatmen, unaccustomed to so much *cash*, spent it freely on wine. Only Chen Song stayed sober. Donning his official uniform, he composed a long memorandum describing the Mongol deployments which he read to Guang, who listened attentively. By now he had gained stewardship of a fair portion of the scholar's ready money in the form of an honourable loan. At a tailor's shop in a waterside town Lord Yun insisted on purchasing a suit of gaudy silks that emptied Guang's purse, while his son chose plain but respectable clothes for himself.

A few days before they reached the Twin Cities, the actors' boat was forced to find a mooring for the river ahead was full. A fleet of paddle-boats and oar-propelled war junks laboured in formation up the rain-quickened Han, bound for the borders. There were swift destroyers and huge, many-storied floating castles, accompanied by darting dragon boats. Guang watched silently as ships laden with crossbowmen and warriors passed slowly, their fine flags drooping in the humid air. Officers in full armour strode the painted decks and the fleet advanced to a steady drumbeat. Its potential filled Guang's imagination. He paced up and down the shore until the fleet passed.

'A powerful force,' remarked Chen Song.

'I should be with them!' cried Guang. 'I could direct our new weapons so the enemy fled back to their miserable steppes!'

Chen Song nodded.

'Yesterday I consulted the Book of Changes concerning your future,' he said. 'I saw fire. Rest assured your time will come.'

Later they heard rumours that a great land army had marched west from the Twin Cities of Nancheng and Fouzhou.

Their spirit was said to be overwhelming, their commanders uncommonly resolute. Guang took the news badly. He returned to the boat and found Lord Yun drunk before an audience of actors, who had also been drinking heavily. The old man, shaking as he spoke, was describing how he cut his way out of Whale Rock Monastery.

'The first one I chopped like this!'

Lord Yun slashed at the air and the actors cheered.

'The second fell like this!'

The actresses squealed behind their fans.

'The third was a tougher fellow, oh yes, but I knew what was good for him, so I took my sword. . .'

One of the actors leapt up and chopped at the air until his arms were tangled in a knot. His audience clapped appreciatively. Father looked from face to face, his mouth trembling.

Gradually they became aware Guang was staring at them. The actor who had mocked Lord Yun scratched his arms awkwardly, ashamed and afraid. Guang strode forward. For a moment he paused, his hand raised, then he slapped the actor so hard across the face that he fell overboard with a splash. Guang glared at the others while the boatmen fished out the drowning man.

'Never annoy Lord Yun again,' he said, quietly. 'You are common filth. He is noble.'

He took Father's arm and deposited him next to Chen Song. Tears clouded his eyes. The old man was muttering wildly again and Guang cringed inwardly as he caught the word 'fishes'.

'Lord Yun will be my constant companion for the rest of the journey,' declared Chen Song. 'It would be the greatest honour for me. I beg you to allow it.'

Guang wondered at this kind friend who had saved him a dozen times. He longed for a chance to repay the debt. At the cost of his own life, if need be.

A few days later they glimpsed the Twin Cities.

竹子

Guang's acquaintance with Fouzhou and Nancheng stemmed from failure.

After his graduation from the Western Military Academy he had several commissions in the Army of the Left Hand, gaining a reputation as a ruthless and efficient Captain of Artillery. On one occasion his men set fire to a dozen pirate ships, drowning all aboard, including their families. Yet promotion evaded him. He was too blunt, too often right when superiors were wrong, traits certain to provoke disfavour. So he found himself cast loose in Nancheng at the start of winter, petitioning for a new commission alongside dozens of other officers, many from influential families.

A time he did not care to recollect. . .

Wind whipped freezing dust through the streets and the wooden frames of houses creaked with frost. Soon his stock of *cash* had run low, for he refused to demean himself by eating like a petty cobbler or peasant.

Then, one afternoon, as he walked down Bright Hoop Street, wrapped against the cold in his quilted jacket, Guang had seen his own face pushing towards him through the crowd. At first he wondered if hunger and cold had numbed his brain. Or whether fox-fairies had cast a spell on him. The man was his double! He wore a doctor's sober robes and a black, ear-flapped hat. He carried a case of needles. Guang refused to believe his eyes.

There are moments in all men's lives when destiny wraps itself round a spot of time. At first he doubted the most obvious conclusion, even the rapid beat of his heart. Who was this stranger? Yet no stranger could mirror one's own face or body so exactly. *Ah*, he heard himself murmuring, the truth slowly gathering, *ah*, as though his voice belonged to someone else, and he speculated how tall and handsome a small boy could grow, so that a tiny lost face might shine with adult intensity. More than that, the face shone with sentiments Guang had felt too little in his harsh life, so very little during fight after bloody fight. The face pushing towards him was marked out by habits of sympathy and kindness. So that Guang felt this strange, shared face somehow reproached him in ways he could not explain.

And, of course, it had been Shih, the twin he had not seen since they were eight years old! Confronted by each other they had stared, afraid to glance away, afraid the lost brother they had imagined through long lonely years would suddenly vanish. At last, tentatively, Shih raised his arms and stepped forward. Guang had flinched at first, unused to affection. His shoulders had tensed. For a moment they swayed towards each other, then wept at exactly the same time, and embraced.

A crowd soon gathered, as it will at the slightest excuse, exclaiming and pointing. 'They are *Shen* and *Men*!' cried a pious old man. 'They will guard against evil spirits! It is an omen! Any who witnesses their meeting will be blessed with good luck!' Afterwards, this man insisted on sending statues of *Shen* and *Men* to Apricot Corner Court; one a red-faced god, the other ghostly white. They were set up in the gatehouse with much ceremony, each holding a long mace and dressed in paper armour.

Naturally Guang had gone to live with Shih. For both it was a time of happy discovery. They talked every evening, finding much in common – and many differences of character. Yet their conversation always returned to the occupation of Three-Step-House and the death of Mother and Father. For word had reached Guang that their parents perished in the fighting against the Mongol invaders.

All winter he had remained as his brother's guest, developing a deep respect for his plain but practical Sister-in-law, Cao. Finally the arrival of spring – and too much home-brewed wine – provoked his oath to deliver a letter to the ancestral tomb.

*

For all these reasons, Guang's heart leapt as the Twin Cities rose on the horizon.

'I would die a hundred deaths for this place,' he informed Chen Song. 'Nancheng delivered a lost brother and now Father to me. Without Nancheng I would have no family!'

As their boat drew parallel to the city walls and watchtowers, the scholar caught his enthusiasm. 'Destiny worked through you and your brother,' he said. 'That is quite clear. Twin cities and twin brothers. The authorities must take notice!'

Their craft approached the Floating Bridge linking Fouzhou to Nancheng, one of the Empire's wonders. This pontoon bridge, three *li* long, was wide enough in places for two carriages to pass. Wooden palisades and elevated platforms for archers protected it from waterborne attack. A man-made island had been laboriously constructed in the middle of the river. On it stood a tall brick and stone fort. Ships travelling up and downstream were obliged to pass through wooden swing bridges and channels of sharpened stakes. By this feat of engineering, the enemy were denied access to the heartlands of the Empire.

They joined a queue of laden river craft until the walls of Nancheng towered above them. Guang stood in the prow as they paddled to the Water Gate of Morning Radiance. Its huge bronze-bound doors stood open. Beyond lay a dark tunnel lined with downward pointing rams to trap unwelcome boats. Then they were through, emerging onto one of the many canals latticing Nancheng. The boat entered a large water basin surrounded by warehouses and hostelries. Guang heard a bellow from the shore. A man in an officer's uniform trotted along the quayside, keeping pace with their gliding boat.

'Yun Guang! Is it really you?'

'Have you gone blind, my friend?' Guang shouted back, joyfully. 'Or are you too drunk to recognise me?'

'Did you deliver the letter?' asked the soldier.

'Better than that, I have my father in this boat, rescued from the Mongols.'

They docked, the boatmen casting out and mooring ropes. As Guang excitedly told his story a crowd formed. Labourers and porters craned to hear his words. Guang was relieved that Father stayed quiet. Soon the crowd comprised many dozens. He could sense the rumour of his story swelling up and down the quayside.

Guang climbed stiffly ashore, then helped Lord Yun onto dry land. Triumph made him light-headed.

'Father,' he said. 'I will take you to a place where you will be treated with great honour.'

So many were listening that Guang wondered if his words were intended for the old man or the crowd.

'Follow me, Father.'

They proceeded down the street, stepping aside for hand-carts and mule-wagons. Many of the people on the quayside followed, some out of curiosity, but most because the snatching of a Family Head from the barbarians excited their ideals.

A mere *li* from the Water Basin, they arrived at Shih's shop. Throughout their long journey Guang had pretended that Lord Yun would join his own household. Now he could pretend no longer. Yet he was afraid to tell the truth in case Father, who had maintained a dignified face so far, disgraced them all. The old man tugged his son's sleeve like a child.

'Can this be the fine house you spoke about?' he asked, gazing doubtfully at the shop and common courtyard it fronted.

Guang resorted to another lie. Or half-truth.

'Step inside this doctor's shop, Father,' he whispered. 'And you shall receive medicine to make all your parts strong again. Perhaps we shall find some fishes. . . This way, Father.'

He bundled the old man into the shop, motioning Chen Song to follow, and slammed the door behind them.

The crowd murmured as it waited outside. Yet Guang was naïve to think his connection with Shih was not well-known. The twin brothers had caught many people's eye during the winter they lived together, as all exceptional things do.

*

The travellers found themselves in a wide room lined with clay jars. The mingled scent of a hundred herbs was sweet and acrid, an intoxicating aroma, suggestive of renewal. A fat youth sat beside the counter. His expression passed from wonder to delight.

'Captain Guang!' cried the apprentice. 'You're alive! I must tell Master.'

Before he could be stopped, Chung disappeared into a back room. Guang said awkwardly: 'Father, someone you least expect will walk through that door in a moment.' He cleared his throat nervously. 'It is your Second Son, Shih.'

At first the old man seemed not to understand.

'Shih? How is that possible?' he said. 'I sent him away. Far, far away. Besides, he is dead. Shih is a paper puppet. He does not exist.'

'Father,' said Guang. 'I beg you, stay calm! For all our sakes, but most of all your own.'

'I will go straight to your house,' declared the old man. 'I do not wish to see a doctor or a paper puppet.'

'Father,' cried Guang. 'I must confess a great fault. I lied to you so you would not feel distressed. It is Shih you must live with, not I. You see, I have no means to provide for you.'

This confession wrenched his pride. He would rather Chen Song had not heard it. Even the scholar, tolerant and wise, looked away. Now Father was trembling.

'I cannot live here,' he protested, stepping towards the door. Guang blocked the way.

'Why is the door locked?' demanded the old man, suddenly afraid. 'Shih is not my son! I cannot share a prison with another ghost! Your mother is bad enough with her nagging and reproaches!'

Chen Song cleared his throat.

'Lord Yun,' he intervened. 'This is no prison. Your second son appears to be a physician, no doubt honoured by his patients.'

Guang was grateful for this help.

'Father, you will be safe here. . .'

He fell silent. Shih stood in the doorway. For a long moment he did not move, staring at Lord Yun in disbelief. A look of horror crossed Shih's kindly face. He blinked at the floor, then glanced at Guang accusingly.

The old man seemed to have trouble looking at his discarded Second Son. At last he understood the significance of Shih's stained doctor's robes and, for a moment, seemed puzzled. Then Lord Yun's lips twitched with contempt.

'A doctor!' he said. 'You will not deceive me so easily! No son of Lord Yun could be so humble! A little doctor in his little shop! Does Khan Bayke appoint a shadow to be my gaoler? Guang, tell me you did not rescue me for *this*!'

Shih hesitated then lowered himself to his knees, his face dark with emotion.

'Father,' he said, dully. 'We believed you were dead. Where is Mother?'

The old man's grave composure cracked.

'Washed away!' he cried, addressing Guang and entirely ignoring the existence of Shih. 'Washed away by the stream! I am only here because of the fishes' spells! They are powerful, even if they are demons and tempt me to hell as the Abbot Jian says.'

Confusion crossed Shih's face, replaced by watchfulness.

'Tell me about the demon-fishes, Father,' he said, softly. 'Do they speak to you?'

But the old man was muttering to himself, laughing at some secret thought. Shih listened attentively, fingering an amulet on his belt. He turned to Guang. Their eyes met, holding each other's gaze. Though time and trial had altered the twin brothers in subtle ways, their brown eyes remained peculiarly alike. Something of the sorrow and fear and pain Guang had endured in rescuing Lord Yun passed between them, and Shih nodded, as though silently acknowledging these sacrifices. But when his gentle, intense gaze returned to Lord Yun, darker passions might be read in his face.

'I see how things stand,' he said. 'I will take Honoured Father somewhere he may rest. A chamber must be prepared. Wait here for me, Guang, there are many things I need to know.'

He walked over to his unexpected guest, who shrank back in alarm.

'Come with me, Father,' he said, briskly. Then Shih appeared to support Lord Yun while firmly directing his steps so that Guang marvelled at how well he managed the old man. For the first time he glimpsed the strength of will within his brother, and thought of bamboo.

'We have a fine room for you, Father,' said Shih. 'You must be hungry after your long journey. . .'

His reassuring voice faded down the corridor until a door closed. Chen Song stirred uneasily.

'A most filial scene,' he said, awkwardly. 'I must leave you now and report to the authorities.'

A great reluctance to stay in Shih's shop made Guang step after him.

'Chung,' he said, addressing the apprentice. 'Tell Dr Shih I am called away on urgent business of state. Tell him. . . I will return soon to explain all that has happened. Now I must accompany my friend to Peacock Hill.'

Chen Song looked puzzled.

'Should you not tell your brother yourself?' he asked.

Guang shook his head doggedly and led Chen Song to the door.

'Shih will understand Father's malady better than I,' he said. 'There is nothing more I can do.'

As they emerged onto the street, the waiting crowd cheered and clapped. Guang strode towards Peacock Hill and with each step an unbearable burden in his heart grew lighter.

竹子

Their destination was a fashionable teahouse at the foot of the former Palace complex. Onlookers turned to watch the two travellers and the excited crowd accompanying them. As the idle naturally will, many joined the throng to share any gossip going. Idlers were a common enough sight. Year by year more peasants drifted into the Twin Cities, harassed by their landlords' exorbitant rents and taxes benefiting only the Son of Heaven's extravagant court.

'It is as I predicted,' Chen Song said, happily. 'Word of your exploits spreads like a filial fire! We must use this to your advantage. But Guang, you seem troubled.'

'More is happening than I expected,' he confessed.

'I beg you to remain here until I return,' said Chen Song. 'I shall go straight to the Bureau of Internal Peace with my memorandum. Given your favourable reception in the city, I shall request that you are granted an early audience with His Excellency Wang Ting-bo.'

Guang bowed to his friend.

'That would please me above everything,' he said.

Chen Song nodded.

'Guang, why not step onto the balcony and acknowledge your admirers. I believe you have acquired a new name.'

Reluctantly, he parted the curtains and went outside. He was confronted by a hundred up-turned faces. At the sight of him, the people began to clap and Guang heard a strange name called out. At first he wondered if he had been mistaken for someone else.

'Captain Xiao!' they called. 'Captain Xiao!'

Who was this captain? *Xiao* meant filial piety, the highest moral duty admired by all. Indeed the authorities compiled thick volumes describing notable examples of such piety, so all might be instructed. Could he really have acquired such a name?

On stepping back into the room, he found Chen Song smiling at his flustered face.

'You are the centre of the hour, my friend. Yet all hours pass. Now I must call on the Bureau Chief.'

Guang was left alone in the room. Servants brought fresh

tea, eager to acquire gossip concerning Captain Xiao. Several singing girls loitered round the door suggestively strumming their lutes, but he ignored their services. A woman was the last thing he needed.

He chose not to appear on the balcony again that evening. The adulation of the crowd elated and disturbed him. When he peered through the paper curtain he could see wine and tea sellers circulating. A portable puppet show had been established on the street. Guang could hear the shrill voices of the performers as they acted out an impromptu version of Lord Yun's rescue.

Night had fallen when Chen Song returned. He smelt of wine and seemed well-satisfied.

'It was good of you to wait for me,' he said. 'I feared you would lose patience and return to oversee the reception of your Honoured Father.'

Guang had considered doing just that. To be apart from Father felt strange, and he longed for Shih and Cao's friendly company, to tell them all that had happened while they gasped and exclaimed. But Guang sensed he must establish his independence or risk losing it. Besides, as hours passed in solitude amidst the noises of the city he began to remember his hopes. All his adult life he had been alone, free to act as he chose. Liberty was something he could not surrender lightly. Why should he tend Father, day after day, month after tedious month, when Shih was so better suited to the task? One did not ask a tiger to pull a plough.

'My time with the Bureau Chief has passed pleasantly,' said Chen Song, filling bowls of wine for them both. 'More importantly, His Excellency Wang Ting-bo has ordered you to attend his morning audience with the city commanders. Rumours of your heroism have reached the Pacification Commissioner's ears. Now, tell me, are you not pleased?'

Guang drained his cup in one. It washed away awkward doubts.

'Or perhaps I should now address you as Captain Xiao,' said

Chen Song. Then he added wistfully: 'There are many who would give much for such a name, but are unworthy of it.'

Dawn brought a visitor while they breakfasted on mutton stew and fish-head broth. Shih's portly apprentice bowed low as he entered, his eyes drawn to the fragrant dishes.

'Well, Chung,' said Guang. 'I take it Father has settled?'

The apprentice nodded so doubtfully he might as well have shaken his head.

'It was a long night, sir,' he said. 'But Master finally persuaded Lord Yun to take a little tea flavoured with. . . something cooling to the spirit. After that, he slept soundly.'

'So everything is settled,' declared Guang.

'Master requests that you visit him at once, sir.'

'Did he say why?'

The lad stood awkwardly.

'That was his message, sir.'

'Tell him I have urgent business with the Pacification Commissioner. As soon as it is concluded, I shall visit.'

After Chung had gone, Chen Song watched his friend carefully. Whatever was in his mind did not reach his tongue.

The streets were already busy. Officials drifted to their bureaux alongside merchants and artisans. Beggars squabbled over pitches for the day. Stalls and booths specialising in breakfast dishes lined the approach to Peacock Hill. Guang and Chen Song were forced to step aside for carriages bearing high officials from their residences in Fouzhou and the garden wards within the city walls of Nancheng.

'That was the Pacification Commissioner's nephew, Wang Bai,' Chen Song murmured, bowing as a carriage passed, its bells tinkling. 'And the horsemen with a retinue of archers are the two Zheng cousins, our foremost commanders in the city. Perhaps we will meet them at our audience with His Excellency.'

They reached an imposing gatehouse decorated with carved

serpents and phoenixes. Chen Song produced a pass with a flourish of pride.

'This simple piece of paper,' he told Guang, 'is a dragon one may ride to the very heart of a dragon's abode. Think of it! I shall treasure this document always and bequeath it to my children.'

Guang had no reply to such flights of fancy, other than a smile.

Although he did not know it, they followed the same route through the former palace of the Kings of Chu that Shih had taken on the occasion of Little Tortoise's sickness. Finally they were led to an octagonal pavilion Wang Ting-bo used for audiences with his highest officials, built among artificial ponds and walkways, floating lilies and fragrant shrubs. The pavilion's advantage was that no one could easily overhear the conversation within.

When Guang entered, it became apparent they were late. An orderly waved them to floor space on the outskirts of the circle surrounding the Pacification Commissioner. A bushy-bearded man Guang recognised as General Zheng Shun was earnestly addressing His Excellency. Zheng Shun was the hero of several notable victories over the Mongols in the last campaign; so much so that he had been posted well away from the frontline by envious officials to prevent him gaining too much influence. He had a reputation for inelegant bluntness – a failing Guang shared.

'Our stock of crossbow bolts is insufficient,' said General Zheng Shun. 'As for the other necessities for a siege, we gather them too slowly. If the Army of the Right Hand is driven back, we can expect the enemy on our doorstep within a few weeks. We must redouble our efforts. The authority can only come from yourself.'

Guang was amazed at the general's boldness. Wang Ting-bo listened patiently.

'I agree,' he said. 'The requisition of supplies must take precedence.'

Yet he did not state how this would happen.

Then Zheng Shun's cousin, Admiral Zheng Qi-Qi, broke in: 'Your Excellency, our river fleet is sadly weakened by ill-repair and a shortage of supplies.'

Admiral Qi-Qi was a less daunting personage than his cousin. Whereas Zheng Shun was naturally irascible, a courteous smile played round the corners of Admiral Qi-Qi's mouth. 'Should the enemy fall upon us,' he continued, 'my boats will be the mouth through which the Twin Cities are fed. I fear we will go hungry.'

Again Wang Ting-bo pursed his lips in agreement.

'No one would deny the validity of your opinion,' he said.

The Pacification Commissioner's nephew, Prefect Wang Bai, spoke up: 'Your Excellency, I can report happier news. Due to my great efforts, the city's underground granaries could withstand a siege of several years. It is true the peasants in the surrounding districts have been taxed hard to achieve this. I make no apologies. Whatever malicious tongues say, none of the impounded grain has been used to force up prices in the market. At least as far as I know.'

The Zheng cousins exchanged mocking glances.

'I commend your diligent work,' said Wang Ting-bo.

Then he noticed Guang and peered at him in surprise.

'Have I not met you before?' he asked, wonderingly. 'Only then you were a doctor. Now you wear a Captain of Artillery's uniform.'

Chen Song coughed apologetically.

'Your Excellency,' he said, bowing deeply. 'Forgive me for speaking. May I humbly inform you, Captain Yun Guang here is the twin brother of the doctor who cured your son. No wonder you mistake one for the other!'

Still Wang Ting-bo gazed at Guang in amazement.

'I have every reason to thank the good doctor,' he said. 'He did me a great service. Now my son is healthier than ever before. Are you the one they call Captain Xiao?'

Guang advanced and knelt before the great man, his mouth

dry as salt. He could not think how to justify his presence. Luckily, Chen Song spoke for him.

'Your Excellency,' he said. 'I beg your permission to tell this exalted company how Yun Guang earned the title *Captain Xiao*.'

He spoke eloquently, outlining his own mission and what he had learned concerning the Mongols' dispositions. How he had chanced upon Guang in Chunming, after the latter gentleman had valiantly killed the despoilers of his ancestral tomb and liberated his father. It was a story deserving the utmost attention.

'All this is true?' asked Wang Ting-bo.

'As I kneel here, sir,' replied Chen Song, solemnly. 'May I add, the heroic Yun Guang, though too modest to proclaim his own virtues, is a notable commander of artillery, a master of the latest weapons. By a lucky chance he has no commission at present.'

Chen Song subsided. His glance flickered round the circle of notables. Wang Bai was smiling thinly, as though appreciating a private joke.

'Ah!' said the Pacification Commissioner. 'I shall send a memorandum concerning this to the Son of Heaven's First Minister! Let the clerks take note that Captain Xiao shall also be awarded five thousand *cash* from public funds.' He looked at Guang curiously. 'There is something strange here. Your twin brother saves my heir when all other doctors despair. Now you appear, just when I lack a Commander of Artillery. How do you explain that?'

The Pacification Commissioner addressed Guang directly. He sensed his whole future depended on his reply. The other officers were watching. Guang lifted his eyes so they boldly met Wang Ting-bo's.

'Your Excellency,' he said. 'Perhaps it was meant to be so. If the enemy besieges the Twin Cities we will need every weapon at our disposal – thunderclap bomb, whirling tiger catapult, fire lance and naphtha. Our traditional weapons will not suffice. We must construct tactics they cannot anticipate. If I were your Commander of Artillery, I would ensure our siege equipment outmatches their own. That way, they could not even approach the walls – except to perish.'

Wang Ting-bo stared at him thoughtfully.

'First your brother saves my son,' he said. 'Now you promise to save the city. Can Heaven's hand be in this?'

The Zheng cousins stirred. Admiral Qi-Qi laid a restraining hand on his cousin's arm.

'Your Excellency,' broke in General Zheng Shun, his cheeks flushing. 'Perhaps we should learn more about this valiant captain before he is promoted to Commander of Artillery.'

Wang Bai had been silent for some time. Now he spoke so courteously that General Zheng Shun seemed a coarse, disagreeable, unsubtle fellow in comparison.

'I, for one, have heard Yun Guang's name mentioned with honour,' he said, 'as a man of courage and filial piety. One might add that in rescuing his father he used our latest weapons to startling effect. So he clearly knows his trade.'

Wang Bai had everyone's close attention, especially his uncle's.

'In addition,' he said, 'I fear that reinforcing our defences will involve hardship for many in the city – I refer to the confiscation of valuable property, forced labour, the levelling of homes. Yun Guang's deeds seem to have gripped the people's imagination. Very good. If *Captain Xiao* oversees this work, grumblers will find it harder to argue. Yet I agree with General Zheng Shun to this extent. . . any appointment should be temporary and I myself will direct all his actions.'

'As an administrator you should not oversee military matters!' burst in General Zheng Shun.

'What do you say, Honoured Uncle?' asked Wang Bai, ignoring the interruption.

'I would beg His Excellency not to make a decision without further enquiries,' urged Admiral Qi-Qi. His voice held little hope. He knew Wang Ting-bo all too well.

'First, my son, now this,' mused the Pacification Commissioner. 'Let it be as both Wang Bai and Zheng Shun suggest. I hereby appoint Yun Guang as *temporary* Commander of Artillery. He shall receive half the normal salary until he proves competent. With regard to strengthening the city's defences, he shall report directly to my nephew, Prefect Wang Bai. Today's audience is over. Good day, gentlemen.'

One by one the assembled officers and high officials left the pavilion, the Zheng cousins and their supporters muttering angrily amongst themselves. Guang followed until he heard Wang Bai calling his name. He bowed deeply to his new benefactor.

'You spoke for me, sir,' he said, fiercely. 'I shall never forget your faith in me.'

Wang Bai smiled.

'One should not forget one's debts,' he said. 'Remember also how the Zheng cousins opposed your promotion! Yun Guang, you must justify my faith in you. As soon as you are settled in your new quarters – I have rather a fine house in mind – inspect our defences carefully and report what might be improved. Remember, I am your patron now.'

'I will do as you say,' said Guang, fervently.

Wang Bai examined him for a moment without speaking.

'Outwardly you resemble your brother, but the inner is quite different,' he said. 'Only inferior minds look no further than appearances. Now I shall order an official to conduct you to your new residence. I think you will find it rather splendid.'

Love for Wang Ting-bo and his nephew filled the new Commander of Artillery. He noticed Chen Song hovering to one side and felt a brief guilt. Perhaps he should argue for his friend's promotion. But Guang adopted a haughty expression and followed Wang Bai into the Pacification Commissioner's private mansion. Chen Song was left alone in the garden where small birds twittered.

竹子

Guang spent the next two days in ceaseless activity, inspecting every inch of the ramparts, too busy to visit Apricot Corner Court. A team of clerks noted the potential location of catapults and giant crossbows, muster-points and arsenals for thunderclap bombs. It was an absorbing study. His new patron, Wang Bai, read the completed report in Guang's presence.

'Did you have any help in this work?' he asked, suspiciously.

'No, sir.'

'You are energetic, unexpectedly so. I shall give you a list of properties we need to confiscate. Make sure you add it to your memorandum. And next time, submit your reports directly to me alone, rather than ordering your scribes to prepare a copy for the Pacification Commissioner.' Wang Bai smiled thinly. 'That way we can ensure there are no errors.'

Convinced he had made a good start, Guang rode his new horse to Dr Shih's modest shop. As usual the attention he attracted was gratifying. People called out *Captain Xiao* as he passed. Mothers instructed their children to stare at him. For all his fine horse and uniform, Guang felt oddly alone as he trotted through the streets. He realised it was not Yun Guang from humble Wei Valley these people admired, but a giant they had created as an antidote to their fear. He felt these things but could not articulate them. Chen Song would have known how to express the thought. Yet Guang was ashamed that his conduct towards his friend had been ungrateful, and so avoided him.

He led his horse into Apricot Corner Court, a place he knew intimately from the winter he had spent there as his twin brother's guest.

Widow Mu's children and Old Hsu's grandchildren ceased their game and stared in wonder at his painted armour and tasselled sword. Flies buzzed around the horse's eyes and it snorted impatiently. A distant rumble of thunder echoed from the mountains west of Nancheng.

'Hey, Little Melon,' he called to a boy too thin for such a

round name. He was bolder than the other children and crept curiously towards the horse. 'Not afraid he might bite?'

'I'm not afraid!' came the shrill reply.

'Ask your mother if you are allowed to earn a string of *cash* for tending my horse.'

Little Melon gasped.

'A whole string!'

It was a week's income for a poor family. The boy ran into Widow Mu's dumpling shop and emerged with his mother, who at once bowed very low.

'You are too noble to visit us, sir!' said the widow, sweetly.

Old Hsu stuck his head through his workshop window and glowered at Guang's armour and sword.

'There would be no more war if men did not wage war!' he called out. 'No more murderers if men reformed their vicious ways!'

His head disappeared back into the house. Widow Mu waved her eldest daughter forward to present Guang with some dumplings wrapped in a banana leaf.

'Take no notice of Old Hsu,' she whispered, confidentially. 'Since his son was conscripted he can't abide the sight of a soldier.'

Guang had always considered the old man to be a madman or, at best, a buffoon. He was half tempted to report him to the Ward Constable for possessing unorthodox opinions. Even so, the exchange dampened his mood.

He was still eating his dumplings when he entered Shih's shop by a side door. He found no sign of his brother or apprentice. Madam Cao sat on a low stool by the counter, drinking tea and examining a ledger of accounts. At the sight of him filling her doorway, she gasped with pleasure.

'You have come at last!' she said, bowing with exaggerated respect.

His sister-in-law's elaborate courtesy contained a veiled reproach.

'I could not visit earlier. I have been engaged on official business, following my promotion.'

'So we have heard.'

Cao poured him a fresh cup of tea and offered her seat to him with another deep bow.

'We never stood on ceremony before,' he said, finding a stool lower than her own. 'Let us not do so now.'

Her troubled expression cleared a little.

'Well then I won't, even if everyone is calling you Captain Xiao. Oh, *Captain Xiao*!' She chuckled but stopped suddenly to check whether he was offended. Reassured, she continued: 'I won't pretend we didn't weep with relief to see you return. While you were away, Shih could hardly sleep for fear of the dangers you faced. Yet it seems everything you asked for in your letter has been granted.'

Guang sipped his tea and glanced at the closed door leading to the family apartments.

'Father is within?' he asked.

'Why yes,' said Cao, as though more might be said.

'How is he?'

Her eyes widened.

'Lord Yun keeps to his room and mutters. We have provided him with a basin of golden carp and they suffice for company. Shih has discovered a strange thing. Honoured Father-in-law believes favourable demons are acting through the fish, that their circling of the bowl somehow protects him. Shih says curing such a malady is like unpicking a tangle of invisible threads.'

Guang sipped his tea morosely.

'I tried my best,' he said. 'There was such danger in the Mongol lands, Cao! We were lucky. Or our ancestors helped us.'

Her eyes descended to his fine chest and shoulders.

'You are what you are, Brother-in-law,' she said. 'You saved Lord Yun from one danger. Now Shih must protect him from another.' She hesitated, adding: 'I never met Honoured Father until you brought him here. I suspect that if the Mongols had not seized Three-Step-House, we would never have seen him at all.'

'Misunderstandings,' muttered Guang. 'Foolish errors. Father was always demanding. I mean, if he felt – rightly or wrongly – that he had not been shown filial respect. . .'

'Is that why Shih was sent away?' asked Cao, doubtfully. 'Did Shih not show him sufficient respect? He was just a little boy when Lord Yun. . . Oh, I shall say no more! It all happened long ago. But I must tell you, Brother-in-law, my own father always found Shih a respectful apprentice.'

A helpless shrug was Guang's only reply.

'Perhaps it is best not to ask these things,' said Cao. 'Yet now Lord Yun lives in our house – and very unwillingly. He seems to believe we are gaolers working for a demon called Khan Bayke and that Apricot Corner Court is a sort of prison.'

Her comment made Guang redden. As Eldest Son, his obvious duty was to provide a home for Father. There were many rooms in his new pavilion on Peacock Hill and a dozen servants to tend Lord Yun's needs. Yet Guang shrank from such a responsibility.

'You can imagine,' continued Cao. 'How little Lord Yun relishes depending on Shih. As for me, I am too common. And plain. He does not notice me. We are half-afraid Lord Yun will order Shih to divorce me. After all I have not borne the Yun clan a son to please your ancestors.'

Guang retreated into his tea. Cao's anxiety did not seem entirely misguided. He looked round the clean room with its fragrant jars and woodcut print of the Yellow Emperor.

'When will Shih return?' he asked.

Cao shrugged.

'It could be hours. Ever since he healed the Pacification Commissioner's son, we have been besieged by fancy folk convinced their own heirs have the dry coughing sickness. Not that there isn't plenty of it about. Perhaps you'll find him at the

North Medical Relief Bureau. He spends more and more time there.'

'So you prosper?' asked Guang.

'We have plenty of money, if that's what you mean.' Cao looked at him sharply. 'No doubt you have heard that Lord Yun is not our only Honoured Guest.' She rose hurriedly and began to straighten the medicine jars. 'His Excellency rewarded Shih with more than silver and jade. He gave him a concubine he wished to discard. She is in the room next to Lord Yun. Poor girl. Shih does not know what to do with her. She stays in her room from dawn until dusk.'

'A strange fee,' said Guang.

'You may say so. These noble folk have their own special ways.'

Brother and sister-in-law sat in silence for a while. At last, he said: 'Perhaps I should pay my respects to Father.'

'If you will forgive advice from a woman,' she said. 'I'd wait until Shih returns. It will give him a chance to wash away any dishonourable messes Honoured Father may have around his person.'

'You mean. . . Ah, I see.'

Guang felt a deep desire to be away from Apricot Corner Court. He could not bear the thought of Father soiling himself. Besides, he had so much business to undertake – a visit to the papermakers' guild to requisition supplies for the manufacture of thunderclap bombs – there was no end to it. Father was probably sleeping anyway.

'I will come back soon,' he promised.

Cao rose, too, evidently alarmed.

'You must dine with us! Please wait! I will send for wine. Perhaps I have said too much and you are offended.'

'No, I must go. But I shall return soon.'

He bowed to her with feeling.

'Whatever Father may think, my brother is lucky in his wife,' he said. 'She never says too much. And unlike many a painted lady, everything she says is honest. Tell Shih that I. . . I honour how he helps Father. That I see how difficult it must be.'

Cao laughed her dry laugh.

'I'll tell him, Captain Xiao. But do come back soon. We will be offended if you do not.'

'I dare not risk that,' he said.

As he untied his horse, Guang glimpsed a lady looking at him from a side window. His mouth opened in surprise. Her green eyes were perfect pools of jade. He could not equate such beauty with Apricot Corner Court. Her perfect make-up and oval face belonged in palaces, not Water Basin Ward. Yet her look was wrenchingly sad. She reached up a slender arm and the bamboo curtain descended with a clatter. The spell was broken and Guang was left blinking.

As he mounted his horse, he tossed a string of *cash* to Little Melon.

'Here is another for your mother,' he said. 'Tell her it is in payment for her fine dumplings.'

Guang trotted into the street, resisting an urge to dig in his heels and gallop all the way back to Peacock Hill. Then he realised why he did not want Father to stay in his new pavilion. His promotion was only temporary. When the commission ended, his new home would pass to another. It would be wrong to accustom Lord Yun to a new home then snatch it away. Quite wrong, even unfilial. Whereas Shih could address Lord Yun's most intimate problems with a practised hand.

When Guang arrived home his melancholy did not lift. He drank wine alone in his courtyard garden, listening to the trickle of the fountain and recollecting the lady with green, unsettling eyes who had hastily lowered the curtain so as not to be defiled by his gaze. No doubt Wang Ting-bo's former concubine considered herself far too precious a sight for a mere soldier. Guang smiled scornfully. After all, what was she except a discarded ornament? All his thoughts should be concentrated on strengthening Nancheng's defences and, above all, on winning honour and respect.

Still he felt unsettled. So Guang sent out a dozen servants to scour the city for Chen Song, each bearing an invitation to dine at the most expensive restaurant in Nancheng as Captain Xiao's personal Honoured Guest.

憺

five

'In the time long ago, all followed the teachings of the Wise Sages, who taught that moral weakness, poisonous influences and harmful minds were to be avoided at one's peril . . . They never entered the chamber of love in a drunken state, lest their *qi* energies be wasted. How, therefore, could sickness or corruption find a place among such pure people?'

From *The Yellow Emperor's Classic on Internal Medicine*

竹子

Water Basin Ward, Nancheng.
Mid-Autumn, 1266.

Dr Shih and Apprentice Chung made a surly pair as they hurried down North Canal Street.

'You forgot the soup of ground ox bones and honey,' said Shih. 'And the infusion of raspberry leaves. How many more times must I remind you? Rigour and insight are the twin mountains on which our art nestles!'

The apprentice bowed miserably and his master frowned but said no more. Sensing he was forgiven, Chung lifted his head. He gestured surreptitiously to an acquaintance loitering on the opposite side of the street as if to say, *not now*. The latter, a young man in an apprentice apothecary's robes, nodded and melted into the crowd.

It was mid-autumn, that time when summer's discomfort fades into memory while sufficient warmth lingers. The evening had only just commenced. Half the city was outdoors, leaving crowded rooms and courtyards to drift from one diversion to the next.

A crowd of fresh-landed boatmen passed, singing and jostling one another like wide-eyed youths. Dr Shih envied their freedom to roam through the pleasant twilight.

'I'll buy wine for us both after we've finished tonight,' he told Chung, 'though really you don't deserve it.'

Now they walked with better feeling and soon came to the paper manufactory of Ibn Rashid in Date Palm Alley.

Ibn Rashid's father had been indentured to a paper-maker in his youth as payment for a gambling debt and now the family trade was in its second generation. Their religion was outlandish, but Dr Shih was too delicate to mention it.

Before he could examine Ibn Rashid's Third Son, a veiled daughter of the house brought out a lacquered tray of mint tea and Turkish pastries.

'We have been greatly honoured this last week,' said the paper-maker, while Shih nibbled the corner of a pastry greasy with sheep's butter. 'I, Ibn Rashid, am ordered to set aside all my paper. Do you know why?'

Shih shook his head, and quietly placed the pastry back on its plate.

'Not for books, sir! Rashid's paper is for thunderclap bombs!' Ibn Rashid looked at him shrewdly. 'I believe you know about this already. For it is your own brother, Captain Xiao, who demands every paper-maker in the city soak and pound from dawn until dusk.'

At the mention of his brother Shih's bland face flickered. He wondered if Ibn Rashid noticed. It was his private sorrow that Guang seldom visited Apricot Corner Court. He was too busy revelling in his reputation as Captain Xiao while others endured the consequences of filial piety. Yet when the humble doctor walked his rounds, a hope of meeting his illustrious brother accompanied him; and he often thought of that joyful day when they met by chance on Bright Hoop Street after two decades apart. Just as often, his feelings would drift from nostalgia to resentment – a bitterness he was ashamed to acknowledge except in secret thoughts.

Dr Shih's next patient lived in Xue Alley. This narrow, zigzagging street had been named after the clan who occupied two-thirds of it. Children with similar faces hung around doorways, resembling their parents like a stand of young bamboo. For all their wealth in numbers the Xue Clan were poor, so Dr Shih often halved his normal fee. Yet they took up more of his time than any other family.

He was met on the street by their clan head, Carpenter Xue. Dr Shih had once diagnosed him as suffering from an excess of the seven sentiments – love leading to fear, sadness, then anger, especially in summer. This evening he had entered a phase of anger.

'Dr Shih! You took your time, sir! No doubt you have better patients than us Xue since you cured the Pacification Commissioner's son!'

'I have no better patients,' said Shih.

He was led to the carpenter's eldest daughter, who had suffered bleeding since the birth of a stillborn son. An hour later Shih emerged sweating and took Chung by the arm.

'If she lives they will say it is because Xue blood is thicker than millet-broth,' he said. 'And if she dies, they'll blame me. Let us buy that wine we talked about.'

Shih drank alone in his shop while Chung proudly carried a large jug into Apricot Corner Court. The apprentice shared it beneath a tree with Old Hsu's youngest son and one of his friends, an apothecary's apprentice. Although Dr Shih considered it his duty to counter the weaknesses in Chung's character, tonight he let the lad gamble at cards. He invariably lost, as his father had before him, with the result that his son failed to inherit a plump tailor's business. Shih had liked Chung's father and still remembered him with sadness.

As he drank, Shih considered their most intractable case. Although his shelves contained hundreds of medicines and a whole library of treatises, nothing seemed to shake Lord Yun's madness. A noise made him look up. Cao stood in the doorway wearing nightclothes. He gestured to a chair beside him.

'Take a cup with me,' he said. 'Only poets and morose people drink alone.'

Brushing back her disordered hair, Cao took the place he offered.

She poured him a large bowl, then another for herself. They sat in silence, at a loss for words not concerning shop or food, unsettled fees or patients.

'I'm worried about Father,' he said.

She looked at him in the soft lamplight. He sensed she wanted to mention Wang Ting-bo's former concubine, that she desired reassurance concerning his feelings for the girl. He continued doggedly: 'I cannot understand Father's sickness. Sometimes I think it would be better to take away his bowl of fishes, but that would be cruel.'

Cao laughed nervously. 'What could ever replace them?'

'You express the matter exactly. Tomorrow I will speak frankly with him. Perhaps I shall learn how to restore the balance of *yin* and *yang* in his brain.' He looked up darkly. 'Not that his former self was worth restoring.'

Cao shook her head. 'Do not say such things! It will bring us bad luck.'

'It is the truth.'

He wondered why they did not laugh as they drank. Should not wine awaken mirth? In the early years of their marriage there had always been humour and amused gossip. Surely that was better. Shih blamed himself, for Cao was naturally mirthful.

The couple drank cup after cup, exchanging a few desultory words. Both were dulled by the day's long labours.

'I will speak to Father tomorrow,' said Shih, his voice slurring as they prepared for bed. 'Then we shall see.'

Cao's fragrance attracted him as he lay beside her, until thoughts of Father awoke an old anxiety, one he shrank from, and all his ardour failed. He rolled over, pretending to sleep.

竹子

Dr Shih rose at dawn like most of the city and found Cao preparing breakfast in the kitchen, the bamboo curtain rolled up. As she worked, his wife watched Widow Mu's children playing round the apricot tree. She called out words of praise when Little Melon tossed his wooden ball over the branches and ran beneath to catch it on the other side. Her bright look faded as Shih arrived and this grieved him.

'I will take Honoured Father his breakfast,' he said.

When he knocked on the door there was no reply. Shih entered and found the room deserted, apart from the bowl of slowly circling carp. He sniffed. Old man's smell filled every corner, acrid and musty. At first he felt alarmed, wondering if Lord Yun had developed a firestorm of the head and thrown himself into the canal. Then he heard a creak from the ceiling.

Dr Shih quietly mounted the steps leading up to the tower room, where he liked to look over the rooftops as he prepared medicines. He found Lord Yun peering round a corner of the window into Apricot Corner Court. Lord Yun was a little deaf and did not notice his approach. Intrigued, Shih stealthily positioned himself so he could see what engrossed the old man. The tower provided a clear, slanting view of the Widow Mu's back room. Through a gap in the upper half of the window, her daughter, Lan Tian, could be seen washing small breasts, a dreamy expression on her face. Father stared, his mouth slightly open. Dr Shih's own eyes narrowed.

'Come away from there, Father,' he said, sharply.

The old man started in alarm. Then flushed.

'You were spying on me!' he said.

'Your breakfast awaits you, sir. I have laid it out in your room.'

Father's composure had recovered by the time the meal was over. It had been eaten daintily, with much dabbing of the clean napkin he insisted on. Lord Yun had rediscovered his fine manners since escaping from Whale Rock Monastery. When he looked up he seemed surprised to see his son still there. For a while they sat in silence, Shih's hands folded on his lap, until the old man grew uncomfortable and pulled his chair close to the bowl of fishes. His entire attention focused on the circling carp. Still Shih did not move.

'I would hate to place a lock on the tower room door, Father,' he said. 'But I will if necessary.'

No reply. Shih knew he had been heard.

'I will say no more on that matter. You know my resolve.'

The old man suddenly looked up. His eyes were cold and fathomless, so that Shih recoiled inwardly, remembering how he had felt as a boy when Father examined him.

'What do you know about resolve?' asked Lord Yun. 'You are not Guang. You are not even my son. I am doubly dishonoured that Bayke chose someone like *you* for my gaoler.'

Shih struggled for composure.

'You are wrong, Father. Of course I am your son.'

'Not if I don't want,' said the old man, triumphantly.

The purpose of their interview seemed to be slipping away. Shih tried again: 'You are not well, Father. If I could be permitted to take your pulse, I might find a name for your sickness.'

The old man snorted.

'You are not fit to touch my wrist,' he said. 'Where is Guang? When he comes you shall pay! I have seen what he will do on my behalf, especially to dishonourable weaklings. And eunuchs.'

Now Shih barely concealed his distress.

'You know you are not a prisoner! Tell me, do you ever hear voices whispering when you are awake? Voices no one else can hear?'

This seemed the heart of the matter. Yet he drew no closer to it, for Lord Yun resumed his vigil of the fishbowl, deaf to every question. Shih wondered if he should make enquiries with other members of the guild. Venerable Dr Ku-ai was said to have an interest in maladies of the two souls. But that way, Dr Du Mau might get wind of Father's shameful condition and use it against him. Perhaps he should hire a magician skilful at taming demons.

Defeated, Shih sought out Cao and asked her to prepare a tea tinctured with hemp pods. After that he felt more at ease.

'Did you learn the cause of Father-in-law's illness?' she asked, taking a cup herself.

He shook his head.

'Only this,' he said. 'We must prevent him from entering the tower room or I fear an unpleasant scandal. If only Guang would come more often! I believe Father is a little afraid of him. Perhaps if Guang spoke sternly. . .' He left the thought unfinished. 'I must go to the Relief Bureau.'

Before he left, Dr Shih happened to meet their other Honoured Guest in the corridor. He felt himself flush and stammered a hope she was well. Lu Ying merely nodded in reply. His thoughts were guilty as he hurried through the streets, preoccupied by someone other than Cao or Father.

竹子

There had been a time when only Cao filled his mind – and senses.

Such a long ago evening! Ten, eleven years had passed since then. In the hours following old Dr Ou-yang's funeral they had not known where to turn. Her duty was plain: to marry the man chosen for her, Fifth Cousin Wen. Yet neither Cao nor

Shih could countenance separation. Since childhood they had been all that was kind and worthwhile to each other. Such tenderness he had known breathed through her lips.

Even then he understood Cao's strength. She was the green jade all sensible people hang from their belts. Without her, he would be nothing. In the capital, a city of two hundred thousand families, she alone cared whether he flourished. Yet he had hesitated before speaking.

'Beloved,' he had said, gazing down at her hopeful face. 'I told you there may be a way. But perhaps we should forget dreams of a better life.'

'No,' she said. 'I will drag out your thoughts. . . with a hook, if I must.'

It was as though they had been in a sad play, acted out in the silent house of dead Dr Ou-yang. Small birds chattered around the eaves, building their nests. Hawkers of snacks and fresh water cried out their wares.

'I will make my suggestion,' he said. 'And you will believe I never honoured you.'

So he had described his plan, if so wild a venture deserved such a name. That they should pack clothes and what little they possessed, defying all decency. In short, they should elope. He subsided, expecting an angry reply. Instead she nestled against him tightly. He felt her heartbeat against his own. The scent of her hair fascinated him.

'Are you not concerned how we will live?' he had asked, amazed at their recklessness.

'No,' came her muffled reply.

'If we flee together, no doctor in the capital will hire me,' he said. 'This scandal will always follow us.'

'Then we will go far away,' she said. 'And set up your own shop.'

'With what?' he had asked. 'My savings are small. Everything you might have inherited has been pledged to your uncle, as a dowry.'

Cao had stepped back, still holding his hands.

'Have your things packed by the next bell,' she said. 'If you are still true to your plan, you shall find me ready.'

So he had waited by the front gate, a single sack at his feet containing all he owned. She had appeared with far heavier bags, loaded onto a wheelbarrow.

'We should not take that,' said Shih, anxiously. 'The barrow belongs to your uncle now.'

He had seen the beatings criminals received in the market-place; such a theft, tainted by unfilial conduct, warranted a hundred strokes of the bamboo. Enough to leave him crippled for life. She ignored his protests and trundled it into the street.

'It is mine,' she said. 'Father gave it to me. I will explain later.'

They went to a hostelry south of the city, taking a tiny room near the waterfront. Shih's stock of *cash* extended that far. Though they shared a bed, still they dared not open their joy together. He remembered staring up at the low ceiling while she slept beside him, snoring softly. The scent of her skin reminded him of warm dough.

At dawn the next day he went from boat to boat, enquiring about destinations. The sailors seemed uncouth folk, but he struck up a rapport with a fellow from Nancheng and found he was willing to take them there for a small sum, on condition they provided their own food and Shih acted as physician to the crew.

'You'll have to find a place in the hold, young man,' said the captain. 'That is all I promise.'

Shih rushed back to Cao.

'Nancheng is said to be a great city far to the west,' he said. 'I have read that several kings of Chu resided there before Our Holy Ruler's ancestors gained power. If only we had money for provisions!'

To his surprise, Cao produced the necessary *cash* from her bags. That was when his suspicions began. He asked no questions, simply relieved to be on their way before her uncle notified the magistrate about the loss of his wheelbarrow.

Many pass whole lives without a single glimpse of the sea, but Shih never forgot that passage along the coast to the Yangtze delta. Most of the time was spent below decks, wedged between barrels of southern wine. When he climbed the ladder from the hold and stood at the rail spray broke on his face. The air flowed with a strange, heady tang and the passing shore was full of interest. The Captain admired his sea legs and asked if he had sailors in the family. Shih replied, perhaps inspired by his wise ancestor, Great-grandfather Yun Cai: 'We are all floating, especially when on land.' After that the captain treated him with more respect.

The Yangtze estuary was a hundred silted islands and villages on stilts. Slowly the boat made its way west against the great river's course. Shih tried not to think of the future. Cao remained out of sight in the hold, in case her presence provoked the sailors. Otherwise they talked and slept, existing on the millet and pickled vegetables she had purchased.

The journey improved as they headed up river. Great cities and towns passed by, and sometimes they stepped ashore, never venturing far from the dockside, to replenish their provisions. Cao lived in constant anxiety that the baggage would be stolen, though Shih joked any thief would gain little.

Nancheng became a secret promise between them. Only they knew the true meaning of its name. Hours were spent in chatter and speculation; in all the years of their acquaintance, he had never seen her so happy. Though gloomy by temperament, he began to glimpse the fine future she described and sense it might be possible.

Summer had commenced when they arrived in Nancheng, passing through the Water Gate of Morning Radiance. By now Shih's resources were at an end. They had only youth to preserve them.

On the dockside, as they stood gawping at warehouses and porters, wondering where to go next, Cao had revealed her secret.

'Husband,' she said, softly.

Shih was noting the layout of the streets. How might he find a doctor willing to employ him?

'I must confess to a great fault,' she said.

'What?'

'Shih,' she said, more sharply. 'I must confess that you are not entirely poor. Look in the blue bag, the one I told you it would be unlucky to open.'

He did so and gasped. Within lay a box of *cash*, several strings of a hundred coins and, more importantly, Dr Ou-yang's case of needles, as well as half a dozen vital books – even a pestle and mortar. All he needed to set up in business that very afternoon!

'Cao,' he said, shaking his head.

'Surely it belongs to me more than Uncle!' she blurted, shame-faced. 'I am Father's only child. Do I have no rights to his property, merely because I am a girl?'

Shih looked round the busy street anxiously.

'Do not speak so loud. We are little better than thieves. All this belongs to your uncle.'

She grasped his hands.

'You will use the needles to make sick people well, as Father taught you! You will use the *cash* to set up a medicine shop and bring happiness. Uncle would have spent the money on loose women or fine clothes. As for Father, I believe he would desire this. Consider how unkindly his family treated him! Besides, I have only taken the tiniest portion of Father's wealth. Uncle can hardly complain.'

'This will haunt us,' he said, ruefully.

Then he looked through the bag of precious objects and sighed with relief.

They hired two small rooms in Apricot Corner Court adjoining the street, and set up a hemp awning to provide shelter against rain and sun. At first trade had been slow. In the first year they barely earned enough to feed themselves. In the second year, Cao began to produce the common preparations her father had taught her, selling them to other doctors in

Water Basin Ward. Shih was grateful for her assistance but did not expect it to last. When children arrived she would have little time for work. But children did not come. Instead, she ventured into new medicines, bargaining in the East Market for rare herbs imported from distant provinces. Where possible, she commissioned the growing of special roots and plants by local market gardeners. Most of all, patient by patient, his practice spread tendrils, one cure encouraging another, until they moved from the two smallest rooms in Apricot Corner Court to their current home. An extravagant house for a childless family, but the rent was cheap. Water Basin Ward was one of the poorest in the city.

So many rooms. Year after year passed without them being filled by children. Meanwhile their business prospered, Cao selling medicines to doctors of all kinds, Shih building his round.

Always he wondered if their childlessness was a punishment. Cao had defied her father's will and he had encouraged her. He never doubted his complicity in her crime. Even now, he used his old master's case of needles. Sometimes, when drunk, Shih suspected Dr Ou-yang had decided she was unworthy of her ancestors. That he was a faithless apprentice, who must be cursed. When his head cleared, the fear persisted. An ancient proverb stated that no good deed goes unpunished. What then of bad deeds?

竹子

The North Medical Relief Bureau stood on a humble street near the Water Gate of Morning Radiance and consisted of a few small wooden shacks and a courtyard surrounded by a high wall. The east-west orientation of the buildings contained few pairings between the green dragon and white tiger, and one might wonder how a place of healing came to be established there at all – until one realised the land had been cheap.

It was flanked on one side by a butcher specialising in offal and, on the other, by a house for itinerant labourers bursting with noisy lodgers. The miasmas created by such neighbours were a constant source of unease to Dr Shih.

He was fortunate to possess even these premises. The Prefecture had provided the money grudgingly, persuaded by the great monasteries at the foot of Peacock Hill which found themselves overwhelmed by needy supplicants.

After the purchase of the buildings, only basic medicines could be afforded. As for a salary to appoint a doctor, a bare pittance remained each year, so Shih received less than many peddlers of cheap amulets. When it came to herbs and medicines, he often had to beg from other doctors, who naturally viewed the Relief Bureau as damaging to their own trade. But not all cures rely on costly medicines. He used massage and the needles, aided by applications of moxa, whenever he could.

The Relief Bureau had struggled along in this way for three years until word of Dr Shih's good work spread beyond the destitute, even reaching the attention of the guild. It had been a cursory attention. After all, a lean dog shames its master.

One morning Shih arrived at the Bureau with Chung in tow and found a crowd of patients outside. His one assistant, a soldier turned monk then doctor's orderly, was admonishing the assembled sick.

'It does no good to shove,' protested Mung Po, addressing a famished-looking man. 'I warn you! Step back!'

At the sight of Dr Shih he seemed relieved, and bowed low.

'Like locusts today, sir,' he remarked.

Dr Shih frowned at the babble of beseeching voices, avid elbows, hungry eyes.

'They must wait outside until I am ready.'

Mung Po took up his bamboo staff with alacrity and cleared the entrance.

Apart from a monk's shaven head, Mung Po retained few

outward signs of his former profession. His arm muscles were prominent from hefting patients and corpses, as well as pounding bucket-loads of poultices. He generally grinned mirthlessly, upper teeth resting on his lower lip.

The morning passed like many others. One woman could not stop retching and Dr Shih diagnosed an overheated womb, prescribing a concoction to make the blood sluggish. Another man was unable to work, having broken his arm while unloading barrels. Dr Shih set the bones and advised him to avoid sour foods. One youth sweated inordinately, his pulse so fiery that Shih wondered if he would survive the day. He ordered Chung to conduct him to the small infirmary on the opposite side of the courtyard.

After a simple lunch of rice and fried vegetables, fetched by the orderly from a street stall, Dr Shih made his way to the infirmary, where the most serious cases were housed.

A dozen lay on mats and threadbare blankets. Flies buzzed round open sores and dull, spiritless eyes. Despite Dr Shih's insistence on every means of ventilation and cleanliness, the room stank. This was the last place many would see on earth. Only those without family came to die here. It was a terrible thing to lack a son or daughter when the last days came.

As he went from mat to mat, Mung Po followed with a wooden stool so his master might sit beside the sick person. Dr Shih leaned forward and took the pulse, ordering whatever simple remedies they could afford, especially distillations of poppy. Often he massaged to lessen the pain, for there was nothing more to be done.

The last patient, a middle-aged peasant and refugee from the north, seemed asleep. Shih took up his wrist then gently let it fall. He hunched on his stool and regarded the dead man's face. He turned to Mung Po, who as an ex-monk, understood answerless thoughts.

'Let us hope the poor fellow is reborn closer to Emptiness,' said Shih.

Mung Po shrugged. 'From his feverish talk, I gathered he was once a bandit. A favourable rebirth seems unlikely.'

'Yet we must hope. Also, we must not distress the other patients. Chung, take his legs. We'll load him in the handcart, then you can dispose of him as usual.'

Mung Po grasped one arm while he lifted the other. The corpse was surprisingly heavy. As they carried it into the courtyard, a group of silk-dressed men, their fans fluttering like painted butterfly wings blocked the way. They were so incongruous in this drab place that Chung almost dropped the dead man's legs.

'Gentlemen,' said Dr Shih. 'Pray, step to one side, so we may reach that handcart.'

Dr Fung frowned at this impudence and sniffed.

'I see your treatment has been ineffectual,' he remarked.

Realising his senior colleague was reluctant to move aside, Shih motioned to his assistants. They gently lowered the emaciated body to the ground. Now he was free to bow deeply.

'We are honoured by your presence, Dr Fung!' he said, wondering what might occasion it.

Dr Fung sniffed again. He had detected the aroma of rotten meat from the butcher's next door. A dozen heads protruded from windows overlooking the Bureau's courtyard, staring at the gorgeous visitors and exchanging ribald remarks.

'I must advise you,' said Dr Fung, in his soft, fluttering voice, a voice that had reassured many of Nancheng's wealthiest people. 'We have been sent by the guild to inspect your *standards*.' He laid peculiar emphasis on the word. 'In managing the Prefecture's benevolence to the common people.'

Dr Shih looked at him suspiciously, then at the corpse by his feet.

'You'll find everything in order. Perhaps others in the guild persuaded you to take up such a duty?'

He was referring to Dr Du Mau, as Fung understood perfectly well.

'We must not let standards slip,' said the doctor.

'Sir,' broke in Mung Po. 'What about our friend here?'

They loaded him onto the handcart and the orderly trundled it away to Crow Tree Cemetery, having first covered the man with a hemp sack.

'Please honour me by sharing a little tea,' suggested Shih. 'But since we are here, first let me show you the infirmary.'

Fung stuck his head through the door and recoiled at the stench.

'Good,' he declared. 'I have seen enough.'

'I would welcome any suggestions you might make, sir.'

Fung nodded sagely.

'I have seen enough,' he repeated, fluttering his fan.

In the front office, Dr Fung outlined his intentions more fully.

'We are concerned that all revenues and medicines are not properly accounted for. I take it you may provide records?'

Dr Shih noticed his visitor did not deign to touch the cheap tea Mung Po set before him.

'We keep accounts,' he said, cautiously. 'Whenever we can.'

'I see.'

'Sir, I am too busy tending the patients for brushwork. But you may look at what we have.'

Dr Fung and his assistants spent a long hour reading the Bureau's ledgers. Shih suspected they had already decided what they would find before opening them.

'Your records are a matter of grave concern,' said Dr Fung. 'I shall have to report your lapses, and recommend the Bureau be closed until the matter is investigated thoroughly.'

Dr Shih nodded.

'Before you do so,' he said. 'Please consider one thing. If the Bureau closes, who will help these people? They are destitute and have no family. You are well known as a good and kind man. Consider who will really suffer, sir.'

Dr Fung looked at him steadily then watched Mung Po lead a shivering wretch to the infirmary. He frowned. Dr Shih waited with downcast eyes.

'If only the world allowed one to be as good as one wished,' sighed Dr Fung. He pursed his lips. 'Perhaps the irregularities are minor. . .Yes, I shall report that to Dr. . . to the guild. But make sure your accounts are more detailed when I visit in a month's time! Remember, wind snaps the stoutest pine.'

Shih understood that gale to be Dr Du Mau. He nodded gratefully and conducted Dr Fung to his waiting carriage, which had attracted a gathering of street urchins and licensed beggars. He remained by the Bureau doors until it rattled away.

竹子

An hour later, Dr Shih lifted his hand to knock on Lu Ying's door, and let it drop again so it hung restlessly by his side.

Cao had gone out to the market and Chung was still at the Relief Bureau, pounding medicines. As for Father, no sound escaped his room, not even the interminable conversations he conducted with himself or the demons speaking through his fishes. Probably he was asleep.

Shih and his nominal concubine had the house to themselves. The possibilities of such a situation brought on restless feelings. It was as if he could not quite trust himself, though how, or why, he did not care to acknowledge. Shih was well aware that, if he chose, he could apply pressure on Lu Ying to submit herself. Had not Wang Ting-bo himself sanctioned such a union? Few men would scruple to pleasure themselves in such a legitimate way; and a barren wife could hardly complain when it was his clear duty to furnish the ancestors with a fresh supply of sons.

Tiny beads of sweat formed on his forehead. Again Shih raised his arm, this time knocking softly on the crude plank door. She did not call out a warning, so he opened the door a crack.

It was a small room, containing little furniture. A heap of lacquered boxes and chests, relics of her days in the

Pacification Commissioner's mansion, were stacked against a wall. At once he became aware of a musky fragrance.

'Lu Ying,' he said. 'May I enter?'

He heard a rustle of silks within and took it as assent.

'I trust I do not intrude?'

She sat on the long divan that served as a bed, looking up at him fearfully. For a moment he did not recognise her, then realised why. When he had seen Lu Ying before, her face always wore a white mask of elegant make-up. Today she was uncovered, apart from a fan held over her face.

The blinds were down except for a crack, allowing a beam of sunlight to pool on the floor. Dust motes circled aimlessly. Dr Shih blinked at her in the gloom.

'Lu Ying,' he said. 'May we talk?'

'Dr Shih,' she said, with sudden force. Her voice was melodious in a trained way, its sing-song not quite refined. 'Please return in an hour, when I have had time to prepare myself.'

His instinct was to obey. Then he frowned.

'That is not convenient. In an hour I must visit my round of patients. Please do me the honour of a short conversation.'

Lu Ying sighed.

'I am hardly in a position to argue,' she said.

Dr Shih perched awkwardly on the only seat available, a large chest decorated with intertwined songbirds.

'You must forgive me for not enquiring about your health more often,' he said, examining the floor. Finally his gaze settled on the lady. She was no coy girl, that was certain, for all the modesty of a raised fan. As at their first meeting he found it hard to see beyond her beauty. Without make-up, her complexion was flawless, emphasising her green eyes. Little wonder the Pacification Commissioner had noticed her when he entered the women's quarters. Yet Shih recollected that such coloured eyes were said by some to denote evil intentions.

'Lady Lu Ying,' he said. 'Have you everything you need?'

She lifted her fan slightly so that only her green eyes showed.

No, Shih could not believe they concealed a malicious spirit.

'I have everything,' she said, stiffly. 'You and Madam Cao are most generous.'

'We are concerned for you,' he said. 'You keep to yourself too much. I understand how unwelcome your stay here must be.'

'If it is His Excellency Wang Ting-bo's desire, it is very welcome,' she replied. 'I mean, for the moment.' Then she added. 'Besides, I am used to waiting.'

Shih considered this. What exactly was she waiting for? Had she received word from Wang Ting-bo that her exile would soon end? Her words implied as much. No letter had come for her from Peacock Hill, unless it had arrived secretly. Perhaps she was warning him not to demand all he might from her; all that the giddiness in his heart and pulse urged him to demand.

'Nevertheless, I am concerned that you are unhappy,' he said. 'The change in your situation is extreme.'

She sat quite still. Only her eyes, staring at the opposite wall, moved to blink.

'I am not unhappy,' she said.

'If you left your room more often you might be happier still. Not that we wish you to spend time away. You may come and go as you please.'

'I know that, sir.'

Shih hesitated. His eyes travelled down her figure to her feet, then hurriedly glanced away. As though possessed by another's will, Shih found himself rising, so that he stood quite close to her chair. For all her evasions he sensed her awareness of his power. Where else had Lu Ying to go, after all, if he drove her from Apricot Corner Court? For a moment wide enough to consume a dozen loves, he hesitated. Lu Ying shrank into the divan, her breast rising and falling hurriedly as though in agitation. Then his tense shoulders relaxed, and a puzzled look replaced the hungry, hawk-like expression on his high cheek-boned face.

'I shall inconvenience you no longer,' he said, smiling his usual sad smile.

Yet still he did not move. So little had been learned! And yet too much. He was left only with questions he dared not ask.

'It is too early to speak of the future,' he said. 'Be assured that we will help you establish a new place in life, in as far as we may.'

'This conversation is distressing to me, sir!' she exclaimed. 'I am quite, quite content to obey His Excellency until he requires me again.'

'Then we shall leave it at that.'

He closed the door behind him. It was a relief to return to his familiar shop. He decided not to tell Cao about his conversation with Lu Ying. What was there to say, except the lady was miserable? Possessing that secret knowledge, little as it was, excited him strangely.

憺

six

'One may often see cheap woodcut prints of the Moon Goddess, Cheng-e, on sale during the Water-borne Moon Festival. Always she is shown as a fine lady admiring herself in a bronze mirror held aloft by a dainty maid while a second prepares tea. Two children admiring a hare stand beside her. The 'hare in the moon' uses its pestle and mortar to grind cinnamon bark into magic powder capable of granting immortality, but only the Most Sage know that this fabulous creature sometimes uses dried bamboo rind instead. . .'

From *Diverse Matters of Interest to Curious Minds* attributed to Ch'i Po

竹子

Apricot Corner Court, Nancheng. Autumn, 1266.

After Dr Shih had gone, Lu Ying remained motionless on her divan. Movement might be taken as a sign she wished to renew their conversation. What he wanted was obvious; and dangerously tempting. Yet she must never allow herself to be swayed by a kindly face again. What were such things worth, after all? Lu Ying listened to the creak of oars as a boat passed on the canal beneath her window, the boatman calling out his wares – purest spring water from Mount Wadung's blessed streams – and she wondered how much longer she must endure this vulgar house.

Although Dr Shih's manners were pleasant, she found his earnest goodwill tiresome. Yet he was attentive in his way – if a little odd – and, despite all the reasons she had for hating him, Lu Ying thought it prudent to appear gracious. At least he showed no signs of forcing himself upon her.

Lu Ying risked a loud sigh. When she finally left Apricot Corner Court, floating in a gilded palanquin carried by six – no, *eight* servants – she would toss Dr Shih an absurd present of *cash*. The guarded pity in his eyes would change to awe. His wife, with her vulgar, lop-sided nose and enormous feet, would bow in consternation. The bells on her palanquin would tinkle, as each step carried her closer to Peacock Hill. . .

Lu Ying realised she was trembling. Images lingered and faded. She must guard against dreams. Had she not even learned that? She pinched her bare arm with unpitying fingers. Once. Twice.

Her glance flicked from corner to corner. It seemed all her life had passed in narrow rooms. Even the widest grew close when morning and night were spent waiting for a visit or summons. Then one fell prey to yearning, despair at the limits of four walls. One imagined what was happening beyond, rivals biting each other like toads in a box. Eagerness for any rumour, however unreliable, made one flatter and bribe the servants.

Oh, she knew all about rooms! How every object becomes intimate: a favourite vase where one arranges and re-arranges flowers, never content with the result; or the silken covers of a divan, its colours and textures; sounds, too, maids on their rounds clattering buckets, splashes of dripping rain, the silence of snow.

One became sensitive, just as she had learned the rustling language of the mulberry tree behind Father and Mother's house as a little girl. A wise tree, witness to a dozen generations. Each autumn Mother had sold its leaves to a silk-worm merchant.

Lu Ying listened to Dr Shih's house. It was a quiet, achingly dull sort of place. In the room next door Lord Yun was muttering. The fat apprentice could be heard whistling as he visited the storeroom they used for chamber pots. No doubt they sold the household waste to a dung merchant. Anything for a little *cash*. This brought an unpleasant idea. Henceforth she would throw her own into the canal beneath her window, even though it was illegal, because the common people used it for drinking water. No one in this place must ever conceive of her as like them.

Lifting the curtain a little, Lu Ying looked out furtively. On the opposite bank of the canal, a girl with absurdly large jade mountains was yawning and stretching outside Ping's Floating Oriole Hall. The girl offended her, though she could not say why.

Lu Ying let the curtain fall and returned gracefully to her seat. One's deportment must be ineffably elegant. One should act as though being constantly observed. In the Pacification Commissioner's mansion, there had been enough spy holes to make that probable, day or night.

She resorted to her favourite cure for low spirits.

The porcelain pots and jars of cosmetics were half-empty, though she contrived a hundred ways to spare them. When Lu Ying first came to Apricot Corner Court, following Dr Shih in a hired carriage, her supplies of make-up had seemed plentiful. After all, it would not be long before Wang Ting-bo summoned her home. Everyone knew he could not live without her. She could recall a thousand instances of power, it was why people feared her. But days became a week, then a month, and her stock seemed less secure.

Lu Ying held back from a letter requesting fresh supplies, though Wang Ting-bo could hardly refuse. She understood the situation perfectly. In a moment of weakness he had made an absurd oath, manipulated by that fox-fairy of a First Wife. Given his position, a decent interval must pass before her recall. After all, he was no use to anyone if he failed to maintain his standing. She had been willing to smile obediently and play along, for a while.

Thirty days into her banishment, the joke tasted vinegary. Lu Ying found herself walking up and down a room crowded with boxes of clothes and knick-knacks. So little space, one could hardly find the most necessary things. Every dawn brought the certainty of a summons back to Peacock Hill. She dressed and applied make-up, sure the evening would find her in his company. When that happened, Lu Ying was determined to be gay and delightful, to disguise reproach, to pour joy through his eyes and mouth. After that, how his wife and scheming nephew would pay! She had learned all their harsh tricks now.

If only Wang Ting-bo possessed more virility, more essence of *yang*! Despite First Wife and half a dozen concubines he had only managed a single son. When she returned to Peacock Hill, everything would change. Reputable magicians and doctors would be consulted until boys were conceived one after another. . .

In the meantime she must wait. Dragging hours became an enemy one could only oppose with frustration. She was used to loneliness. Was not everyone alone? But however hard Lu Ying tried to avoid the fact – and indeed she struggled – Wang Ting-bo had assigned her to a mere doctor, a quack lacking even a degree from the Imperial Medical Academy. It was incomprehensible. And the petty neglects she suffered! To be obliged to eat when Dr Shih's household ate, even if that meant a tray brought to her room. (She refused to accept food under any other circumstances). And what food it was!

Her pride felt like a delicate painting lying in scraps on the floor. But the more she suffered to maintain Wang Ting-bo's face, the greater would be her reward.

So she applied make-up to feel better, painting her own face white, paying particular attention to her neck. Soon she was pale as a ghost. The mirror revealed a strange, frightened mask. Grief rather than beauty.

Lu Ying turned to her eyes, darkening lashes and lids with

blends of kohl, traces of rouge. The eyes in the mirror blinked. She tried several smiles. Broad and thin, decorously amused, a saucy arch of the lips. Her expression reverted to hardness and she made it playful again. Rouge brought life to her cheeks, followed by a reckless dose of fragrance.

For a long while she stared at her reflection. Then she paced up and down, waiting for Wang Ting-bo's knock on the door. The make-up might summon him like a spell or charm.

At once, she felt a thrill of power. He would re-discover her loveliness and gasp! She almost heard him swearing to divorce his wife and make her. . . she dared not think what.

Lu Ying grew aware tears were ruining her perfect make-up. Always she had been stupid! Clever, dainty women wrote noble letters or poems to express their grief at being abandoned. She was stupid, walking up and down this tawdry room. Then Lu Ying realised she must remind Wang Ting-bo of her existence. She must send a splendid present. A fine gift to rekindle the joys he had abandoned.

Lu Ying heard a boat passing on the canal beneath her window. A voice called out in gentle mockery and oars creaked. It was the spring-water seller returning; his wares soon sold in the market place. Oh, she must not surrender to the loneliness enveloping her like fog! Too easy to grant intimacy to someone comforting.

The brightness of day softened into evening, then night, until she was forced to wash away her precious mask, for it made her skin itch.

竹子

A headache woke Lu Ying from painful dreams. She had been back on Peacock Hill, obliged to bow while First Wife admonished her in an exasperated drawl. Her heart beat quickly until she recognised the plain room in Apricot Corner Court and she rubbed a throbbing pulse on her forehead.

Lu Ying recalled this was a doctor's house. Well then, let him practise his trade. She had plenty of money for a fee. Wang Ting-bo had filled a whole lacquered box with *cash* before she left the palace.

As ever, preparations were necessary. An hour later, Lu Ying shuffled into the corridor on silken slippers, wincing extravagantly. At once she encountered the doctor's father, a fine-looking old man, furtively creeping down the steep staircase from the tower room. He looked uneasy, then puffed out his chest.

'My fellow prisoner is well, I trust?' said Lord Yun.

Lu Ying massaged her forehead without touching the skin, in case it smeared her make-up.

'I do not know if Lord Yun finds me quite well,' she said, pouting.

She knew the story of his rescue from the Mongols and remembered glimpsing the old man's saviour, the one they called Captain Xiao, a most attractive fellow, stronger and broader chested than the doctor who so closely resembled him. But Lu Ying had never favoured military types – though she suspected their simplicity might be intriguing.

Lord Yun seemed not to have heard.

'I have been spying out the extent of our prison,' he whispered. 'It is a remarkably common place.'

Then he examined her in a way she found unpleasant.

'I know how to make a lovely lady better,' he said. 'But Bayke will not allow it.'

She bowed, remembering the warning that Lord Yun's mind was not whole, and shuffled to Dr Shih's shop. Here, Madam Cao was filling out a ledger of accounts. There was no sign of Dr Shih.

'Madam Cao,' she said, plaintively. 'I would not interrupt you, except for my extreme discomfort.'

Cao blinked at her, a brush laden with ink poised above the ledger. Reluctantly, she laid it on the wooden rest.

'Is Dr Shih available for a consultation?' Lu Ying asked.

'He's occupied at the North Medical Relief Bureau.'

'Oh.'

The name meant nothing to her guest, as Cao evidently realised, for she said: 'It is a place for poor people when they are sick.'

Lu Ying considered such an idea.

'How do they pay for their medicine?' she asked.

'They don't. It is done by charity.'

'How strange.'

She recollected the vanished days before she joined Wang Ting-bo's household. There had been nothing like that in the village. When poor people fell sick they either died or recovered.

'So who pays the honourable doctor for his services?'

'The Prefecture, though I can assure you, it's little enough. My husband does the work because he likes to see people happy. Even low people.'

Lu Ying detected a hint of reproach in Madam Cao's voice. It reminded her of First Wife.

'How strange,' she repeated, with an edge of coldness.

Cao lifted her eyebrows.

'What is your extreme discomfort?' she asked.

'I will await Dr Shih's return,' said Lu Ying, haughtily. 'Pray inform him that I am indisposed. Naturally, I will pay his usual fee.'

There was a long silence.

'I'm sure my husband will not require it,' said Cao. 'You are our Honoured Guest.'

'That will not be necessary,' replied Lu Ying. 'Let the usual fee apply.'

She turned away, intent on regaining the safety of her room. Cao said more gently: 'Miss Lu Ying, tell me what troubles you, and perhaps I can suggest something. Is it a woman's complaint?'

Lu Ying hesitated.

'I have an insufferable headache,' she said. 'My temple. . . it is as though there are lights.'

Cao's expression softened. She sighed, as if at a private thought.

'I'm sure you have every reason for it. Sit down and I'll bring something I myself find helpful. Perhaps little red sister has come? If the tea does no good, Dr Shih can help.'

Lu Ying sat stiffly. This simple woman had read the situation exactly. She awaited Cao's return, eagerly watching people pass on the street. Some looked interesting and she wondered where they came from, what they sought. Her headache was much improved by the time Madam Cao returned with a steaming pot. She drank the infusion cautiously. It tasted coarser than she had expected. Soon a sense of well-being filled her body. Cao watched, her eyes stealing down to Lu Ying's slippers, then took a cup herself.

'I feel surprisingly better!' announced the girl.

Indeed, she felt disturbingly at ease. If Wang Ting-bo came upon her now, he would gain the shameful impression that somehow she belonged here.

'Pray tell me how much *cash* is required?'

Madam Cao regarded her curiously.

'Miss Lu Ying, when do you intend to leave our house?'

The girl looked away in confusion. She understood what troubled the plain woman before her, with her bent nose and absurd feet. The reason was all too familiar. She could have her husband any time she chose. Lu Ying would have laughed at the irony, but she was used to maintaining a bland face. So ridiculous a situation! And horribly demeaning. A cruel impulse inspired her next words. Yet it was Wang Ting-bo's wife she wished to punish, not Madam Cao.

'I would be most appreciative if Dr Shih took my pulse,' she sighed. 'I imagine he takes one's pulse very sweetly. His touch must be gentle.'

Now Madam Cao looked alarmed.

'A lady always appreciates the attentions of a diligent doctor,' continued Lu Ying. 'Especially one dedicated to one's welfare.'

Cao responded by taking up her brush and dipping it into the ink-slate. The neatness of the ledger mocked Lu Ying. She could barely write, apart from her signature. It seemed their interview was at an end. She left awkwardly and Madam Cao did not look up from her task.

竹子

Instead of the shifting street glimpsed through the window of Dr Shih's shop, Lu Ying was confronted with stacks of shiny, lifeless boxes. Her feelings were uneasy as she closed the chamber door. One might possibly describe her behaviour as faulty – though it had felt pleasant to be superior. That way she might remember who she truly was. But Lu Ying knew she had offended Madam Cao and regretted it. The doctor's wife reminded her of Mother. Yet Dr Shih was a handsome man and he had every right to admire her, whatever his wife might think.

Sleepy from the bitter tea she had drunk, Lu Ying lolled on the divan. It had once stood in the Pacification Commissioner's mansion. Memories clung to it, traces of perfume, vanished words. . .

Lu Ying had first passed through Wang Ting-bo's gatehouse a year before her ceremony of hairpins. A great honour, denoting his wish that she receive a thorough training before entering concubinage.

The time before that was vague. Her father had held a lowly position in the Waterways Bureau, assisting the local sub-commissioner for fords and bridges. His duties often took him away from home. Mother said he had been unjustly overlooked for promotion.

Blessings eluded him in other ways, too. Although Mother delivered half a dozen daughters, no son had been forthcoming. Yet Lu Ying always knew herself to be valuable as any son. People could not help glancing at her and often marvelled over

Father's good fortune. Such a daughter, they said, would attract splendid wedding gifts.

Only Mother did not seem to appreciate her worth. She kept Lu Ying out of sight, forcing her to mind her sisters because she was the eldest. Nevertheless, it was Mother who bound her daughter's feet, and though it was painful, Lu Ying felt proud. None of her sisters' feet were bound. That honour belonged to her alone.

Father would return every few weeks. Apart from complaining about his superiors, he often talked about a child's duty to provide for her parents – just as he had cared for his own in their old age. Lu Ying rolled her eyes when he could not see.

'You shall come with me to the village,' he announced one day. 'The Sub-prefect is to hold an examination.'

An examination! Did not scholars undertake the Son of Heaven's examinations? Lu Ying wondered if Father would be promoted at last, though he was surely no scholar.

Then the local matchmaker arrived. Whispered conversations took place in the kitchen, so secret that Mother stood guard by the door. Lu Ying crept beneath the window outside and heard her name mentioned, as well as *ba-bao*, precious things. Then everything made sense. Why the village boys came by, whistling to attract her attention, and older men, too, speculation in their eyes. It was because she was precious and would bring Father luck. He ordered her to bow before Madam Matchmaker.

'This lady will prepare you for a great event,' said Father. 'You must do exactly as she says.'

She stood very still while Madam applied make-up and dressed her in borrowed silks. Mother fluttered anxiously.

'This is our great chance,' she murmured. 'Be placid and obedient.'

That afternoon Father took her to the village square where the Sub-prefect had set up a temporary court. She waited in the tavern owned by Madam Matchmaker's husband, her cheap silks and make-up constantly adjusted. Lu Ying did not know why they hid her away. She wanted everyone to admire her new clothes.

At last Father appeared and led her into the village square. The Sub-prefect sat beneath an awning, conspicuously bored. When he caught sight of Lu Ying his expression changed. Dozens of other girls her age stood awkwardly, but she was the one he noticed. A calculating look came into his red-rimmed eyes. He ordered her to come forward.

'What is your name?' he asked, in a strangely effeminate voice.

'Lu Ying, sir,' she said, bowing as Madam Matchmaker had instructed.

'Show me your feet.'

She hesitated, then raised her skirt a few inches. He chuckled and clapped his hands: 'This one will do!'

She had wondered what exactly must be done.

As Lu Ying dozed on the divan in Dr Shih's shop, pictures filled her inward eye. A journey in a curtained carriage. Stripping naked while doctors examined her gravely, recording on scrolls and consulting astrologers. She was one of fifty girls from all over the province. Some gossiped excitedly when they thought themselves unobserved but Lu Ying had known better. They were never unobserved. It rarely crossed her mind that these rivals were more beautiful than herself. When it did, Lu Ying went cold inside yet smiled so gaily, and modestly, that even the doctors' grave expressions softened a little. For all her smiles, she did not trust them. Ever after, the presence of doctors made her anxious – ivory does not come from a dog's mouth.

A sudden noise startled her. Dr Shih was pounding medicines again. She did not care to consult him now; not after her conversation with Madam Cao. Once more her thoughts drifted. . .

When Father left the Pacification Commissioner's mansion on Peacock Hill, he was pushing a specially purchased hand-cart, laden with bolts of silk and boxes of precious things.

'Do not disgrace us,' he told her. 'Remember, if you are ever banished from here our doors will be closed. Never forget your duty to us!'

She had waited, head bowed, expecting some sign of affection. But Father seemed inordinately pleased with his bargain and vanished into the crowds of Nancheng. He did not look back though she waved and waved.

She never saw him again. Years later she heard that Wang Ting-bo had received a letter from the Sub-prefect, explaining a flood had drowned Father and Mother. As for her sisters, she never learned what became of them. No one showed her the letter and she was too afraid to ask. Besides, Peacock Hill filled her mind and senses.

Lu Ying could not remember when First Wife noticed her. She had been so little regarded. At that time First Wife was pregnant with Little Tortoise and a brittle atmosphere ruled the ladies' quarters. Everyone feared the unborn baby would not live long enough for its ceremony of the scarlet shirt.

Darkness of midwinter, clouds rolling across a star-lit, frosty sky when Wang Ting-bo at last honoured her with a summons. She was fifteen years old. The servants led her to a huge canopied bed decorated with gilt and dragons and instructed her to disrobe. She was sure what followed had not been painful; at least, only a little. She stayed awake all night in case he required more but he snored peacefully, his breath scented with garlic and wine. At dawn the Head Butler's urgent, silent gestures called her away while the Pacification Commissioner slept on. That month her red news came as usual. . .

The pounding upstairs had stopped. Lu Ying registered the change and curled up on the divan, hugging her chest.

After that, her position in the household subtly altered. Wang Ting-bo summoned her infrequently and First Wife regarded her with a mocking smile as she held her baby boy.

'Lu Ying,' she said. 'I hear you eat a great deal. Indeed, I have witnessed it. A girl in your position must deserve her food.'

She kept her head lowered.

'Yes, Madam.'

'Really there are too many concubines!' First Wife exclaimed to her confidante, an old crone of little wealth who echoed her mistress in everything. 'Before the birth of Little Tortoise, I understood the need for girls like this. Now she is quite unnecessary.'

The child on her lap began to cry and First Wife awkwardly bobbed him up and down, unsure what to do.

'Lu Ying,' she said, irritably. 'I hear your parents were washed away by a flood. I suppose we're stuck with you. Will this child never stop crying! Lu Ying, hold him for a moment.'

She took the Pacification Commissioner's son while Madam First Wife fanned her streaked face. Years of looking after baby sisters had taught Lu Ying what troubled the child. For a moment she wondered whether to let on. It was amusing to see First Wife in a fluster. Then Lu Ying took pity on the baby – so sweet a little thing, after all – and winded him on her shoulder. He let out a huge milky belch. First Wife watched the boy settle then reached out angrily.

'Stupid girl! You are not worthy to touch my son! Pass him back at once!'

Lu Ying did so, bowing shamefacedly. But the river of her feelings had changed course. It no longer ran smoothly. Hatred for Madam First Wife brought purpose and strength.

After that Lu Ying became more mindful of Wang Ting-bo, observing him closely. Years passed, until she celebrated her nineteenth birthday. She noticed he liked to laugh among friends, whereas First Wife always spoke to him coldly. That he seemed uneasy with the mother of his heir. His eye often descended to his concubines' jade mountains, so she contrived to make her own more prominent. Most of all, she sensed the loneliness of his august position. That was the weakness to work upon.

Lu Ying eagerly awaited her summons to his bedchamber.

After the birth of Little Tortoise, his attentions were naturally directed towards First Wife. Finally, the interminable hours spent in her chamber came to an end. The Pacification Commissioner's personal servant ordered her to follow him and that night she tested her plans.

First, she archly suggested that he leave a candle burning and encouraged him to revel in her ivory mounds. Saucy tales of the palace servants diverted him so he laughed out loud. Once his ardour had extinguished itself, she enquired about the day's business, hoping His Excellency had been caused no annoyance. He seemed surprised, but explained about certain emissaries from the court, and she sighed admiringly at his wisdom.

As she lay on the divan in Dr Shih's house, Lu Ying hugged herself more closely. Her breath quickened. What followed was the happy time. The most dangerous of times. At last First Wife truly took notice of her existence. . .

'Lu Ying, you displease me,' she had said, when the women of the household were gathered for the Vigil of the Water-borne Moon. Silence among the ladies. Lu Ying knew she should feign humbleness, yet would not.

'How have I displeased you, Madam?'

'Don't think your tricks go unnoticed,' chided First Wife. 'Many a silly girl before you thought she could supplant her betters. It always ends badly.'

'Who is this silly girl Madam refers to?' asked Lu Ying, wide-eyed. 'She must be very bad.'

First Wife paled at such impudence.

'Go to your quarters,' she commanded.

That same night Wang Ting-bo called her to his bedchamber, defying the admonishments of his wife. He was drunk and his flame required coaxing before it would burn steadily. Then her moon filled the night sky.

For two years he doted on her. She was assigned quarters scarcely smaller than First Wife's. He took her on excursions to fashionable waterfalls and monasteries, smiling at the chatter she rehearsed to amuse him. She was the being in his eyes, everyone acknowledged it. Servants whispered the fearful word *divorce* and officials treated her with exaggerated respect.

Extravagant clothes and perfumes were all supplied without question, some as gifts from officials hoping to buy future influence. She even risked offending Wang Ting-bo's great adviser, his nephew, Wang Bai, concerning an appointment. Amazingly, the Pacification Commissioner followed her suggestion. Afterwards, she had wandered her suite of rooms, drunk on the fragrance of perfumed clothes and exquisite furniture, the metal-smell of ornaments – and most of all, power. First Wife would no longer speak to her, but Lu Ying pretended not to notice. Each slight or rudeness encouraged her to beg something new from Wang Ting-bo and he never refused.

But no child came. Every month her scarlet general grasped the door. Gradually the Pacification Commissioner became less manageable. He even began to mock her inability to write well or recite noble poems. Then, like a flood unleashed by Heaven, his heir fell sick. And Dr Shih – kindly, earnest Dr Shih – did the rest. If the boy had obligingly died, as most reasonably could have been expected, then the divan on which she curled would still stand in the mansion on Peacock Hill.

Lu Ying's headache returned. At least she had a plan now. A fine present would remind him she was waiting. It was impossible he had forgotten her. But she must not empty her box of *cash*. Without wealth, what was anyone?

Then Lu Ying had another idea. Dr Shih had received a considerable reward for taking her into his household. He could hardly have spent it all, given his modest ways.

Lu Ying's flower-bud mouth pursed as she calculated. Because of Dr Shih's obvious fascination with her, she would soon persuade him to pass over a considerable sum. The main obstacle, his dowdy wife, was hardly worth mentioning. But even as she thought these things, Lu Ying felt a flicker of unease. How weak she was becoming! Henceforth, whenever she felt pity for Madam Cao, she would pretend First Wife's face sat upon the plump woman's shoulders.

There was another danger. What if Dr Shih assumed that providing the money for Wang Ting-bo's present entitled him to intimate exchanges of the 'bathing in orchid blossom' kind? Lu Ying hugged her chest and wondered at her own feelings; for such a prospect did not disgust her exactly as it should.

Rising, she paced the room full of boxes. The lacquer on their sides reflected her movements as a blur.

竹子

The autumn night was unseasonably warm. While the household slept, Lu Ying lit a candle and quietly opened her chamber door. She listened for a long moment. No one stirred. Not even a creak as the wooden walls settled. The central corridor of the house was entirely dark. Lu Ying ventured out, naked of make-up, her long hair disordered. What would happen if Dr Shih found her in such a state? She was in no position to prevent anything.

Lu Ying bit her lip and held the candle high, its light steady in the breathless corridor. Step by step, she made her way to the black tunnel of the stairs. Pausing on the bottom step, she detected a faint snoring. No telling whose room it came from.

Then Lu Ying climbed the steep staircase, silk slippers scraping faintly. On reaching the tower room, her fears subsided. She laid her guttering candle on the floor and stood by the south window. Rooftops formed a confused jumble, leading all the way to Peacock Hill, where lights burned late in the Pacification Commissioner's residence.

A half-moon varnished the wooden rooftops. Clouds rolled northwards, obscuring the moon momentarily. Lu Ying felt that the Moon Goddess, Cheng-e, shone for her alone.

Vague warnings crept across her soul. She shivered. The moon was lonely, too. She could see its reflection in the dark, placid waters of the canal below. Tears filled her eyes. How tiresome life had grown! The moon lay on the water like a half-open door, tempting her to enter. If she jumped from the tower, no one would hear. And she could not swim. She shivered, imagining the struggle for breath, the darkness closing as she sank. Perhaps she should dress in her finest, heaviest silks, weigh herself down with jewellery, and find peace at last. Wang Ting-bo would miss her then. Her pale, beautiful face would float upwards, just as the moon's reflection drifted on the inky, drifting water.

Lu Ying stared out across the sleeping city. In the morning she would order a gift for Wang Ting-bo. And now she knew what it must be: the moon had taught her. She would commission a round, silver mirror, the characters of her name etched like shadow beneath the shining metal. When he glimpsed his face in it, her name would lie across his reflected image. Then he would be entranced and come to her.

She bowed solemnly to Cheng-e. The moon did not reply. Back in her room, Lu Ying barely slept, wondering even in her dreams how to find the *cash* for so costly a gift. At last, she recollected that Dr Shih had received a bar of pure silver from Wang Ting-bo. Everything was ordained. This thought quite settled the matter. Towards dawn she fell into a deep slumber.

Lu Ying was no stranger to commissioning costly objects. At the height of her power she had developed a passion for embroidered silks. Then there were the amulets and hairpieces she ordered from her favourite jeweller. He had done well by her patronage.

All morning she paced her room, awaiting a visitor. When someone knocked tentatively, she arranged herself on the divan in an attitude of amused ease.

'Enter!'

The fat apprentice bobbed in the doorway, grinning nervously.

'A visitor, Madam.'

'Well, send him in, Chung.'

He ushered into the room a neat, clean-shaven man. Her visitor looked round curiously, hands hidden in his sleeves. Instead of bowing low as in the old days, he merely nodded. Lu Ying's condescending smile grew brittle.

'Fu Sha! Do come in and close the door. Wait outside, Chung.'

The jeweller stood in the centre of the room, taking in the stacked boxes, the meanness of her quarters. Tales of her situation would make salty gossip. Some might even reach the Pacification Commissioner's palace. There was no help for it now.

'Fu Sha,' she said. 'As you can see, my store chamber is a little cluttered at present. Alas, my audience chamber is being refurbished, so this will have to do.'

'I am honoured,' he said.

She shot him a glance. So smooth a face gave no sign of whether he believed her.

'Good. Well, let's to business. I have a commission for you, Fu Sha.'

She outlined her wishes. That the mirror's radius should not exceed two hands. Its borders were to be decorated with dragons and phoenixes. The characters of her name should be like a shadow beneath the mirror's silver face. He listened attentively.

'A most unusual design,' he said, at last.

She nodded, pleased by his reaction.

'I need it very soon. How soon might it be complete?'

Fu Sha's glance was wandering again.

'How soon?' He bowed slightly. 'Such a great piece of work would take many months to accomplish.'

'That is too long!'

'The border decorations alone would occupy my entire workshop.' He looked up at her sharply. 'Honourable Lady Lu Ying must realise that even humble Fu Sha has not lacked commissions since her. . . change of abode.'

A flush crept through her make-up.

'Then there is the matter of payment,' he said. 'I take it the account should be sent to His Excellency, as before?'

'No,' she replied. 'Your fees will be met by myself.'

He frowned.

'I see. I am most grateful. May I request that my fee of ten thousand *cash* be settled in advance? With so unique a piece of work. . . I'm sure Madam understands.'

Lu Ying understood very well. But ten thousand! Her box of *cash* contained only a third that amount.

'What if you were to receive a large bar of silver?' she asked. 'You might begin at once.'

Fu Sha seemed embarrassed.

'As I say. . .'

'The silver shall be sent to you today.'

'Even so. . .'

'Then it is settled.'

Indeed it seemed so to her, as though the mirror was already waiting in its silk-lined box for a messenger to rush it to Peacock Hill. He pursed his lips.

'I would be honoured by your commission, when I receive full payment in advance.'

She barely heard him. At last her troubles were receding! She felt like a sick person informed her disease is on the mend.

Lu Ying realised the door had closed. Fu Sha no longer stood before her. Had she given him permission to go? Yet he was gone. Her fan tapped against her knee. The bar of silver must be sent without delay, before all hope slipped away.

Lu Ying had always prided herself on her energy. Once Wang Ting-bo had gazed at her in wonder as they lay entwined on moist sheets. 'When you bear me a son,' he said, 'he shall have the vigour of a tiger.'

So now she did not hesitate. Dr Shih must be found at once. The rest would be simple. Lu Ying waited a decent interval for Fu Sha to leave Apricot Corner Court, then hurried to the shop. Fortunately, there was no sign of Madam Cao. Dr Shih's witless apprentice was polishing jars of medicine without any discernible effort.

'Where is your master?' she demanded.

He blinked at her stupidly. 'At the Relief Bureau, Miss,' he said.

Her breath hissed with annoyance.

'Master's due home soon,' he added.

'I shall go to this precious Relief Bureau straight away,' she announced. 'Where is it?'

She listened impatiently to his directions, wondering whether Wang Ting-bo's payments to the doctor amounted to ten thousand. Five would do. The remainder might be raised by selling a few jewels.

Purpose renewed her strength. She hurried into the street before Chung finished his directions. He had told her to seek the Water Basin. That was easy enough. The masts of boats could be seen in the distance. Blurred faces surrounded her but Lu Ying took no notice. Walking as quickly as her bound feet would carry her, she denied the fluttering of her heart. How strange to be outside! To be in the city, among common people! She was so far above them that she felt invisible. They were easy to ignore. They didn't exist if she ignored them. It was like walking through the Pacification Commissioner's pleasure gardens, only the carved pavilions and belvederes had been replaced by filthy warehouses and taverns, shops and mean houses. One might pretend the jabbering voices were birds singing as they fluttered from branch to branch. She would find Dr Shih, bend him to her will.

Lu Ying at last became aware a curious crowd had gathered and were blocking her way. She went very still, drew herself upright. Coarse eyes sullied her exquisite silks and make-up. People muttered. Then she realised her folly. To be out on the street, unchaperoned! Lu Ying realised with a dreadful certainty that news of this would reach First Wife. How had she allowed it? First Wife must have hired a sorcerer to send her mad! Lu Ying began to tremble. Someone laughed behind her. Were they jeering? She felt hot tears in her eyes. Her make-up would run. She looked round desperately. Essential to retrace her steps, regain Dr Shih's shop. But she did not recognise the broad street lined with shops selling vegetables and hempen clothes. In her haste, Chung's directions had flown far away.

Just as she was about to cover her face, a tall figure appeared before her. Through her tears she glimpsed armour, a sword. Yet the soldier possessed Dr Shih's face. Trembling, she looked up, and her heart leapt. The broad-chested officer seemed displeased and puzzled. A dozen soldiers and clerks accompanied him.

'How is this?' he demanded.

His voice was uncannily like Shih's, though harsher, and there was something daunting about his manner. She recognised him from his visit to Apricot Corner Court a few weeks earlier – and the look of disapproval in his glance showed that he remembered her just as clearly.

'I'm seeking Dr Shih,' she mumbled, afraid people in the crowd might hear. Again he frowned and turned to the gawping circle of faces.

'Move on!' he ordered. 'Sergeant, clear these people! They cause a public nuisance.'

Soon the street flowed as before.

'Sergeant, form a close escort round the lady,' he commanded.

Miraculously, she found herself hidden by a forest of burly men carrying halberds.

'You are Dr Shih's brother,' she said, regaining sufficient composure to flutter her fan. 'You are Captain Xiao.'

He glanced at her. She sensed he felt as awkward as she did.

'So they say. Now I'll escort you to my brother.'

The tall soldier walked a few paces ahead of her and the crowd parted before him. No one noticed her now. All eyes were drawn to the splendid Captain Xiao, just as one admires a plumed drake while the drab duck waddles behind. Lu Ying glanced up occasionally at his straight back. Mostly she kept her eyes lowered. Despite gratitude at being rescued, she did not care for his tone. After all, he was just a soldier. Hardly a gentleman at all.

When they reached Apricot Corner Court, Guang nodded at the door.

'That is where you belong,' he said. His large brown eyes narrowed. 'Next time, ensure you have a guide when you seek my brother on the street. Water Basin Ward is a den of rogues.'

Lu Ying found herself nodding obediently. Before she could make a pretty speech of thanks he marched off, too busy for one like her. She watched him disappear round a corner. It surprised her that he did not look back.

An hour later Lu Ying sat in Dr Shih's consulting room. Tea bowls lay untouched on a low table between them. Once again she was trembling, but now with ill-concealed fury.

It seemed the whole world was unreasonable. First Fu Sha and the gawping peasants on the street, then the arrogant Captain Xiao; and finally, this provoking doctor, with his way of setting one at ease when a formidable stiffness was required. His wife watched from the doorway with a cold vigilance Lu Ying recognised from her battles with First Wife. If only Madam Cao had not broken into their conversation! Dr Shih might have been managed easily otherwise.

'Lady Lu Ying,' he was saying. 'I still do not understand. You request as a loan the bar of silver I earned for saving His Excellency's son? But that was my entire fee. The monthly stipend we receive from the Pacification Commissioner merely pays for your food. I was given to understand that he had provided you with a large sum for any special items you might require.'

'Sir,' she said. 'I believe His Excellency gave you gifts in trust, intended for my welfare. Now I need them urgently. It is quite simple. When I resume my former position I shall double, no triple, anything I borrow now.'

Dr Shih glanced at his wife, who at last stirred: 'You'll find my husband spent all the fees we received on buying and repairing this house, which formerly we rented from the Landlord Hsing Wa.'

It amazed Lu Ying he allowed his wife to speak for him. She despised men ruled by women. Ignoring Madam Cao, she said stiffly: 'Dr Shih, if you could send for the bar of silver, I would be most grateful.'

'How can we give what we no longer possess?' he asked, clearly taking pains not to embarrass her.

'What of His Excellency's other gifts?' she demanded, shrilly.

'Lady Lu Ying,' said Dr Shih, a note of warning in his deep voice.

Anguish clouded Lu Ying's beautiful face. She realised Dr Shih was watching closely, as though she were a patient in need of a cure.

'You are distressed,' he said. Then Shih hesitated, and turned to his wife: 'Perhaps Wang Ting-bo intended a little of my fee for her needs, though no mention was made at the time. What is your opinion, Cao?'

Lu Ying recollected similar debates between Wang Ting-bo and First Wife. Always she got her way in the end. She allowed herself a sideways glance of triumph at Madam Cao.

'I think,' said the plain woman. 'We owe nothing. In fact, the obligation lies entirely the other way around.'

'But His Excellency clearly intended we should take care of her,' suggested Shih. 'If it will lift her spirits a little. . . Tell me, Lu Ying, what exactly *are* you asking for?'

Quite unexpectedly, the doorway where Cao had been standing became a closed rectangle of wood. Lu Ying and Shih stared in surprise at the blank face of the door. They heard Madam Cao's hurried footsteps retreating down the corridor. The street door opened and closed with a bang. Lu Ying felt all the bitterness of her triumph.

'Generous sir,' she whispered. 'I require at least five thousand *cash*. There is a piece of jewellery I must commission and the wretched jeweller. . .'

Quite suddenly, as a cloud swiftly hides the sun, Dr Shih's expression became one of contempt. A change she had never imagined possible from him. The silver mirror and all her schemes suddenly seemed foolish, even vulgar.

'You create dissent in my household for *that*?' he said. 'Can you really not see how we live here?'

'Dr Shih, perhaps. . .' she muttered, but he did not hear, for he had bowed curtly and followed his wife through the door. Lu Ying was left alone to finish her sentence: 'Perhaps I have misunderstood.'

For long moments she cruelly pinched the softest, most tender places on her arm. If only she had given Wang Ting-bo a son! Then she would not be here, wretched and ashamed. She would not have to return to that suffocating room, crammed with mocking boxes. Or wear silks too fine for her new position in the world.

And now there was a new fear. Dr Shih and Madam Cao might defy the Pacification Commissioner's displeasure and insist she leave Apricot Corner Court. No one would blame them. Everyone hated her. Lu Ying imagined the cold waters of the canal closing over her head. Wearily, she retreated to her chamber.

憺

seven

'I recollect a drinking party in autumn when we ordered our carriages to bear us to Mount Wadung, though it was the middle of the night. Our intention was purely a love of insight. Sub-prefect Hui Chi contended that, when the sun rose, we would be able to discern whether Fouzhou lay in shadow longer than Nancheng. Thus we might be able to attribute *yin* and *yang* to the different cities. Slowly dawn cast a glow upon the land and realms of stars retreated to the emptiness where they hide themselves during daylight, dazzled by the sun. At last Hui Chi announced: 'Fouzhou is *Yin*-mountain!' and we muttered amongst ourselves, quite aghast. For '*Yin*-mountain' lies in the Sixth Hell and is populated by souls more sinned against than sinning. . .'

From *Remembrances of A Western Terrace at Twilight*

竹子

The Floating Bridge, Nancheng. Autumn, 1266.

Dr Shih left the shop, hurrying into the crowded streets of Nancheng. Faces swam before his eyes, tens of thousands drifting to a food stall or home after the day's labours. The argument with Cao echoed in his mind.

Shih never quarrelled with his wife, a matter of pride to him. Yet it seemed their oneness was crumbling like earthen walls during a flood. Even his distress seemed ignoble. The single quality he respected in himself was calmness, or its show. Now he avoided the eyes of those he passed, however humble.

The city bell tolled the hour mournfully. He should have been starting that evening's round of patients. Many were grievously sick. For the first time in ten years he ignored duty and walked blindly on through Slaughter Pig Alley where carcasses on hooks dried in the wind, then the Street of Jade where jewellers flattered wealthy nobles and merchants, all oblivious to his distress, all intent on their own bargains.

At last he reached the Gate of the Vermilion Sparrow. To ensure public order a dozen bored soldiers inspected people crossing the Floating Bridge to Fouzhou on the far shore. Lanterns glowed in the dusk-light. Shih paused, leaning on the parapet and watching the river below. The wood and bamboo bridge creaked continuously from the footfalls of passers-by.

Though he grew calmer, a dull ache beyond the power of needle or drug would not fade. Sickness of the spirit requires invisible cures. Often virtue is the only medicine. He recollected how Dr Du Mau's spite had led to Lu Ying's presence in his household – and Cao's distrust, a thing he had never expected to see.

The river rippled in shifting patterns as he gazed down. It smelt of cleansing and decay, somehow fetid, even lewd. Then Shih imagined Lu Ying's naked body beneath his own, her firm jade mountains and the fragrance of her black rose. Eyes reaching out and clasping. Murmurs and cries. So strong was the unbidden image that he felt dizzy leaning over the low parapet. His heart raced. Control struggled for mastery.

By right he could possess her anytime he chose. Was she not his concubine? At least, if she forgot Peacock Hill – if she made that pact with him – if he could betray Cao who had surrendered her entire happiness to his care.

Another part of him asked coldly, was he not a man? Lu Ying might bear him a son. Her essential breaths reeked of warm health, and that implied fecundity. Yet if he took what dangled, he would lose something ineffably fine. Once water was poured into wine, neither could be itself again.

Dr Shih looked up at the battlements of Nancheng and recognised a silhouette against the thinning sun. At once he hurried after it, pursuing a shadow. Passing through the Gate of the Vermilion Sparrow, he climbed an earthen ramp. A dozen carpenters were working at the foot of the walls, sawing wooden beams. As many rope-makers arrived in a convoy of wheelbarrows filled with hemp coils. At last he spied his brother on a platform, observing the loading of a whirling tiger catapult.

Guang raised his arm and barked out a command. Twenty bare-chested men hauled on as many ropes, flinging a rock high over the battlements. An observer on the walls fluttered a yellow flag and Guang nodded happily. Finally he noticed Shih and summoned him with a wave.

'Brother, did you see where that stone landed!' exclaimed Guang. 'Had it been a thunderclap bomb there would have been a dozen Mongol widows!'

Shih listened to predictions of burning ships and drowned men, his smile forced and fixed. At last Guang became aware of it.

'Is something wrong?' he asked. 'Is Father unwell?'

'Father is exactly as he was when you deposited him at my gates,' said Shih.

'Put it where I ordered! Over there!' bawled Guang at a squad of soldiers carrying a huge crossbow. 'What were you saying?'

'It is not important.'

Guang scowled at the hammering and confusion around them.

'This is all I hear from dawn until midnight! I say, let them get on with it. I can always mend their mistakes tomorrow. Now Little Brother stands before me and I am thirsty. So let us drink.'

Soldiers saluted as they left the ramparts. Soon the bright

doors of a large teahouse came into view, festooned with banners and glowing lanterns. The Five Breeze Loft occupied both sides of the street, a confusion of balconies and tiled roofs. A flying bridge connected the two buildings and waiters with steaming dishes on lacquered trays scurried over the hats of people on the street below.

'This place will do,' said Guang. 'The owner knows me.'

Shih hesitated. He could barely afford the simplest of dishes in so grand an establishment. Besides, he had heard Dr Du Mau often came here.

'Don't worry, Little Brother,' said Guang. 'You are my guest.'

The arrival of Captain Xiao caused a stir among the waiters. They were led to a sumptuous private room, its balcony overlooking the rooftops of Nancheng. Across the river, Fouzhou was dotted with lights. Above the Twin Cities, constellations glittered in a blue-black sky.

Flasks of warm and chilled wine arrived, along with a dozen dishes.

'*Now* I feel better,' said Guang, downing his first bowl. 'The truth is, I'm busier than a nest of wasps.'

Shih toyed with his wine for moment, then swallowed it in one. Unworthy feelings crept through his breast. He envied his brother's apparently uncomplicated nature. That he seemed to live without doubt.

'You might wonder why I'm so busy,' continued Guang, swallowing a coloured egg stuffed with minced quail. Yellow crumbs clung to his moustache. 'The truth is, we have received messages that the Army of the Right Hand is in full retreat. Our generals will not risk a fight, the dogs!'

'That is bad,' said Shih, dully.

'If only I was there! Try one of these chicken wings, Little Brother, the sauce is a wonder.'

For the first time, Shih smiled. Sometimes Guang reminded him of a guileless boy who draws one into his games through sheer enthusiasm.

'I'm glad of your company, though,' continued Guang. 'I

need a wise head, and a discreet one. What do you make of this?' He bent forward to whisper. 'My patron, Prefect Wang Bai, constantly asks what properties we are confiscating. He's even given me a long list of places. The strange thing is, half the houses have no military value. And once they've been seized, I'm forbidden to pull them down. Some say that he packs them with tenants as soon as their owners have been evicted. Of course, that cannot be true. Yet I suspect a dirty business. Corrupt officials must be to blame. What do you say?'

Shih shrugged and drained another large bowl. His third.

'No doubt,' he said.

Guang stroked the wisps of his beard thoughtfully.

'You're thirstier than a clam tonight,' he said. 'How is Father? Still talking to the fishes, eh?'

'To Lord Yun, I am Khan Bayke's hired gaoler,' said Shih. 'He refuses to acknowledge me as his son. Well, there is nothing new there. But he asks after you, Guang, really you should visit him more often. It might help him rediscover his true nature.'

Other reproaches could have been added. That the one they called Captain Xiao in honour of his filial piety neglected his own father. That the old man was a burden in every possible way. But some truths may not be spoken, so he took Guang's advice and tried a chicken wing. The sauce was indeed a wonder.

'I hear you spend much time with your new lieutenant,' said Shih. 'The fellow who helped you escape the occupied lands.'

'You mean Chen Song!' said Guang, warming. The mention of Father had dampened his spirits. 'Now, there is a fine gentleman, Shih! Without his assistance in Chunming we would surely have been taken prisoner. I tell you, Chen Song is a man for difficult times. He is both scholar and soldier – and fine company, too.'

Shih glanced out of the window. Jealousy of one who had saved the lives of his dearest relations was surely ignoble.

'I'm glad you take pleasure in his company,' he said, stiffly.

'Yes, we've had a few wild nights since I got back.' Guang leaned forward conspiratorially. 'When we visit an oriole flower hall. . . Well, let us say the welcome is warm.'

He chuckled and splashed more wine into their cups. Shih felt oddly disconcerted. Though he knew Guang intended nothing by it, half of Lu Ying's name meant *oriole*. Against his better judgement, he began awkwardly:

'Actually, I would welcome some advice concerning a lady. You know about the Pacification Commissioner's concubine, who has joined my household?'

'Who does not know? Try these snails, you won't be disappointed.'

Shih persevered. After all, Guang was Eldest Brother. It was his duty to offer useful advice.

'Today Lu Ying caused a quarrel in our household,' he said. 'Even with Cao. . . Well, especially with Cao.'

Guang's chopsticks froze in their work of pouncing on snails.

'No need to say more! I always take Honoured Sister-in-law's side! She is jade to me, solely for her loyalty to you. This Lu Ying must be kept in her place. If need be, drive her from your doors.'

'Matters are slightly more complicated than you suggest,' said Shih. 'I fear the Pacification Commissioner would hardly forgive our family for throwing her on the street.'

Guang nodded.

'You are right. Then lock her in a small room for a day. That'll teach her a lesson.'

'Is she a criminal?' asked Shih. 'Am I to be a gaoler as Father believes? You see, I pity the lady. Of course I have not felt it appropriate to enter into *relations* with her. It would break Cao's heart. I try so hard to do well by everyone, Guang. But that seems impossible.'

Guang tugged at his chin, then poured more wine.

'I met the lady myself today,' he said. 'She was wandering round the streets, dressed like a peacock. Perhaps she is mad. You must keep a tighter grip on her, Little Brother! She claimed to be looking for you, but it was nearly a bad business. A crowd had gathered to stare at her as though she was a puppet show!'

Shih frowned.

'No one told me,' he said.

Somehow he did not welcome the thought of Captain Xiao talking with Lu Ying. The two brothers downed another bowl to fill an awkward silence.

'I have the answer,' said Guang. 'I shall admonish the girl sternly. Remember, I am Eldest Brother, and given Father's condition. . . Well, let's not bring Father into this. I shall command her to follow Cao's instructions, as is only proper. Lu Ying will certainly obey me.'

'Actually, the young lady is generally obedient to Cao,' said Shih, hurriedly. 'Thank you for your advice. There is no need for you to speak to her. I now see how to proceed.'

'As you wish,' said Guang. (Was there disappointment in his voice? Shih could not tell). 'If her conduct gets worse, come and see me. I know a thing or two about women.'

Guang tapped his forehead, then drank another cup. His expression suddenly grew morose. Shih was used to such shifts of mood in his brother.

'I have never forgotten how you and Cao helped me,' said Guang. 'You shared what little you had when all the world viewed me as a worthless, hungry dog on the street. Some would say it was merely your duty. But I have seen many betray their own brothers. Honour me by relating our conversation to Sister-in-law. Tell her I will always defend her.'

Then Guang's flame brightened again. His frown smoothed and he returned to favourite topics: how he had overcome a thousand petty obstacles to gather thunderclap bombs; how he had gained praise from the Pacification Commissioner himself and even won the grudging respect of the Zheng cousins, those brave commanders who had initially opposed his promotion.

Guang arranged the flasks and bowls on the table to represent the Twin Cities, showing how an attacker would be ground like rice until the husks floated away down the Han River. Shih drank so steadily his head swam. He did not mention his troubles again; it seemed easier to listen and admire.

When he returned to Apricot Corner Court, he found that Cao had not waited up for him. Neither did she stir as he awkwardly undressed in the dark, or even when he murmured drunken endearments by way of good night. Her back was strangely rigid for one who slept.

竹子

Peace returned to his household the next day. At least, outwardly. If intimacy is two boughs fluttering beside one another so their leaves mingle, Shih sensed Cao's branch lean away, and filled the empty space between them with sad thoughts. He also feared that she suspected his intemperate desires.

Lu Ying kept to her room and he wondered what she was thinking. Not of plain Dr Shih, that was certain. Yet, sometimes, he imagined she might wish him to approach her.

That afternoon, his duties at the Relief Bureau fulfilled, he returned home and mounted the stairs to the tower room. As he emerged on the first floor he found Lord Yun by the window, half-hidden by a bamboo curtain, peering like a watchful hawk down at Apricot Corner Court. Shih had little doubt what fascinated the old man. A few swift strides to the window confirmed his fears.

Widow Mu's daughter, Lan Tien, was playing with her brothers round the apricot tree, bending and brushing back her fringe. Dr Shih released the curtain so that it fell with a clatter. The old man shuffled back a few paces, his sensitive almond eyes staring into empty space.

'You demean yourself, sir,' chided Shih. 'The city has many noble sights. This is not one of them.'

'Do not talk to *me* about demeaning oneself!' replied Lord Yun. 'You claim to be my son, yet what do I find? A doctor. A *peddler*.'

Shih went pale.

'If I am *just* a doctor, as you say, then who is to blame? It is you, Father, who chose that destiny for me. Have you really forgotten?'

'Ah hah! That is what Bayke taught you to say! I'm aware of your game! If only Guang was here, he'd make you grovel.'

'Father, have you really forgotten how I came to be a doctor?'

There was pleading in Shih's voice.

The old man pushed aside bunches of drying herbs that hung from the rafters and descended the steep wooden stairs. A door slammed below. For a moment Shih stood indecisively, wondering whether to follow. Drawing up a stool, he sat at his workbench and stared across the rooftops at Peacock Hill, listening to the children play outside.

Later he walked across Apricot Corner Court, nodding curtly to Lan Tien and her brother on the way. He found Widow Mu fanning herself in her dumpling shop.

'I have come to enquire about your health,' he said. 'Among all these rumours of war and Mongols.'

She watched him cautiously.

'As I told Madam Cao only this morning, with so many soldiers in the city, business has never been better,' she said.

Shih realised his wife had been gossiping. Widow Mu probably knew more about their troubles with Lu Ying than he did.

'So you are well,' he said.

'Even if we were sick,' she replied. 'Since you healed His Excellency's son, we couldn't afford your fees.'

'I never charge fees for a neighbour.'

Widow Mu continued to fan herself.

'It is strange you mention the Mongols,' she said. 'Last night Lan Tien woke up crying and said the barbarians were spying on her.'

He shot her a sharp glance. Was there reproach in Widow Mu's tone? He could not be sure.

'She will sleep well tonight,' he said, hastily. 'I will send Chung over with an infusion and an amulet I have found useful in such cases. You must wave it over Lan Tien's forehead five times.'

Widow Mu looked suspicious, even while she bowed with every sign of gratitude.

'It is kind of you to remember us, sir. What with so many changes in your household.'

'Ah,' said Shih. 'Yes.'

'I take it Madam Cao is happy with the changes?'

An insolent question! Here was proof his wife had been gossiping. Soon everyone in Water Basin Ward would become experts on their intimate business.

'Five times over the forehead,' he repeated. 'And ensure the blinds are kept lowered at morning and evening, lest day or dusk gather in the rafters and confuse your daughter's sleep.'

Shih left, refusing her offer of a dumpling. He had done all he could. As ever, it did not feel enough.

竹子

He went to the East Market to buy merit. On the ground known as Lone Willow, three criminals' heads were being fixed to hooks dangling from the market gates. A dozen others grinned in various states of decay.

Nearby stood a pond surrounded by a maze of stalls. Here monks sold lucky spells and blessing-merchants tended golden carp in wooden troughs, scooping them out with long-handled nets. Shih selected a fat one, its scales dappled silver and grey. Chanting a short sutra, the merchant reverently placed it in a square bucket painted with favourable symbols.

Dr Shih prayed for merit in this life and the next as he set it free in the pond. For a moment, the fish quivered as though stunned, then vanished into the dark water with a flick of its tail. Its liberator examined the pond. A few carp floated belly up. On a small island, long-legged cranes paced. One darted its long beak and seized a writhing fish. Its gorge worked rhythmically. The fish vanished.

He wondered why the blessing-merchants did not scare the greedy birds away. Perhaps they were necessary. Without them, the pond would soon grow full. Perversely, Shih recollected how the Mongols plucked up whole nations in their beaks and devoured them whole.

Once the rite was over, he walked swiftly towards the North Medical Relief Bureau. The narrow alleys of Water Basin Ward were muddy from last night's downpour. Dogs and children played in puddles. Low black clouds rolled like his thoughts. He longed to unburden himself, to be empty like the Enlightened Ones. All his life Dr Shih had struggled to forget so many things.

At last he reached a junction. One way led to the Relief Bureau, the other to the Water Gate of Morning Radiance. Unpleasantness awaited him at the Bureau. Expensive herbs had gone missing and the matter must be investigated. He hesitated, then followed the line of the ramparts until he entered a narrow, brick-lined tunnel reeking of urine and green slime. The tunnel took him outside the city walls, where the wide river spread into the distance.

He followed a path along the riverbank, beneath the impregnable towers and ramparts of Nancheng, soon reaching an isolated wooden jetty. There he sat, leaning against a mooring post. Closing his eyes, he allowed memories to surface, like the round, hungry mouth of the carp he had freed. His daring surprised him, for with those memories invariably came anguish. . .

The boy had been tall for his age. It was a family trait. People in Wei Valley called them the Stilt-Yuns, though not to their faces. The nickname implied barbarian forebears and other unflattering things. When the peasants came to Three-Step-House, paying half their crop in rent, Lord Yun towered a head above his tenants. Shih always remembered that. As Eldest Son, one day he would be Lord. The servants told him this many times, as did Mother. Father rarely noticed Shih among his many concerns.

Father was the sky and Mother the moon floating across him. Little Brother, who resembled Shih exactly, was a star hanging beside his own, glimpsed through the bamboo curtains of the room they shared. Little Guang cast a light of mischief and laughter. Though Shih was the eldest, he often deferred to him.

They were five years old and Shih might have been completely happy, except when he was not good enough. Father applauded Guang's bold antics and Shih tried to copy them, discovering that to imitate is to be ignored. Worse, to earn unfavourable comparisons.

One winter night, as they dined on twenty dishes, Shih said to Father that families in the village were very hungry. He had seen them boiling bark and old hooves for soup. That was the year when the harvest failed because of too much rain, then too little. Father's only reply was an unblinking, owl-like stare. Later, Mother whispered it was better not to mention these things because Father refused to lower the rents. Shih did not know what rent might be. He suspected it made people unhappy.

A serious little boy, he stared at the plum trees above Three-Step-House, noticing how they changed according to the season. Guang climbed to the topmost branches, clambering and making noises like a monkey. If Father chanced upon them, he watched the pair coldly. Shih understood, without ever a word being said, that he should be the one grappling the highest branches. When he tried to describe how the trees grew from bareness to blossom to fruit, Father seemed angry.

'That is why we hire gardeners,' he said, sternly. 'Our duty is to eat the best of the plums and sell what is left.'

Shih felt foolish but Guang piped up: 'I don't want anyone but *us* to have all the plums!'

Father rewarded such splendid words with a new wooden

ball. Shih received nothing. Though he never doubted the justness of Father's admonishment, he still noticed the plums turned from sour to sweet, and wondered why. Surely it meant that people or animals would notice and eat them? Whereas if they remained sour and small, no one would pay attention and the fruit would be safe in its tree. He kept those questions to himself.

Father hired troupes of performers, who he met on his frequent trips to the provincial capital, Chunming. Acrobats and actors, fire-eaters and musicians. Mother explained that Lord Yun was easily bored and required diversion. Shih knew these people were a bad thing, because he once heard Mother pleading with Father to consider the expense.

'I will do as I like!' he had raged. 'What I want, I shall have!'

After that Lord Yun would not speak to anyone for a week.

Shih pondered Father's words in the darkness of his room at night. Of course, Father was right. But he had never forgotten the year when the harvest failed and wondered whether Father should hire hungry peasants instead of acrobats. He mentioned this to Mother and she sighed: 'One might talk to the river, but it does not listen.'

Guang was more delighted than anyone by the actors. He particularly loved fire-eaters and begged Father to let him learn how to breathe out flames. He was rewarded for this brave suggestion by being taken in the carriage when Father toured the district, gathering rent with his bailiff. Shih stayed at home, wondering what he had done wrong. When Guang returned he did not seem happy. 'A lot of the peasants were insolent and started crying,' he whispered. 'One of them called Father a thief, and Father ordered his whole family to be beaten before our eyes and to leave our land forever.'

A thief! Shih considered this silently for a while.

'Father,' he said, quite suddenly, as they ate one of their miserable dinners together, where not even Mother dared speak. 'Why do the peasants call you a thief?'

The table fell silent. He realised, too late, that it was a

wicked question. Yet he meant no harm. He simply wanted to understand. Father glared at him.

'Go to your room!' he bellowed, sweeping a bowl of rice to the floor.

A hungry night followed. Shih heard Father praising Guang extravagantly in the courtyard as they fired arrows at a target.

Then Aunt Qin arrived, carried up the valley in a jolting cart laden with her boxes. Mother told the boys that with the death of her husband, Aunt Qin had no home except Three-Step-House. Mother's face was bright for a change, her eyes no longer downcast. So Shih was glad to welcome Aunt Qin.

She was younger than Mother, though not so beautiful, and always carried a purple fan which she fluttered gracefully whenever hot winds arose. At first Father seemed pleased by her presence.

Aunt Qin was no delicate lady like Mother. She laughed heartily at simple things and did not yawn when Shih explained the mysteries all around them. He was eight years old, of an age to dote. Yet he was suspicious at first, wondering if secretly she was mocking him.

One day they walked hand in hand by the river and he found the courage to explain all he had noticed: the plum trees and other plants and animals in the valley. He pointed out where monkeys gathered and birds laid their eggs. She replied that a little nature makes all things kind. They looked at nests together, collecting speckled, turquoise eggs.

For once he did not care that Guang was back in Three-Step-House with Father. Besides, when he came home from these expeditions, he often found Guang impatiently awaiting his return. They would play without quarrelling and Guang seemed envious of his walks by the river. A happy time. Aunt Qin helped him learn his characters, for the tutor Father appointed spent more time drinking and amusing his employer than guiding Shih's brush.

In six months he mastered so many characters that he began to read the many books and scrolls left by Great-grandfather

Yun Cai. Mother clapped her hand to her mouth and wept silently when he read out a poem written by their great ancestor. But Father scowled, loudly ordering a servant to fetch wine. Later, Mother told him Father had never been patient when it came to reading or writing, but that it did not matter because he was Lord of Wei.

Once he found Aunt Qin crying. She said her husband's absence weighed heavily on her spirits. As he listened helplessly, Shih made a silent promise. Whenever he saw a lady weeping he would make her happy. So he took Aunt Qin's hands in his own and said: 'I shall marry you when I am older, then you won't miss him so much. For you shall have me.'

Aunt Qin looked at him in surprise. He met her gaze without looking away. For once he did not feel foolish.

'I see you will keep me quite safe, Honourable Yun Shih,' she said, bowing. 'And I need someone to protect me. . . But I must be calm. Remember, Shih, whatever happens, one must be calm.'

She did not explain why she needed a protector. Her eyes filled with tears and she hurried to her room. Yet Shih felt proud. It was something to be needed by a beautiful lady like Aunt Qin.

'I am Aunty's protector,' he told Guang. 'If anyone treats her in a low way, I shall punish him when I become Lord of Wei.'

Words spoken in childhood. Remembering that promise made Dr Shih feel vengeful and afraid. He opened his eyes. The rough bark of the post chafed against his back. The river flowed, dimpled by light. He felt a great reluctance to remember more. What was the use? It did little good to grieve twenty years too late. He should hurry to the Relief Bureau, where he might do some good before night fell. But once awoken, Aunt Qin's words could not be forgotten, like an unburied ghost hungry for satisfaction. *I see you will keep me quite safe.*

*

Rain fell for days. He remembered that. Everyone in the household feared Father's restlessness when he could not visit the neighbours or gallop to places of entertainment. With the monsoon came heat. Even in the mountains, the air was motionless, sweating like fever. A time of prickly boredom.

Lord Yun paced the hall in the Middle House, drinking wine and ordering the boys' tutor to play endless games of chess, washed down by wine. Needless to say the tutor made sure he lost every game. Then Father summoned the bailiff and berated him for a whole hour, his loud voice echoing round the hall. Mother declared herself indisposed and kept to her chamber. Then Shih watched more trays of wine and food brought to the hall.

He crouched in the doorway of the topmost house, which stood on the hillside above Middle House, listening to the plash of rain as it ran from the tiled eaves. Why could Father not be like the servants and Mother, who ignored the discomfort of the monsoon? Surely he should be glad. Rain made crops grow on hillside terraces. Plants must drink just like people. Besides, he found it amusing to watch ducks on the river, followed by lines of paddling ducklings, quite oblivious to the downpour.

Shih noticed a servant hurrying up to the family quarters from the Middle House. A few minutes later Aunt Qin descended the plank-lined steps, protected by a bamboo and silk umbrella. She disappeared into the Middle House.

Shih stirred uneasily. He wished Mother was not sleeping in her room. He didn't like Aunt Qin being alone with Father. It seemed a bad thing, though he did not know why.

Recollecting his promise to Aunt Qin, he trotted down the slippery steps. Gusts of rain blew on his shaven head. He entered Middle House by a side door, softly lifting the latch. The hall was strangely still. Shih sensed all the servants had been sent away. The only sounds were water noises, dripping and splashing from the roof. Shih crept down the corridor and peered through a half-open door.

Because the blinds were unaccountably down, the hall was

gloomy. No lanterns had been lit. Aunt Qin was on her knees paying homage to Father, who paced up and down. Several empty flasks stood on the table. One lay in pieces on the floor.

'You have come to my house!' he roared. 'You make no effort to please me! Who is your master here?'

Aunt Qin was trembling. Shih longed to dart forward, to take her arm and lead her away. Instead he hid, paralysed.

'Everyone must please me,' continued Father. 'Can you not think of a way?'

Father was also trembling. He stepped towards Aunt Qin and leaned over her, gazing down. His arm was raised, as though about to strike.

'I'm sick of you all!' he cried. 'Sick of this dull place! None of you know the meaning of respect.'

Shih watched in horror as he seized her shoulders, thrusting her towards his high-backed ebony chair. Great-great-grandfather's chair. The Lord of Wei's chair.

'You'll learn to enjoy your duty, you slut!'

Now Aunt Qin was moaning. Her distress brought Shih to his feet. Still he dared not move. Then something unaccountable happened. Father forced her face so that it pressed against the seat of the chair and stood behind her. He tore aside her clothes, revealing Aunt Qin's white behind. Father was fumbling with his own robes. He took out a fierce, swollen, ugly thing that filled Shih with disgust. He knew it meant only harm.

Aunt Qin was pleading: 'No! No! Please!'

Father grasped her buttocks and at last Shih found the courage to act. All he knew was that Aunt Qin was afraid, that he had promised to keep her safe. He bustled loudly through the door and into the hall. There he drew himself to his full height like the actors Father hired.

At once both adults noticed him. Father shamefacedly readjusted his clothes. The ugly thing vanished. Aunt Qin, sobbing and hiding her face, stumbled to join the little boy. Though she was almost twice his size he felt tall and noble like Great-grandfather Yun Cai.

He spoke the first words in his head: 'Aunty, come with me! Father, it is very wrong of you to make Aunty cry!'

Before he could say more his feet rose from the ground. He found himself being half-carried, half-dragged out into the rain, up the slippery steps to the Top House and the family rooms where Mother was resting. When they reached the corridor Aunt Qin clasped him, weeping silently.

'Brave boy,' she sobbed. 'Oh, you honourable boy!'

He swelled with pride. Now everyone was happy, or almost happy. Except for Father. But somehow, though he knew it was very wicked, he did not care for Father, and decided to avoid him. It was not difficult. That same afternoon Lord Yun rode to Chunming, accompanied by his friend, the tutor.

Then came bad times. Scattered memories from a scattered life. Aunt Qin leaving in the rain, her sedan carried by four drenched peasants. Mother weeping in the doorway, dabbing her eyes with a sleeve. One of the servants whispered that Aunty had gone to a monastery, that it was a great pity. Shih never saw her again and never dared ask after her. Aunt Qin had become unmentionable.

When Father returned from Chunming with an astrologer and a gentleman in an official's uniform, he ordered that Shih should be locked in a store room with a tiny, high window. Hours passed slowly and he heard raised voices in the house. It shocked him to hear Mother angry. He never imagined Mother could be so angry. Most of all he longed for Guang to play with him, but his brother was forbidden to come near.

Finally, the door was unbarred. The astrologer entered and said, after coughing repeatedly (he had a terrible cough), that a grave mistake had been made. Yun Guang, not he, was Father's First Son and heir. He said that he feared Shih had been planted into Mother's womb by a fox-fairy.

'Where is Mother?' Shih had wailed. 'I must speak to Mother!'

The astrologer held his arm in a steady grip and led him outside. Bags were piled in the porch and a horse-drawn carriage stood in the rain. The astrologer ordered Shih to enter it. Then he banged on the roof and a whip cracked.

As they jolted away, Shih stared back at Three-Step-House. Suddenly he cried out and tried to open the carriage door. His guardian struggled to hold him down. For Mother was running down the hill after him, pursued by Father and the tutor. She slipped in the mud, falling to her knees. The carriage entered Wei Village and he could no longer see her through the buildings and pig-sty fences, the mulberry trees and roof-tops.

An hour later they were in a strange country and the astrologer sat morosely beside him. Shih sensed the man was ashamed. The boy stared straight ahead, determined not to cry. He always remembered what Aunt Qin had taught him: that he must be calm. Soon he would return to Three-Step-House. Then he would play with his dear brother, Guang, on Wobbly-Watch-Tower-Rock, as they always had. People would remark how they were like each other's shadow, and Shih would feel safe again. He hugged himself as the carriage struggled through mud and monsoon, heading always east, towards the capital.

竹子

Shih opened his eyes. Wiped away tears. How used he was to feeling the past as a dripping sore.

Then came a new thought, so uncomfortable he sensed it must be true. His reluctance to share his essences with Cao, finding excuses in work and its wearisome duties, stemmed from that moment in the Middle House.

Was that why no children filled the empty rooms of their home? Because of what he had glimpsed, so long ago? Because of Father?

He thought mournfully of Cao. And Aunt Qin. Of Lu Ying. And Cao again.

The river, speckled by ripples and light, flowed ceaselessly. A family of grey geese paddled towards the jetty. Shih stared at them blankly until a commotion on the river made him stir.

A fleet had appeared round the sweeping bend of the river. A dozen warships limping toward the Twin Cities. Shih rose, shielding his eyes for a better view. Several seemed burned, their hulls splintered, decks stubbled with arrows. As he watched, a gaily-painted paddlewheel destroyer listed violently, the crew that cranked its many gears and handles emerging like desperate rats from hatches. Suddenly the sailors' cries for help were drowned out by beating wings. The family of geese had taken fright, skimming over the wide expanse of water between Fouzhou and Nancheng. Shih hurried back in alarm to the Water Gate of Morning Radiance.

竹子

Cao's eyes were downcast as she threaded through the streets – and not solely due to a respectable woman's modesty. Her heart ached. She hesitated and straightened her dress. Hasty words could not be unspoken. Once uttered, they altered life's flow. A storm may change a river's course, washing away houses once snug and dry.

Perhaps she wished to punish herself. Really it had not been necessary to ignore Shih so steadily over the last few days. Cao was not the kind to sulk. Their guest was welcome to pre-eminence in pouting and fragile moods – along with all her other dainty ways. Mostly she wished for the reassurance of her husband's face.

Her destination lay only a *li* or so from Apricot Corner Court. When she reached the Relief Bureau she found the medical orderly, Mung Po, anxiously watching the street.

'Where is Dr Shih?' she asked.

Mung Po bowed, upper teeth resting on his lower lip in a nervous grin. It was one of his affectations to treat the humble doctor's wife like a dowager empress, yet today he spoke with more excitement than decorum.

'Madam Cao, I had hoped you would answer that question.'

'I thought he was here, Mung Po,' she said. 'Has he not attended his duties this morning?'

Mung Po shook his head. 'Madam, I was about to enquire if he was sick.'

Cao flushed, wondering if her coldness had infected her husband with a malady. She knew how much he hated dissension.

'No doubt he has been called upon urgently,' she said. 'I will sit and wait.'

The orderly made a show of polishing the Bureau's best chair with his sleeve, then returned to examining the street from the doorway.

'Mung Po, are you quite well?' she asked.

'Madam, forgive me. Dr Shih would not welcome me discussing official matters, even with your honoured self.'

'Come now, there are no secrets between my husband and I.'

Mung Po nodded with relief.

'Of course, Madam, forgive my stupidity! You are aware that Dr Fung inspected the Bureau a few days ago, on behalf of the guild? And that he claimed to have discovered irregularities in our accounts?'

Cao bit back an angry name for Dr Fung.

'My husband mentioned it. He told me the good doctor would return in a month or so. He said there is nothing to worry about.'

'Then Dr Fung deceived him,' said Mung Po. 'This morning no less a person than Dr Du Mau came here, accompanied by an official from the Prefecture. Dr Du Mau was very cold. He inspected the place from top to bottom and persuaded the official to confiscate all our ledgers. The word corrupt was whispered.'

Cao stood up angrily.

'Dr Shih would never sell medicines intended for the poor! Not like the superintendents of other Relief Bureaus I could mention. His honesty is a reproach to men like Dr Du Mau. That is why they hate him. Du Mau is merely angry because the

Pacification Commissioner has refused to let him set foot again on Peacock Hill!'

Mung Po shook his head.

'I must tell you that some of our most valuable medicines have been disappearing. When I mentioned it to Dr Shih yesterday, he said the matter must be investigated.'

The pair stood in silence.

'Dr Du Mau seemed quite triumphant as he left,' added Mung Po.

'His triumph will be short-lived,' said Cao, uneasily recollecting Lu Ying's demands for *cash*. But surely her husband could not stoop so low, unless, of course, there was some secret understanding between them to satisfy the girl's requests. She stilled her thoughts. Horrible, unworthy thoughts.

'I tell you, Mung Po,' she continued. 'If Dr Du Mau hopes to snare my husband, he would do well to consider who saved the Pacification Commissioner's heir. And who is the brother of Captain Xiao. Though I am a woman, I am no fool and understand these things.'

The orderly seemed relieved. 'Madam's opinions are forthright and wise,' he said, bowing.

In her heart she was less sure.

'Has the apprentice been here?' she asked.

'I thought he was with Master.'

'Chung left Apricot Corner Court two hours ago. Did he not arrive at all?'

'I have not seen him.'

'Then he is at fault,' she said. 'I shall return home. Tell Dr Shih I would welcome his company.'

'I understand,' said the orderly.

'Mung Po, have you told anyone else about Dr Du Mau's visit?'

At this he seemed embarrassed.

'My own foolishness, Madam, though great, does not extend so far.'

'Of course. Forgive me. You are a good man, Mung Po.'

*

As her straightest way home led through the disreputable warren known as Xue Alley, Cao took a roundabout route. It led her to the Water Basin near the Water Gate of Morning Radiance. As usual, boats lined the dockside. Grain and goods were being unloaded from all over the Empire and beyond – even the fabled lands of Cham and Calicut, places entirely savage.

Wandering sailors attracted hawkers. The cries of their wares, tea or pastry, cheap wine or water from a secret spring blessed by Immortals, joined the rumble of barrels and bartering voices. No one troubled Cao as she passed through the crowd. Several people bowed respectfully to the good doctor's wife. Where so many were low it was not hard to be high.

Outside a tavern with a bad reputation she encountered an ungratifying sight. Chung knelt beside a blanket on the dusty road, alongside half a dozen wastrels. *Cash* coins were stacked neatly before him. As he rolled the dice, worry crept across his plump face. The other gamblers' piles of *cash* were higher than his own. One of the wastrels clapped his hands and made a great show of kissing a tin amulet. Chung ruefully pushed over the last of his *cash*.

When he glanced up, the apprentice encountered Cao's reproachful gaze. He rose hurriedly and bowed, his floppy black fringe falling across his forehead.

'Madam,' he said. 'I was just. . .'

She said nothing. His fellow-gamblers muttered among themselves, evidently sharing a little fun. It would do Dr Shih's reputation no good for his apprentice to be seen gambling before a low tavern.

'Why are you here?' she whispered, leading him up the street. 'Why are you not at the Relief Bureau?'

Chung shrugged miserably.

'I have only just left there,' he blurted. 'At least, I. . .' His voice trailed away. 'I beg you not to tell Master!'

Cao shook her head doubtfully. Of course it was her duty to

tell Shih. Yet their quarrel concerning Lu Ying lingered. Chung's disobedience might be the cause of yet another argument. All she longed for was peace in her household. For life to resume its old patterns – as it had been before Lu Ying arrived with her boxes and impossible lotus feet. Besides, Cao had a softness for Chung. He reminded her of Shih's neediness, long ago, when he first came to Father's shop in the capital.

Chung was also a child of misfortune. He had joined their household on his eleventh birthday, a week after his father's suicide, his large brown eyes blinking slowly at the strange world of Apricot Corner Court.

He had been alone in Nancheng without friends or relatives, for Chung's mother had rejoined her family in a village far to the south, taking three daughters with her. The journey had been paid for by Shih, who had sometimes drunk tea or wine with Chung's father at one of the neighbourhood stalls, for he was an entertaining fellow and a fine talker. But a love of reckless wagers finally brought him to disgrace. On the night before his landlord and other debtors stripped the last of his family's possessions, he had fastened a silk cord to the rafters and jumped from his own shop counter. Shih, in memory of his lost friend, purchased the indenture of Little Chung at a price they could barely afford. At first Cao had opposed such generosity. When she saw the boy's big, liquid eyes she went the other way.

'It's little wonder your apprentice finds it hard to pound herbs,' she had told Shih. 'After all the terrible things he has seen.'

She was referring to the fact that Chung had discovered his father creaking and swaying.

'I only set him simple tasks,' countered her husband, mildly.

It was true. Shih was indulgent as masters go. Her own father, Dr Ou-yang, would have taken a bamboo rod to the boy.

A year into his indenture, even Cao began to wonder if he

would ever make a doctor. Shih struggled to make him learn anything difficult. He had a talent for shortcuts, most of which ended badly. When he explained the reasoning behind his mistakes, lips trembling, it was hard to feel angry. If he was sick – a disturbingly common occurrence considering he dwelt with a doctor – Cao fluttered by his bedside and fed him fish-head stew.

Dr Shih laboured hard to teach the lad his characters. One time, Chung failed after many reminders to copy out the characters of the Seven Sentiments, and his master resorted to slapping him round the face. Cao put her arms around the weeping boy when Shih was not looking. Sometimes she discovered small items of food missing from the pantry, but said nothing.

So years had passed. Now Chung was twenty, a mere year from his capping as a man and the end of his indenture. She liked to chat with him if work was slack; like his poor father, he possessed the knack of lightening a dull mood. She forgave his sly evasions and, once, in an unguarded moment after drinking too much hemp-flavoured tea, revealed the circumstances of her marriage. Chung blinked at her with wide eyes and she immediately grew afraid. If Shih found out he would be angry. Such a story might damage his reputation beyond all repair.

But Chung had yawned and said he was hungry. She made him a dish of rice sweetened with honey and sesame seeds, his favourite. The matter had never been mentioned again. No doubt, in his sleepy way, Chung had forgotten. He certainly forgot most things.

Cao trailed back to Apricot Corner Court, the apprentice beside her. She worried where he found cash for gambling and how she might explain it to Shih. Meanwhile, Chung was relating a droll piece of gossip concerning a neighbour. She half listened, though usually such stories made her smile.

Dr Shih startled them by stepping quickly through the gate

of Apricot Corner Court, looking pale. She sensed at once he had learned about Dr Du Mau's visit to the Relief Bureau and the confiscation of his ledgers. At the sight of her, he hurried forward.

'Chung has been walking me home,' she said, quickly.

The apprentice shot her a grateful look.

'Never mind that,' said Shih. 'Chung, clean the shop until we return. I must speak with Madam Cao.'

They stood together in the street, watching the endless bustle of sedan chairs and laden mules and camels and passers-by. A boat heavy with chicken cages drifted past on the canal in the direction of North Market.

'There is something I need to tell you,' he said, softly. 'We must find a place where we cannot be overheard.'

Before he could say more, a beggarly man came running down the street. Cao recognised him as one of Water Basin Ward's most notorious drunkards. Now he was swollen with news.

'The enemy have come! The barbarians are only fifty *li* distant!' he yelled.

People stopped their business, stared.

'The enemy! Notices are going up all over the city! The Mongols draw near!'

A flurry of excited voices mingled with cries of fear. Bustling filled the street. Suddenly everyone wanted to find relatives and loved ones. Confusion blew through the Twin Cities like a hot wind. Such popular moods had fanned riots in the past.

'Let us go inside,' said Shih. 'I'm afraid there will be disorder before night falls.'

War

战争

憎

eight

'I, the Great Khan, Khubilai, order my armies to advance by sea, river, land and mountain. Those of our enemies who do not resist shall be spared slaughter or confiscation of all they own, not least their liberty. Those who serve us by persuading the treasonous to submit to our just rule shall be rewarded. Those who persist in foolish opposition and resistance shall endure every woe imaginable. . .'

Proclamation of War

竹子

The City Ramparts, Nancheng. Autumn, 1266.

Captain Xiao, firmer than the ramparts he defends, gazes everywhere. His eyes shoot out approval and reproach. He thrusts out jaw and chest. Autumn winds may whip around him but he will not flinch. Captain Xiao must justify that title every moment of every day. Die a thousand cruel deaths, sooner than risk dishonour.

So Guang imagined himself, waiting on the battlements of Swallow Gate. As he stared west, a commotion started in the city behind but he did not turn. Along with hundreds of officers and soldiers lining the ramparts, his attention centred on Wadung Mountain and the broad valley leading to

Nancheng. It had become a wasteland, every village burned and every field flooded so the enemy might find nothing useful. Relays of smoke signals and coloured flags awaited their arrival.

'Perhaps they have chosen to halt their advance,' he remarked to Chen Song who stood close by, splendid in a new suit of lamellar armour.

'Our beloved land frustrates them,' declared the scholar-spy, now turned warrior. 'This is poor country for cavalry, even during the autumn drought. It is my firm conviction. . .'

He stopped and looked round in irritation.

'What is that noise? One might think the barbarians were already within our gates!'

They used their elevated position to examine the disturbance. Soldiers were pulling down a row of houses near the ramparts. Meanwhile officials, bright as parrots in green and blue uniforms, attempted to stop them. Chen Song frowned.

'Those officials are in the service of Prefect Wang Bai!' he said.

Guang reluctantly followed his friend's pointing finger.

'Yes.'

'Do they not know those houses should be demolished?' asked Chen Song. 'The enemy could easily set them ablaze. The whole ward might burn. I shall intervene. . .'

'No, I order you to remain here.'

Chen Song halted in surprise.

'Forgive my presumption,' he muttered.

Since Chen Song's appointment as Captain of Artillery at Guang's suggestion their friendship had changed, though not weakened. Duty formed new channels between the two men; and water parts, as well as connects.

'Wang Bai has instructed me to spare those particular buildings,' said Guang, more gently.

'Tell that to General Zheng Shun,' said Chen Song.

Indeed, the General of Land Forces had joined the dispute below. Within minutes carpenters were stripping the roofs, dispatching precious timbers to government lumberyards for use in the siege defences. Guang sighed. His patron would surely seek to punish Zheng Shun. Amidst the bickering, victory would run ahead of them like a fleeing deer.

Chen Song remarked solemnly: 'Little ponds reflect the same clouds as great seas.'

'How so?'

'Here squabbling holds us back, but affairs in the capital are no different. At court one party opposes another. The Emperor bends this way, then that. No one agrees how the war is to be conducted, so nothing is done.'

'Speak more softly,' cautioned Guang, glancing at the common soldiers tending an enormous crossbow nearby.

'I hear,' muttered Chen Song, 'our defeat at Willow Fords was caused by General Liu's refusal to engage the enemy. He claimed to have orders from the Chancellor. In the rout we lost ten thousand good men.'

Such talk trailed wisps of treason.

'A soldier's duty is to follow orders and fight,' said Guang, doggedly.

'Not to die without reason,' murmured Chen Song. 'For it weakens our cause.'

Guang resorted to dignified silence. Still no signal rose from Wadung Mountain. Where were the cursed barbarians? He longed to end the months of uncertainty, to bury unsettling thoughts in action.

As he looked westward, Guang wondered if Khan Bayke rode among the Mongol horde. Could destiny be that generous? Though killing the usurper of Wei Valley and Three-Step-House would restore neither title nor property to his family, he wished for it fervently. But then Bayke would simply be replaced as Lord of Wei by another Mongol.

An hour later, the watchers received their reward.

They came like black clouds, obscuring the land. Dust hovered above endless columns of horses and wagons. The pale autumn sun glinted on steel and, even at a distance, bright banners broke the dull, grey monotony of the advancing horde.

Thousands, tens of thousands. Guang noticed that the beasts of burden far outnumbered men. Camels pulling carts; huge domed wagons dragged by twenty oxen; and horses, horses beyond count. Impossible to kill them all. The neighing and whinnying was incessant. A slow drumbeat summoned regiment after regiment to positions marked out by standard bearers.

Guang scanned the ranks for siege engines. Catapults and cloud ladders, wheeled towers and gigantic crossbows, these were to be his special prey. A clerk perched on a low stool by his feet, recording all he saw.

The orderliness of the barbarians amazed him. They wasted no time in raising round steppe-huts of hide and wood, as well as pens for their animals. One might call their army a people on the move, their camp a mobile city. He recollected they had defeated a formation equal in size, sent by the Chancellor to pacify the frontier. For the first time he felt something new. Was it doubt? He glanced back at the houses and rooftops of Nancheng, the splendid markets and pavilions. No, he must not doubt. The city would stand forever if brave men held firm.

A large group of Mongol officers galloped towards Swallow Gate and halted beyond bowshot, examining the moats and towers. Their stillness was both a challenge and menace.

'That must be General A-ku himself!' exclaimed Guang, pointing at an officer wearing golden armour. 'He is no older than myself and definitely a short fellow. Do you not think so?'

Chen Song did not reply. Perhaps he was awed. Rumours had circulated through the Twin Cities, spread by spies, that the Great Khan had appointed General A-ku to subdue them as a reward for conquering Sichuan Province. It was said he never failed, whatever the cost. Certainly A-ku's horde was vast. As was his reputation for cruel determination.

Guang looked hopefully at a cairn of stones between the city and enemy lines. It was studded with flags insulting the Great

Khan in bold characters. Guang had ordered its construction at the far limits of crossbow range that morning. Yet it seemed the Mongols might never take the bait. At last a group of officers from the general's entourage cantered over to the mound of taunting flags.

'Prepare the siege crossbows!' ordered Guang.

He felt Chen Song's excitement beside him. Teams of soldiers cranked winches, tensing the giant machines.

'Aim as you have been instructed.'

When the horsemen reached the cairn, Guang ordered the fluttering of a yellow pennant. Loud cracks followed as a dozen huge crossbow bolts were released. Moments later the six foot shafts fell among the horsemen, bringing several down. Flaming bolts followed, trailing yellow smoke, whooshing across the cleared ground before the city. Suddenly the pile of stones packed with thunderclap bombs ignited. The explosion echoed all the way to Wadung Mountain. Flying rocks crushed mounts and riders. One Mongol officer was on fire, rolling on the ground. Even General A-ku's horse reared and bucked.

Loud cheering spread along the ramparts. Guang's own men were beside themselves, for they could boast the honour of first blood.

'Captain Xiao! Captain Xiao!' they bellowed, waving halberds and crossbows.

In the midst of his triumph, Guang became aware an officer was saluting him, fists pressed together, head bowed.

'His Excellency requires your presence, sir.'

Reluctantly, he turned to go. The enemy were still spreading out to surround Nancheng. Guang glanced back at A-ku, hoping he had heard the name of Captain Xiao. If not, he would learn it soon enough.

竹子

The doors of Wang Ting-bo's summerhouse stood open. Scents from the Pacification Commissioner's pleasure garden entered the room: chrysanthemum and orchid, many-petalled fire-bell and lord's whisker, lilies floating on glassy ponds beside ornate rocks. One might have expected a gathering of scholars, a literary drinking party. Instead a long trestle table had been set up in the summerhouse. Men wearing armour or the vermilion uniforms of high officials sat in strict order of precedence around a relief map of the Twin Cities made from sculpted cooked rice.

Guang could assess his own status at the meeting by his neighbours. He had been seated at the far end of the table, away from Wang Ting-bo and the other Commanders, as well as his patron, Wang Bai. The fellow on Guang's immediate left was responsible for waterways and sewage. On his right sat an actuary. He itched to draw the great men's attention and advance, place by place, closer to His Excellency.

'Gentlemen,' began Wang Ting-bo, tugging at his wispy beard. 'Our worst expectations are realised! Even as I speak the barbarians draw a noose round our necks. As all know, it is difficult to get off a tiger's back.'

General Zheng Shun and his cousin, Admiral Zheng Qi-Qi, stirred a little but said nothing.

'We are the anvil and General A-ku wishes to be our hammer!' continued the Pacification Commissioner.

Guang detected something wrong with this comparison but couldn't say what. Admiral Zheng Qi-Qi coughed politely, the corners of his mouth rising a fraction.

'Your Excellency, between a hammer and anvil one frequently finds molten iron,' he said. 'Yet our mettle is hard and cool.'

All present exclaimed at so clever a pun. Here was how civilized men derided danger! Only Wang Bai, handsome and sleek, seemed unmoved.

'Quite so, quite so,' said Wang Ting-bo, hurriedly. 'Nevertheless, this is a grave meeting.'

No one quibbled over that.

'The purpose of our council is to determine the best way to proceed.'

'Sir, I advise spiritual tactics,' said Admiral Qi-Qi. 'Our moats and walls are a rock they will break against.'

'Indeed, sir,' added General Zheng Shun. 'Stealthy waiting will teach us the strength of their forces, while concealing our own. It is the only proper way!'

His eyes narrowed and he turned to Guang.

'For that reason,' he added, fiercely, 'I was surprised by your display this afternoon, Commander!'

Guang blinked. He had expected hearty praise for his exploding pile of stones.

'How so, sir?'

'Because now A-ku will be doubly wary. When they attack in earnest we shall kill less of them. That is why.'

An uncomfortable silence settled round the table. Guang felt the officials beside him inch away a little. Wang Bai cleared his throat delicately.

'General Zheng Shun is wise,' he said. 'But I must venture to disagree. Yun Guang scorched A-ku's pride and lent heart to our troops.'

However, Guang could not dismiss General Zheng Shun's words so easily. Surprise had indeed been squandered in a way one might call foolish. Besides, he doubted Wang Bai's motives – and confirmation came at once.

'May I add,' said the Pacification Commissioner's nephew. 'It will hardly raise morale among the people to pull down perfectly serviceable houses near Swallow Gate. Your Excellency, I petition that such decisions are left to myself in future.'

General Zheng Shun snorted.

'You refer to my own decision?'

'I do,' said Wang Bai. 'A most regrettable action.'

'Because the tenants pay their rent to you?' asked Zheng Shun.

'That is irrelevant.'

Again the council of war lapsed into silence. Guang looked from face to face. Could they really be debating such things at such a time? Even Wang Ting-bo seemed displeased with his nephew for raising the matter.

'Gentlemen! To business!'

They waited for him to define it. He waved his hand, then clapped decisively.

'These are grave times,' he said.

'Your Excellency,' broke in General Zheng Shun. 'I repeat, our strength lies in our defences. We must await a relief force sent by the Son of Heaven to raise the siege. We cannot risk open battle until then.'

'Ah!' said the Pacification Commissioner. 'Ah! Now that is the moot point.'

'Our moats are wide,' said Admiral Qi-Qi. 'If they try to cross them, their casualties will be absurd.'

Guang tried to look wise as he followed the debate. The Zheng cousins' policy seemed undeniable, so that Wang Ting-bo's response, when it finally came, surprised him.

'We must be bold!' announced the Pacification Commissioner. 'I have decided that a counterattack should be launched from the city as soon as possible. The Court expects nothing less and I am loathe to disappoint them.'

'Your Excellency!' protested General Zheng Shun. 'There are at least forty thousand cavalry out there.'

'It must be accomplished,' said Wang Ting-bo, doggedly.

'I concur,' broke in Wang Bai. 'It will send the clearest message of our resolve to His Imperial Majesty.'

Guang knew he should support his great patrons. Yet all his instinct revolted against wasting brave men's lives.

'We must burn their camps,' insisted His Excellency.

'If we ever reach them, sir,' retorted Zheng Shun.

For a moment the Pacification Commissioner wavered. Then his nephew spoke up softly.

'If we are afraid, there is little hope of victory.'

General Zheng Shun went pale.

'Afraid? No one used *that* word.'

'Nevertheless. . .'

'If His Excellency commands, I will lead the attack myself,' declared Zheng Shun. 'Though I strongly advise against it.'

Again Wang Ting-bo seemed torn.

'We must consider how the Court will perceive a failure to counterattack,' said Wang Bai, addressing his uncle directly. 'They are noting our strength of will and might conclude our resolve is wavering. Or that. . .'

'We value maintaining our strength?' interrupted Admiral Qi-Qi.

Wang Bai smiled, apparently unconcerned by the disrespect he had been shown.

'Naturally.'

His Excellency Wang Ting-bo scowled in a most martial manner, as though the Son of Heaven would somehow see his resolve and reward him as he deserved. Yet the capital lay far, far away.

'Our resolution knows no wavering!' he announced. 'Gather our forces. We shall attack at dawn and General Zheng Shun shall lead the assault.'

'Your Excellency. . .'

Guang found himself speaking. He had not meant to speak. It was undoubtedly best to say nothing. But he admired Zheng Shun and wished only to help him. For a moment he groped for a means. It came in a flash.

'Your Excellency,' he said. 'Though you propose an infantry attack, perhaps my artillery might be of help. The enemy have foolishly built their camps at the far range of my siege crossbows and catapults. I suggest delaying an attack until the wind favours us. Then we shall direct combustibles upon them and follow with fire. In the confusion, General Zheng Shun's forces could gain surprise and at least burn their outer camps.'

He became aware everyone present was observing him closely. He sensed, for the first time, something like respect.

'That sounds right,' said Zheng Shun. 'A limited foray to dent their confidence and burn their catapults. Then we could retreat before their cavalry bear down on us.'

Wang Bai waved his hand impatiently.

'Never mind the wind! Astonishment is our great ally!' he said. 'If we attack at dawn, as His Excellency has already decided, victory is certain.'

Guang could not remain silent.

'Fire breathes wind, sir. Let us wait until the wind is right.'

General Zheng Shun nodded so fiercely that once more Wang Ting-bo hesitated.

'Fire breathes wind!' he chuckled. 'How true. Then let them burn. Yes, we shall delay until the wind is favourable.'

Guang turned to Wang Bai and flinched. He had never expected to see such cold rage in his patron's usually urbane glance.

'Your Excellency,' said Wang Bai. 'I wish to mention another matter. Although Yun Guang has been appointed as our *temporary* Commander of Artillery in Nancheng, may I suggest that another is appointed for Fouzhou? Then if Yun Guang is wounded or if he displeases you, a replacement is instantly to hand.'

Guang hid his confusion with a bow. He had been warned. If he did not support Wang Bai in everything, another man would wear his uniform, occupy his new house, and acknowledge the bows of ten thousand subordinates.

'Why not?' said Wang Ting-bo. 'A single man cannot be in two places at once. Carry on, gentlemen. I will send a message to the Court that we shall attack imminently.'

His Excellency beamed, plainly satisfied he had pleased everyone while still getting his way. The sickly-sweet aroma of autumn flowers stole into the summerhouse.

竹子

Guang spent the entire night moving catapults and supervising alterations to giant crossbow shafts. From his vantage point on Swallow Gate, the barbarians' campfires glittered like a thousand angry red stars, scenting the night with burning.

A day passed. Mindful of General Zheng Shun's reproach, Guang instructed his men to conceal their range and ignore tempting targets. He noted several enemy encampments close to the city. Did their proximity denote contempt? Or over-confidence? Perhaps the wooden walls and ditches were a trap: the Mongols were notorious for feints and manoeuvres.

Dawn mists rolled on the river; the future swirled in on itself. He tried to use each hour wisely, drilling the catapult crews and amassing stores of poison bombs and rocket arrows.

On the evening of the second day, Guang peered at the moon above Mount Wadung. A curved sword parted high, drifting clouds. Soon it would be in the lodge of *yi*. Where moonlight was watery and unsteady, surely a great wind would arise within three nights.

'Chen Song,' he said, staring across the moat and killing-ground to the Mongol camp. 'Do you see what I do?'

A line of twenty enemy catapults were lobbing stones into the night sky. One crashed into the darkness beyond Swallow Gate. A terrible shriek followed.

'Why do we not reply in kind?' asked Chen Song.

'Because their catapults have given me heart,' said Guang. 'I would not damage them for the world. Where they have stones, they will store burning-powder and thunderclap bombs. It seems A-ku has provided me with something to set ablaze.'

'Unless he anticipates us,' muttered Chen Song.

Three nights later the wisdom of the Ancient Commentators was confirmed. Invisible fingers tugged the defenders' hair and uniforms, making banners flow stiffly on their poles. General Zheng Shun joined Guang as he watched the enemy from Swallow Gate. The Commander of Artillery bowed respectfully to the more senior officer.

'As you predicted,' drawled Zheng Shun. 'The wind is up. I take it you have no objection to dawn?'

'None at all.'

'I shall order my regiments to gather in silence by the gates.

Any who make a noise will pay with their tongues. Will your men be told the same?'

'Yes, sir.'

Zheng Shun seemed pleased.

'Good. We are of one mind. Dawn is three bells away. Be prepared.'

'I am ready.'

The older man chuckled.

'I believe you are, though I still don't like this. Everything seems too easy.' He looked at Guang shrewdly. 'Of course, attacking is madness. But then, it is insane that the barbarians have been allowed to reach the Twin Cities at all. Unless one blames treason. Not every great man in the Empire would be sorry to see the Son of Heaven humbled.'

He waited for a reply but Guang found such thoughts unpalatable. General Zheng Shun chuckled dryly and strolled away.

The hour before dawn is a time of fitful dreams. Vague shapes floated through Guang's mind, trailing fears and clutching fingers. It is said the nails of fox-demons are twisted like sea-shells and caked with their victims' blood. That they wait to carry off souls denied an honourable burial. Guang recollected these stories as he peered down at the companies squatting beneath the shelter of the walls. He caught glimpses of white eyes. Glints of steel reflected torches on the ramparts. Slowly, far to the east, the direction of the capital and Court, a red glow hardened behind distant hills.

At last General Zheng Shun trotted on a grey stallion towards the gate, followed by a band of cavalry holding bundles of oil-drenched torches.

'Incendiary thieves,' muttered Guang to Chen Song. 'They will ride ahead of the infantry and hurl swallow-tail torches into the camp.'

'Then they are brave,' said Chen Song.

Zheng Shun stood in his stirrups and raised his arm to

Guang. With a decisive motion, he let it fall. At once Guang addressed his officers.

'Release!' he roared.

Flags waved up and down the city walls. Great cracking sounds filled the air as when an ice-bound river grinds and breaks apart. The sky was streaked by meteors – giant crossbow bolts laden with flasks of oil and fuses – catapults hurling bombs in high arcs. Guang rushed to the rail to see where they landed. He barely noticed the cavalry galloping across gaps in the moat, their torches ablaze. Or the companies of foot soldiers streaming after them.

'Release!' he bellowed, again and again.

By now incendiary bombs were striking the nearest sections of the Mongol camp, planting flowers of spark and flame. Nearly every catapult in the city had been brought to this area of the ramparts. Guang noted oily clouds billowing from the line of enemy artillery. A huge explosion made one catapult tumble.

'As I foresaw!' he exclaimed to Chen Song. 'We've hit their thunderclap bombs!'

By now the incendiary thieves had galloped into the smoke-filled camp, whirling their flaming torches. The regiments of infantry had covered half the ground, advancing at a brisk trot. There was time for a final volley. Guang ordered the fluttering of purple flags. A flight of stones and crossbow bolts arced towards the camp and vanished in the smoke.

'Cease!' he bellowed. 'Fresh teams to the catapults! Chen Song, order all officers to watch my flags. If I show the yellow, any who fail to obey the signal shall be punished. Order the rocket-arrow flame-archers to take up position on the south western ramparts.'

Yet it seemed he would not need to fly the yellow flag, the signal he had chosen to denote their most desperate strategem. General Zheng Shun's infantry were pouring into the barely defended camp. A bedlam of cries and hammering floated to the city. The air was tainted with burning oil and naphtha, a sweet, heady scent that always made his nostrils flare. Guang stared avidly into the burning siege lines.

Dark specks were visible, rushing this way and that. Perhaps General A-ku had been caught unawares. If Zheng Shun's halberdiers reached the horses, a startling victory might be achieved, one to enter the annals and be debated by strategists for centuries to come. And would not the name of Commander Yun Guang be weighed among the others? He could not doubt it.

Time passed. Still no sign from Zheng Shun. Guang mastered an urge to abandon his post and gallop into the Mongol camp. If only he could meet A-ku sword to sword! Or better still, Khan Bayke!

'Chen Song,' he said, trembling. 'What is going on in there?'

His friend peered across the battlefield.

'I have a bad feeling,' he said, dully.

This was so unlike him that Guang frowned.

'Why?'

'That smoke to the south is not from fire,' said Chen Song. 'It looks like dust.'

Now Guang strained with every nerve in the direction of his friend's pointing finger. He blinked. Looked again. Then panicked.

'The rocket-arrow flame-archers on the south western ramparts must take up position!' he shouted. 'Quickly! They are seeking to outflank us!'

Mongol cavalry were indeed gathering. Perhaps a whole division of ten thousand. Was it a trap after all?

'Chen Song, go there at once! All regiments of crossbowmen must line the battlements. When their cavalry are parallel to our ramparts, command the men to loose everything they have!'

Chen Song rushed along the walkway while Guang stared to the south west. Turning to the officers around him, he ordered. 'Prepare noxious bombs, but hold back until I command.'

Now Guang fixed his attention on the Mongol camp. To the

south his catapults had not commenced firing. How long would Chen Song take? Each moment's delay might cost a hundred lives. Above all, a charge must be prevented. It would sweep all hope before it.

Groups of Zheng Shun's infantry were emerging from the burning camp. As they re-formed, more appeared. They were being driven back. If the Mongol cavalry to their right could not be deterred, a massacre must surely follow.

At last thunder-crash bombs had started to arc towards the advancing lines of Mongol horsemen. It was a shrewd choice. Chen Song had picked the only weapon truly feared by the barbarians – and more importantly, their horses.

'Steady!' Guang shouted to the men round Swallow Gate. 'No firing in this part of the walls or you will hit our own men!'

On the far flank came a huge explosion. Then another. Horses were down. Others panicked at the noise, their riders struggling to control them. Still the Mongols formed a dense phalanx as they rode along the sides of the moat and ramparts, eager to fall upon Zheng Shun's retreating forces. More missiles were falling. Battalions of archers and crossbowmen on the ramparts were loosing steadily, so the air filled with flitting swallows. For a moment Guang feared it would not be enough.

Then the flame archers lit their rocket arrows. Barbed shafts poured out in a ceaseless rain of smoke and sparks – thousands falling on the packed ranks of horsemen. The carnage among the cavalry was immediate – everywhere warriors and horses were pierced, some by several arrows. The remaining Mongols halted in confusion then broke, galloping back the way they had come.

Guang turned his attention to the struggling mass of General Zheng Shun's infantry. Their retreat was surprisingly disciplined. Yet now the first sign of what had driven them back emerged through the black smoke – masses of armoured cavalry, Genreal A-ku's best men.

'They intend a charge as we retreat!' Guang cried.

It was true. Zheng Shun's regiments, horribly reduced by the fight in the camp, were halfway back to the city, yet the Mongols had gathered in force and were preparing a final, decisive attack.

It was a possibility Guang had anticipated. He judged the force of the wind by examining a loose pennant. It still blew strongly from the east.

'Fly the yellow flag!' he bellowed. 'Fly the yellow flag *now*!'

Then he began to count: one, two, three. . . before he reached fifty a volley of spinning, smoking balls flew over the heads of the fleeing troops. Wherever they landed, small flashes scorched the ground. Almost at once the air filled with clouds of fumes. Powdered lime and arsenic spread in a sickly green and white mist. Mongol horses were rearing, riders and mounts unable to breath. A steady wind blew the noxious cloud onto the lines of advancing heavy cavalry.

'More!' screamed Guang, beside himself.

Seizing a giant crossbow lever, he thrust the soldiers aside and sent off the bolt. It missed the Mongols and stuck in the dry earth.

The first wave of infantry reached the moats. A few flung themselves in and swam desperately to the ramparts where ropes were lowered, hauling them up to safety. Most re-entered the city in a jostling stream, cramming the bridges with men. But there was no fatal cavalry charge from the Mongols. Guang's noxious bombs had succeeded in deterring them. Finally, the gates banged shut.

A strange silence settled on the ramparts. The open spaces behind them were full of wounded, smoke-blackened men, mingling confusedly with the exhausted catapult crews. There came no cheering from the Mongol camp either.

竹子

Guang found General Zheng Shun inspecting the treatment of the wounded. His cheek was bleeding from a sword gash. Men lay on the ramps leading up to the battlements, groaning or staring sightlessly. Many had abandoned their weapons during the retreat, a dispiriting sight.

'Ah, my boy!' said Zheng Shun.

Guang offered a half-empty wineskin. A great portion of it was sloshing round his empty stomach. Zheng Shun took it and drank eagerly. Yellow wine dribbled down his chin.

'Better!' he said, at last. 'Good.'

The two men examined the scene around them.

'They were waiting for us!' said Zheng Shun. 'There can be no other explanation. We penetrated deep into their camp. I tell you, they paid dearly for that. Then we were attacked by their cursed cavalry. How could they have formed so soon? It must have been treachery.'

The older man took another drink.

'If you had not stopped them with your noxious bombs I would have lost my whole command. A sorry business. As it is, we lost a third of our men out there.'

Guang grunted.

'So many?'

'Three thousand, Yun Guang! In less than an hour! The worst of it, my boy, is that a great many were trapped in the camps. I hope for their sake they died fighting.'

Then the illustrious General Zheng Shun did something Guang had never expected. He bowed his head a fraction.

'We may commend your foresight, Captain Xiao. You anticipated every event.'

Tears filled Guang's eyes. He brushed them aside. Protestations of duty touched his lips but remained unspoken. He knew Zheng Shun honoured deeds not words.

Later that day, the defenders of the Twin Cities were confronted with a spectacle of General A-ku's making. Hundreds of prisoners, their hands bound, were paraded before the still smouldering camp. Wang Ting-bo stood with his commanders on Swallow Gate to watch what followed. A slow and deliberate affair. Guang positioned himself beside his patron, Wang Bai, who surveyed the business curiously.

'How wasteful to use crossbow bolts shot in the back of the head!' he declared. 'I'm surprised General A-ku allows it.'

'I suspect the shafts are removed afterwards, sir,' said Guang.

'Ah! Of course. Yet surely, many must break.' Wang Bai watched the executions proceed for a few moments. 'I hear remarkable stories about your catapults, Yun Guang.'

'Thank you, sir.'

'Quite remarkable,' said Bai thoughtfully. 'You do me great credit.'

Guang kept his eyes fixed on the next group of prisoners. They did not plead for mercy. He wondered how bravely he would behave in their position. A vague unease formed in his soul, strangely like fear. He stifled it and examined Mount Wadung.

'The executions are taking a long time,' said Wang Bai, at last.

'We must watch until the end, sir,' broke in General Zheng Shun, a hint of reproach in his stiff voice. 'Our martyrs deserve that honour, at least.'

Wang Bai raised an eyebrow

'I will watch even if it takes a week,' he said, gravely.

They fell silent. A-ku's demonstration continued for another two hours rather than a week. When it finished Guang returned to his gilded pavilion and stared into an ornamental pond where lilies floated. Servants brought bowl after bowl of wine. He summoned Chen Song, who insisted on playing his lute to settle their spirits and the twanging continued until both were properly drunk.

竹子

That evening the moon unfurled. Ivory fingers touched the Mongol encampment and the Twin Cities alike. The moon knew no favourites. Humble or noble, soiled or brave, it did not care who gazed at its sad face.

Now its soft light stole across Apricot Corner Court. The

fruit tree's leaves were shrivelling in obedience to autumn. As the moon stared down, a single leaf fluttered to earth. The yowling of cats broke the silence then faded, their quarrel drowned by the vastness of night. Moonlight caressed the bamboo curtains of Old Hsu's workshop, filtering into the darkness within.

The fan-maker sat at his bench, opening and closing a fan painted to resemble a peacock's tail. In his youth, it had won him admittance to the Fan-maker's Guild. Old Hsu had kept it ever since, even during hungry times. One must preserve one's soul or become a person chosen by others.

His thoughts spread wide, then narrowed like the fan. He dreamed of the vanished world described by his beloved philosopher, Mo-Zi, before men's hearts were corrupted – the Time of Great Togetherness, a hundred generations ago. His vision excited an ardour and hope he had almost forgotten. It made him feel young again. Could Universal Harmony be impossible, when it had once existed, however long ago?

Then, the Great Dao had truly prevailed! Leaders were elevated due to talent and virtue; they spoke sincerely, scattering peace as the sky does rain. They thought nothing of wealth. They did not resemble Wang Ting-bo and his grasping clan. Folk possessed a single family – each other.

Old Hsu's hands trembled as he recalled the secret meetings he and his comrades had held, debating such matters. They had been led by a wandering preacher who never revealed his true name. Then the authorities took their Wise Father away. No one learned what became of him. The members of the Society drifted apart like a fleet deprived of rudders. Dullness and disappointment filled long years. He had observed former zealots becoming everything they once abhorred.

Old Hsu shook his head to clear it. With the coming of the Mongols they needed Mo-Zi's vision more than ever, lest the world drown in anger, fear and despair.

The old man realised he was tapping the precious fan against his knee. Even here, in Apricot Corner Court, discord seeped from neighbour to neighbour. That afternoon, amidst news of the failed attack against the horse-people, an unpleasant conversation had occurred. As he and Widow Mu stood in the gateway, watching wounded men jolting on carts to temporary hospitals she had spoken with unexpected savagery.

'I hope Captain Xiao burns every one of them! I'd fry General A-ku in oil like my dumplings!'

Old Hsu had frowned.

'War will never vanquish war, madam,' he replied. 'Of course we must defend ourselves. But kill them all? Then we would be no better than our enemies. Besides, one day they might become our friends.'

To his surprise, instead of her usual deferential sigh or sideways glower when he tried to instruct her, she turned on him.

'Traitor's talk! Have you forgotten what they did to the prisoners?'

'Widow Mu!' he had pleaded.

'I shall report you! Those scum would rape Lan Tien if they could and enslave my dear boy. How can you talk like that?'

'Madam, calm yourself!'

Widow Mu slammed the door of her dumpling shop. With a heavy heart he had watched the procession of wounded men.

Mournfully, Old Hsu spread the splendid fan across his legs. If only the Society of the Great Togetherness still existed! It might become a burning seed, lighting the sky with reason and compassion. He remembered lying on his bed when he was barely twenty, imagining the Middle Kingdom as a land of joy. Why should that vision taste so sour now?

In the room next door his wife snuffled in her sleep. Old Hsu carefully put the peacock fan back in its lacquered box.

竹子

Old Hsu was not alone in sleeplessness. Across the moonlit courtyard a lesser light burned. Cao sat in the shop, hemp-scented tea on the low table beside her. She warmed her hands round a cup decorated with plum flowers. Shih was late back, as so often. It did not surprise her. The city choked on its casualties. All doctors had been conscripted to tend the wounded and the North Medical Relief Bureau must play its part. She did not expect to see her husband before dawn.

A tray of covered food bowls waited on the counter. Though she was hungry, Cao had set aside her own portion. Shih and his apprentice would be famished when they returned. Yet the scent of rice and salt-fish distracted her.

Instead of food, Cao digested the day's news. Whispered tales had reached Apricot Corner Court. How the prisoners captured by the Mongols had died, one by one, while Wang Ting-bo mournfully watched from Swallow Gate. It was said thousands had perished, and not all bravely. For a moment Cao listened, imagining horsemen galloping through the dark streets. But it was just a single rider, no doubt a messenger, his harness jingling.

Cao pulled her robe close round her shoulders. Everyone knew how the Great Khan and his forebears had conquered half the world. The mountain of skulls must reach higher than Mount Wadung! Madam Cao, as was customary in the city, viewed the blessed peak as a symbol of hope. People prayed to the mountain in times of drought, urging it to nudge passing clouds so they opened their granaries of rain. It was remarkable how often their mountain listened. Yet why should it care for Pan-Gu's fleas? Or the frivolous city at its foot?

Such speculations were unwelcome. She glanced round the familiar shop. They owned this room now and all those behind and above. Yet when they first arrived in Nancheng they had possessed nothing but love. And youth, of course. What vigour she and Shih had shown to win this house! To build his practice from a case of needles. To win the trust and regard of neighbours, so that tradesmen bowed to Dr Yun Shih's wife when she walked through Water Basin Ward. Was all that slow gain to be burned by the barbarians until only rafters and the charred outlines of walls remained?

Become nothing Shih sometimes said in spiritual moods provoked by drink. Cao did not want to become nothing. Except for the children destiny had denied them, she liked her life. Perhaps they were lucky, after all. Children in times like these would be an unbearable anxiety. No, they did very well. Or almost well. Except for that dainty, heedless creature up the hallway.

Cao drank another cup of tea. Her thoughts swirled elsewhere. Brother-in-law was the only Commander to win honour in today's battle. His exploits passed from courtyard to courtyard; how he had driven off the barbarians and saved thousands of men to defend the city. Yet one could not help worrying. The Mongols would hate him for his success. Perhaps they would seek his death because they feared him. And he looked so fine in his doughty armour! His up-thrust sword hilt made her think strange things.

A hand tested, then rattled the door. Cao grew stiff, half-expecting Guang, summoned by her thoughts. When she unbarred the door, Apprentice Chung slipped past, his shaved head lowered.

'Where is Dr Shih?' she asked.

Chung settled on a low stool by the counter. An irritable flush covered his face.

'Still at the Relief Bureau.'

'Then why are you here?'

He cast a longing glance at the pot of tea. Cao poured him a cup. He drained it with a loud slurp.

'Master sent me for moxa and other medicines.'

Chung frowned uncertainly, producing a scrap of paper.

'He made me take this list in case I forgot.'

'Give it to me,' said Cao. 'I will gather what is needed.'

Chung's eyes were fixed on the tray of covered dishes so she served him his food. While she measured out medicine, Chung shovelled with his chopsticks.

'How is the Relief Bureau?' she asked.

His chopsticks paused. Resumed again. Though Chung had not been spared the sight of death in his young life she had never seen him so troubled.

'Why must a single a man contain so much blood?' he asked, wonderingly.

He started to tremble and grains of rice fell back into the bowl.

'Madam, I heard a rumour that all apprentices are to be pressed into the Militia. Is it true?'

'I do not know.'

'Yet I heard it.'

She continued to spoon out dried raspberry leaves.

'Perhaps it is true. The city needs men on its walls or it will fall.'

He swallowed another mouthful and chewed morosely.

'Madam,' he said. 'I cannot be a soldier.'

'I have no power over that, Chung.'

'But you do,' he insisted. 'Master is Captain Xiao's brother. He could ask him to arrange for me to stay as I am.'

'You are upset,' she said, soothingly. 'Eat some more and drink that tea.'

His fist banged on the counter.

'If you had seen what I have tonight, you would know I cannot join the militia! You must persuade Master! I insist on it!'

Despite her surprise, Cao looked stern.

'*Insist?* You should understand there are limits, Chung! Among his many concerns Captain Xiao can hardly intercede for an apprentice, however dear to us. His business is very pressing. We must all do our duty.'

Chung glared at her in an unseemly way. His red-rimmed eyes showed no agreement with her plea. When he spoke again, it came quietly.

'You forget, Madam, that I know all about the circumstances of your marriage. For you told me yourself.'

A deep emptiness entered Dr Shih's cosy shop. Assumptions

of the past, mists of friendship and loyalty, parted to reveal a void within. Cao's breath held for that moment. Her eyes fixed on his familiar face. It was sullen and resolute. Then she breathed out.

'Oh, Chung!'

'You heard me.'

They tested a silence years of trust had once filled. Cao realised she felt tearful. Chung's eyes lowered and she understood he was ashamed.

'Take this parcel to Dr Shih,' she said, coldly. 'Tell him everything on the list is here. And take these bowls of food for him, only be careful not to spill any.'

Chung rose reluctantly. He flapped plump fingers.

'Madam will understand I am distressed!' he cried. 'But I am not a fool. Not what everyone thinks – oh yes, I know how little I am respected! Why should I suffer what might be avoided?'

Her face showed no expression.

'I mean what I said. I cannot be a soldier. I will not!'

'I shall speak to Dr Shih,' she said.

He departed without saying more. Cao was left to the comfort of her tea. Chung's threat filled the shop like an unwholesome odour.

竹子

While mistress and apprentice spoke, Lu Ying was negotiating a misty gateway. Her silks were so heavy they weighed her down as she advanced through the fog. Her jade and silver hairpiece bent her neck like a yoke. When she emerged into daylight there was no need to walk further. For she had become a fluttering oriole, skimming over a vast city.

At once she knew the place and marvelled. Below spread Kaifeng, the former capital, generations ago before the Middle Kingdom was divided in the reign of the Emperor Huizong. How well she knew that monarch's sad story! A play about it had been performed in the Pacification Commissioner's mansion. Most marvellous of all, she realised Emperor Huizong wore a familiar face: Wang Ting-bo's!

But her master was displeased. As Lu Ying flew she understood it all. How disappointing the people were, how ungrateful!

A great royal pleasure park grew before her eyes. A Daoist monk had once told His Majesty that building the park would lead to many sons – and see! Babies, boys, youths, all trailing after their father.

Lu Ying fluttered between precious rocks and rare plants, a high hill constructed by thousands of labouring peasants. Water cascaded down cliffs into a pool of serenity. Flocks of geese and ducks formed patterns to please His Highness and on the shore gibbons howled mournfully. All around the city people scurried through field and swamp, scrabbling in the earth for curiosities to grace the Son of Heaven's park. Officials stood over them and flicked thin whips. Those offering nothing were beaten with bamboo sticks.

Now Lu Ying grew afraid. What had she to give? His Imperial Highness was frowning again. He had noticed her as she flew this way and that in distress. The horizon grew dark with the drumming of hooves, barbarians galloping towards Kaifeng. At once the city was ablaze.

Lu Ying groaned in her sleep. Sweat moistened her hair. Her dream shifted. . .

She was no longer an oriole, but a concubine weighed down by precious silks. The pleasure-ground lay in ruins, barbarian horses fed on the bodies of geese and plumed ducks, tearing at the gibbons' fur with protruding yellow teeth. Wang Ting-bo cried out that he had been betrayed.

Again Lu Ying murmured as her dream changed. A grotesque cavalcade marched wearily across grassland stretching as far as one might see. Courtiers and eunuchs in splendid uniforms, young and old, wives and concubines, herded across the endless plains towards dishonour. Lu Ying realised she was the Emperor's beloved First Wife. As they stumbled over the hard ground in thin slippers, horsemen selected the most beautiful of the ladies, dragging them into the grassland to satisfy unspeakable pleasures.

Suddenly a barbarian officer stood before them and Wang Ting-bo recoiled. She felt all her royal consort's shame.

'This is Heaven's punishment!' railed the officer. 'You deserve what you have become!'

His Highness was trembling.

'You have lost the Mandate of Heaven!' jeered the officer.

What did the insolent barbarian want? But she knew. They both knew.

'Do not be so miserly,' continued their tormentor, in a sly voice. 'Share what you have lost!'

Then rough hands dragged her away and Wang Ting-bo did not even protest. Indeed he smiled strangely.

'Take her,' he said. 'I have plenty more.'

Lu Ying curled into a tight ball on the bed. The sweating man was on top of her, his breath reeking of garlic and wine. He tore aside her silken clothes, revealing that triangle it was criminal to show. When he lay exhausted and panting, pressing her onto the hard earth, Lu Ying saw it was not a barbarian who had raped her. The man possessed Wang Ting-bo's face. He was gazing lasciviously, quite pleased with his conquest.

She sat upright, gripping the sheets in distress. For a moment she was in many places at once – on the unyielding soil – then a half-forgotten girl in the Pacification Commissioner's mansion – and finally herself, in a room of hard shapes, a room of strange darkness. For a long while Lu Ying hugged her knees, until her heartbeat slowed.

Still half-asleep, she rose and stumbled from her bed. How close this room felt! It was suffocating her, night after night. No wonder her dreams were bad. She walked into the corridor and groped to a side-door. A simple desire to look at the moon's sorrowful face led her outside.

The apricot tree stood as always, leaf and bough forming tangles of shadow. No one else was about.

Lu Ying breathed deeply, the night air slowly dispelling recollections of her dream. She settled on the bench beside the tree, a thick shawl round her shoulders. Dawn would come in a few hours.

She had heard all about the defeat outside the city walls. Proud and ambitious, Wang Ting-bo's feelings at such a reverse were predictable. . . but she did not like to think of him, not so near her dream.

Suddenly she grew alert. A tall, burly silhouette filled the gateway. She felt eyes upon her and glanced back at the safety of Dr Shih's house. The man advanced through Apricot Corner Court into the moonlight. Her heartbeat quickened.

'Captain Xiao,' she said, faintly.

Guang halted a body's length away, looking down at her. His face lacked the haughtiness of their previous meeting. He seemed troubled. She smelt wine on his breath and her hands instinctively pulled the shawl tighter, covering the line of bare, white soft skin where neck meets shoulder.

'I had a terrible dream,' she said, feeling a need to explain her presence in a public place so late at night. 'I wanted. . .'

She gestured at the sleeping courtyard around them. Unexpectedly, he did not reproach her, as he had the first time they met. All harshness seemed to have drained from his manner.

'Then we are alike,' he said. 'I also came here seeking comfort.'

He remained standing before her as she sat on the long bench. Yet Lu Ying did not feel afraid.

'I wanted to see how my brother is faring – and Madam Cao,' he added.

His words were a little slurred. Lu Ying realised how absurd she must appear, lacking make-up or respectable clothes. In the moonlight and at such a time of danger, it did not seem important, as though ordinary rules of conduct had been set aside.

'You were our city's hero today,' she said. 'I'm sure everyone is grateful.'

'Tonight Nancheng is full of widows and fatherless children,' he said, with some of his former curtness. Lu Ying sensed he was ashamed of his failure to preserve more of their men and felt an unexpected desire to touch his arm – or be warmed by it. Instead, she shrank deeper into the bench.

'I believe your brother is tending wounded soldiers at the Relief Bureau,' she said. 'Still, a light burns in Dr Shih's shop, so I suspect his wife waits up for him. She usually does.'

Guang glanced over at the golden rectangle round the curtain.

'Little Brother is lucky,' he said. 'He does his duty and someone waits for him to return.'

Again he looked at her doubtfully.

'No one should meddle with that,' he warned.

'Madam Cao is a most respectable lady,' said Lu Ying, blushing. Then she added: 'I am not all bad, sir. However I appear, I am not all bad.'

'Younger Brother deserves happiness,' he muttered. 'There has been too much suffering in our family.'

Part of her wondered at the implications of his words. Perhaps the brothers had been talking. Power touched her with its familiar hunger. Why should she not be a wife, even to one as humble as Dr Shih?

'Perhaps Captain Xiao desires a little tea?' she suggested, to change the subject. Somehow she did not wish to consider Dr Shih right now.

Though truly, she had no idea how tea might be provided. Lu Ying realised she must learn how to make tea for visitors. Except then she would be no better than Madam Cao.

Guang yawned and stretched. She watched his limbs carefully.

'I am not thirsty,' he said. 'And I do not require ceremony in my own brother's home. Here I am plain Eldest Brother, not Captain Xiao.' He glanced at her. 'Do you understand why?'

Lu Ying sensed she was being tested. Images of dull, formal exchanges in the palace, more ritual than conversation, crossed her mind. Oh, she understood the importance of a title or name! One's whole destiny might be changed by a few words.

But Lu Ying did not know how to explain her thoughts, so she said: 'Commander Yun Guang is very wise. I'm sure he knows the answer to his own question.' Then she added: 'Perhaps you might send word to Dr Shih that his wife is waiting for him? I'm sure it would comfort his labours in the Relief Bureau.'

How strange the world was! A few months ago she had not known such a lowly place existed. Now she used its name quite naturally. For the first time since they met, Guang smiled at her.

'Goodnight,' he said. 'I will tell him myself. I have heard the Prefecture is sending a magistrate to inspect Water Basin Ward tomorrow. It would be sensible for Shih to greet him when he arrives. The official concerned has a certain reputation.'

After he had gone Lu Ying sat with the moon, her heart breathing new sensations. She forgot the horde encamped round the ramparts and even her dream, which had seemed so terrible.

竹子

'Are we to be punished?'

Widow Mu's querulous voice spoke for many in Apricot Corner Court. It was the next morning. All the courtyard's residents except Lu Ying and Lord Yun were gathered round their guardian tree, united by neighbourliness – and its dangerous obligations. The laws of collective punishment were remorseless in siege-time. Unless, of course, one had influential relatives.

'I heard the Sub-prefect who is to inspect us ordered beatings for several families when he inspected Xue Alley! Carpenter Xue received three strokes for not bowing to His Honour quick enough.'

No one disbelieved her. Half the world's gossip flowed through her dumpling shop. That is, if one's world was Water Basin Ward.

Dr Shih cleared his throat for silence. It felt uncomfortable that a woman should lead their talk. Besides, he had grievances against Widow Mu so delicate he barely acknowledged them to himself.

'Madam,' he warned.

At this the nervous virility of Apricot Corner Court stirred.

'She speaks with the authority of a Dowager Empress!' cried Old Hsu.

Everyone laughed at this new title except Widow Mu, who glared at the fan-maker.

Dr Shih's position meant he must act like a father to the courtyard.

'I advise you to resume your normal business until His Honour the Sub-prefect arrives,' he said. 'I shall stand watch by the gatehouse and Chung shall beat the gong when His Honour graces us.'

Cao shot him an approving smile as she withdrew. He was pleased to note that even Old Hsu trailed home. If anyone was likely to offend the authorities, it was the fan-maker.

Shih sat before the gatehouse on a three-legged stool. The street was quiet. The siege ordinances severely restricted trade and few found a reason to wander the city. At night a strict curfew was enforced.

He watched a ragged collection of undesirables being driven down the street: tinkers, travelling magicians, entertainers and itinerants of every kind, forced from the city in case they were spies. Plumed creatures no longer allowed a perch. They shuffled like weary beasts, eyes downcast.

When they had gone Shih felt a terrible sadness. Only last night he, too, had been forced to taste the bitterness of exile from a place he once believed safe.

The previous evening Dr Du Mau had graced the Relief Bureau, accompanied by a smooth-cheeked young man, a Dr

Du Tun-i. The lad was little older than Chung. But while the apprentice was plump, Du Tun-i rose like a tall sapling, his doctor's hat with its long ear flaps slightly too large for his head. He had a strangely angular face, all cheekbones and chin. Yet Du Mau announced that this young man, his nephew, had been temporarily appointed to oversee Dr Shih's work as Bureau Chief, pending an official enquiry into missing medicines. His tone implied Dr Shih should consider himself lucky he had not been thrown in the Prefectural gaol – and that such an event was still probable if Dr Du Mau got his way.

In that moment ten years' labour floated away like clouds! Shih had sensed the pointlessness of arguing. He could not quite believe what was happening. After all, Dr Du Tun-i was only replacing him nominally – and temporarily. Indeed Shih had continued to direct cures for a hundred wounded men all that long night. His own misfortune seemed a small thing compared to losing one's sight or limbs. Agonising deaths caused by poison arrows. He had returned home at dawn, stumbling through the grey morning light, driven by Guang's warning that His Honour the Sub-prefect would surely inspect Apricot Corner Court that day.

Shih was saved from further speculation about the Relief Bureau by the arrival of a palanquin and entourage on North Canal Street. Others were also keeping watch from their gatehouses and within moments every courtyard on the street buzzed with alarm.

His Honour turned out to be a small, spare man with a lean face and bushy eyebrows. He led a party of officials and guards into Swifts-At-Sunset Court, emerging half an hour later with a prisoner, who was promptly dragged off to the Prefectural gaol.

'Chung,' called Shih, softly. 'Tell everyone to gather round the apricot tree.'

His Honour processed over the humped canal bridge, his tasselled umbrella carried by a clerk. He paused outside Apricot Corner Court and Shih prudently sank to his knees. Dr

Shih dared not lift his head as the official studied him impassively.

'You there! Is this Apricot Corner Court?'

His accent suggested humble origins. Shih nodded.

'Your name?'

'Dr Yun Shih, sir!'

His Honour consulted a list. Evidently he did not connect the kneeling doctor with the saviour of Wang Ting-bo's heir. Shih wondered if he should mention it.

'Make way!'

Soon His Honour was inspecting the assembled people. His glance flickered over their bent heads to every corner of Apricot Corner Court.

'There is no communal cooking fire set away from the buildings,' he said.

No one had an answer to that.

'Where are the buckets of sand? And the wet hempen cloths demanded by the ordinances? A single fire arrow could set your whole ward ablaze!'

'Your Honour,' said Shih. 'If there is to be blame, let it fall on my shoulders.'

Potentially, blame meant a dozen lashes of the bamboo.

'One would think this a nest of traitors!' declared the official. 'I have heard there are people with unorthodox views in this ward. Do any dwell here?'

Widow Mu was casting anxious glances at Old Hsu. Certainly the fan-maker's views were unorthodox and Shih realised a frightened accusation might billow from her lips. To forestall her, he rose from his knees.

'Sir,' he said, quietly. 'Are you aware my eldest brother is Captain Xiao? There are no traitors here.'

Intakes of breath greeted his words. He had diminished His Honour's face in notable ways: first by his tone, then by pointing out an ignorance. Lackeys looked away, pretending not to have heard.

'Of course,' blustered His Honour.

'Forgive me, sir,' said Shih. 'I am foolish to mention what you already know.'

Slightly appeased, the official looked round for someone to humiliate. His eye found Old Hsu's mocking expression.

'Old fellow, you seem to have something to say for yourself,' he growled. 'Out with it!'

Again the residents of Apricot Corner Court held their breath. Such an invitation was like lighting a fire-lance – moments later it would discharge with a whoosh of smoke and flame. Old Hsu flushed and was about to speak when the side-door of Dr Shih's house swung open.

Lord Yun emerged in a fine suit of silks, clutching his bowl of fishes. Water sloshed to the ground. His high cheekbones and balanced features denoted nothing but handsome nobility. Lord Yun surveyed the official with brazen contempt.

'Tell Khan Bayke I will defy him to my last breath!' he shouted. 'He shall have nothing more that is mine!'

Then the old man threw down the bowl so that it bounced on the earthen floor. Water spread out grasping fingers. Silver-bellied carp flapped helplessly, drowning in air. His Honour went pale, then very red.

'What is this!' he spluttered.

In a blur of motion Cao rushed to Lord Yun and bundled him back into the house. She moved so swiftly he was too surprised to resist. The door closed behind them. Silence in the courtyard, interrupted only by the dying exertions of the fish. A breeze stirred the apricot tree.

'Captain Xiao's father,' whispered Shih, conspiratorially. 'A delicate family matter. Captain Xiao is most sensitive about it.'

Again His Honour bit back angry words. Defeated, he stalked to the gatehouse, Shih following deferentially. He had the uncomfortable thought that if Guang ever fell from grace, His Honour would make them pay for hiding behind the name of Captain Xiao.

'A displeasing inspection,' he grumbled. 'Dr Yun Shih, I hold you directly responsible for the future conduct of Apricot

Corner Court. If anything is amiss you must answer for it with the full force of the law. And let me assure you, I shall keep a close watch.'

Shih believed him. As His Honour the Sub-prefect departed, an angry bellow came from the house.

A clerk was left behind to teach the courtyard what must be done. He was quite as grim as his superior. First he recorded names and occupations, indicating that Chung and the other serviceable men were liable for conscription. Then he ordered everyone except Madam Cao to take buckets and dredge the canal for mud. Miserable work, but finally the roofs and buildings were covered with thick layers of silt, impervious to fire arrows.

Meanwhile, Shih and his wife stood in Lord Yun's room, listening to a remarkable speech.

'You! Yes, you!'

'Father, calm yourself.'

'Since you claim to be my son, I have a test. A son obeys his father in everything, is that not so?'

Cao and Shih glanced at each other.

'Perhaps you require refreshment?' offered Shih, hopefully. 'One of my cordials perhaps?'

'I require you to divorce this woman immediately! How dare she manhandle me! It is a crime.'

Indeed, by any interpretation of the law, laying hands on one's father-in-law could be punished severely. Assuming Lord Yun brought an accusation, there was no shortage of witnesses – including His Honour the Sub-prefect. Shih told himself that given the city's condition and Captain Xiao's influence, no magistrate would be interested. But one day the Mongols would leave. Such a serious charge might be revived at any time. Cao, evidently shaken, hid her face. Shih laid a gentle hand on her arm.

'Father will be pleased to learn I have ordered a new bowl of fish for him. . .'

'Damn your fish!' replied Lord Yun. 'What use are demons if they do not aid me? I have heard enough of their tedious whispering! No, if you are my son you will divorce this woman today. I command you to marry that heavenly creature next door. She has the capacity to please me.'

'Father is unwell,' said Shih, severely. 'I shall prepare something very calming.'

Even as he spoke, disreputable thoughts stirred. A father's word in such matters held the weight of law. If he wished, he could obey and many would applaud his filial piety. As so often, the haunting image of Lu Ying, the flush of her cheeks and the promise of soft thighs, made his mind gulp for clean air. As always, he despised his own feelings.

'Father needs medicine,' he muttered.

He led Cao to the shop and stared at the floor, unable to meet her eye.

'Fetch me the tincture of poppy,' he said, dully.

When he glanced up, his wife's expression was anxious. She had glimpsed his doubt. Neither spoke as he prepared a remedy.

竹子

An hour later, Shih trailed through subdued streets towards the North Medical Relief Bureau. He had left Father slumped in a chair. Perhaps the old man would never awake. Certainly the medicine he had drunk was known to sometimes cause paralysis.

Dr Shih chafed inwardly at the prospect. Imagining such things, alongside all his other vile thoughts, surely proved his wickedness. Why else had Father banished him to the capital as a boy? Because he was deficient. Something wrong with him. Though he tried so hard to be good, it counted for nothing.

Shih realised Chung was talking excitedly and forced himself to listen. The apprentice's usual amiability was strained – clothes smeared with mud from dredging the canal, hair disordered. Exertion never brought out the best in Chung.

'It is quite wrong, sir, quite wrong!'

'What is?'

'I have just explained that.'

Was that exasperation in Chung's voice? Dr Shih met his eye. He was in no mood for nonsense. The prospect of deferring to young Dr Du Tun-i filled him with disgust. It was not that the new Bureau Supervisor was malicious. His face shone with goodwill – as long as he felt himself treated with the diffidence and solemn respect his new position warranted. No, what angered Shih was the certain knowledge that Dr Du Tun-i's skills were inadequate for healing those in the Relief Bureau's care.

'The official took my name for a conscript but I cannot join the militia, sir,' continued Chung. 'I'd do anything rather than join the militia.'

'If you are summoned, then you must answer,' said Shih. 'None of us like the situation. Personally, I abhor it.'

'I will do anything to avoid the militia,' repeated Chung, doggedly. 'Has not Madam Cao mentioned it?'

'Mentioned what?'

'Captain Xiao, Master! He could speak on my behalf.'

Shih recollected some talk of a petition.

'That is hardly likely,' he snapped. 'With the enemy at our gates, Yun Guang has no time to visit his family, let alone compose petitions for apprentices.'

For a moment Chung seemed admonished, then he glowered.

'I *do* expect it, sir. Did not Madam Cao explain?'

Shih stopped. They were in Xue Alley and he had no wish to be accosted by Carpenter Xue.

'Chung, speak more plainly. What has Madam Cao to do with this?'

His apprentice's tongue was out a little, as a child expresses fear. The youth's behaviour had never been more ridiculous.

'I do not like to say, sir. You have been very good to me. . . But I cannot join the militia. I mean to say, I *know*.'

Chung looked at him significantly.

'What on earth do you *know*?'

'About. . . Did not Madam Cao say, sir?'

Chung was clearly in agony. Sweat shone on his plump face. In more favourable times Shih might have been patient or curious. Now he scowled.

'I mean, sir,' said Chung. 'I know things others would profit to hear.'

Shih had a strange thought his wife had been indiscreet. It was not a suspicion he cared to pursue. Chung was evidently referring to the charge of embezzlement at the Relief Bureau and old habits saved Shih from further speculation. He had long regarded his apprentice as an empty jug and took no notice when Chung struggled to pour.

'Be quiet and follow me,' he commanded. 'Now is not the time for this.'

A few minutes later they reached the Relief Bureau.

Two soldiers were talking by the front entrance. One's arm was in a sling and his friend offered a gift of late-blooming orchids, crimson streaked by yellow. Shih paused, glimpsing in those petals the civilization they were defending. Flower-lanterns the barbarians wished to extinguish forever.

He politely stepped round them and entered the surgery. Here he found Mung Po tearing bandages from a hemp sheet. The orderly's weathered face broke into an expression of relief; then he glanced furtively around.

'Where is our new superior?' asked Dr Shih.

'Dr Du Tun-i took one look at all the new patients then went back to his family across the river in Fouzhou. Where have you been, sir?'

'Even I must go home sometimes,' said Shih.

'We've had a hard time. . . Well, you shall see. A hundred more were transferred here this morning.'

Shih hurried through the surgery into the courtyard. Every inch of the dirt floor was occupied by lines of wounded men on blankets. Between the lines were narrow passageways as one finds in a market. His trained nose detected the iron of blood, amidst pus and putridity. The whole courtyard swam with baleful miasmas. Such a reward for heroes seemed scandalous and wasteful. Could the city really squander its defenders so needlessly?

He bent down to examine a young man clutching his stomach and lifted the single blanket protecting him from the autumn chill. A few bloated flies rose angrily. The lad was gasping, staring up at the sky. Shih noticed a thin, watery excretion between the soldier's legs and wrinkled his nose.

Glancing round the courtyard he looked for some sign of a latrine. Nothing. Those strong enough crawled or tottered from their blankets and relieved themselves against a wall. The rest soiled their beds.

'Mung Po,' he said. 'What of food? Fresh water? When did these men last eat?'

The orderly looked uncomfortable.

'Sacks of grain have been sent to us, sir. They're stacked in the infirmary. Dr Du Tun-i told me to touch nothing until he returned.'

'When will that be?'

'He said he needed to ask his uncle's advice, sir, and headed back to Fouzhou. But he left his assistant with strict orders to keep an eye on me.'

Shih stood in the centre of the courtyard, hands hidden by long sleeves, head lowered. Finally, he took off his coat and ordered Chung to hang it on its old peg.

'Mung Po, inform the Supervising Officer's assistant that I am in charge here until his master returns.'

For the next six hours Dr Shih's voice rose above groans and pleas for assistance. First he set aside a corner of the courtyard for cooking fires. Soon a gruel was bubbling and at the smell men cried out desperately. Shih ordered that all available wine jars be breached.

While his assistants went from mouth to mouth with bowls, Shih persuaded a dozen occupants of the neighbouring lodging house to construct canvas canopies over the wounded, paying them with bowls of rice-gruel. Then he marked out each row with numbered paper squares fixed to sticks and broken spear butts. Finally, he drew up a long list of the wounded, noting name and regiment, the nature of their hurt. Above all, he changed the dressings of those most grievously injured, washing wounds in an astringent tincture.

It was dusk when he paused to take the tea Mung Po offered. Yet Shih felt satisfied with the start they had made. He turned to find a youth dressed in turquoise silks peering into the courtyard, his angular features passing from astonishment to vexation. Shih hurried over, still holding his steaming cup.

'Dr Du Tun-i! Thank goodness you are here. We have a great need of you!'

The younger man tried to look stern.

'What is going on?'

Dr Shih sipped his tea. The Supervising Officer flushed at such disrespect.

'I did not authorise these. . . changes,' he said. 'By whose authority have they happened?'

Elated by work and energy, Shih could not help smiling.

'I suppose, since you are our father here, it must be your authority,' he said.

Dr Du Tun-i bit his lip and looked around. There was no denying the new sense of purpose in the Relief Bureau. With it came calm, the perseverance of men reassured by order and efficiency in a dark, chaotic hour. Even misery is bearable when one believes it tends towards progress. Dr Tun-i noted a fresh sack of millet being emptied into a cauldron and restrained a comment.

'You have anticipated my intentions,' he said, uncertainly. 'Yet you did not consult your superior. I must inform my uncle.'

Shih lowered his cup.

'Dr Du Tun-i, a great many of these men need moxa or needles to settle their pain. Will you not administer the treatment?'

Dr Du Tun-i wavered, then looked stern. Shih remembered himself at that age. How strange it was for an older man to be bullied by youth!

'Uncle warned me you are insubordinate,' declared the young man. He struggled for the decisive last word. 'But you have done well to follow my intentions so exactly.'

There was no deceit in his tone. He believed what he said. That anything good must be attributed to his own virtue, anything bad to the incompetence of others.

'I am glad you are pleased,' said Shih. 'Perhaps you should send your uncle a memorandum describing how well you have done.'

For a moment Dr Du Mau's nephew looked at him suspiciously. That moment soon passed.

The Supervising Officer walked with quiet dignity to his desk. Chung, who had been listening to the conversation, followed Dr Du Tun-i into the office while Shih and Mung Po bent over a patient.

An hour later the apprentice hurried across the Floating Bridge towards Fouzhou where Dr Du Mau's residence stood. In his hand was Dr Du Tun-i's freshly composed memorandum. It was a message Chung had earnestly begged to deliver. Especially as Dr Du Tun-i had ordered it should be delivered directly into his illustrious uncle's own hands.

憺

nine

'It is said that Nancheng and Fouzhou are like two raised fists holding back invaders from the North. How so? Why not march round Nancheng's impregnable walls and moats, striking deep into the Empire's stomach and bowels like a tiger tearing out mouthfuls of soft flesh, swallowing whole cities in gulps while the blood of our people drips from its ravening jaws? The answer is simple. Any invaders foolish enough to leave this great city full of resolute men, will soon find all communications severed. They will be harried before and behind, and on either side. Thus invaders dare not enter the Yangtze region without first securing the Twin Cities. . .'

From *Dream Pool Essays* by Shen Kua

竹子

Peacock Hill, Nancheng. Winter, 1266.

Neither side prospered as the siege entered its fourth month. Yet if the Twin Cities fell, the Yangtze River would lie exposed like a pulsing vein leading directly to the Empire's heart.

Nancheng's wide moats and walls endured assault after assault. When a desperate attempt to storm Swallow Gate littered the ground with broken towers and thousands of corpses, General A-ku changed tactics. The best weapon he retained was hunger. So his forces, swollen by Chinese conscripts from the North, tightened their siege lines. Even this great blockade proved a sieve. Messages and supplies entered the city through the river fleet led by General Zheng Shun's cousin, Admiral Qi-Qi.

The Mongols' frustration was matched by that of the defenders. Although Wang Ting-bo risked another attempt to break out, it fared as badly as the first. After that, the Pacification Commissioner resolved to diminish the enemy by other means.

Guang was solemnly ordered to deploy his artillery day and night. They had few other ways of hurting the barbarians. Boulders flew back and forth, sometimes so thick in the sky that rocks ricocheted off each other. Both sides sent streams of fire arrows into the night until stars were hidden by streaking meteors. No one burned much of value. As long as General A-ku kept his forces behind the palisade of the Mongol camp Guang lacked targets. This excuse barely appeased Wang Ting-bo who hungered for favourable reports to send to the Imperial Court.

Day after day Guang toured the city ramparts, observing slaves without number dragged from their villages to construct Mongol ditches and ramps. He did not hesitate to view the unfortunate conscripts as targets. They were aiding the enemy, whether by choice or coercion – force subjugating force was all that mattered now.

When he snatched a little sleep, scurrying peasants crushed by his boulders crowded Guang's dreams, chattering angrily and accusing him of murder. He would wake and reach for the flask he kept beside the bed to drive him to another day's grim work.

One evening Guang remembered his conversation with Lu Ying in the moonlit Apricot Corner Court. That night the air had been strangely still, as though the humble courtyard floated like the Isles of the Blessed where only Immortals dwell. It puzzled him how the memory filled his mind, vivid as a dream. Then Guang recollected that Immortals never dream, for they have transcended desire, and wondered what made him think of her. Yet that night, as he slept, her beauty softened his troubled soul.

竹子

Wang Ting-bo summoned his commanders and high officials to the Hall of Ineffable Rectitude. As Guang knelt he sensed the presence of ghosts, watchful spirits, spying on their council of war. Long ago the hall had been the audience chamber of a petty king, before the Son of Heaven's ancestors re-united the Empire. Did Wang Ting-bo's choice of this room denote a hidden ambition?

One might speculate – especially as his nephew, Wang Bai, sat beside the Pacification Commissioner on a small throne. Several generations of the Wang clan had ruled this province. For the first time Guang wondered how far their hopes extended. If politeness was any guide, Wang Ting-bo's face was genial enough to dispel suspicion.

'Gentlemen,' he said. 'We find ourselves like pheasants beaten into a corner of the forest and penned in by huntsmen.'

Wang Ting-bo was evidently pleased by this comparison and glanced at his nephew for approval.

'Your Excellency,' said Admiral Qi-Qi. 'I believe we are faring better than you suggest. We are more like tigers who retreat to an impassable gully, where we glare down at our enemy and roar whenever we choose.'

Wang Ting-bo frowned.

'No, Zheng Qi-Qi, we are exactly as I have said. Pheasants in a forest.'

The room fell silent.

'His Excellency means to express disappointment,' broke in Prefect Wang Bai. 'The siege is over four moons old yet we have not forced the Mongols to retreat. No one could deny we are hemmed in.'

'With respect, sir,' said Admiral Qi-Qi. 'The advantage lies on our side. We are well-supplied and their blockade is ineffective. In a few months, spring will bring the heat and moisture our enemy finds intolerable.'

'We must see things as they are, sir,' added his cousin, General Zheng Shun. 'It is pointless to hope our forces in the city can drive them off. The court must gather an army capable of lifting the siege.'

Wang Ting-bo's expression hardened.

'Yet I am displeased.'

'Sir,' said General Zheng Shun, grimly. 'If you intend another attempt to break out, I will state plainly that I oppose it. Too many good men have already perished that way.'

Once again Wang Ting-bo glanced at his nephew. Was it for reassurance? To confirm some prior conversation? Guang could not be sure. He detected weakness in the man appointed by Heaven to win victory. But even Wang Ting-bo would find it hard to oppose Zheng Shun's advice. The general was beloved by both his soldiers and the people.

'We can never rest secure until we understand the enemy's intentions,' said Wang Bai. 'Therefore I must reveal a startling offer. . .'

The assembled officers listened avidly, for it appeared a great fish had swum willingly into their net. A message had been received from one of General A-ku's Northern Chinese mercenary commanders, offering to defect. It seemed he had grievances of a deep nature against the Mongol general. However, he would only cross over to Nancheng if accompanied by a senior officer from the Twin Cities, who must join him in the Mongol camp. He had even sent his brother-in-law to act as a hostage and guide. In return, he offered information that would expose all the weaknesses of the Mongol army. Silence filled the Hall of Ineffable Rectitude.

'An obvious trap!' declared General Zheng Shun. 'Why else would the fellow insist on a senior officer sneaking into their camp?'

Wang Bai smiled patiently.

'We need a brave man,' he announced. 'I had in mind Admiral Qi-Qi.'

The latter did not hide his surprise.

'I have never lacked courage,' he said, coldly.

'Cousin, do not think of it,' broke in Zheng Shun.

All eyes were upon the unfortunate Admiral Qi-Qi.

'We might gain information that will end the siege!' said Wang Bai. Then he sighed. 'But if Admiral Qi-Qi is. . . anxious.'

General Zheng Shun laid a restraining hand on his cousin's arm. Though Guang had remained silent, looking from face to face, at last he saw his chance.

'I will gladly be that senior officer,' he announced. 'Let it be me!'

If Guang expected praise from his great patron he was swiftly disappointed. Wang Bai's vexation was obvious.

'I did not have you in mind,' he muttered.

'Gentlemen, I have experience behind the enemy lines. Think how I rescued my father.'

The other commanders were examining him in wonder.

'That's settled,' said Wang Ting-bo, beaming. 'Really, Commander Yun Guang, you ceaselessly impress me. Truly you are worthy of your great ancestor.'

To Guang's embarrassment Wang Ting-bo began to recite one of Great-grandfather Yun Cai's most famous poems, the long one about the lotus every schoolboy was forced to learn by heart. His Excellency's deep, sonorous voice echoed round the splendid chamber, emphasising the rhymes. Guang had always found the lotus poem obscure – its relevance to their current predicament escaped him entirely.

When the audience was over, General Zheng Shun shook his head sadly and stalked from the Hall of Ineffable Rectitude. Guang, however, was in such high favour with the Pacification Commissioner that His Excellency insisted he share tea.

竹子

'Can you really not see this is a trap?'

Chen Song was pacing. Guang had seldom seen him so animated.

'If His Excellency trusts this renegade, who are we to doubt?'

His friend seemed not to have heard.

'You tell me Wang Bai wished Admiral Qi-Qi to be the bait tempting the turncoat,' continued Chen Song. 'That tells me much. Everyone knows His Excellency's nephew hates Qi-Qi. What better way to be rid of him?'

Guang had not realised his friend was so well-informed.

'You may have a point,' he conceded.

'Yet still you volunteered!'

'I am not afraid!'

'Fear is not always weakness.'

Chen Song ceased to pace and sat before the wine-tray. Amber liquid had spilled on its lacquer surface. They were in Guang's pavilion, all shutters closed against a cold wind from the north.

'My friend,' said Chen Song, finally. 'Though your pride and courage are admirable, I must advise you to change your mind. I am astonished His Excellency has been so easily duped.'

Guang poured another bowl. Its fire could not dispel a gnawing, incipient dread.

'I cannot,' he replied. 'Today His Excellency honoured me with tea. Think of it! He told me he craves stirring reports to send to the Son of Heaven's court. If I were to disappoint him, all hope of advancement must cease. I might even lose my place as Commander of Artillery.'

'It is said the grave is a cold, dark place,' said Chen Song. 'We may be sure A-ku would not let you enter it painlessly.'

Wind rattled the shutters and Guang sensed it was changing direction. He knew it would drop soon. Then dense fogs would fill the river all night until dawn. To change an unpleasant a subject he mentioned this prediction to Chen Song.

'Are you sure?'

Guang prickled.

'I am seldom wrong on weather matters – even if I am Wang Ting-bo's dupe!'

Chen Song nodded and said: 'Then there may be a way. After all, our spies come and go through the Mongol camp. I shall return in a few hours.'

While he was gone the lamp and candles flickered. Finally, Guang fell asleep in his chair. When he awoke Chen Song stood before him.

'I have commanded the servants to fetch tea,' he said.

While they waited for refreshments, Guang listened. His friend had been busy that night. He claimed to have selected a handful of men proficient at entering the Mongol camp undetected – and more importantly, at leaving the same way. It seemed Chen Song was still in communication with his old associates among the spies, especially one from Fukkien Province. The Fukkien had explored the artillery companies facing the city using a stolen quartermaster's licence to sell wine and had learned many useful things. On such a dubious fellow Chen Song asked Guang to surrender his entire trust.

'Your intentions must be hidden if you are to survive,' he declared. 'Your tactics must be unconventional.'

He outlined a plan so daring, yet in essence so simple, that Guang wondered if he had underestimated his friend.

'It is essential the Mongol turncoat has no prior warning. No one must be told, not even His Excellency. The Fukkien will manage everything.'

'Our great patron would hardly approve,' said Guang. 'In fact, you are proposing that I deceive him.'

Chen Song answered with a little smile.

'If it works he can hardly complain.'

'And if it does not?'

'You will not complain either. Or not for long. But you may yet win through! Remember the old proverb: when the map is unrolled, the dagger is revealed.'

Guang chuckled at this wit, though he seemed to recollect

the historical incident that inspired the proverb had ended very unhappily.

竹子

Two days later, on a winter's night when the moon had deserted the Middle Kingdom, a flat, narrow boat slid away from the shadow of the pontoon bridge connecting the Twin Cities. Six men crouched low as they paddled. Fog rolled over the mile-wide river and they travelled almost blindly. Dark waters were revealed; then left behind.

Occasionally the rowers detected light through the murky air – watch fires and lanterns from Nancheng and Fouzhou. In siege-time the ramparts were well lit at night so the barbarians might know the defenders' valour still glowed.

Soon the Twin Cities were left behind and the boat entered channels formed by gravel banks. The boatman at the prow half-rose as they neared an island of silt and driftwood. The danger was less about getting stuck than making a noise. He directed the boat towards the southern shore, the side of the river where Nancheng lay, and where General A-ku had constructed his largest camp.

Now the lights filtering through the fog resembled a thousand glow-worms, each a fire tended by men born in dry lands with flat horizons. Uncouth men whose only reason to be here was conquest. Men who despised the watery people they sought to subdue.

Scents tainted the thick air; roasting meat, wood-smoke and something acrid, elusive, the fetor produced by tens of thousands living in close proximity. The rowers heard song-snatches, random shouts, sounds distorted by the fog. Once they heard a braying laugh, quite clear, and knew they had paddled too near the shore. At last the helmsman held up his hand and the boat drifted slowly on the current, back the way it had come. In the silence one of the rowers rose and whispered to their guide.

'Is this the place?'

The boatman nodded, gesturing at a gravel-bank.

'Set us ashore,' murmured Guang. 'Remember, wait at the place we agreed. If you fail me, His Excellency Wang Bai. . .'

He need say no more. The Pacification Commissioner's nephew had recently gained a new title – Ineffable Assessor of Disloyal Conduct. Whole families hung from trees in the East Market, punished for a wayward relative's treason.

The boatman guided the boat towards the shore. Curtains of mist opened and closed before them. A faint bump and their senses strained the night for movement. Nothing. Just ripples of river, muffled splashing as they waded onto dry land.

Once on firm ground the five formed a huddle. They were a ragged sight. Deliberately so. Sacks of grain and skins of cheap wine hung on their backs. If challenged they could reply that they were bearing supplies to their company and produce a passport written in the strange Mongol script to prove it. They wore the uniforms and armour of North Chinese auxiliaries loyal to the barbarians, even down to their weapons.

Now Guang must surrender even the pretence of command. He did so reluctantly.

'Well, my friend,' he said, addressing a grizzled man with a scar across his cheek. 'We are in your hands now.'

The man nodded. He was Han Chinese like those he had undertaken to lead through the camp.

'I still do not see why I was given no notice,' muttered the scar-faced man. Indeed, the Fukkien had forced him into the narrow boat at knifepoint. 'Surely I must warn my kinsman you are coming.'

'I wish to communicate His Excellency's assurances to your relative then leave,' replied Guang, in a low voice. 'He needs no warning for that.'

'I have another idea,' said the guide. 'Why not wait here? Send your boat to hide in the mist while you stay on the shore. I shall return with my brother-in-law. It will be safer for us all.'

The Fukkien stepped closer to him and the scar-faced man grew uneasy.

'No,' said Guang. 'We will follow your original plan.'

A furtive look crossed the man's face.

'As you wish. It's all the same. Follow me.'

Their guide strolled into the mist, the Fukkien close by his side. The rest of the party followed, assuming casual expressions. They climbed the high riverbank then took a muddy path to a palisade of wooden stakes. As their guide had predicted it was unguarded. The reason was plain to see – and smell. Even as they watched, a stoop-backed peasant in rags trundled a wheelbarrow full of human ordure down a short wooden jetty and dumped it in the river.

'This way,' said the guide.

Beyond the palisade they entered a world of conical, animal-hide tents. The fog revealed humps and glowing fires. Upright shapes moved through the grey air. Here the scents they had detected on the river were so concentrated Guang almost retched. Their guide walked quickly, his head lowered, the Fukkien just behind. If they became separated from the scar-faced man, Guang did not care to think how they would find a way back through A-ku's camp. He had already decided to perish sooner than be captured. In his belt was a dagger sheathed in fast-acting poison to make certain of it.

Each step took them deeper into the fog-shrouded camp, the air thickened by clouds of drifting smoke. They passed circles of lolling men, spear-thickets and sudden voices. Once they blundered into a crowd of Mongols taunting two blinded and naked prisoners to fight with fists and teeth alone. Skins containing fermented ewe's milk circulated among the jostling warriors. The air was full of wagers. No one challenged them.

Their guide stepped past an enclosure where huge iron pots bubbled over fires. Slaves fed the flames, depositing naked bodies into cauldrons. A sickly sweet smell filled Guang's gorge with bile. He had heard rumours of this place. Everyone knew the Mongols rendered down the carcasses of fallen enemies. Grease was essential in war, whatever its provenance.

Then they circled a pit of cowering prisoners weighed down by heavy wooden yokes. Their scar-faced guide began to speak to a guard in their uncouth tongue. Before he could say more than one word the Fukkien had taken his arm and was whispering urgently in his ear, evidently sharing a joke. The warrior looked at them in contempt, then spat down on the men below. Guang caught a glimpse of white eyes before they moved on.

Next came a regiment recruited from the north: Han Chinese, and more dangerous than Mongols for they took more notice of their own kind.

Yet no one disturbed their progress. Chen Song had hired a reputable sorcerer to chant favourable spells through the long night to ensure their invisibility and perhaps his magic worked. They travelled the enemy lines, skirting corrals of camels and horses, dung piles and mountains of straw, until they reached the catapult companies facing Nancheng. At last their guide halted. Even in the darkness his long white scar showed plainly.

'I will take you to my kinsman,' he whispered. 'We must pass through that line of catapults. Beyond lies his tent. You must wait here until I return. Perhaps I can bring horses, as I promised.'

The man's forehead was shiny. The exertion of their dangerous journey had been too much for him. Unless, of course, he feared a different kind of discovery. Guang inspected his men: they were remarkably calm. The Fukkien seemed quite at ease. Guang caught the latter's unblinking gaze and slowly lowered his eye-lids.

They stepped aside for a drunken soldier staggering to the palisade wall, muttering to himself as he released a steaming jet. Guang stepped close to their guide, his face inches from the livid scar. When the soldier had blundered away and vanished in the fog, he murmured: 'Tell me, my friend, why did your brother-in-law insist that a senior officer come to fetch him? It hardly makes sense.'

Their guide looked from face to face. Guang detected the acrid scent of fear.

'So he. . . he would know you are in earnest,' said the man.

'I am,' said Guang.

He shoved the short dagger concealed beneath his cloak into the fellow's stomach, twisting it so the poison worked quickly. The Fukkien had already covered the man's mouth. Their guide was carried to a ditch and laid out of sight almost before he had slumped. Hidden beneath his own dark cloak, he looked strangely at peace, like a man sleeping.

The Fukkien motioned and they walked towards the upright shape of a catapult, vague in the mist. If all had gone according to plan, they were near the corner of the camp, beside the river. Guang realised he was shivering and wondered if his men noticed. He must not think of the dead man. He was gone. Quite behind him. He must never think of him again.

'You are sure this is the artillery company you mentioned?' he asked the Fukkien.

'Yes.'

'And you can identify the officer you told me about? You are sure of his name?'

The Fukkien looked at him curiously.

'Talk puts us all in danger,' he murmured.

Guang repressed panic. He must rely absolutely on the Fukkien or perish here.

They approached a catapult rising like a huge gallows. Half a dozen Han Chinese crouched at its base round a fire of dried dung and wet leaves. Clouds of smoke added to the fog. Little surprise the artillerymen were Han, for the Mongols possessed no skill in such matters. A short officer wearing an embroidered coat squatted closest to the flames. Even in the bad light his deep tan suggested a curious story.

The Fukkien stepped forward.

'Is this the catapult nearest the corner tower?' he asked. 'I cannot tell for the fog.'

'It is,' said the officer.

'Ah!' said the Fukkien. 'You are the one they call Li Tse! Don't you remember me?'

The officer glanced up wearily. He struggled to place the Fukkien's face. Certainly there was something oddly forgettable about him. In the same way, his words did not linger in one's mind when he spoke.

'No. . . Ah! Now I do! The quartermaster with wine that should not be his! Ha! You have more?'

'Much more. And at the same price.'

The other artillerymen stirred expectantly.

'Here!' said the Fukkien, offering a wineskin. 'Try this, my friend.'

The officer took it and tilted.

'Good!' he said. 'A little bitter, but good!'

The bitterness bore a scent of cloves. Before long anyone who tasted the wine would be fast asleep.

'Let your men try it too,' said the Fukkien. 'And keep your voice down. Our business must be private.'

Reluctantly, the officer surrendered the wineskin. It passed from hand to hand.

'What is your name again?' asked Li Tse, suddenly suspicious. 'Which regiment are you attached to?'

Guang looked round. It was a miracle their conversation had not alerted the neighbouring catapult crews. But nearly everyone was asleep and the fog deadened those noises it did not distort.

'Step aside with me, sir,' said the Fukkien. 'We will agree a price in private.'

'I asked what regiment?' repeated the officer.

Guang could bear it no longer.

'I told you we should sell it to Bayke!' he hissed, addressing the Fukkien. 'Let's go to him now.'

The Fukkien shot Guang a look of surprise, then his face went gravely blank. Meanwhile the artillery officer reached for the wineskin circulating among his men.

'Hey, not so quick!' he said.

'Come with us or stay here,' said Guang.

He turned to leave and sensed the Fukkien follow reluctantly. Everything depended on the next moment. Guang had taken a huge risk. If the officer did not join them all they had endured, the danger and fear, the murder of their guide, would be for nothing. And they would still need to escape the camp.

Guang led his men deeper into the mist. It seemed his ploy had failed. Then Li Tse appeared behind them through the fog.

'Hey!' called the officer. His last word that night. Concealed by the rolling air, they clamped hands over his mouth. He writhed until a blow stunned him, and the Fukkien's poison was forced down a tube between his lips. A few moments later they slid his unconscious body into a long sack tied with hemp cords.

Guang listened. The camp was full of noises. Whinnying horses and snorting camels. Crackling log fires and mournful singers. The voices, snuffles and snores of countless men. Perhaps they had not been heard.

'Quickly!' hissed the Fukkien.

They made their way to the wooden palisade and earthworks overlooking the river. A single sentry guarded this portion of the wall, for the Mongols had grown careless as the siege dragged on. It was through this part of the camp that the Fukkien was accustomed to come and go, using a drainage ditch beneath the palisade. Yet a single vigilant guard would be enough to raise the alarm and they were too large a group to risk the Fukkien's usual method. The guard's silhouette paced above them, stamping to keep warm. The Fukkien nodded at one of his men who climbed stealthily onto the siege ramparts. There was a sudden grunt: the sound of something sliding to earth.

'Where is the drain?'

'Here.'

'Pick up the bag containing the prisoner.'

'Leave the rest?'

'Yes.'

'Quickly.'

This last whisper came from the Fukkien. Then they were crawling through a short tunnel reeking of human filth. Guang did not care. In a moment he would be free of this hellish place. He scrambled out, his boot sinking into something slippery and soft. There was a crack of bones. Peering down Guang smelt rather than saw the corpse. As his moan of surprise died away everyone froze. But Chen Song's magician must still have been chanting his spell. Even that indiscretion remained unpunished.

They carried their prisoner to the riverbank. Li Tse did not stir or groan and Guang hoped the Fukkien's poison had not been too strong. Their feet crunched sand and gravel.

The final test was one of faith. If the boatman failed them, all they need do was wait for dawn to reveal their position. Or flee desperately across the killing grounds to the city. But the guards on the palisade were sure to see them, weighed down by their prisoner. Then would come horses, a certain end.

Guang gestured to the Fukkien, whose bamboo whistle produced sounds uncannily like goose calls. No dark shape broke the fog rolling over the river. Again, Guang gestured impatiently, but before the Fukkien could raise the whistle a prow parted the mist.

Later, their laden boat approached the pontoon bridge connecting the Twin Cities. Only then did the raiding party relax. By now the prisoner was beginning to struggle in his sack.

'Tell me, sir,' asked the Fukkien. 'How did you know they meant to betray us? That the scar-faced one should be killed?'

Guang loosened his cloak. Despite the chill he felt unaccountably hot, almost feverish. All he longed for was wine to wash away pain and fear.

'I didn't,' he said. 'But before one drinks, one should remember the source.'

The Fukkien laughed harshly at the old proverb and his companions murmured praise for Captain Xiao, who had triumphed yet again. Guang peered back into the fog. He was certain a hungry ghost floated wordlessly after him, reaching out crimson fingernails.

竹子

The next morning Guang found himself wandering through streets free of fog. The sky was cold and pale above Nancheng. Reluctant to reach his destination, he stopped at a floating oriole hall and ate an absurdly expensive breakfast of rice and pig's kidneys fried in spices. The singing girls fussed over noble Captain Xiao. Their attentions emboldened him, and by the time Guang reached the Prefecture he looked as confident as his reputation required.

A guard led him through courtyards surrounded by bureaux where officials administered the siege. Abacuses clicked amidst quiet conversation. Here was proof of the Empire's superiority. On a whim, Guang struggled to remember a patriotic poem to express this feeling but of the many he had sung or read, he could recall none. Chen Song was able to recite dozens. That was why he was fit for high office.

Guang grew morose. Soldiers of his kind only won honour in desperate times. When the barbarians were driven back, his worth would vanish, just as one welcomed clouds in a drought but feared them when fields were well-watered.

He was conducted to a hidden courtyard at the rear of the Prefecture. Guards stood by the door. All bowed respectfully to Captain Xiao.

In the centre of the sandy floor a prisoner hung by his wrists from a bamboo frame. The interrogation had already begun – and badly, by the look of it. One would hardly bother to torture the hapless artillery officer had he proved co-operative. Guang was surprised to find his patron, Wang Bai, seated on a high-backed chair, fanning himself though the air was cold. General Zheng Shun paced up and down before the prisoner, evidently displeased.

'Ah, Yun Guang!' said Zheng Shun. 'I'm delighted to see you still alive. What happened to our friend with the scar?'

Guang pursed his lips. Clearly the Fukkien and the other men had stuck to their story.

'He died well,' said Guang. 'We had to take what we could get.'

'Really? Well, it hardly matters. This fellow is knowledgeable enough but very obstinate. Aren't you, dog-man?' Zheng Shun wagged a reproving finger. 'We're not finished with you yet, my fine fellow!'

Guang sat beside his patron while the interrogation proceeded. Wang Bai watched curiously, displaying no emotion. Pincers were applied to tender organs and Li Tse grew more amenable.

'What. . . wish. . . know?' he gasped.

'How many men does A-ku field?'

No one welcomed the figure he mentioned – or that another three divisions of ten thousand were on their way.

'How many catapults?'

Again the numbers astonished the assembled officers. Worse was the news that the enemy had almost completed the construction of a secret fleet, in the hope of closing the river as a means of supplying the Twin Cities.

'I'm sure this is useful,' said General Zheng Shun. 'Certainly it will discourage His Excellency from another pointless attempt to break the siege. We must send more messengers to the court requesting reinforcements. Now I want my breakfast.'

Wang Bai rose with him but waited until Zheng Shun had gone. His cold eyes found Guang.

'You did well to capture this man,' he said.

Guang could tell the Pacification Commissioner's nephew was shaken by what they had learned. The forces ranged against them were an endless stream, threatening to wash the Twin Cities away. Then Wang Bai's guarded face took on an expression of wonder.

'How do you achieve these exploits?' he asked. 'First rescuing your father, then seizing this man. . . Are you without fear? Is that the answer? Captain Xiao does not care whether he lives or dies?'

It was the first time Wang Bai had addressed him by that title.

'I am. . .' Guang hesitated. 'I am loyal, sir. That is all. I am loyal.'

The word barely explained his confusion. He could not describe what drove him to recklessness. But Wang Bai seemed satisfied.

'Then I expect your loyalty,' he said. 'Whatever happens – and I foresee strange things – do not allow it to waver from the clan of Wang.'

With that he swept from the courtyard.

Guang frowned. Should not His Excellency's nephew have urged him to remain loyal to the Son of Heaven? Instead he had mentioned the house of Wang. A hoarse, hacking laugh disturbed his thoughts. The prisoner had been listening throughout their conversation.

'That gentleman sniffs the wind,' said Li Tse. 'Cut me down, Captain Xiao! I'll tell you more than I told the others.'

Guang indicated it should happen, that wine be brought. The prisoner gulped down a large bowl, his throat working like a bellows. When he had finished, he glowered at Guang.

'You're the one who burned our catapults and blinded us with poison bombs. You killed General A-ku's own cousin with your tricks. Oh, A-ku would like to have you!'

Li Tse retched wine mingled with blood and mucus. Guang did not reply.

'Let me tell you, sir,' said Li Tse. 'So you know what is coming. Perhaps you will let me live.'

While Li Tse spoke, noon shadows inched across a floor covered in fine white sand to soak up the prisoner's blood.

竹子

An hour later Guang sat in his fine pavilion, resorting to the same comfort that had made Li Tse so voluble. Only Guang did not speak his thoughts aloud. They seemed disreputable. He tried to judge the man's story.

Certainly it seemed credible that Li Tse had been born, as he claimed, forty years earlier, when the mighty Kin Empire fell to the Mongols after the second siege of Kaifeng. And he might well have been conscripted into the artillery. The barbarians had enlisted numerous Chinese. That was their genius, constantly learning from conquered enemies until the advantage lay entirely on their side. Several notable commanders of the Great Khan were Chinese – Guang had even heard that such generals commanded Mongol nobles in battle. All merit flowed from an officer's usefulness; once proven, the highest positions followed.

Guang snorted. How different from the Middle Kingdom! Here one must pass the Emperor's written examinations to gain influence, just as the wise, beloved Wang Ting-bo and Wang Bai had done. Of course, birth helped. How could it be otherwise when most scholars were the sons of scholars? A mere soldier dared not hope to eclipse a scholar. Such was the natural way of their ancestors. Guang's forehead felt pinched. One should not speculate too deeply.

Could the rest of Li Tse's story be true? He had spoken of a great army marching west to the world's end, a hundred thousand horsemen followed by trains of vassals. So many sheep and horses they devoured the lands they passed through like locusts. Li Tse had described how they subjugated a mountainous kingdom. 'You would not feel so sure of your walls,' he had said, 'if you had seen the mountain fortresses we laid waste.'

Led by General Hulegu, they had marched to a vast city, one Li Tse called the greatest on earth.

Guang poured and drank swiftly. Here was proof that Li Tse lied. Everyone knew the Son of Heaven's capital, Linan, was the epitome of all cities. Outlandish lands filled with barbarians could never produce a better. Still the artillery officer had seemed definite. He had even given the place an absurd name *Quagdad*.

Li Tse said the city surrendered after a short siege. Its entire populace were ordered to gather on the plain before their shattered ramparts. They had expected to be treated mercifully in return for paying homage to their new masters. When General Hulegu ordered the slaughter to begin, their wails of surprise could be heard several *li* away. For three days the Mongol cavalry herded and massacred the people like a vast field of deer or sheep. Li Tse witnessed it with his own eyes. From the way he hesitated, glancing away furtively, Guang wondered if he had played a part.

Then the Mongols poured into the streets and burned everything they could not steal. Only a wasteland remained.

Guang could believe the barbarians had slaughtered everyone – had he not witnessed such sights himself? But to say fifty times ten thousand had perished! The vastness of such cruelty strained the imagination.

Silence fell on the courtyard when Li Tse finished. Guang, though uncomfortable, managed a scornful laugh. One of the attendant officials nervously asked the prisoner: 'How are you here, if you went so far to the West?'

Even to that Li Tse had an answer.

'The Great Khan died. Most of the army returned from whence it came. It was necessary to choose the successor and every noble in the army wished to be at the *kuriltai*.'

Guang looked up.

'Did those Mongols left behind in the ruins of your fanciful Quagdad prosper?'

Now it was Li Tse's turn to look uncomfortable.

'I heard they were defeated and could conquer no new lands to the west.'

Guang slapped his knee.

'That will happen here!' he said. 'They shall never be our masters, however many tales you tell. We are not frightened and our strength is the root of mountains. Of Mount Wadung, in fact.'

The officials in the courtyard broke into applause at these words. But Li Tse, beaten and scarred, looked at him mockingly.

'Do not be so sure,' he said. 'I tell you these things so you may know the truth, Captain Xiao.'

'Even if what you say is true, your friends will never reduce the Twin Cities.'

Li Tse shook his head.

'You have not seen what I have seen. Now let me live, sir.'

Guang had risen and left without replying. He had no idea what would happen to Li Tse and did not care. For a wavering moment he wondered whether his family would survive if the Mongols triumphed. Surely Khan Bayke would track them to Apricot Corner Court. Then he ordered more wine, sending out a servant to summon Chen Song. For a long while Guang stared through the open window at passing clouds, his forehead furrowed.

憺

ten

'Heaven has ordained that in this world there are risings and fallings. Each of the ten thousand creatures arises from the Primal Emptiness and must return there in due course. So it is with our dearest feelings. So it is when we seek to plant seeds in the earth and wait in hope for them to grow to our advantage. . .'

From *Remembrances of a Western Terrace at Twilight*

竹子

Water Basin Ward, Nancheng. Spring, 1267.

The stars shifted and the sun grew brighter. Fish of the nibbling kind thrived in the moats of Nancheng. A patriotic recipe was invented: pike or roach barbecued on a communal cooking fire in a paste of Sichuan pepper, wild garlic and chives. Chives were everywhere. Thrifty folk sowed them on roofs layered with mud to deter fire arrows, so that high buildings resembled green hilltops.

Mists no longer clouded the broad river. It was blossom-time, tantalisingly brief. Fruit trees planted to strengthen canal banks wore dense robes of white and pink.

Despite the siege, people greeted spring with the same songs and rites as the year before – and a thousand springs before that. They had reason to celebrate. The first sultry rains made the river rise, covering soil and gravel banks exposed during the winter drought. As heat began to swirl, the ground before the city used for paddy fields filled with rain. Accustomed to dry steppes gnawed by wind, the Mongols suffered in the humid atmosphere. Their hardy horses fell sick, plagued by fungus round nostril, hoof, and lower orifice.

The Twin Cities could afford to breathe more easily until autumn. They had defied A-ku's horde for six critical months. Supplies remained plentiful in the huge underground granaries beneath the Prefecture. Those who had cursed the Pacification Commissioner's nephew, Wang Bai, for impoverishing the whole province, now marvelled at his foresight.

竹子

One morning a work party of women gathered round two wheelbarrows in Apricot Corner Court. They were five in number, a lucky figure: Madam Cao, Old Hsu's Wife, Widow Mu and her daughter, Lan Tien, as well as one who hovered on the edge of the group. While her companions exchanged jokes about watery breakfasts, this fifth woman's expression remained stiff and aloof. Her clothes were outlandishly large for they had been borrowed from Madam Cao. Her attention was on the street, as though she feared someone might witness her disgrace. The women ignored her and noticed everything she did.

'We should go now,' said Madam Cao.

Lu Ying hung back a moment, fiddling with her peasant's clothes. She thrust back a straying lock of hair beneath her broad-brimmed, conical hat. When she looked up, the wheelbarrows had already left Apricot Corner Court. A long-handled hoe lay by her feet. Did they expect her to carry it? Madam Cao had told her she must justify her rations like everyone else in Apricot Corner Court. It was both a test and reproach.

Lu Ying flushed. Oh, one who had been weighed down by

the richest brocade and jade could carry anything! Nor would she be shamed now. She made an exceptionally attractive figure in plain clothes – like a new Mulan or other patriotic heroine forced to set aside her silks. Then, despite her intention to be brave, Lu Ying felt something close to despair. Why deceive herself? No one would notice her, except to mock. Perhaps it was better to be invisible like all poor, toiling folk. Yet Lu Ying feared her jade green eyes would always draw unwanted attention.

Picking up the hoe, she shuffled after the other women. They were some way ahead. She followed with downcast eyes, occasionally glancing up at the trundling wheelbarrows. Her bound feet struggled to find balance as she carried her hoe. By the time they reached the Water Gate of Morning Radiance she was sweating and distressed. Nevertheless she met Madam Cao's look of concern blandly. That was a kind of triumph. More and more she had begun to view Cao with the distaste once reserved for Wang Ting-bo's First Wife. Lu Ying leant on the hoe, shoulders and arms aching. A sergeant descended from the Water Gate's parapets and nodded courteously.

'So you meant what you told me, Madam Cao,' he said, examining the other women, who burrowed their gaze into the ground.

'Indeed, sir,' said Cao. 'If you will allow it.'

He pursed his lips.

'It'll do no harm. From what you say it might even do good. But at the first sign of trouble get back inside double-quick.'

Madam Cao bowed respectfully.

The procession of wheelbarrows advanced into a brick-lined tunnel cut through the earth walls, emerging on a thin strip of wasteland between rampart and river. The soldier on guard gestured Lu Ying through, then bolted the iron-fretted door behind them.

Every place has neglected borderlands. Ground where glorious blooms might unfurl given a chance. Lu Ying realised this as they surveyed the soil before them. She recollected one of Wang Ting-bo's concubines, a plain, unsophisticated girl with broad thighs. She had miscarried in her sixteenth year after the Governor's attentions and been ignored ever after. Yet Lu Ying had always feared that girl, sensing her ripeness. Once she asked him about her and he had replied that her smell was displeasing. Lu Ying, with a woman's insight, had known he was a fool. Here was one who would surely bear the sons he craved. Now, as Lu Ying smelt the rank, peaty earth before them, she recognised the same potential. It was an unlovely strip of land, high with weeds and wild peonies.

Madam Cao turned to them.

'We clear today,' she said, mildly. 'And plant tomorrow.'

Hours of labour lay in between. Lu Ying was directed to hoe, yet found her lotus feet could not grip properly as she turned the soil. Tears of humiliation stung her cheeks, tactfully ignored by the women alongside her. They advanced across the earth in a line until she lagged behind. Soil rich with roots and grubs revealed itself to her hoe. The other women began to sing but she did not join in. Their words were strange to her. They sang as though born to it:

Chop, chop, we clear the elms
And pile branches on the bank.
He neither sows nor reaps.
How has our lord five hundred sheaves?
He neither traps nor shoots.
How do badger pelts adorn his courtyards?
Those lords, those handsome lords,
Need not work for a bowl of food.

Lu Ying listened attentively. The ancient words were vulgar. She must not be moved by them, lest she became a peasant herself.

When she glanced up, she found that Madam Cao had not joined in either. For a moment their eyes met, sharing a secret knowledge of being raised for a different place in this floating world. Then Cao cleared her throat politely and the singers fell silent.

'Dr Shih says he needs mugwort and bletilla tubers. Also, big thistle and ginseng. For those herbs suppress bleeding.'

Her gentle tone held great authority. How could it be otherwise? Of the four women she addressed, three lacked husbands, unless you counted the ghost of Mu's spouse – as his widow obviously did.

'I will ask my husband to advise us when it is best to sow,' declared Widow Mu. 'He will visit me in my dreams tonight.'

'We shall plant them as soon as the soil is bare,' said Cao. 'And harvest them in late summer and early autumn, when the moon is auspicious.'

Old Hsu's Wife laughed sadly.

'In the autumn there'll be plenty of bleeding for your herbs to cure,' she said. 'So we'd better grow plenty.'

The five women toiled beneath the ramparts of Nancheng. The air swirled with gnats and heat. As they worked Lu Ying occasionally looked around, for she felt exposed outside the city ramparts. Further upstream, the Mongols were raising two fortresses to prevent supplies from reaching the Twin Cities by water. She could see earthen walls and hundreds of slaves swarming like ants. Across the broad river lay Fouzhou, smaller than its sister-city. It was only recently that General A-ku had established a comprehensive line of siege-works around it, declaring he considered Fouzhou to be the lips hiding Nancheng's teeth, and that he would strip it to the gums. Everyone in the city knew that story. Spies and treacherous agitators circulated it at the great general's order.

竹子

As Lu Ying's hoe severed stems and turned sticky soil, her thoughts turned over an unexpected meeting that had occurred a few days earlier, while Madam Cao and Dr Shih were both away from Apricot Corner Court.

A pounding on the front door of the medicine shop had made Lu Ying rise in alarm. There are many ways of knocking on a door. This knock was heavy with its own importance. She waited for Apprentice Chung to answer until it became obvious he was away with his master and that only she and Lord Yun were in residence. Lu Ying hesitated, wondering whether she should beg the old man to greet their caller, but when she checked, his room stood empty. No doubt he was hiding somewhere in Apricot Corner Court, as he often did these days, peering and muttering to himself.

Bang. Bang. Whoever was knocking clearly had urgent business here. Lu Ying hurried from her room to the deserted medicine shop, concealing her face behind an elegant fan depicting the Moon Goddess, Cheng-he, on painted silk.

'Who is that?' she called out.

A moment's silence was followed by a harsh, official-sounding voice: 'Open the door at His Excellency Wang Ting-bo's command! I bear a message for the Lady Lu Ying!'

Abruptly her fear melted into incredulity, then exhilaration. With trembling hands she undid the heavy wooden bolts. A single servant stood in the street, his expression more vexed than respectful.

'You took a long time to answer,' he muttered.

Lu Ying shrank back. This was not how she had imagined Wang Ting-bo would summon her to back to Peacock Hill! Where was the awe and reverence she craved? The elaborate ceremony such a summons naturally required? Instead the servant thrust a letter – not even a bound scroll – into her hands and turned on his heels with the curtest of bows.

Lu Ying hurriedly examined the street for witnesses to his insolence. A line of mules laden with military supplies was being led down North Canal Street, drawing a crowd of urchins. One beast chose that moment to release a load of dung, provoking a fight amongst the urchins over who should claim such saleable fuel. Lu Ying hastily closed the street door, forgetting to bolt it behind her.

Then she opened the letter. The characters were tightly written – long, neat columns in such a precise hand that she suspected they had not been written by Wang Ting-bo. He was well known for his careless style of writing; at least that was what people who understood such things whispered in the women's quarters. Lu Ying's own ability to read was so feeble, worse even than her writing, that she had never been able to judge for herself.

Then she had another thought. Why shouldn't Wang Ting-bo employ a scribe for his most intimate business? Would it not make his private concerns somehow more official, and so enhance her status upon her return to Peacock Hill?

Lu Ying retained this comforting idea as she tried to decipher the dense script. Certainly she recognised her own name several times in the document; beyond that she was less certain, and fell back to tapping her leg with the letter.

Of course she might ask Dr Shih or Madam Cao to read it for her, but she did not trust them. What if Wang Ting-bo was not restoring her to her former position as she hoped? What if he was reproaching her for sending no splendid presents to regain his affection?

Lu Ying bit her plump, bud-like lips and used the letter as a fan to cool her forehead.

No, she must not ask them. Already Madam Cao held her in contempt after her attempt to borrow a little *cash*, an episode she bitterly regretted now. She would find another person, one she could trust.

Then Lu Ying realised there was no one she could trust. Not a single creature in this wide world. She had no one; no one but herself.

The thought dispirited her enough to stare desperately at the baffling characters, perched on a stool by the tall maple counter of the shop. Stray words floated through the mists of her ignorance: *cash, His Excellency, generous* – or was that *very generous*? She really could not be sure. But other characters were numbers, she felt quite certain, lots of different numbers. . .

Lu Ying was biting her lips again, so intent on the letter that she did not notice the unbolted door swing open and a tall, broad-chested figure step inside. When, at last, her glance flickered up and noticed him, she cried out in alarm.

The soldier watched her quizzically and bowed.

'Lady Lu Ying,' he said. 'Forgive me for startling you.'

She reached for her silk fan depicting Cheng-he, but it was in her bedchamber. For a moment she used the letter to hide her face until an impulse, a desire for him to look at her, to see her just as she was, made her lower it.

'Captain Xiao!' she exclaimed, twisting the letter in her hands. 'I trust you are quite well?'

His tired face remained grave.

'Quite well,' he said. 'But where is my brother? And Honoured Sister-in-law?'

Lu Ying sensed implications behind his use of the word *honoured*.

'Not here,' she said in an over-bright voice. 'I have no idea when they will return.'

'Ah.'

He looked at her sharply, then glanced at the floor.

'What of Lord Yun?' he asked. 'I take it *he* is at home?'

Lu Ying coughed apologetically.

'I assume so,' she replied. 'Though I could not find him earlier when I looked.'

'I see. Then I must seek him out.'

Yet Captain Xiao seemed in no hurry to find the most important relative one can possess. He stood uncertainly in the middle of the shop lined with tightly sealed jars and burdened shelves.

'Perhaps I shall wait for my brother first,' he said.

Lu Ying watched him curiously. After a moment he appeared to recollect himself.

'Please wait for me here,' he said. 'I have some questions to ask you. First I shall speak to Father.'

He was gone no longer than ten minutes. When he returned Lu Ying was waiting quite demurely on a stool in the medicine shop, having used the interval to apply kohl to her eyebrows and refresh her pale cheeks with a blushing powder. Yun Guang appeared decidedly ruffled as he entered the shop.

'Is Lord Yun unwell?' she asked

Yun Guang waved a casual hand, as though making light of her question.

'A little,' he muttered. 'At least, I believe so. I found him in the tower room. It seems some loud knocking had disturbed him and he thought the enemy had come to take him back. . . but let us not mention it. Shih will know what medicine to give.'

'Forgive me,' said Lu Ying, 'but Lord Yun often finds places where he can be concealed. There is a demon, or perhaps person, called Bayke. . .'

She let the name dangle. Guang shot her a quick glance.

'Quite so. His fear is. . . a distressing sight.'

She detected the possibility of tears in his voice. This seemed so very far from proper for Captain Xiao that she hastened to divert them.

'Commander Yun Guang,' she found herself saying. 'I have a request for you.' Then she hesitated, caught in a bird's nest of tangled vanities. 'Please read this letter for me,' she said in a quiet voice. She could tell he was surprised. 'You see,' she said. 'I read less well than I would like, which is to say, hardly at all.'

It was difficult to interpret his grave silence. No doubt he viewed her as deficient, an imbecile. Her face coloured with conflicting emotions. Yet to her surprise he bowed.

'You honour me with your confidence,' he said. 'You will be interested to learn that Lord Yun himself is an indifferent reader of characters. In fact he can barely read. So you see, gentlemen of noble birth share the weakness for which you reproach yourself. And they are men, while you are only a woman.'

Lu Ying nodded gratefully. 'I am indeed a woman,' she conceded. His glances at her person showed he saw it only too clearly, so that Lu Ying's blush deepened further, though now her discomfort felt oddly like pleasure.

He held out his hand for the letter.

'It is. . . from His Excellency Wang Ting-bo,' she said. She watched him read, noting Guang's sensitive brown eyes were better suited to a scholar than a mere soldier.

'It is from the Chief Steward of Wang Ting-bo's household,' he said. 'Firstly, he would have you know that His Excellency commends himself to you and that he has decided to increase the rations of grain and other food to be sent each week for your use. There is another message. The steward says that His Excellency orders him to pass on the following words: *Rivers and mountains are more easily changed than a man's nature.* He adds: "His Excellency advises the Lady Lu Ying to maintain her portmanteaux and boxes in readiness." After that comes a list of the extra supplies you will receive.'

Guang folded the stiff sheet and handed it back. Lu Ying trembled as she gripped the paper.

'I shall return to my chamber,' she said, faintly. 'You were kind to help me, very kind.'

As she opened the door to the inner corridor his deep voice halted her: 'Wait, please!'

Without turning, she paused in the doorway, so that he spoke to the back of her head and the layered mound of glossy black hair held in place by a silver pins.

'Let me say, as one who wishes you well, that His Excellency's words can be read in more than one way.'

Lu Ying did not know how to reply, so she glanced back at his handsome, concerned face, and bowed as she closed the door behind her. The tone of his voice echoed long after the exact meaning of his words faded.

That had been days ago. Strangely, perilously, handsome Commander Yun Guang occupied her speculations almost as much as the implied promise in Wang Ting-bo's message. As she laboured with her hoe, Lu Ying wondered what Captain Xiao would think if he spied her from the ramparts during an inspection or patrol. Such a prospect was mortifying, yet part of her – a secret, scarcely acknowledged part – desired it.

Towards noon Lan Tien screamed, throwing down her spade. All eyes followed her shaking finger. A swollen body had floated onto the muddy shore. The women regarded it in silence. Then an eddy of the current freed the corpse, so that it drifted downstream. For a long moment no one spoke.

'A bad omen,' said Madam Cao. 'We should attempt no more today or our herbs will be unlucky.'

It was also time to prepare the men's dinner. They trailed wearily back to Apricot Corner Court and more work round the communal cooking fire.

Lu Ying soon fell behind. For every two steps of the others, she took one. This time she did not fear getting lost. Water Basin Ward was becoming familiar, its features no longer menacing. Few noticed Lu Ying in her plain clothes, her hat concealing the beauty of her face, and those who did assumed the outward denoted the inward, that she was a simple woman engaged in common labours. Any who idly wondered at her lotus feet concluded she was a singing-girl without a place, or a fine lady impoverished by widowhood or misfortune. This respite allowed Lu Ying to observe a curious sight when she reached the Water Basin.

A palanquin of moderate splendour stood in the street. She shrank back, recognising its occupant at once. His expressionless face and small, slowly blinking eyes filled her with distaste. Dr Du Mau had attended her often in the palace, once for ill-health, but more usually because Wang Ting-bo sought to assess her receptiveness for child-bearing. Lu Ying had frequently bribed the good doctor to ensure favourable reports. If he saw her dressed like a labourer, word would fly to the Governor's wife. Then all hope of restoration must wither.

Lu Ying shrank against a mud-wall, her face hidden by the broad peasant woman's hat.

But Dr Du Mau had no leisure to examine the street. He was absorbed by a conversation – and that was the curious thing. For the most senior physician in the Twin Cities was leaning down and addressing a kneeling figure. Of all the people in the world, the illustrious Du Mau had deigned to notice Dr Shih's apprentice, Chung.

At first Lu Ying could not quite believe it. Yet it certainly was Chung. He spoke and gazed eagerly up at the palanquin, pressing his forehead into the muddy street. Whatever the young man said, it made Dr Du Mau smile faintly. A smile one might not call kind or mirthful. He motioned to his bearers and with a tinkle of bells they departed, leaving Chung in a position of profound abasement. When the bells faded he rose, brushing dirt from his knees. The apprentice looked round warily. Lu Ying kept her face hidden. He gave no sign of noticing her and hurried towards the North Medical Relief Bureau, shoulders hunched.

As she approached Apricot Corner Court, Lu Ying found Madam Cao waiting for her at the gatehouse. The older woman clicked her tongue sympathetically.

'I was beginning to worry you were lost. You must stay with us when we go out. It is not safe to be alone on the streets.'

Lu Ying's silence was her reply.

'I have left food in your room,' said Cao, timidly. 'You have certainly earned it.'

'Madam Cao, where shall I put this hoe?'

'I shall take it.'

Lu Ying was trembling from the morning's exertion. For a moment she considered telling Cao what she had seen. After all, Chung's strange behaviour hardly boded well for Dr Shih. Everyone knew Du Mau hated him for healing the Pacification Commissioner's son. She vaguely remembered hating him for the same reason herself.

'Where may I wash?' she asked.

Cao shrugged.

'In your room, I suppose.'

'But. . .'

Lu Ying stopped herself. Asking her hostess to fetch the water could hardly help her position in the house. She noticed movement in the tower room above where they talked. Apricot Corner Court was as bad as Wang Ting-bo's mansion for eavesdroppers. A silhouette was revealed momentarily. Lord Yun, no doubt spying on the girls in Ping's Floating Oriole Hall across the canal.

She filled a large bucket and hobbled back to her room, spilling half on the way. There she stripped and slowly washed herself with what little soap she still possessed. It smelt of mint and peas. The cool water made her gasp for pleasure. Then Lu Ying noticed her closed curtain stirring. It could not be attributed to the wind. In a moment, she had covered herself with a thin shift. Her eyes glittered angrily and she hurried over, hauling up the bamboo curtain with swift jerks. She was just in time to see the retreating back of Dr Shih's father, who had been loitering in the narrow strip of land between the canal and the back wall of Apricot Corner Court.

'Lord Yun!' she spluttered. 'How can this be? To find you outside my window!'

The old man struggled for something to say. As ever, she marvelled at the nobility of his features. Even in age, he was an epitome of *yang*. It was a shame neither son had inherited such exquisite looks. In his youth he must have been formidable indeed.

'You mistake the situation,' he said, gravely.

Lu Ying put her hands on her hips.

'I fear that I do not!'

'Ah, my dear,' he said, shaking his head, but looking round as though afraid of spies. 'If only you knew how I contrive matters to your advantage.'

This made her hesitate.

'In what way, sir?'

Lord Yun chuckled, his eyes flicking over the wet shift so that Lu Ying uneasily covered her jade mountains with folded arms.

'If I were to have my way – and I always have my way – there shall be a new mistress in this hovel. Then I will expect my reward.'

Lu Ying watched in surprise as Lord Yun disappeared through the side door into the house, evidently pleased with himself. His tone and words had been surprisingly balanced. Then again, Lu Ying seemed to recollect Madam Cao remarking that his madness could wax and wane a dozen times within a single hour. Perhaps he was not really mad at all and would somehow help her. She let the curtain fall in case any of the singing girls from Ping's establishment were watching and stood for a while in silence.

All that afternoon she slumbered on her divan, speculating even in her dreams about the old man's meaning, Guang's unexpected kindness, and Wang Ting-bo's letter.

竹子

Madam Cao was quite as weary as her unwanted guest. Clearing ground by the river had unearthed a doubt. Her father would have blushed to see his only child scrabbling among roots, spade in hand. But desperate times breed change. Though Shih had initially opposed her intention to venture beyond the ramparts, calling it unfit work for his wife, as well as dangerous, she had held firm. Concern for the wounded finally won him over, as she knew it would. Besides, if His Honour the Sub-prefect inspected Apricot Corner Court again, Shih could cite the women's labours for the common good as proof of their loyalty. And the Mongols were hardly likely to fall upon the Water Gate of Morning Radiance without being detected.

Cao sighed, examining blistered hands. When her fingers grew hard with calluses, would Shih find her attractive? As it was, he scarcely noticed her. Yet everything she did was for his sake.

She added an extra pinch of precious, soothing leaves to her pot and stirred. Of course he would be grateful if the medicine jars were replenished. A doctor's prosperity and reputation depended on cures. Yet all she really desired were warm glances.

When the tea had done its work, Cao wandered across the courtyard to visit Widow Mu. She found her chiding Lan Tien.

'Did I not tell you to gather herbs from the ground beside the canal? Is that all you could find?'

Lan Tien pouted sulkily.

'People were there before me!'

'My daughter is disobedient,' said Widow Mu, appealing to her visitor.

Cao took the offered seat.

'I'm sure Lan Tien did her best,' she said, tentatively. 'Everyone is after herbs to add to their rice. One cannot survive on grain alone, however generous the rations from the Prefecture may be.'

Widow Mu subsided and turned to her daughter: 'Madam Cao is soft-hearted. Go and play with the other children.'

Unexpectedly, Lan Tien stood firm. She hugged her arms, torn between defiance and habits of deference to her mother's whims.

'I am not a child anymore!'

'Oh, but you are!'

For a moment the argument hung in the balance. Then Lan Tien bowed and left for the apricot tree where her brother was playing ball.

'I despair of that girl,' said Mu, heavily. 'Her breasts grow a little and she calls herself a woman. Yet I remember when she could not walk.'

Cao listened silently. She had little to say about raising children. Instead she offered a saucer of leaves for Mu to brew.

'I could not help smiling today,' said the Widow. 'Seeing

your guest fanning herself with a hoe instead of silk and gauze.'

'It brought me no pleasure.'

Cao wondered for the hundredth time whether her motives had been pure when she insisted Lu Ying join the other women. Yet no one else in Apricot Corner Court was exempt from labour except Lord Yun, and that was solely due to his noble title. One would expect a healthy girl like Lu Ying to earn her share. Even the mistress of the house did as much.

'Still, I smiled,' said Widow Mu.

The two women bent over their steaming cups.

'I noticed Lord Yun bowing to your Honoured Guest the other day,' remarked Mu.

Cao licked a shred of leaf from her lip.

'Her presence seems to please him,' added Widow Mu, dryly. 'Lord Yun has a sharp eye. He likes to notice what there is to see.'

'My husband's father is a most observant gentleman. It is a shame his health is impaired. Often he misunderstands the things he sees.'

Widow Mu smiled.

'For one so venerable, he seems to have plenty of faith in his own *yang*.'

'A misplaced faith, I fear, at his age.'

'Well, he's a man like any other.'

Cao resisted the urge to share a confidence. Bad enough that her mad father-in-law should be so set against her, without circulating details amongst the neighbours.

'Poor man!' she sighed. 'His losses have been great.'

For a while they discussed herbs on the riverbank then Cao returned home, troubled by the conversation.

In the shop she found no respite. Chung stood with one hand resting on the counter, staring into space. His eyes, as he glanced up, were bright.

'I hoped to find you here,' he said. 'Master wanted to send me back from the Relief Bureau. He said I deserve a rest. But Dr Du Tun-i wanted me to clean his bureau and I would have done, only I was tired, so I stole away when Dr Du Tun-i was not looking.'

Cao wondered at the defiance in his voice. She stepped behind the counter so it lay between them.

'Is Dr Shih also tired?' she asked. 'He has been at the Relief Bureau for nearly a whole day now.'

Chung yawned and Cao sensed he was on the verge of something.

'I received a message today,' he said, dully. 'From the Prefecture. It seems I am to be spared the militia because of my trade. They say I must report to the Bureau of Righteous Fire. I have been ordered to make poison bombs for flinging at the enemy.'

'Then your wish has been granted!' she exclaimed.

His plump face quivered.

'Do you really not know this is worse? Dr Liang's apprentice was ordered there and died of arsenic poisoning after his face turned green!'

'Nevertheless, it is not the militia,' she said. 'Perhaps Dr Liang's apprentice was careless.'

'But I heard from Dr Chu's apprentice that he toils from dawn until long after dusk – and he receives a single bowl of millet as pay! My friend's skin is quite withered from the lime and burning powder. I tell you, it is not for me. And I have been ordered to live in a dormitory with a hundred others. Dr Chu's apprentice says it is a vile place.'

Cao glanced sideways. She was too sincere a woman to pretend the news was not welcome. How could she be comfortable with someone who made her afraid?

'It will not be for long,' she said.

'It will not be at *all*!' he replied, flushing. Then he added with grave significance: 'Madam, I must tell you. . . what I said once before still applies.'

He waited for a reply. When she remained silent, he grew angry. 'Must I state it openly?' He hesitated, held back by a thousand kindnesses and gestures of affection.

The excited cries of Lan Tien and her brother as they played ball entered from the courtyard. Cao realised she was clutching the counter.

'It seems I must be plain,' he said, heavily. 'If I cannot continue as Dr Shih's apprentice then I must find another master. A master with influence, who can protect me.'

Had fear shaken his mind? What other doctor would be so forbearing as Shih? Who else would ignore Chung's lazy ways and half-learned lessons?

'Such a one might be hard to find,' she said, cautiously.

'Hah! Not so, Madam! You see, there are those who would offer me a position in return for. . . certain information.' Breath quickening, he rubbed his forehead. 'I do not want any of this! You know how I honour Dr Shih. You have been a mother to me. And he a father. But I love my life and making poison bombs will kill me as surely as it did Dr Liang's apprentice. Can you not urge Captain Xiao to intercede on my behalf? Then we shall live as we did before.'

Cao's head remained low.

'You refer to something I once confided in you,' she whispered. 'Thinking you a friend.'

Chung could not meet her eye.

'I do refer to the circumstances of your marriage,' he muttered. 'And I give you until this evening, Madam, because I have been ordered to report to the Bureau of Righteous Fire by sunset.'

The familiar shop blurred through tears.

'Very well, I shall ask Captain Xiao today,' she said, wiping her eyes. 'This afternoon I shall see him. Yes, I shall.'

Chung bowed and walked stiffly to his room. Yet she glimpsed a look of triumph on his once-dear face as he left. It frightened her more than his words.

竹子

Cao hurried towards Swallow Gate. Many noticed her sorrowful expression, but in that she was unremarkable.

Who did not grieve as they wandered through these days?

Uncertainty might be glimpsed in every corner of the Twin Cities. Public wells guarded day and night in case spies poisoned them. Splendid mansions empty, their noble occupants having gone over to the Great Khan. Silent markets and restaurants – who knew when they might re-open? Cherished sons walked out to take their turn on the ramparts and returned in wheelbarrows, head or limbs broken.

As she walked Cao endured a siege of her own. Wounded thoughts surrounded her. She and her husband had gazed on Chung's sleeping face when he was a boy, glancing at each other and smiling shyly. His smell had been of purest bean curd. They had saved him from the utmost poverty! How could he repay her with threats?

Most of all Cao feared Shih would never forgive her. Her stupidity had put everything in danger. He risked being revealed as the seducer of his master's daughter and might even be denounced as a thief. Cao did not care about her own reputation, but she knew that Shih, already so uncertain in himself, would wilt before the world's scorn. Then he might cast around for someone to punish. It would be natural.

If only she could make time rush backward and undo what she had done! But Shih might find a more realistic remedy. Assuming they were even married in the law's eyes, a most questionable thing, he had every justification for a divorce. Lord Yun's command to divorce her could be cited. It hovered above her head like raised bamboo – and it might even come to the bamboo stick for both of them if their false marriage reached the magistrate's attention.

Such thoughts hastened her steps until she approached Swallow Gate, Captain Xiao's customary station of command.

High battlements rose above the rooftops and Cao became aware she had chosen a poor moment to beg for help. Black dots arched through the sky between columns of smoke. Alarms and shouting could be heard ahead. A handcart containing sheaves of arrows trundled towards the ramparts and the porter looked at her in surprise.

'Hey, lady! Get away from here! Go home while you can!'

Cao pressed onwards. Chung had demanded an answer that very evening. If she perished, so much the better. His threats could not harm Shih then.

When she reached the cleared ground behind Swallow Gate, her courage faltered. A dozen catapult crews were hauling ropes, urged on by bellowing officers. Among them were many peasant women, wearing the same grimy clothes as their men. A house was on fire, filling the air with acrid smoke, and a human chain passed buckets from the nearby canal. Hundreds of armoured men crouched in the ramparts' shadow in case the Mongols broke through. As Cao watched, a rock descended lazily from the sky, crushing a man pulling a catapult rope. It happened quite suddenly. A crowd gathered round him and she caught a glimpse of his caved-in chest and sightless eyes. Then his body was dragged away.

She darted through the siege engines to Swallow Gate. There she met a familiar face, hurrying down the steps with a rolled-up order. The officer wore splendid lamellar armour and carried a Mongol bow. They stared at each other in surprise. She recognised him as Chen Song, her brother-in-law's dear friend. The man frowned.

'Madam! Are you not Yun Guang's sister-in-law?'

His question was drowned by roars from the catapult crews as they loosed a dozen missiles at the enemy.

'Sir, I must speak with him!'

'This is no place for you,' said the officer.

'I have news concerning Yun Guang's brother. Please take me to him.'

A ragged flight of burning arrows came back over the wall. By some miracle they struck only earth.

'The news is urgent?'

'It is.'

He hesitated, then sighed.

'I will lead you to him, but whether he will speak with you, I cannot say.'

She followed him up the steep steps until they reached the middle parapet of Swallow Gate. Chen Song waved her to a sheltered embrasure from which she could survey the battlefield through a slit and summoned over an orderly.

'Inform Captain Xiao his Honoured Sister-in-law is here. She carries an urgent message.'

Then he bowed to Cao.

'I forbid you to go further,' he said. 'Wait here until Commander Yun Guang summons you. You should be safe.'

He vanished the way they had come, his horseman's boots clattering. Cao was left alone, fearfully looking out.

Though she did not know it, the unfolding battle was a pinprick compared to General A-ku's previous assaults. One might wonder what the Mongols hoped to achieve by it.

A thousand foot soldiers had deployed in the open ground before the ramparts and moats. Tall shields on wheels, known as wooden donkeys or goose wagons, protected many from the defenders' arrows and crossbow bolts. Less fortunate warriors lay face down on the muddy earth. Cao's eye was drawn to a high wooden tower on wheels, decorated with defiant characters and carved dragon heads. Slaves pushed and dragged it across the churned earth before Swallow Gate. On its topmost parapet observers waved coloured flags to direct the Mongol catapults, for the movable tower allowed a clear view of the city below. Certainly their aim was accurate. As Cao watched, a boulder struck one of the giant crossbows on a nearby turret, splintering the weapon and scattering its crew.

Then Cao noticed Guang on the highest parapet of Swallow Gate.

He stood in full view, with only a low rail between him and the attacking horde. He seemed more statue than man, full-chested in his bulky armour, leaning on a halberd decorated with a vermilion pennant. Standard bearers crouched around him, each carrying a collection of signal flags. Guang stepped aside to address a lieutenant and a boulder fell where he had been standing a moment before. It bounced and hit a standard bearer with a heavy crump. His scream tore the air. Guang's flinch was momentary. A clamour rose from those around him.

'Captain Xiao! You must move! They have your range.'

To Cao's astonishment, Guang climbed stiffly onto a footstool, making himself even more exposed. His reply came in the form of a defiant taunt, so loud all the defenders of Swallow Gate heard him clearly.

'That would not be proper. If I move, the hearts of my men will move as well!'

All eyes were upon Captain Xiao. A wild cheer spread from rampart to rampart as his words passed from man to man. If courage is a spell its magic worked. Guang ordered a flutter of pink flags and boulders rose from the city, curving down, down, until by some miracle one struck the mobile tower's parapet, quite destroying it. Men and signal flags tumbled to the earth fifty feet below. Another boulder struck the base of the wobbling tower, breaking a huge wooden wheel. Suddenly the movable castle toppled, slowly at first, then rushing towards the earth. It fell with a crash. Hundreds of slaves fled for their lives. One by one the Mongol companies retreated back to the safety of their camp, dragging goose wagons and wooden donkeys stubbled with arrows.

Soon the battlefield was silent, except for the pleas and cries of the wounded. Guang stood upright as before, ignoring the delight around him. He seemed duty's expressionless creature, barely a man at all. His shoulders sagged briefly then stiffened again. Turning, he pushed past bowing subordinates to the stairs. There he encountered Madam Cao, peeping out like a child from her embrasure in the parapet.

His harsh face melted in astonishment. Stepping forward swiftly, he gripped her arm with a gauntleted hand. Cao winced, but did not wish him to let go.

'Sister-in-law! What madness is this?' he whispered.

'Forgive me, I had to see you. . .'

'They are targeting me! It is not safe to be near me on the ramparts. General A-ku has declared a reward for any who brings me down.'

He looked around, waving aside his orderlies so they could speak unheard.

'Is Shih in danger? Or Father? Is that why you have come?'

She could not match this flustered, anxious man with the ineffable figure who stood unmoved while boulders fell around him. Then Cao realised how unseemly it would be to mention Chung. How shameful after all the sacrifices she had witnessed. He let go of her arm and she noticed his hands were unsteady, that he squeezed them together to hide his weakness.

'Brother-in-law,' she said. 'I know it was wrong to come here. I wished you to know that they have demoted Shih. One of Dr Du Mau's relatives holds his position in the Relief Bureau.'

He blinked, struggling to comprehend her words, as though the world beyond Swallow Gate was somehow unreal.

'Demote. That is bad. I'll speak to Chen Song about it. Enquiries. Yes, he must make enquiries for me. . . Why didn't Youngest Brother tell me himself? Could you not send a message?'

He looked at her suspiciously.

'Shih does not know you are here, does he?'

Cao shook her head like a naughty girl.

'I thought. . . Oh, forgive me, Guang! Do not tell him I came! I know he is too proud to ask for your help so I came myself. I did not understand how dangerous it would be.'

'Leave us!' Captain Xiao commanded an underling with the temerity to approach. 'These are family matters, damn you!'

He turned back to her.

'Please do not tell him,' she repeated.

Guang sighed, rubbing eyes circled by shadow.

'Very well, I will not. And I shall do what I can to help him. But I must tell you in confidence, Sister-in-law, I will not be around to see the matter through.'

'You are leaving us?'

'My departure is a great secret, yet it is very imminent. The safety of the Twin Cities depends on our mission. I know you are always discreet. I shall be gone for a few months.'

She bowed her head.

'Do not be afraid!' he chuckled. 'These are matters a woman cannot comprehend. In any case, a little absence is good for me. You saw how close things came today.'

She nodded submissively.

'Go home now. I shall visit you in Apricot Corner Court before I go and pay my respects to Father.'

'You will not tell Shih that I came here?'

Again he frowned.

'Yes, though it is a fault in me. Nevertheless, I promised. Enough. Go home.'

He walked down the steps and mounted a fine horse tethered to Swallow Gate. Half a dozen cavalry waited as his escort. Their hooves clattered on flagstones, then they had gone. Cao ached inside as she walked through the exhausted catapult crews. Chung's face danced across her inward eye – and it was angry.

憺

eleven

'It is not without reason that Nancheng Province is known as 'the land of fish and rice'. Rivers and lakes in abundance fill the central plain. One may look West, North, East and see ranges of snow-capped mountains. When I was a young man I travelled through an endless bamboo forest unvisited by man. It lay several days walk from the Twin Cities and teemed with peculiar animals and birds. Yet its strangest denizen was a monk who had lived for two hundred and fifty-three years, sustained by a diet of sunbeams and dew. . .'

From *Dream Pool Essays* by Shen Kua

竹子

Apricot Corner Court, Nancheng. Spring, 1267.

Midnight had become a dull hour in Water Basin Ward since the curfew. The drifting crowds of revellers who once haunted its streets had vanished, replaced by patrols of Watchmen.

Shih sat in the tower room he used for preparing medicines, hands flat on his knees, eyes half-closed, mind fluttering between one place and the next. Though he had learned the *dao* of meditation from his orderly, Mung Po, it would not come. Peace would not come. Perhaps the former monk had taught him badly. But Shih seldom blamed others for his own failures and did not now.

An unpleasant farewell had driven him inwards. That dusk had seen Chung's departure for the barracks attached to the Bureau of Righteous Fire. His apprentice had been ordered to report there before the curfew bells tolled across the city. A melancholy parting. Cao had felt it, too, showing womanly frailty by hiding in their bedchamber until the lad had gone.

Chung's anger puzzled Dr Shih. As he stood in the doorway the youth's portly face showed many emotions, none friendly, as though he somehow blamed his master for the Prefecture's decision to conscript him.

'Well then,' Shih had said, hoping to lend a better heart. 'Remember you are always welcome here. A single life consists of many risings and goings to bed. Before you know it, the war will be over and then you may return to us. I still have much to teach you.'

He had expected gratitude. Implicit in his words was a promise. Despite the apprentice's manifold failings, his master was willing to indenture him. But Chung had scowled.

'So you thought it best to ignore Madam Cao's warning!' said the youth, bitterly. 'I won't forget it! A greater doctor than you shall indenture me. Then you'll be sorry.'

With that Chung carried his bag into the fading light and Shih had watched, lips parted to utter soothing words – though really he should be the angry one. Soon Chung would be sleeping in his new barracks, there was no changing that. Arguing with official decrees is like shaking a fist at the sun. Shih had wondered why his apprentice seemed to despise him, and self-doubt escaped its cage, so familiar and deep-rooted he could not reason with it.

Now Shih sat in the tower room, seeking meditation's temporary comfort. Once again he laid open palms across his knees as Mung Po had instructed. One must feel solidity beneath one's feet, connecting down, down through timber beams, down to the earth-truth. Yet his mind was full of monkey chatter. Questions. Half-answers. How could he evade thought? He imagined roots, thirsty for moisture, pointlessly railing at sandy soil for being dry. Was he such a plant? Only Cao understood his potential to bloom, his dear wife who he betrayed daily through lustful desires. Shih stirred uneasily, opening his eyes. Hurried footsteps were mounting the steep stairs to the tower room; then Cao's head bobbed through the hatch.

'Husband! Come quickly! Father has vanished!'

Shih reluctantly rose.

'What do you mean?'

'He is not in his room. I cannot find him anywhere.'

'Come now, he never goes far.'

'He is not to be found in Apricot Corner Court!'

Her eyes caught star-sheen from the open window. Shih followed her down the stairs and examined Father's chamber by candlelight. The wide bowl of circling fish formed a yellow moon on the floor.

Those without clan must depend on their neighbours. Shih went from doorway to doorway and soon the residents of Apricot Corner Court gathered round the tree, many still in nightclothes. Clouds and constellations patterned the sky.

'I humbly apologise for causing inconvenience,' said Shih, holding up a guttering lamp. His neighbours waited nervously.

'Lord Yun is missing,' he continued. 'You all know of his great infirmity. How could you not? It is of mind, not body. I beg you to help us search the ward. I am afraid he will come to harm.'

Old Hsu's youngest son stirred uneasily.

'What of the curfew?' he asked.

Shih had no answer to that. Then Cao was at his elbow.

'Husband, might not Captain Xiao's name reassure the watchmen?' she asked, quietly.

He was reluctant to rely, yet again, on the protection of his brother. Was he never to escape that shadow? Never become his own man?

The decision was taken out of his hands. Old Hsu took the lead, ordering his sons to explore Xue Alley while he searched nearby canal banks.

'I shall go to the Water Basin,' said Shih. 'Madam Cao must remain here to await news.'

One by one they vanished into the humid night. Only Widow Mu hesitated.

'Dr Shih,' she said. 'I could tell my son to look beneath the bridges, but I do not think Lord Yun is there.'

'Then where is he?'

Widow Mu bowed.

'You might find him across the canal.'

'Do you mean in the neighbouring ward?'

'I mean, sir, in Ping's Floating Oriole House.'

She averted her eyes from his frown.

'It's only that Lord Yun once mentioned the place to my daughter. No doubt I am wrong.'

Dr Shih's face was blank as he left Apricot Corner Court. He did not go to the Water Basin but crossed the humped canal bridge until he stood outside Ping's establishment. Despite the curfew, a red lantern dangled from the lintel. Within he could hear laughter and the lazy twang of a lute. A woman's voice wailed a song of betrayed love.

He rapped on the painted door. A wooden bolt scraped open and Ping's doorman appeared. Shrewd eyes read the mood of both caller and street. Without a word, he was ushered inside.

Shih entered a central courtyard wreathed with flowering creepers. A dim lantern burned in obedience to the curfew restrictions. A few customers, mostly local wastrels protected from conscription by family influence, were listening to the singing girl and drinking yeasty, home-brewed wine. The proprietor rose to greet him and the two bowed. Ping was a wiry fellow whose heavy-lidded eyes hid many passions. Shih had often attended to the health of his girls, but never trusted their master.

'Dr Shih! Most pleasant surprise, sir!'

'Alas, my business is not pleasant,' he replied stiffly. 'I seek the dearest relative a man may have. If he is here, you will understand my meaning.'

'Mysterious!' exclaimed Ping, smiling at his guests, who chuckled.

Shih felt himself redden.

'Then it seems I have disturbed you for no reason.'

The sound of giggling came from behind a screen, followed by a familiar laugh. Though it was unmannerly, Shih walked over and listened. He frowned at Ping's insolent expression.

'I have come to take him home,' he said. 'Perhaps your girls should now delight another customer.'

It was the brothel-keeper's turn to glower.

'I never disturb a guest,' he said. 'It's bad for business.'

Shih reluctantly removed his hand from the screen.

'Perhaps you will make an exception to your rule?'

Ping laughed hollowly and spread out his hands.

'You can see for yourself how my business flourishes! Before the curfew my rooms were full. Now I treasure every customer like jade. Why not let an old man have fun? When his *cash* is gone, you may take him home with my blessing.'

The other guests applauded their host's wit.

'My brother, Captain Xiao, will be displeased,' said Shih, quietly. 'Gravely displeased.'

Ping licked his lips.

'Ah! Captain Xiao is not a little doctor. He is a man one respects.'

Shih's blush deepened. Indeed, the brothel-keeper had aimed well. How swiftly he resorted to his brother's name! It had become almost a mannerism. Nevertheless, Shih slid open the door concealing his Father.

Within, Lord Yun lay on a divan, surrounded by three mirthful girls. The reason for their good humour – and Ping's annoyance at losing such a customer – was obvious. A varnished, maple *cash*-box lay on the table. Shih recognised it as belonging to himself.

One of the girls raised her head from Lord Yun's parted robe and Shih caught a glimpse of feeble ardour. He glanced away hurriedly, his legs suddenly weak. An image of the dark hall at Three-Step-House, of Aunt Qin pleading, made his heart clench unbearably. When he opened his eyes, the foul image lingered. Lord Yun's clothing had been hastily adjusted. The loathed reminder was out of sight.

Shih reached down for the *cash*-box. It was nearly empty. He scooped it up and held out a hand to Father. For a moment he thought Lord Yun would argue. But perhaps the old man also remembered that terrible afternoon, so long ago. Perhaps he was simply too drunk to resist. Shih gently pulled him to his feet.

Pausing only to check Lord Yun had his shoes on, he led him shuffling though the courtyard full of curious eyes. Ping's mouth opened mockingly until the doctor's expression cut him short. Bowing, he followed them to the entrance, murmuring a hope that Dr Shih's honoured father had enjoyed himself.

When they reached Apricot Corner Court, Shih slackened his pace. A platoon of Watchmen were approaching in the distance. Without a word he bundled Lord Yun inside and closed the heavy door.

'Do not speak!' he hissed.

Inside the shop they found Cao waiting. Shih wiped moist palms on his robes.

'Your behaviour is unseemly, Father,' he said. 'You waste our *cash* when what little we have is needed for food. Surely you are aware that the stipend we receive from Wang Ting-bo scarcely feeds Lu Ying, let alone us. We have nothing to spare! Then you blatantly defy the curfew. Even now our neighbours are searching Water Basin Ward, at risk to themselves, for we feared you were in danger. And to visit a haunt of criminals! It diminishes us all.'

If he expected remorse, the old man's bloodshot glare taught him better. 'Hah!' jeered Lord Yun. 'Where is Guang? Where is my only son?'

'I am also your son,' said Shih, icily.

Then, provoked beyond endurance, he emptied his heart as an archer will fire frantically until his quiver is bare.

'I am your firstborn! I am the true heir to Wei Valley and Three-Step-House! Do not talk to me of *only* sons! This game of not remembering will stop, Father! It will stop now!'

Lord Yun laughed scornfully but Shih detected a flicker of unease.

'I will not listen to Bayke's lies, *Doctor*! You shame my ancestors by pretending to be my son. If you were a man you would be fighting Khan Bayke! You would avenge our ancestors. You cannot be my son.'

Shih's expression was strange throughout this tirade. Yet his hands were busy, preparing an infusion from a jar hidden in a secret drawer beneath the counter.

'If you were my son,' continued Lord Yun. 'You would have possessed your concubine! I'll do it for you. And I always get my way.'

Shih spooned more herbs into the cup. Then he hesitated. Was it too much? One had to be careful. But he must silence that vile, taunting voice. He dipped the spoon and stirred the infusion. While he worked, his eyes did not stray from Lord Yun's angry face. He could sense the demons inside the man were weakening.

'I am your firstborn son,' he repeated. 'Father, you are full of odious deceit!'

Cao shrieked in distress, covering her face. To abuse one's father was to defy the law. A strange sense of power filled Shih. With it came cruelty.

'Do you remember Aunt Qin?' he asked. 'I sensed it in you earlier. Both of us shared the same thought. Oh, you remember her very well! And that afternoon in the monsoon when I found you with her.'

Lord Yun bristled as a child will, his old eyes filling with tears. He hovered between bluster and defiance.

'Swallow this,' ordered Shih.

He held a porcelain cup chased with blue dragons to his father's lips. The old man gulped, once, twice, then stood panting in the dark shop. Cao moaned.

'Lead Father to bed, wife,' said Shih. 'I've had enough of him.'

Already the thin figure was drooping and it required both of them to help him to his chamber.

Shih stood for a while by the door, candle in hand, watching the dark shapes of the circling fish and listening to the pattern of Lord Yun's breathing. Then he closed the door and went wearily to the seat beneath the apricot tree. One by one he greeted the returning searchers, assuring them Lord Yun was quite safe, and that his whole family were in their debt.

Old Hsu came back last of all. The fan-maker grunted when Shih told his news and mentioned Ping's establishment.

'There's no fool like an old fool,' he replied. 'At my age you hope people forgive you for it.'

Shih watched him enter his house. The first rays of dawn made the rooftops glow.

The next day Dr Shih awoke to dread. Surely punishment must follow his unfilial conduct. But when, after a tentative knock, he entered the old man's room, he found Lord Yun in good humour. Small birds twittered in the eaves outside. A warm breeze wafted water smells from the canal through the open window. Shih bowed awkwardly.

'I take it Honoured Father has rested?'

Lord Yun looked up from combing his straggly hair.

'No thanks to you. But I had a strange dream.' He smiled a secret smile. 'A very sweet dream indeed.'

Shih's eyebrows raised. Could Father have so soon forgotten Ping's brothel? Perhaps the medicine he had drunk possessed deep powers. A single dose of the infusion – one familiar to all learned doctors but seldom deployed for fear of unexpected consequences – seemed to remove unwelcome recollections as a broom sweeps away ash. Shih politely withdrew, reluctant to rake the embers of last night's quarrel.

All day this strange circumstance tinctured his thoughts. Dangerous knowledge is not easily forgotten. Amazing the old man could be so easily tamed! A simple draught, regularly ingested, might restore peace to his household. And he knew enough herbalists to ensure a plentiful supply. Except Shih doubted the virtue of such a remedy. Was he, the son, to reduce the parent to a state of childhood? The consequences for Father's essential breaths were also doubtful. His clutch on sanity, already insecure, might weaken further. Certainly Lord Yun would develop cravings for larger doses, until he begged his son in a plaintive voice for just a little more of the herb, always a little more, in return for being good.

The possibility of such power – or revenge – attracted Shih in an unwholesome way. He retreated to the tower room, anxious to hide his feelings in clouds of meditation. Yet a hot sun peeps through any cloud.

竹子

A week passed. One twilight Dr Shih left the gatehouse of Apricot Corner Court, a full bag on his shoulder. Lately his duties at the Relief Bureau had dwindled almost to nothing. As summer rains dampened General A-ku's tactics so the stream of wounded shrank to a trickle. More importantly, Dr Du Tun-i had tightened his hold on the Relief Bureau, finding little for Shih to do. As Mung Po remarked, meaning to be kind, the new wave breaking on the shore washes away its predecessor's foam.

At first Shih had struggled to maintain his former position until the futility of his efforts became obvious. Besides, there was no denying Dr Tun-i possessed virtues. A plentiful supply of medicine flowed from his influential uncle; and the younger man displayed a talent for administration notably lacking in Shih. Never before had the North Medical Relief Bureau's ledgers appeared so correct – even when funds floated across the river to the Du family mansion in Fouzhou.

Mung Po complained that the new supervisor rarely took a patient's pulse in the course of a whole day. But Shih could not guide Dr Tun-i's hand to a suffering wrist. He could not place needles before the young man and advise where they might do good. He could only accept that all he had built now belonged to another and console himself with the thought that surrendering desire brought one closer to Emptiness.

There were more immediate benefits. The exhaustion he had once accepted as a natural fog, dulling every waking moment, lifted. For the first time since the start of the siege, he resumed his round of private patients.

Stepping out of Apricot Corner Court that dusk, bag on shoulder, Dr Shih felt strangely free, just as when he first arrived in Nancheng afire with youth and hope. Swifts and bats flickered between rooftops; the comforting silhouette of Wadung Mountain seemed to smile upon him.

He glanced back at the shop doorway. Cao was reaching up to wipe the lintel and he returned her wave. For the first time in many months, or at least since Lu Ying joined their household, he noticed her curves and grew confused.

Strange to think of her as a woman after so long a gap between embraces. It made him uneasy. How could he approach her naturally? Maybe she no longer cared for him and would turn to the wall in disgust.

Dr Shih's first patient lived beyond Xue Alley near the Water Basin. As he entered that long, twisting street heads were poking out of tenement windows to summon children. For their part, the children pretended not to hear, stealing one last game before the curfew forced them indoors. Shih half-expected Carpenter Xue to hurry out and demand a consultation, but instead he was detained by a different voice.

Somewhere a woman was singing an ancient, wistful tune. The melody reached down to him from an open window and Shih listened, his heart full of contradictory feelings:

A handsome gentleman
Waited by the gate:
How very sad I did not accompany him!
For him I wear my unlined skirt,
My skirt of brightest silk.
Oh, sir, gracious lord,
Give me a place in your coach!'

Shih realised tears were filling his eyes. Did he think of his dear mother buried far to the West and the coach that had so cruelly taken him away from her? Or was it his last glimpse of Cao as he left Apricot Corner Court? The knowledge their treasured closeness, that had once seemed as immutable as the sun, had faded with youth? He could not say. The old tune seemed a premonition of some nameless, future grief.

Then Lu Ying stole like a fluttering shadow across the image of his wife. Shih's heart quickened. Surely that nonsense was over! He did not respect the girl. She was ignorant and foolish. His only concern was her welfare. Yet Father sneered at him for not having possessed her. Why must he think of her so often?

A loud neighing startled Shih from these questions and he looked up in surprise at a warhorse blocking his path. Features almost identical to his own gazed down from a saddle decorated with silver and red tassels.

'Sister-in-law told me I'd find you here,' said Guang, dismounting nimbly.

The brothers examined each other in the fading light.

'Come with me to Peacock Hill,' said Guang. 'I've ordered a banquet for us both.'

There was a note of entreaty in his voice.

'What of Cao?' asked Shih. 'She will worry if I do not return.'

'I've sent a message not to expect you. Here, climb up behind me! Remember how we would ride Father's horse round the plum orchard above Three-Step-House? Only then you were the one in front. Do you remember how I clutched you?'

Shih laughed nervously.

'I've grown more accustomed to walking since then,' he said.

He finally agreed and Guang hauled him up, fastening his doctor's bag to the pommel. They trotted through streets full of people hurrying to evade the curfew. Some looked up in surprise at the twin brothers, one in painted armour, the other wearing a humble doctor's blue robes and grey hat

At last they cantered through the gatehouse at the foot of Peacock Hill and Guang slowed the horse. He led Shih to a small, ornate pavilion with an upward-curving tiled roof. A servant hurried out to take the reins.

Two hours later they had drunk a dozen toasts to Wang Tingbo, Wang Bai, the brave General Zheng Shun and Admiral Qi-Qi, even the Son of Heaven himself. They had dined so finely Shih almost forgot there was a siege. Wild duck dipped in sweetened vinegar. Kidneys in a sauce of bitter fruit. His head span from the wine. He said the first thing swirling among the fumes in his brain: 'Guang, what is the cause of this? I hardly hear from you in months, though we live only a few *li* apart. Then this!'

Guang shook his head ruefully.

'I have been at fault,' he said. 'It is an elder brother's duty to guide you. But I have been too busy killing Mongols! You must forgive me.'

They laughed and Shih glanced round the splendid hall. Carved friezes of noble banquets lined one wall. On another hung paintings and delicate calligraphy. Such fine things were quite beyond his means, though he brought people life not death.

'Besides, I needed to see you for a reason,' continued Guang. 'I have been honoured, Little Brother! I am to accompany

Prefect Wang Bai to the capital on a secret embassy. The fate of the Twin Cities may depend on it.'

Shih poured himself another bowl of wine, emptying it in two gulps.

'You are to leave us?'

'For a few months at most. We will travel overland through the siege lines, using a secret route, then join a waiting flotilla a hundred *li* further downstream. I shall return in the autumn at the head of a great force. One that shall drive the barbarians back to the borders. Then Three-Step-House and Wei Valley shall be restored to us.'

'Wei Valley,' said Shih, dully. 'I think of it sometimes. I suspect even Father no longer believes it will be ours again. . .'

Shih placed his bowl on the lacquered table. A change of mood made his heavy eyelids blink.

'Guang, when was the last time you visited Father?' he asked.

'Tonight, of course! Father was asleep so I could not speak to him. A great pity. Cao told me he had taken his medicine and would not wake until morning.'

'Why not before tonight?'

Guang blinked in surprise.

'My duties. . . I did visit him once when you and Cao were not at home. He was hiding in the tower room. How fearful of Bayke he has grown! I fear his sanity has worsened. Thank goodness he has your medicines to help him.'

'He pours scorn on us everyday!' broke in Shih. 'He abuses my manhood. I tell you he is unmanageable without your influence!'

'You should not speak of Honoured Father in that way!'

Shih laughed harshly.

'The Honoured Father *you* neglect! Since you abandoned Father at my gate, you have visited him fewer times than I have fingers! What of me, who you also neglect? Don't criticise me, Yun Guang! Day and night I strive to please everyone.' He gestured wildly. 'Everyone but myself!'

'Little Brother! You are drunk. Your words are not proper.'

Shih chuckled as he poured and swallowed another cup. It burned his throat. He felt giddy, intoxicated by something headier than wine.

'No,' he said. '*You* are not proper, Captain Xiao! What is filial piety if not patience and respect? What reason have I for that? Don't you remember how Father discarded me? How he abandoned me? Have you really forgotten?'

'Little Brother!'

'Now I will laugh! Truly I will! You still call me by that name! But you know it is a lie. I am not *Little Brother,* that name belongs to you.'

The two stared at each other, appalled. Guang's hands were trembling as he held his half-empty cup. At last Shih looked away uneasily.

'I am not afraid of the truth,' he muttered.

He stared into a corner of the room. The storm that had billowed so unexpectedly died away, revealing hollowness: 'I'm sick of this life! Sick in my being!' he cried. 'Whatever stern words you use can't change that.'

Shih laughed again, his drunken eyes blinking furiously. Anyone seeing him would not have recognised this wild, bitter man as the kindly doctor from Apricot Corner Court, who did so much good for the scantest of rewards. Yet one self flowed from and through the other.

'My heart is empty, Guang!' he cried. 'That is why I am never at ease. Even with my dear Cao I am never wholly at ease! When Father sent me away he drained my heart. . . Oh, what does it matter? We both know the truth.'

Guang's tongue showed between his lips, as when a little child displays fear.

'You must not speak ill of Father,' he said. 'I will not allow it.'

Shih steadied himself in his chair. It seemed for a moment he might fall to the floor.

'You are drunk,' continued Guang. 'That is why you speak such nonsense.'

'Yes, I am drunk.'

'I will pretend I did not hear.'

Shih nodded. 'Yes, let us pretend.'

'I shall instruct some of my servants to escort you home.'

'Very well.'

Guang hesitated before calling his men.

'Listen, Shih, I must leave in an hour's time. I hoped we would embrace and laugh as friends do, as dearest brothers do! But please, look after Father in my absence. Can I trust you to protect him?'

Shih nodded sadly.

'I'm good for that,' he said.

But a strange glint in Shih's eyes made Guang hesitate before he said: 'I know you are.'

'Then you know me better than myself.'

They parted stiffly. The night became a floating world of lanterns on poles and tramping feet. Shih shivered inwardly. Guang would never forgive him for speaking aloud their family's shameful secret. One was only permitted to brood over such things, year after year, until the spirit wearied of itself.

He sobered a little as Apricot Corner Court came into view. Despite the late hour a carriage waited on the street. Several soldiers of the City Watch stood guard.

The curtains of the carriage lifted as Shih approached, revealing Dr Fung's anxious face. He had not seen him since the day Dr Du Mau ordered an inspection of the Relief Bureau.

'Dr Shih!' called out Fung in his soft, fluttering voice. 'I have been sent by Dr Du Mau who has instructed me, in his capacity as head of the guild. . . Why, I beg you to come closer to the carriage.'

Shih noticed Cao's frightened face looking through the shop window. He felt an impulse to rush back to Guang and implore his protection, but it was too late for that.

Dr Fung held open the carriage door and Shih peered unsteadily into the dark box, his nostrils detecting an acrid odour. Then he recognised Dr Fung's companion and understood at once what such a presence meant. How the journey from old Dr Ou-yang's medicine shop in the capital had always been destined to end this way, that *karma* was remorseless. The alcohol and rich food in Shih's stomach churned; for a moment he struggled against nausea. Suddenly harsh hands were dragging him away and he vomited over his own clothes.

憺

twelve

'Lesson 24. The Capital! Centre of the Five Directions! On one side lies the West Lake, startlingly clear, and on the other a broad river rich and cloudy with sediment! (*Yang* lake, *yin* river). Canals pattern the districts into lattices of dense, tall wooden houses. One can traverse the city by means of these canals quite as quickly as by the roads. (*Water element*: canal; *Earth element*; road). All the natural laws are followed where the Son of Heaven dwells!'

From an untitled woodcut primer, intended for students studying the First Examination.

竹子

Linan, Eastern China. Summer, 1267

Guang approached the capital on a paddle-driven destroyer. They had made swift progress from the Yangtze, following the Grand Canal south. The coolies cranked the paddle shafts under the watchful eye of their overseer. The Wang family banner of three yellow chrysanthemums flew from prow and stern. No one recognised it as a noble symbol. Indeed, one wastrel, leering down from the balustrade of a high curved bridge, had enquired whether they belonged to the 'Chrysanthemum Brigade', meaning prostitutes trained to sing 'southern style'. Guang had to be restrained by Chen Song from leaping ashore to administer a beating.

At last, after weeks on the river, their flotilla entered the outer suburbs of Linan, the Empire's capital, seat of Heaven's Chosen Son, and Guang had succumbed to awe. Though he had visited many great cities nothing had prepared him for Linan's sheer scale. The outer walls stretched for *li* after *li*. High houses and low, warehouses and grand markets, people scurrying after ten thousand kinds of reward. Guang's attention was drawn to the military encampments they passed. It seemed most of His Highness's army had gathered round the capital though the Mongols were attacking far to the north west. The soldiers looked listless, reduced by boredom to ill-discipline.

'Sir,' he said, seeking out Wang Bai, who lolled in state on a high-backed chair beneath a splendid silk awning. 'How is it so many regiments are here?'

Wang Bai's smooth face flickered with a darker emotion.

'It is a question my noble uncle has raised in several memoranda to His Majesty.'

Guang waited for more but Wang Bai waved him away and resumed his steady, watchful brooding. He joined Chen Song at the prow. The scholar-soldier seemed inspired by the bustle and prosperity all around them.

'Here one may glimpse why we gladly suffer at the front,' remarked Chen Song. 'These scenes of order and peace confirm His Highness enjoys the Mandate of Heaven.'

'Many defectors to the Great Khan disagree,' replied Guang, quite as formally. 'They ask, how may one explain our reverses on the frontier? Or the loss of our ancestral lands?'

Chen Song shook his head.

'Such turncoats are vile traitors.'

'As for me,' continued Guang. 'I believe these prosperous people you admire have no idea how we suffer on their behalf. I doubt one in a hundred cares that the Twin Cities are besieged.'

He recollected the strange fear and nervousness that had gripped him in their first days away from Nancheng. No longer feeling trapped and surrounded by a pitiless enemy had a contradictory effect. Instead of release, he felt anxiety.

'I cannot believe that,' said Chen Song. 'Nancheng and Fouzhou are the dams preventing the enemy from releasing a flood that would drown our Empire.'

'You are eloquent,' said Guang.

At noon the Grand Canal came to an end, depositing their small convoy on the long wharf of Linan's famous West Lake. Crowds of merchants and longshoremen, beggars and idlers, went about their business. Now it was Guang's turn to feel inspired. The West Lake featured in many of Great-grandfather Yun Cai's most popular and enduring poems. For a moment the old longing to be a poet like his noble ancestor caught him on its rusty hook. He was released by Wang Bai's querulous voice.

'Find a palanquin to bear me to the Palace!' called his patron to one of the servants. 'Commander Yun Guang! Prepare an honour guard led by yourself.'

He did as instructed, asking Chen Song to find suitable lodgings for all the officers, as only Wang Bai and a few body servants were to be accommodated in the Palace.

'I already have somewhere in mind,' smiled Chen Song, refusing to say more.

They hired the finest palanquin on the wharf, decorated with images of the Immortal Liu Hai standing on a three-legged toad. Wang Bai examined it suspiciously. He stiffly climbed aboard, hidden from the eyes of the city by thick, red brocade drapes.

The procession headed east, then south along the Imperial Way, trotting at the double to emphasise Wang Bai's rank. The street was a hundred yards wide. Temples and many-storied buildings with flying balconies lined the way. Flags and banners proclaimed fashionable teashops and restaurants. They hurried past markets where hundreds of stalls devoured wealth from all corners of the world and strings of *cash* formed a serpent long enough to constrict the entire city.

Guang was out of breath, forehead moist with sweat, by the

time he glimpsed the first towering gatehouse of the Palace. He tugged at the palanquin's curtain.

'Your Excellency!' he called. 'We near our destination!'

He expected Wang Bai to part the curtain a little. Indeed, he desired it. Was he, Captain Xiao, hero of Swallow Gate, reduced to a mere escort now the Mongols were far away?

'Carry on!' called a muffled voice from within.

When they reached the first archway decked with dragon and phoenix statues, a detachment of Imperial Guardsmen blocked the way. Guang realised his armour was scuffed and damaged from numerous blows, whereas theirs was flawless. Yet he rose half a head above the tallest.

'His Excellency Wang Bai!' he announced.

The guard officer looked at him uncomprehendingly and seemed inclined to sneer.

'Deposit a petition at one of the appropriate ministries,' drawled the officer. 'No entry without authorisation.'

Then Wang Bai's arm appeared through the brocade curtain. His pale hand held a scroll. With a flick, he let the document unroll. All capable of reading blinked in surprise. It was an urgent summons, bearing the divine seal of the Son of Heaven's First Chancellor. Now the guardsmen fell to their knees. Wang Bai rapped on the roof to indicate they should proceed.

Guang stepped aside as the exhausted porters stumbled forward. The curtain parted and Wang Bai called out: 'Find your own quarters, Guang, but ensure the ships are ready to leave at any time. I shall send word if you are required.'

The palanquin vanished into the palace complex and Guang was left on the dusty road with his battle-hardened soldiers.

'Buy wine and pork,' he ordered, passing over several strings of *cash*. 'Toast the health of Pacification Commissioner Wang Ting-bo! Sergeant, take my helmet and halberd, as well as these gauntlets. I'll join you on the ships before midnight. You have done your duty well.'

'It's your name we'll toast, sir!' called out the sergeant. 'Not the Wang clan.'

Guang ignored this disloyalty and was left alone amidst a hundred thousand people. Litters and plodding camels and donkey-carts filled the Imperial way. Despite retaining his sword, he felt more exposed than when arrows showered down on Swallow Gate.

竹子

Yun Guang paced up and down before the Imperial Palace, one hand resting on the hilt of his sword. Realising that he made a strange sight, he found a tea-stall further down the Imperial Way. Then he drank bowl after bowl, the hot tea failing to cool his fevered thoughts.

Of course, others of his family had visited the capital before. Shih had lived here for over a decade after Father banished him. Most illustrious was Great-grandfather himself. But Yun Cai seemed too fabulous a personage for comparison.

Guang blinked as he sipped another scalding cup. The leaves were bitter, over-brewed. Clearly the vendor had decided he was a gull flown in from the provinces, ripe to be plucked.

Recollections of Shih made his forehead furrow. Guang could not forget their parting conversation – the accusation that Shih, not he, was Eldest Son. Those words had pursued Guang throughout the long journey to Linan. Intolerable thoughts he could not settle.

His brother had used the word 'pretend'. But how could he expect Guang to remember what had happened all those years ago? They had been seven, eight, surely no older. Who could remember things from their eighth year? Not clearly, at least, or honestly. One must discount many memories. Guang did not like to think how many. He gulped the hot tea. Then, quite unexpectedly, a name came back to him from their eighth year: *Aunt Qin*, like a ship emerging from dawn mists, *Aunt Qin. . .*

Aunt Qin had always favoured Shih, he remembered that much, but it had not mattered to Guang because Father so obviously favoured him. And Father was Lord. Yet he did recollect envying his brother. When Aunt Qin walked and talked with Shih by Wei River she was full of tender enthusiasm for her faithful nephew. . .

Guang gripped the hot cup tighter.

Something had happened during his eighth year. A monsoon of endless rain. Three-Step-House filled with weeping. No one explained why – Mother, Aunt Qin, Shih, even the servants, all had seemed frightened. He remembered Father galloping to Chunming in the pouring rain, his face a mask of rage. When he returned a few days later, he summoned Guang and held out a high, silk-embroidered hat.

'This is yours,' he said, examining his son strangely. 'Wear it with pride.'

Guang had seized the hat gladly, thinking how jealous Shih would be. No other child in Wei Valley possessed so fine a hat! Not that he wished Shih to be unhappy, but he had so many empty places to fill in his soul. When he placed the hat on his head it was too big and settled over his eyebrows.

'There is more,' continued Father. 'You are forbidden to see Little Brother – if he is indeed your brother – ever again. He will be leaving soon. Then you must never mention or think of him, for he will never return. *Never*.'

The eight year old boy detected hysteria in the way Father repeated that word. A hell of dishonour. And could not explain why.

'Father,' he stuttered. 'It is I. . . I am Little Brother.'

In an instant Father was towering over him, clutching him by the shoulders.

'You are Eldest Son now, curse you!' he roared, shaking Guang so hard that his teeth rattled. 'Do not *dare* to disappoint me!'

At last Guang broke free and fled to the room he shared with Shih. He expected to find his brother there. Instead a servant was hastily stuffing Shih's clothes into hempen travelling sacks.

'What are you stealing?' he demanded, but the servant did not reply.

When Guang tried to leave he found his way barred by their drunken Tutor of Characters.

'Little Master Yun Guang must stay in his room,' said the man, slyly.

An hour passed, spent on games of chequers and drawing. The tutor customarily had no patience but today he was all moderation. Guang wondered at it, and wore his fine new hat. Here was something else to boast about when he met Shih again.

The sound of Mother and Father arguing reached them from the Middle House. Guang froze in fear. He had never imagined such shrieking. Not from passive, gentle mother.

'Pay no heed!' snapped the tutor. 'Your turn! See, you're winning!'

Yet Guang had lost all taste for the game.

At last he heard shouting and the rattle of wheels. Then, rising through it all, Shih's wail of fear and despair.

After that, Guang could remember nothing. Had he forced a way past his tutor into the rain? Did he ever learn where Shih had gone? Father once muttered that Shih had been planted in Mother's womb by an evil Fox Fairy. Answerless questions, inhabiting a guilty void. Not just his own. No one spoke of Shih after his departure. Mother hardly spoke at all except for the most necessary things and, to Father, never by choice.

Perhaps a secret part of him expected his favour with Father to grow, now that he was Eldest Son, heir to Wei Valley. Yet each time Lord Yun looked at Guang's face he seemed to see the features of another. He would glance away, avoiding his son's eye.

One day Guang discovered some moth-eaten scrolls and books in a lumber-room. They contained Great-grandfather Yun Cai's verses, hidden away because Father thought them dull. He studied them over several months and conceived a strange notion that Great-grandfather was displeased with them all. He tried to explain it to Father but was scornfully rebuffed. Guang kept thinking of Shih and why he had been sent away. For the first time he wondered if he liked Father. Yet when the Lord of Wei bent towards him – less and less often as the years passed – Guang would melt at once, eager for approval.

When Guang was thirteen a furious desire to write poetry like Great-grandfather took hold. He mixed ink and dipped his brush, though he knew Father would greet his efforts with mockery.

Guang remembered that moment always. It was a doorway, to dip his brush in the black ink of truth and push open the door. To wipe it on the ink-tray and peer into a strange house. Dip and form columns of characters. To enter that house of truth. He wrote:

Since	Not	Shadows	Darkness
you	complete	at	between
and	our	evening	plum
I	hearts	grow	trees
parted	wither	long	above
snow	like	as	Three
rain	breaking	sad	Step
sun	bamboo	ghosts	House

Guang read and re-read his poem. Gloried in it. He chanted it aloud while hiding in the ancestral tomb, certain Great-grandfather was listening and that the verse would lift the curse of their ancestor's disapproval.

At last he sought out Mother and recited it. First she blinked, tears filling her eyes, then her voice rose in a wail like a river over-flowing a dam. Father and all the servants came running. She sobbed and rocked over the poem, tears dripping onto the ink so that it blurred. Father snatched the poem from her listless hand. Because he was a poor reader, it took time for him to decipher the characters. When he did his gaze fell on Guang like a thunderbolt. The youth met it for a moment, then looked away, horribly afraid.

'I shall not forgive this!' he roared.

He swept from the room, tearing the poem in two. The paper fluttered to the ground like moth-wings.

A week later Guang was sent away to the Military Academy in distant Nancheng for training in the artillery. A demeaning position for one whose forebears included fully-examined scholars and a poet beloved throughout the Empire. But Guang had not argued, glad to escape the misery of Three-Step-House and Mother's lifeless eyes. There were no more poems, though he longed to write them. Instead he learned a different rigour – that of killing through force and fire.

Guang ceased his pacing. This was what he had been trying to remember! All his life, it seemed. With release came a deep, swirling sadness. At last he understood the reserve that always lay between himself and Shih; as his poem said, there was darkness between the plum trees. For even during their most intimate conversations, both habitually held back, as though intimacy would expose something shameful and secret. At last Guang saw how much false fellowship characterised their relationship and blamed himself. But that was not a fixed thing. They could change. He resolved to share all he had remembered with Shih as soon as he returned to Nancheng.

He swallowed another bowl of tea and solemnly bowed to the Son of Heaven's palace.

竹子

Guang handed back the empty teacup, paying the vendor with a few *cash*.

How he wished he could heal the rift with his brother and their drunken quarrel on the night he left for the capital! Once, during that splendid winter when he had lived with Shih and Cao in Apricot Corner Court, when the two brothers had been reunited by destiny itself, Shih had let slip a street name. It had been a street in the capital – the very place where he had served out his medical apprenticeship to a certain Dr Ou-yang. As Guang stood on the Imperial Way, he conceived of a service he could accomplish for his dear brother and sister-in-law.

'Where is Black Tortoise Street?' he asked the stall-holder.

'There!' cried the man, pointing up the Imperial Way. 'Twenty minute's walk! By the Jade Disc Tea-house.'

Guang strode north, hand on hilt, his back straight. Many eyes were drawn to his fine figure. What he expected to achieve in Black Tortoise Street was simple, yet deeply filial. He hoped to gather greetings for Shih and Cao, perhaps even letters of blessing from Sister-in-law's relatives, then bear them back to besieged Nancheng as a peace offering.

When he reached the ornamental gate leading into Black Tortoise Street, doubts set in. Perhaps no one would remember the little boy from distant Chunming Province or even Dr Ou-yang and his daughter. Guang sensed the fragility of one's hold on places and thought ruefully of his sacrifices for the sake of Nancheng. But surely the people of the Twin Cities would never cease to hail him as Captain Xiao or feel an obligation towards him.

Black Tortoise Street was a bustling thoroughfare, lined with booths and small restaurants serving cordials. Banners hung outside many establishments, promising noble benefits. Apothecaries were marked out by dried calabashes above their doors. It was to one of these that Guang made his way.

A man stood in the doorway, surveying the crowded street. As the tall soldier advanced upon him, the shopkeeper blinked at him in surprise. Then he leaned forward to look more closely, agitation evident on his face.

'Sir!' called out Guang. 'A word with you!'

The man's eyes flicked anxiously towards a particular gateway. Otherwise he tried to ignore Guang, who frowned at such discourtesy.

'Sir! I seek a. . .'

'Is it really you?' asked the shopkeeper in amazement.

'As I say,' said Guang. 'I seek. . .'

'Why are you here?' broke in the man. 'Leave before they see you!'

'What?'

'Go now!' hissed the man, retreating into his shop.

The door closed. Guang was left speechless on the pavement. He paced further up the street to the gateway that had drawn the shopkeeper's glance. It was a doctor's shop. The sign read: 'House of Ou-yang Wen: Health From Cradle To Grave.' Guang stepped into the courtyard and at once the brightness of the street was replaced by shadow. He smelt bitter medicines, confused with sweet, cloying floral scents. A young lad swept the small courtyard.

'Is Dr Ou-yang here?' asked Guang.

'Yes, sir.'

'Then fetch him.'

Guang waited uncertainly. No doubt this Dr Ou-yang was a relative of Shih's former master. He knew from Cao that the old doctor had died soon after their marriage. Suddenly he realised how little he knew of her family. It was a topic Cao and Shih answered with silence.

When Dr Ou-yang appeared in the doorway, fastening his silk girdle as though after a nap, the man froze. He was unusually ugly, squat as a toad, and this gave him a kind of distinction. Guang's polite bow of greeting was cut rudely short.

'You!' accused the man.

At last Guang grasped what should have been obvious at once.

'You do not understand,' he began, eager to explain he was not Shih.

In doing so, he rested his hand on the pommel of his sword. At once Dr Ou-yang recoiled fearfully and ducked back inside the house. The door slammed behind him, followed by a sound of bolts.

Guang debated his next move. Things were evidently happening in the house, for he could hear raised voices. Then the door was flung open and Guang saw six men carrying clubs and wooden staves. At their head, a sour-faced old man in a splendid red silk dressing gown decorated with staring fish. His eyes flicked contemptuously over Guang's uniform.

'Do not think *that* will protect you, Yun Shih!' he cried. 'Do not think your crimes are forgotten. Now I know why that official from the guild out west came asking after you! To the magistrate you will go! Thief and rapist!'

'Sir, you are quite at fault. . .' began Guang angrily, until an uncomfortable thought silenced him. He reeled inwardly. These men wished to arraign Shih for capital crimes. Perhaps his brother was guilty. The shopkeeper at the pharmacy evidently believed so. Then there were the strange circumstances, never properly explained, of Shih setting up his practice thousands of *li* from his former master. Guang began to back towards the gatehouse. Encouraged by his apparent loss of nerve, his opponents stepped forward.

'We shall carry him to the magistrate ourselves!' called out the old man.

'Fetch the Watch, Father!' urged the ugly Dr Ou-yang. 'He has a weapon!'

In a moment they would rush him. Guang drew his sword. It glittered dully in the shadowy courtyard.

'Come closer,' he urged, quietly, stepping towards them.

They halted and looked into his eyes. Then they retreated a few steps, murmuring among themselves. Guang stepped backwards calmly into the street, gently closing the door behind him. For a long moment there was no pursuit. It gave him precious time to sprint down Black Tortoise Street, knocking over a wheelbarrow piled with melons on his way. Voices rose from Dr Ou-yang's gateway: 'Stop him! Fetch the Watch!' Then Guang was running down alleyways, under lines of drying clothes between tenement blocks, past urchins and gossiping housewives who stared as he tore by. He dared not slow his pace. Despite his head start, Guang could hear sounds of pursuit.

He had grown wiry and nimble in the wars. Soon he outpaced his persecutors. At last he found his way blocked by a canal. There seemed to be no one behind him. He hailed a passing boatman, requesting passage to the wharf-side of the West Lake. Soon he was being paddled into a mass of other small boats where he disappeared.

Within moments two panting young men wearing the robes of medical apprentices arrived. They stood gasping for breath until the voice of a beggar who had been crouching in the shadows beneath an awning, called out: 'You look for a tall man? I know where he went!'

竹子

An hour later, Guang gazed at a low pavilion by the lakeside in amazement. It was as though Chen Song had sensed a deep wish.

'Are you sure?' he asked.

'Quite,' said Chen Song, complacently. 'Your glorious ancestor Yun Cai lived here at the height of his early fame.'

'The pavilion is surrounded by other buildings,' said Guang. 'Great-grandfather's poems describe it as standing alone, encircled by a deer park.'

'That was a hundred years ago.'

'This is truly Goose Pavilion?'

'Your noble ancestor will clap immortal hands as you enter,' said Chen Song.

Guang fervently hoped so. It might help to dispel unpleasant recollections of Black Tortoise Street.

Goose Pavilion had become a lodge for travellers to the capital, part of an elegant lakeside inn. The tariffs were high but Guang would have paid twice what the innkeeper asked. He found out from a garrulous servant that the original Goose Pavilion had perished by fire fifty years previously, so that nothing remained of Great-grandfather's haunt but its name. He chose not to mention this fact to Chen Song in case it embarrassed him.

At least Goose Pavilion was pleasant. Several days passed without word from Wang Bai, who remained in the Palace debating the rescue of the Twin Cities. Although Guang sometimes chafed at his role as bodyguard when he should be defending those he held dear, at least there was honour in the importance of their mission. Wang Ting-bo had loaded his nephew with desperate petitions and memoranda to His Imperial Highness's First Chancellor, urging the court to send fresh supplies and troops.

Each morning Guang and Chen Song inspected their small flotilla of paddle-wheel destroyers to ensure the sailors were ready to cast off at a moment's notice. That duty done, the day became their own.

No one they met mentioned the war far away to the west or the daily sacrifices holding back A-ku's horde. The low hills surrounding the West Lake framed slow, exquisite sunsets. Flocks of water-fowl rose and wheeled over the water. Mongols were unreal to the people here.

Guang spent many hours staring at the West Lake, as he suspected Great-grandfather Yun Cai had done. Yet his thoughts were far less noble or lofty than his ancestor's. He often found himself gazing at artfully-dressed ladies who reclined in pleasure craft. Sometimes he drowsed and dreamt of Lu Ying, recollecting their last meeting in Shih's medicine shop with peculiar clarity. Wang Ting-bo's letter had hinted she might be recalled to Peacock Hill soon, though it set no dates; and surely the increased grant of grain and other rations he was sending each day implied a return to favour. It surprised Guang that such a prospect made him uncomfortable. Lu Ying had offended Cao and was clearly a foolish, flighty creature. Yet her parting look as he left Shih's shop had been forlorn, not scheming. Against all sense, he found himself wanting to think well of her. And as he gazed at the lake, her striking eyes – the exact shade of precious green jade – seemed to glint on the water. It was easy to picture her graceful figure and soft limbs.

One night Guang visited a floating oriole hall with Chen Song to rid himself of Lu Ying's image, but returned unsatisfied, troubled by imagining another woman beneath him. It was nearly midnight and a messenger in palace livery waited at Goose Pavilion.

'Commander Yun Guang?'

He offered a letter bearing Wang Bai's personal seal.

'Chen Song,' said Guang, having surveyed its hastily-written contents. 'I must go to His Excellency in the palace. Prepare our ships to leave at dawn.'

Guang donned sword and jade waist-badges, before following the messenger through silent streets. The night was moonless and his guide lit the way with a swaying, circular lantern attached to a long bamboo pole. Instead of entering the palace by a front entrance, Guang was led round the outskirts of the Imperial City to a small gatehouse hidden behind the Bureau of Salt Revenue. Guang glanced uneasily at the high palace walls. He had no wish to enter them, especially by a back door.

The messenger knocked and whispered through a hatch to someone within. The gate swung open and six guardsmen carrying halberds with long, curved blades blocked the way. After more whispering, the soldiers stepped aside.

Then he was conducted deep into less exalted areas of the Palace City, away from the broad avenues and gilded splendour of the Imperial family's quarters, into a dark warren occupied by menials who carried the palace on their shoulders. Despite the late hour, he glimpsed washerwomen and lesser eunuchs bent over ignoble tasks. A line of drudges pushed a convoy of wheelbarrows transporting night soil. Without a guide he would soon have been lost. Flies and moths pursued the bobbing lantern down twisting alleyways. At last the messenger pointed at a low wooden door studded with rusty iron nails.

Guang kept a hand on the hilt of his sword as he pushed it open. A long, low-raftered chamber lay beyond. Then his fears became relief, for Wang Bai sat at a table, writing with great concentration by the light of a guttering candle. Guang noticed strain and anxiety on the older man's usually suave face.

'Ah,' said Wang Bai, barely glancing up. 'Sit on this stool beside me, so we may talk quietly.'

Guang did so. His superior sipped a cup of cold tea.

'I smell wine on your breath,' said Wang Bai.

'Many apologies, sir!'

'You are wondering why I chose to meet you here, rather than in the ambassadors' quarters,' he said. 'It is because I wish our meeting to be private.'

Guang watched in surprise as Wang Bai rose and checked each window for spies.

'Are things so bad, sir?'

'I shall speak frankly with you, Commander Yun Guang. You have always been loyal to my family. My mission has gone well in only one respect. The Son of Heaven's First Chancellor has agreed to send a large fleet to re-supply the Twin Cities. They hope to breach the blockade.'

In his excitement Guang half-rose: 'With fresh supplies, we shall hold off the Mongols until they rot! You are our saviour, sir!'

Wang Bai showed no sign of elation.

'The world is not so simple. I said only one aspect of my mission has been accomplished, no more. It may well be the least important.'

Guang watched as his patron rose and again checked the door. But the messenger had withdrawn a dozen paces up the alleyway and so could not eavesdrop. Wang Bai came over and bent close. Guang felt hot breath on his cheek and ear; the odours of liver and perfume. He shrank from the intensity in Wang Bai's eyes.

'I have a task for you,' he said. 'One that is quite secret.'

Guang blinked uneasily.

'What need is there for secrecy here, sir?' he asked. 'Where can be safer than the Son of Heaven's own palace?'

A hollow laugh greeted this question.

'I merely wish you to deliver a letter and ask no questions.'

'I shall do so, sir. On one condition.'

Wang Bai blinked in surprise.

'*You* have conditions for *me*?

'Forgive me, sir, but you mentioned our mission being unsuccessful. My entire family are trapped in Nancheng. I would know the worst.'

Wang Bai regarded him coldly and Guang understood a judgement was being formed, one that might determine his future.

'Very well,' said Wang Bai. 'Why should you not know? It will be discussed everywhere soon enough. His Imperial Highness has appointed a new Supreme Pacification Commissioner to oversee my uncle. And I have been refused the position of Vice Governor in Nancheng Province. Such a promotion, it was felt, would make the Wang family too powerful. So our great loyalty is rewarded with ingratitude and shame.'

Guang bowed. Suddenly he wished to be far away from the palace and its intrigues, somewhere simpler and cleaner.

'Forgive me, but could not one of the palace servants deliver this message? I should oversee the flotilla.'

'I have spoken and that should be enough,' replied Wang Bai, sharply. 'There is no danger to you, none at all.'

Again Guang might have demurred. But he was used to obedience when it came to the Wang clan and placed his fists together in a salute. A thick scroll was passed over. His patron whispered urgently and Guang's eyes widened as he grasped the strangeness of this duty.

'Furthermore,' added Wang Bai. 'It must be accomplished before dawn.'

'That is only four hours off!'

Wang Bai nodded.

'I depart at sunrise. I recommend you join the flotilla before the fourth bell. Unless you wish to walk back to Nancheng.'

'Yes, sir,' he said, reluctantly.

Wang Bai resumed his writing by the dancing light of the

candle and Guang stepped out into the alleyway, reeling from the news he had just heard. Wang Ting-bo set beneath another! He could barely conceive of such a reversal. What did it mean for his own future? Everyone knew of his loyalty to Wang Ting-bo. He considered hurrying to Chen Song for advice but felt oddly reluctant. Guang realised his palms were sticky with sweat.

竹子

Around the same time that Guang left his patron a small procession approached one of the military wharfs on the West Lake. Chen Song was supervising the loading of provisions onto the paddle-wheel destroyers. They had need of arrows and thunderclap bombs, naphtha and bandages for wounds. The return journey through the Mongol siege lines would be desperate.

Soldiers and sailors worked by the light of flaring torches soaked in oil. A light wind blew from the West Lake and the flames danced. There was a smell of stagnant water in the air.

When Chen Song turned to meet the procession he detected another bad smell – the dangerous odour of law. An old man in fine, dark-blue silks was being carried upon an open litter. Two constables accompanied the magistrate, bearing cudgels and a heavy wooden yoke for restraining prisoners. Chen Song bowed low and waited for the official to reveal his business.

'We seek a criminal,' announced the magistrate, clearly vexed to be about his duties in the middle of the night. A bad sign. Inconveniencing a judge was a crime in itself.

'We are soldiers busy with His Highness's business,' said Chen Song.

An unusually ugly man wearing a doctor's robe and a hat with long black earflaps pushed forward.

'What of Yun Shih! He was seen visiting these ships a few hours ago! Do not deny he is part of your crew! Now we are forced to disturb His Honour because you are preparing to depart!'

Chen Song wished he could do just that – and instantly.
'Yun Shih?' he asked, innocently.
'Yes,' repeated the irascible doctor.
Chen Song's quandary deepened.
'Ah,' he said.

By now Guang had left the palace and stood in a shadowy street. Wang Bai's letter, concealed in his girdle, felt heavy. He wondered if it contained more than words, a golden bribe perhaps or something likely to compromise the bearer. His willingness to serve the Wangs made him complicit in all their intentions. Perhaps he was destined to fall with them.

The lantern-carrying servant had abandoned him as soon as he was ejected from the palace. Now Guang needed another guide. All he possessed were crude directions and a man's name. Linan seemed vast and dark, though far from lifeless.

As he walked – heading, he hoped, for the Imperial Way – Guang noticed poor wretches slumped in miserable huddles against walls and under bridges. Prostitutes of the lowest sort congregated round market gateways. Raucous laughter from teashops and taverns broke the silence of night. He heard a hubbub in the distance but could not guess its significance. At last Guang accepted he was lost.

A great temptation to abandon his duty and find a way back to the paddle-wheel destroyers took hold. He could pretend to Wang Bai that he had delivered the message. But it was not in Guang's nature to deceive those to whom he felt an obligation.

So he stopped a young man wearing a waiter's uniform, evidently returning home after a long evening's labour at a fashionable teahouse.

'I am lost,' said Guang. 'Two hundred *cash* if you'll act as my guide across the city. See, here are the strings of *cash* which shall be yours.'

The young man agreed with alacrity. The value of many a man's wage had been reduced by the Empire's debased currency

– too much *cash* minted to pay for the court's extravagance and endless threats on the frontier.

Now that he possessed a guide Guang made fast progress. Haste was necessary. Already the sky showed hints of day – and Wang Bai had made it plain he would set sail without him. He was led through crumbling ancient walls to an outer suburb bordering the broad River Che. Here lay a district of shipyards used for the repair of merchant junks. Half-finished craft lay on chocks amidst timber stacks. There was a sweet, sulphorous scent of hot pitch.

'I have never been here before,' muttered his guide. 'Foreigners live here. Merchants from strange places. It is said some of them trade with pirates. You asked me for the house of Jo-Set, sir. I have not heard of it. The name sounds foreign.'

'Then we must proceed further.'

Guang led the way down a wide lane rutted by carts. Workshops and isolated houses lay on either side. At last he found a pair of night watchmen crouched beside a lantern, playing dice. Both carried bamboo clubs, for only the Son of Heaven's soldiers were allowed to bear edged weapons in the capital.

'Where is the house of Jo-Set?' asked Guang.

The watchmen looked at him suspiciously.

'I seek one called Mah-Chu,' added Guang. 'May he be found here?'

One of the night-watchmen pointed at a low, rectangular building, resembling a small temple.

'That is the house of Jo-Set.'

Guang strolled over, aware of the watchmen's curious eyes and rapped on the wooden door. No one answered. He balled his fists and banged. At last he heard shuffling feet, then a cautious voice asked in a strange accent. 'Who is there?'

For a moment Guang hesitated, glancing back at the watchmen. Why should he not speak openly?

'I bear a message from His Excellency Wang. . .'

The door abruptly swung open and Guang was confronted

by a thin, tall man, bearing the features of the Western steppelands. For a moment Guang wondered if he was a Mongol. The man urged him into the house, glancing fearfully at the street. Guang's guide was left outside.

'Psssht' hissed the man. 'Do not speak that name so loud! You mad?'

Guang bristled. It would take one sweep of his arm to punish this Mah-Chu for his impudence. The fellow reeked of foreign fox smells. Besides, he had blue eyes, and though Guang had seen such oddities before, they always made him think of devils. He recollected his duty and looked round the wooden house.

It was indeed a temple of some kind. He did not recognise the deity. At the far end stood a crude altar, lit by red candles. A wooden image of a man carved in black wood and apparently nailed to a cross caught his attention. Red wounds had been painted on the criminal's wrists and ankles. Yet the idol's face was serene.

'What Wang Bai message?' asked the man, nervously. 'Did he send letter?'

Guang passed over the scroll and waited while Mah-Chu took it to the flickering candles on the altar and read by their thin light. Guang could not take his eyes from the shameful criminal on the cross. Despite himself, he was reminded of poor Shih.

Finally Mah-Chu folded the letter and returned to where Guang waited by the door, restless to be gone.

'Tell your master,' said the holy man. 'I send at once.'

Guang looked at the foreigner closely. He had not expected any of this.

'Whom do you serve?' he asked.

The monk blinked.

'Why, same as you,' he whispered. 'Do not fear! Serve same as you.'

Guang left and was relieved to find his guide still waiting outside. Dawn was sowing the horizon with seeds of light.

'We must hurry,' said Guang, eager to leave this strange place with its tortured god and furtive holy man. He glanced back just once and saw Mah-Chu watching him from the doorway through alien, blue eyes.

Chen Song was having a most trying time. Lying to the magistrate risked a death sentence, unless one lied to protect one's parents or could afford to bribe a more senior judge. Meanwhile he would be punished severely if the flotilla was not ready to sail when Wang Bai arrived.

'I have no Yun Shih among my men,' he said, for the tenth time. 'I suggest an error.'

Each time the magistrate seemed about to agree and return to his comfortable bed, the remorseless Doctor Ou-yang intervened. He was clearly a person of influence and wealth in his guild; even the magistrate treated him with respect. Chen Song was reminded of Dr Du Mau and the influence he had once possessed with Pacification Commissioner Wang Ting-bo.

'How could this Yun Shih have been seen here, if he was not here?' demanded the magistrate, spurred on by Dr Ou-yang.

Chen Song raised hopeless hands and struggled for a suitable quotation from the Five Classics or at least a proverb: 'One does not seek to catch fish up a tree,' he suggested, feebly.

Guang was stumbling with tiredness through the city. His boots clattered on stone pavement slabs. Yet daylight was gathering in courtyards and thoroughfares. Only the most desperate prostitutes maintained their stations. Otherwise the streets were filling with labourers starting work in the hour before dawn. Finally the West Lake, grey beneath the dull sky, became visible through a canyon of tall, wooden buildings.

When Guang reached the port area and saw the banners of Wang Bai's flotilla, he hesitated. His sharp eyes at once recognised the figure of Chen Song and someone else – a fat official and constables – as well as his sister-in-law's relative, Dr Ou-yang. The official looked suspiciously like a magistrate.

Though he could not understand this turn of events, he was sure it was quite separate from Mah-Chu's letter. Otherwise, why would Dr Ou-yang be present? Guang knew it was Shih they sought and that approaching the ships would invite instant arrest. Just then Wang Bai's palanquin, carried by eight porters, descended on the paddle-wheel destroyers at a double-trot.

After paying off his guide, Guang spent agonising minutes watching from the shadow of a low warehouse. He could hear rats scurrying in the eaves above his head. Somehow he must join the ships. Already Wang Bai had climbed aboard with his boxes of possessions and they were preparing to cast off. His Excellency stood at the rail, admonishing the magistrate, who had decided it was prudent to offer a humble bow. None of this helped Guang. Then he had a desperate notion.

As the paddle-wheel destroyers began to churn water, drums beating to hasten the sailors' pedalling feet, Guang darted forward until he hid behind a pile of empty fish crates on the quayside. Meanwhile the ships began to advance north, towards the Grand Canal and beyond that, the Yangtze. It was vital Dr Ou-yang and the other watchers on the shore did not glimpse him. Luckily they were busy arguing amongst themselves.

The first paddle-wheel destroyer drew parallel to Guang's hiding place and his heart lifted – for Chen Song stood by the helmsman.

'Chen Song! Throw me a rope!'

It took a moment for his friend to notice him on the wharf. Then he was all action. As Guang trotted to keep pace with the ship, Chen Song ordered the helmsman to veer closer to the shore. A long rope curled outwards, landing at Guang's feet. He hastily wrapped it round his chest, tying a tight knot. At once he felt himself being pulled forward. One step, two, he teetered over the short drop to the lake and leapt into the water. Instantly he went under, weighed down by his clothes and sword. A fierce jerk hauled him to the surface. He was dragged like a harpooned dolphin to the destroyer's stern and pulled aboard, gasping for breath.

Wang Bai, who was already seated on his high chair in the stern of the second paddle-wheel destroyer, raised a hand of haughty recognition. No thanks for the dangers Guang had undertaken to deliver the message! Perhaps the Prefect believed he should feel grateful to be noticed at all! Then Guang recollected that Wang Ting-bo's days as Pacification Commissioner were numbered and wondered how much longer Wang Bai's own position would stay secure.

竹子

Guang slept in the raised prow of the paddle-destroyer, muttering his brother's name over and over. Sweat on his forehead caught the starlight. Chen Song, who sat nearby, removed his cloak and placed it gently over his friend, for Guang had caught a river-fever after his immersion in the West Lake. Then he left Captain Xiao to his fitful dreams and wandered towards the stern to share a word with the helmsman.

At first Guang was drowning, trapped underwater by long, tangled willow roots. Everything moved slowly in this aquatic world – his fingers clawing at the surface as though for a handful of air – bubbles floating upwards – flickers of silver he took to be fish. Then the fish became a white, peering face. A ghost's wide-eyed, unblinking face. Shih! It was Shih come to release him! Unless it was his own future ghost, for the face possessed Guang's features. Though his lungs ached for air, he called out: 'Eldest Brother! Eldest Brother!' In a flash of comprehension he knew that he was offering to renounce that title in exchange for Lu Ying, to forego his empty lordship of Wei in exchange for life. Shih's hand reached out, the dream abruptly shifted. . .

She was beside him on the rough-hewn, pine bench in Apricot Corner Court. Night scents mingled with her fragrance. They could not meet each other's eyes. Why could they not?

The answer thrilled and appalled. He dared not acknowledge it. Guang moved his hand along the bench, closer to hers, almost touching her slender fingers. She wore a thin, hemp shift like a peasant girl, her jade mountains prominent. The obviousness of his arousal made him murmur a throaty excuse. For he was afraid Shih would see them together, that he would never be forgiven for stealing his brother's lovely concubine as he had stolen the title of Eldest Brother. . .

Quite suddenly, Guang realised he was awake. Lu Ying had vanished. He stared up at a dark sky streaked with constellations. *Where am I?* he thought. The answer came from the steady creak and splash of paddlewheels, the rough planks beneath his head smelling of tar and resin. Tomorrow they would reach the assembly point on the lower reaches of the Yangtze where His Imperial Majesty's officials had decreed a great fleet should gather.

Yet Guang could only think of the trade he had offered Shih in his dream. To swap a noble title for. . . what? A dream of happiness? A discarded concubine? In any case, Shih was not the real danger. He knew Wang Ting-bo well enough to fear his jealousy.

Guang's bones ached with fever and he pulled Chen Song's cloak tight round his shoulders.

The Grand Canal opened into the Yangtze and Wang Bai's flotilla joined streams of merchant junks bound for trade throughout the Empire. Guang reflected it was no wonder the Great Khan longed to subjugate the Middle Kingdom. What the Mongols could not build through civilization, they must seize by force. And what they seized could be used to subjugate other peoples until all the world knelt in submission.

All day the flotilla paddled against the swollen summer Yangtze until the city of Jiankang came into sight. If Nancheng was a great city, it had its equal in Jiankang. Pagodas and water-markets, mansions and slums linked by countless canals. But Guang's gaze was drawn to a long line of warships bobbing outside the port area. Chen Song clapped his hands for sheer joy at the sight of the fleet.

'See!' he cried. 'Did I not say the Son of Heaven would move mountains to relieve our distress!'

Guang nodded with less certainty.

'Yet this fleet cannot drive the Mongols away,' he said.

'Oh, you are too fastidious!' declared Chen Song, in a way that made one doubt who was the Commander, as though both were student friends in the Metropolitan University debating Imperial policy over wine. 'This fleet is proof of the great love felt by our sovereign for his people.'

'Or perhaps,' replied Guang. 'His Majesty's First Chancellor makes these forces available because he is afraid of losing his position should the Great Khan prevail.'

'That is dangerous talk,' muttered Chen Song, looking round to see if they were overheard. 'Do not believe the lie that the Great Khan seeks to establish a new dynasty like those which have gone before. The Mongols seek to devour the whole world.'

Guang laughed.

'Now *you* are too fastidious,' he said. 'I merely wish to comprehend all sides of the question. Is there not a verse by my noble ancestor:

Always ask why the fisherman casts
glinting nets into sunsets:
he thinks to catch fish
but merely traps drops of light.

So you see, old Yun Cai anticipated me. I, too, am a fisherman in my humble way.'

Chen Song surveyed him for a moment then glanced at their leader, Wang Bai, who was also studying the Ineffable Winged Relief Fleet.

'Nevertheless,' he said. 'Some truths are easier to catch than others. And so are some men's loyalties and intentions.'

One truth was evident enough: the fleet growing hour by hour was equal to anything the great Khan could muster. There were tower ships three stories high with fortified upper decks and portholes for crossbows and fire-lances. Catapults hung limp from the upper decks and fierce tiger faces had been painted on the broad, flat prows. Birds and animals were carved in relief to overawe malicious river spirits.

Around these monsters floated war junks and swoop ships, as well as open decked boats intended for 'the bravest and best' marines. All eyes were drawn to dozens of flying dragon paddle-wheel destroyers. Whirling tiger catapults stood on the decks and marines prepared bombs of many kinds, as well as giant crossbows and fire-lances.

'Are all these to defend the supply ships?' wondered Guang aloud.

A hundred junks lined the wharves, loaded with salt, clothes, burning powder and jars of naphtha, as well as arrows and crossbow bolts, not to mention lime and arsenic. Enough to poison the entire Mongol army and its Chinese auxiliaries.

Suddenly Guang laughed hoarsely and Chen Song laughed alongside him. Whether they were amused by exactly the same thought was less clear. Wang Bai watched them curiously from his high-backed chair. Then he smiled, too.

懀

thirteen

'All who have heard the *ying* (oriole) singing listen in wonder; indeed the *ying* is the bird of music and boundless felicity. One often sees it depicted in paintings to represent friendship. Of course, 'floating *ying*' and 'wild *ying*' are names polite people use to discuss prostitutes. . .'

From *New Remarks Upon the Nature of Birds and Flowers*

竹子

The Prefectural Gaol, Nancheng. Summer, 1267

How low can a ceiling be? As low as you wish to make the person beneath it. Shih's cell was four feet high. For a tall man like him, the roof ensured misery.

His prison lay at the rear of Peacock Hill beside a compound used for storing lesser concubines in the antique days of Chu. Those ladies were long forgotten, replaced by officials and administrators in the interlocking courtyards of the former palace.

The Prefectural gaol was a long narrow building with a central corridor and cells on either side. Dr Shih's iron shackles were attached to a thick wooden bench and only removed when he was scheduled for questioning. In this way interrogation became a relief. It suggested one was still remembered by the longed-for, half-real world outside. That one was still a man.

Despite his cramped position Shih tried to remain comfortable through stretching and breathing exercises. This amused his fellow prisoners who lacked the disadvantage of tallness. Most humiliating was defecating before one's bench in full view, then shoving the foul matter into a central drain with handfuls of filthy straw. Naturally, the stench endured until the floor was sluiced clean every second day. It was a great trial to avoid unwholesome waste adhering to one's hands – a sure path to disease, as Dr Shih knew well. He dared not complain to his captors, in case they applied the bamboo.

'This is your second night here,' confided his closest neighbour, a thin, emaciated clerk accused of abusing his position in the Grain Distribution Bureau. 'When you have survived your fourth month, as I have, you will understand that every breath is a knife-edge. At least His Excellency Wang Ting-bo has a nose for justice.' The clerk tapped his olfactory member, rattling the manacles on his wrists and adding in a voice loud enough for spies to hear: 'A nose, I say.'

'What of injustice?' asked Dr Shih. 'Certainly this place reeks.'

To that, the disgraced clerk whispered anxiously: 'Remember that normal customs do not apply here. Even the Chief Gaoler is immune to bribes. Secondly, the bamboo is the least of it. When they tie you to the willow frame, you are truly lost.'

Between vile dreams Shih recollected his arrest. It seemed no coincidence it had occurred on the night Captain Xiao left the city, so that he could not appeal to his brother for protection. Surely his enemies had anticipated this vulnerability. If so, they possessed an intimate knowledge of Wang Ting-bo's intentions – a frightening thought, for it also suggested his accusers might have influence over the judge.

Shih had been arrested by the same His Honour who

inspected Apricot Corner Court in the early days of the siege. Dr Fung had been present to confirm Shih's identity. It was obvious Dr Du Mau had ordered his fellow physician to play that role. Such unwavering hatred was incomprehensible to Shih. Had it not been enough to steal the North Medical Relief Bureau from him? Or to instruct other doctors in the guild to shun him? It seemed Dr Du Mau desired his utter disgrace. Yet even now Shih was unsure of the charges laid against him.

On the third day, around noon, two guards entered the prison building. Its central passageway possessed a normal roof, so warders and visiting officials were not obliged to stoop.

'Yun Shih!' bawled the elder guard.

Shih hesitated before rattling his chain to indicate his presence. It was the rule that prisoners must not address or even look upon their gaolers unless given express permission. The cell door, made of iron bars so the prisoners could be surveyed from the central corridor, was unlocked and thrown open.

'Come with us!'

He hobbled down several corridors to a long audience chamber. His Honour sat at the far end, accompanied by clerks to record judgements. Shih glanced hungrily at the sunlight outside. He could hear birds twittering gaily and smell the moist aromas of summer plants on the breeze.

'Ah,' said His Honour, when Shih had abased himself sufficiently. 'You are a dark fellow.'

Shih banged his forehead on the ground.

'A dark, dark fellow! I suspect we'll never know half your crimes. I have here a letter, supplied by Dr Du Mau, from the Guild of Physicians in the capital, Linan. It seems you are well known to them. Even your former apprentice steps forward as a witness against you. Have you nothing to say?'

'Sir,' began Shih, feebly. 'I am innocent.'

His declaration was a lie, a hopeless lie, yet true in every essential way – if the law only dealt in subtleties.

'Nonsense!' replied the judge. 'If nothing else, you are taking up my time. Back to the cells with you! If you find the means to win my favour, submit a petition. I'll give you ten days. Remove him.'

Shih shuffled back to his cell, quite defeated. His Honour could hardly have been clearer. Unless a substantial bribe was offered, he would face the full lash of the law. And Shih's crimes, though old, were grave. Most damning was the wooden case of silver acupuncture needles taken by Cao after her father's death.

At first Shih could not imagine how Du Mau had learned about his old master, Dr Ou-yang. In the perpetual night of the Prefectural prison, he pieced together strange remarks and warnings from his former apprentice. At last he understood the extent of Chung's betrayal and a great repugnance filled Shih's soul.

Many of the hours Shih spent chained to the broad bench were occupied by unanswerable questions. Was Cao safe in Apricot Corner Court? Did she even know where he was held prisoner? All thoughts of Lu Ying fled his mind. In this dismal place he realised the depth of his folly, how a simpleton's lust had blinded him to the true pearl in his treasure chest. Too late, too late.

Of course Cao must have noticed his feelings for the girl – she was far from stupid, far from blind. She had merely pretended to see nothing as a loyal wife should. Yet their match was different from common marriages. The only matchmaker shuttling between them when they chose each other, negotiating the wedding gifts and contract, had been love itself. She had placed her entire trust in him; to change, to waver in his affection, to even consider a concubine – though quite proper in the world's eyes – betrayed that great trust. He was sure she loved him less for it. Once poison is stirred into the dish one may not remove it. Had he poisoned their love? Shih grew helpless before that particular accusation. If he was guilty of any theft, as His Honour maintained, it was this: stealing away their long happiness through a foolish craving.

Shih longed to see Cao one last time before His Honour sentenced him. He could not doubt that sentence, for they did not possess a bribe. Even wealthy local families had impoverished themselves to save a beloved family member. Legally, half of Apricot Corner Court belonged to Shih and, should he face strangulation, it would pass to Guang, for a will had been drawn up in order to bypass Father. Of course, as a woman and spurious wife, Cao had no claim on anything except the clothes she wore, and maybe even not those. But if Guang perished in the wars, all would revert to Father. Shih was certain Father would evict Cao the moment he gained sway over Apricot Corner Court. Heaven knew what other abuses the old man might commit. Shih recollected Widow Mu's daughter, Lan Tien, and grew uncomfortable.

When he could no longer bear such thoughts he observed the prison. His training had made him a sharp onlooker. He noticed the prisoners' irregular breaths – not one of them was wholesome, especially the diseased clerk. Shih took the man's pulse and identified a decayed heart.

'You are quite well,' he said, reassuringly.

At other times he noted the comings and goings of the rats and how their movements bore a regularity, as though ruled by the sun. Yet the prison lacked a single window, so how could they know? These questions interested him despite his sorrow, just as he had noted the cycles of the plum trees as an unhappy boy in Three-Step-House.

All the while his hunger worsened. Although he was accustomed to siege rations, existing on a small ladle of thin rice gruel at morning and evening stripped away his strength. Light-headed weakness set in. The disgraced clerk confided that prisoners had been known to gnaw the corpses of those who perished during the night.

'There is no shame in it,' he said, warily. 'It is only natural.'

Eight days after Shih's interview with His Honour a new

prisoner was dragged in, limp from a beating. By the dim glow of a red lantern the Chief Gaoler looked around for somewhere to place him. He spied a vacancy next to Dr Shih and chained the newcomer to the scarred wooden bench, still unconscious. Shih waited expectantly for the man to wake. His heart was full of contradictory emotions. At first, an unbidden, cruel glee that he was not the only one cast in darkness. Then his habits of feeling re-asserted themselves. He touched the man's arm.

'Ping!' he whispered. 'Ping! Can you hear me?'

He knew severe beatings may leave a man temporarily deaf, even blind.

'Ping! It is I, Dr Shih of Apricot Corner Court, your neighbour. Remember, I treated your girls several times.'

At this the oriole hall keeper stirred in the darkness.

'Ah, doctor,' he murmured. 'Ah, doctor.'

'How sad I am to see you here,' said Shih, tears starting to his eyes. 'How very sad.'

Though he bore the wiry pimp no affection, the sight of his former neighbour in this hell made the world seem doubly mad and vile. Yet he wept for himself as much as Ping.

Dr Shih reached out and began to massage the wounded brothel-keeper's shoulder in a choice place. Ping cried out in pain. Gradually his head lolled and he slept deeply. Still Shih continued his massage, for he knew it would ease the patient's circulation in a dozen beneficial ways.

When Ping awoke the pain had not diminished. Dr Shih questioned him carefully and concluded there was internal bleeding.

'Why are you here?' he asked.

'Because one of my girls failed to satisfy that bastard Weng-Pa, the judge's head clerk,' coughed Ping. 'Or to be truer, he was incapable of satisfying her. So I am punished for another man's shame. My crime is that I was foolish enough to joke about it, because I was drunk.'

Shih, wracked by hunger, had a vision of Ping's establishment.

'I remember the charcoal brazier where you grilled pig's kidneys,' he said. 'They were tossed, still sizzling, in sauce and spices.'

'Hey!' shouted an eavesdropper. 'Don't talk like that! It makes my hunger worse.'

'No,' came another voice from the dark, full of longing. 'Tell us more! What else was there? What did you drink?'

That night Ping died quite suddenly and Shih propped the body on his shoulder. When the night warders passed with their lantern, he dared not mention the dead prisoner in case the corpse inconvenienced them. Shih did not fear the dead; he had seen too many arrivals and departures to doubt they were merely points on a circle.

Strange hours followed. Shih's mind swirled with many questions as the dead man stiffened beside him. If the object of justice is correction, what was he to be corrected for? Marrying his master's daughter without consent? But his master had been dead. Stealing from his former master? But he had purposefully taken nothing. Cao, it was true, had carried away a small portion of the inheritance she was owed – a little *cash* and a case of silver needles. Was he, Yun Shih, really complicit in that? He had not discovered the theft – if theft it was – until they arrived in the Twin Cities.

Shih, as was his habit, looked for holes in his own reasoning. . .

One might argue that, upon discovering the needles, he should have rushed back to the capital and delivered them to his master's brother and heir. Perhaps he could have done so, though they had no *cash* for such a journey. Perhaps he should be more perfect than other men.

Shih itched to relieve his feelings by walking up and down but he was trapped, a fetid corpse heavy against his shoulder.

His mournful thoughts shifted from Ping to Mother. Again tears filled his eyes. Poor Mother! Oh, poor Mother! Guang had told him how she had died tending Father through his madness in Whale Rock Monastery. How cruel, as though

Heaven hated his family, yet Mother deserved no punishment at all. Shih felt an overwhelming desire to stamp on Father's absurd fishes until they twitched no more.

Then he bowed his head to another grief. If only he could beg forgiveness of those he had wronged! Guang, for taunting him at their last meeting. Even Wang Ting-bo's discarded concubine. Oh, he was no better than lustful Lord Yun! He had conceived of her as no more than a forbidden excitement, just like Aunt Qin. Shih squirmed inwardly. How vulnerable the girl was behind her layers of white paint.

Shih steadied Ping's corpse so that it did not slip from the bench to the rat-infested ground. After all, it is a rat's nature to eat what is offered. One could not blame them, any more than one could blame humans for making more mouths to feed when half the world starved. Oh, he did not care to contemplate children. The cruel injustice that assigned child after child to dismal parents and none at all to those who would be most loving.

The cell remained in darkness. A faint trickle down the walls indicated it was raining outside. Dr Shih licked the ribbon of moisture thirstily. Then he meditated on his wife's dear face, taken for granted over so many years, yet elevated to a sunrise in this windowless place. Memories of her became all his sunlight and so, quite naturally, she cast shadows.

竹子

Cao sat alone in the silent shop. All the shutters of the windows facing North Canal Street were closed. A little light filtered in from the corridor at the rear of the counter, otherwise there was only shadow. It had been that way ever since Shih's arrest a week earlier. Cao had barely eaten, as though starving herself might bring about his release. Each day she prepared food for Lu Ying and Father-in-law, as well as a dose of the draught Shih used to settle the old man's nerves.

From dawn until nightfall hardly a word was exchanged in

the house. This suited Cao. Her heart was too burdened for talk. Even now, the exact charges against her husband were unstated.

When Cao visited the Prefectural prison that morning she was informed by a surly official that all accusations would be declared when Dr Shih came to justice; in the meantime, an innocent man need fear nothing.

'As for the guilty, Madam. . .' He let his voice trail.

Cao, who felt guilty to her core, blanched in a way the official found interesting.

'When is my husband's trial to take place?' she asked.

The official narrowed his eyes, perhaps considering whether it was disrespectful to ask so forward a question. 'It is tomorrow,' he said.

'Sir,' pleaded Cao. 'May I not see my husband?'

'You are more likely to have an audience with the Pacification Commissioner himself!' replied the official, frowning haughtily.

Yet his voice was tired. Cao sensed he had used these same words a hundred times before and with the same forbidding expression, to as many concerned relatives.

As she walked back to Water Basin Ward through the humid streets, Cao was forced to step aside. A company of crossbowmen were marching south to take their turn on the ramparts. Ever since the onset of the monsoon, the Mongols had ceased their attacks, yet everyone knew the misery of daily assaults would resume in a few months' time. General A-ku was merely resting his forces and using them to strengthen and extend the siege works choking the Twin Cities.

In Apricot Corner Court, Madam Cao found her unwanted guest lifting the wooden lid of a clay storage jar in the kitchen. Startled, the girl let the lid fall with a dull clatter. The older woman met her eye, aware her own were swollen by weeping.

'Are you hungry, Miss Lu Ying?' she asked.

The concubine flushed with relief.

'Oh yes, Madam Cao! Do not mistake me, I quite understand your pre-occupation and why our meals are so late. What with Dr Shih's. . . Well, I'm sure you do not wish to discuss such an unpleasant thing.'

Cao shivered. It was everything she wished to discuss. Yet it seemed she had neither friend nor relative she dare confide in. Even Widow Mu kept her distance, afraid the laws of collective punishment might be somehow visited on Apricot Corner Court. While understanding her friend's motives, Cao felt the betrayal deeply. It appeared Widow Mu's dead husband had advised her in a dream not to get involved and, like any dutiful wife, she had no choice but to obey.

'Miss Lu Ying,' said Cao. 'There is something I hoped to ask.'

Cao hesitated, aware how easily her superiority over the girl had turned to its opposite. Was it not the fate of all women, to float or sink like ships carried by the tides of their men? She laboured on: 'Miss Lu Ying, can you not use your influence with His Excellency to lessen my husband's discomfort? After all, Dr Shih was kind to you. And now he is in danger. His Excellency would surely read a petition from you with great attention.'

Lu Ying met her hopeful gaze. Then glanced away.

'Madam Cao,' she said. 'You exaggerate my influence. It appears to be very little.'

Nevertheless Wang Ting-bo had recently ordered the delivery of extra rations to Apricot Corner Court for his former concubine's sustenance. A small quantity, it was true, but enough to indicate she was remembered – and perhaps more. Cao suspected that communications of a secret nature had passed between Lu Ying and the Pacification Commissioner. A liveried servant from Peacock Hill had called on two occasions since Shih's arrest, conferring with the former concubine in a low voice. Perhaps this humble emissary signalled Lu Ying's restoration was imminent. Yet when Cao had hinted at the possibility, the girl's face went quite blank. One might almost imagine the question caused her distress.

'I might only make such a petition to His Excellency once,' added Lu Ying. 'Not that I do not feel grateful to Dr Shih – and to yourself! Only I am like an archer with one arrow. I must preserve it for myself. Would not anyone do the same?'

Madam Cao lowered her eyes in despair and seemed hardly aware of the question.

'What pains me most,' she whispered. 'Is that our former apprentice conspires in the prosecution against Dr Shih. We saved him from ruin, you know.'

'I never liked him,' said Lu Ying. 'Quite, quite ugly.'

'He was so sad a child, and very thin. Yet between us we restored his health and humour and plumpness. Yet I am told he will stand witness against Dr Shih tomorrow. How can such things be?'

'I must return to my room,' said Lu Ying.

'Yes, go,' said Cao, not bitterly. She was too preoccupied for bitterness. 'Forgive me for detaining you.'

Lu Ying bowed low for the first time since she had arrived at Apricot Corner Court and shuffled away on her tiny, lotus feet.

竹子

It is said: in death, avoid hell; in life, avoid the law courts. Cao remembered this proverb as she rose at dawn and hastily prepared simple meals of grain for those dependent upon her. She dressed in her most respectable silks – a long trailing skirt and sober belted jacket of blue – gathering every *cash* coin and precious thing they still possessed, in case she might yet be able to bribe the judge. Even a small gift might brighten His Honour's mood. On the other hand, it might offend his sense of importance. All their real wealth was invested in Apricot Corner Court and one could hardly hand over a wooden house.

As Cao was about to leave, she heard a knock on the door leading to the inner courtyard.

Upon opening it, she recoiled in surprise. A crowd of forty or fifty people were gathered round the apricot tree, muttering among themselves. Cao was surprised to see Widow Mu at the rear, accompanied by her daughter, Lan Tien. At the front of the crowd stood their other neighbour, Old Hsu. His eyes brightened at the sight of her and he bowed respectfully.

'Madam Cao,' he said, in his rasping voice. 'It is a blessing to detain you before you depart for your husband's – ahem – *arraignment*.' This obscure statement and grand word evidently pleased Old Hsu.

'You see,' said Old Hsu. 'We wish to escort you to the Prefectural court.'

Cao dabbed her eyes. It was an old custom in the city for friends and well-wishers to attend court hearings so that the judge might know the accused was not without clan. Tears welled and Cao bowed at the crowd.

'Behold all the residents of Apricot Corner Court!' said Old Hsu. 'And dozens of Dr Shih's patients, all wishing to testify to his good name. Orderly Mung Po is with us, as are the entire Xue and Rashid clans, and many more besides! It is our intention to sway the court.'

Now Cao blinked in joyful wonder.

'You need say no more,' said Old Hsu. 'You are a woman and silence is best. I shall speak on behalf of everyone here.'

This seemed less sensible.

'Master Hsu,' she said. 'Forgive me, but do you not recall how His Honour singled you out when he came to Apricot Corner Court? You may be sure he remembers you.'

'Madam, it is a risk I must take,' said Old Hsu. 'I am no stranger to taking risks for justice's sake. Only through courage might the Great Society be won.'

Cao scarcely knew what he was talking about, yet felt deep relief. She was no longer alone.

As the procession left Apricot Corner Court, other residents of Water Basin Ward joined them. Dr Shih was a popular man, not least because of his stewardship of the North Medical Relief Bureau. Just as significantly, people knew him as brother to their beloved Captain Xiao, hero of Swallow Gate. It seemed a cowardly thing to many that Dr Shih should be prosecuted when his brother was not in the city to support him. Others tagged along because the long siege had brought idleness. As the authorities understood, there was nothing so tinder-like as an idle mob. Especially during the dog days.

All formal trials in the Empire were public. Yet some were more public than others. When His Honour stepped onto the judge's podium to occupy an ancient chair painted with images of King Chu Jiang, one of the Ten Kings of Hell, he blinked in surprise. Over a hundred people were gathered in the long hall, held back by a dozen constables. Many more were squatting in the dusty square outside, including unchaperoned women. His Honour adjusted the papers and writing materials on his red-covered table. He straightened his moustache and tuft of beard. An officer of the Guard hurried over.

'Sir!' he said, bringing his fists together in salute. 'It seems these people wish to petition for one of the prisoners, sir.'

Madam Cao watched His Honour assess the crowd.

'Do you want them cleared, sir?' asked the officer.

'No,' said His Honour. 'His Imperial Majesty's justice does not hide. It may be seen by all his people, like the sun.'

Cao felt a shiver of premonition. Old Hsu the fan-maker knelt beside her. He raised an eyebrow as Apprentice Chung entered by a side door, accompanied by Dr Du Mau, who sported a golden belt-amulet showing his high office in the Guild of Physicians. Cao recoiled at the sight of Chung in fine new silks. It appeared he was trying to grow a man's moustache. His plump face was flushed, sullen and afraid. His fear was justified: the accuser might become the accused in a moment.

Now she understood it all. How she had delivered poor Shih to his enemies through foolish indiscretions. How Chung had avoided his conscription as a bomb-maker in the Bureau of Righteous Fire. She buried her gaze in the earth.

Finally, another side door opened and Dr Shih emerged,

assisted by one of the gaolers. Two weeks in the Prefectural prison had robbed his face of all colour. His wrists were raw from the chafing of iron manacles, his legs unsteady. Cao gasped at how thin he had grown. Dr Du Mau examined him curiously, too, except the only emotion he showed was a twitch in the corner of his mouth and a brooding glance at young Chung.

The latter seemed to find the floor of great interest – anywhere sooner than look at his former master or the ranks of kneeling people, many of whom were friends from Apricot Corner Court. He was particularly assiduous at avoiding Madam Cao's anxious face.

His Honour watched impassively as the accused fell to his knees and wearily pressed his forehead to the earthen floor.

'Commence with the impeachments against Dr Yun Shih,' he announced in a singsong voice to emphasise the gravity of the situation.

Cao listened to the charges. First Dr Du Mau showed a letter he had received from the Physician's Guild in the capital, Linan. Its contents did not entirely surprise her: that a scandal had occurred, contrary to all natural relations. That an apprentice had eloped with his master's daughter. That property had vanished when they fled the capital with *cash* and valuable medical equipment. No blame was offered against the girl, for it was assumed she must be a dupe to the male in the case. Cao bristled inwardly at these charges: was the best part of her life a crime?

'And you testify, Dr Du Mau,' drawled His Honour. 'That this letter passed through the blockade around our beloved Twin Cities. How strange, sir! Please explain.'

Dr Du Mau seemed surprised by this question, and not a little displeased.

'Everyone knows, Your Honour,' he said. 'That messages and much more besides reach us from the capital, if one is willing to pay a very high price. It is true, however, that a gentleman with great influence was involved. I fear it would be indiscreet to mention his name in so public a place.'

His Honour nodded understandingly.

'I believe there is also a witness.'

All attention shifted to Chung, who fell to his knees. Until now the crowd there to support Dr Shih had maintained a prudent silence. Many present remembered the orphan boy nurtured by the man he now accused. Others recollected Chung's weakness for gambling and that the same fault had brought about his father's suicide. Above all, their sense of *xiao* was outraged. The discomfort on Chung's face revealed an awareness of his unfilial conduct.

'Well then,' said His Honour. 'What are you?'

Chung bowed so many times while naming himself he resembled a bobbing heron.

'What do you know that is relevant to this case?'

Quite unexpectedly, Chung prostrated himself so that he was almost flat on the earthen floor of the courtroom: a sign of respect evidently not displeasing to His Honour.

'Madam Cao over there once told me that she and the master – as he was then, sir, though he is no more, now I am Dr Du Mau's loyal servant – that my *then* master, Dr Shih, ran away with her for love and without her father's permission, for her father, a Dr Ou-yang, sir, or so she claimed, was dead, and so he could not grant it.'

His Honour watched Chung with interest.

'Proceed,' he ordered.

'And, sir,' said Chung, in a rush. 'It means they never married at all. Yet they passed themselves off as respectable people. They deceived the trust of their neighbours, Your Honour, and of His Excellency Wang Ting-bo.'

These last phrases sounded as though they had been planted in the youth's mouth. For a moment there was silence in the long room. The crowd digested his words. Someone behind Cao muttered: 'It is a fault in Dr Shih, but marrying without permission is hardly unknown in Water Basin Ward.'

His Honour examined the top of Dr Shih's bent head. Cao followed the judge's gaze. The lofty thought processes of such a personage were unfathomable. Yet she did not like the way His Honour kept glancing at Dr Du Mau, as though for approval. The Du clan were powerful, especially across the water in Fouzhou. His Honour shrugged, washing his hands of the matter.

'Damning evidence,' he announced, reverting to a sing-song voice. 'Does the accused have anything to say in his defence?'

Dr Shih's head remained bowed for a long moment. Then he slowly looked up. His eyes sought out Madam Cao. Cracked lips tried to smile reassuringly when he found her. After that he did not shift his attention from her face.

'Do you offer no defence?' repeated His Honour, irritably.

Still Shih stared longingly at Cao, so that she felt herself blush before his steady look. The accused man turned towards the judge. A proud and disdainful expression transformed Shih's face, and he seemed about to speak. Never had he looked more like the resolute Captain Xiao.

'The charges against me relate to unfilial conduct,' he said, his voice weak and slightly breathless. 'Yet if I am to be condemned for a love-match, how many thousands in Nancheng must follow? The city is full of such marriages, as all know. True justice. . .' He coughed, painfully. 'Comprehends the human heart.'

Shih glanced again at his wife, the corners of his mouth lifting a little. His gentle brown eyes did not waver as he added: 'And I wish my wife to know that I regret nothing! Nothing! This foolish charge least of all. If I am to be found guilty for marrying such a lady then the law is unnatural. And quite at fault. Not her. Never her.'

Many in the crowd muttered approvingly at this fine speech. Old Hsu, in particular, nodded gravely. His Honour scowled and said: 'Be warned, if you offend me, I shall include your wife in the charges.'

Shih stiffened, his eyes opening wide. Then his shoulders sagged.

'In that case, sir,' he said. 'I have nothing more to say.'

His Honour sniffed, exchanging a look of satisfaction with Dr Du Mau.

'That settles the matter. My judgment is as follows. . .'

Before he could utter it, a slender, angry figure rose stiffly to his feet. Cao tried to persuade Old Hsu to kneel but the old man shook her off.

'I cannot remain silent!' he cried. 'It is obvious this court intends to punish my good neighbour, Dr Shih! And quite unjustly!'

Old Hsu's supporters murmured until their voices filled the room. His Honour watched through cold eyes. The court officials stirred uneasily, taking hold of their bamboo clubs.

'Dr Shih is a good man!' continued Old Hsu. 'Let him be, I say! That is true justice!'

At this the crowd broke into applause. His Honour nodded sagely.

'I am interested in your arguments,' he said. 'Indeed, you are familiar, old sir, from my inspection of Apricot Corner Court. Let the courtroom be emptied of everyone except Dr Shih's close neighbours, then I can question you further.'

This seemed entirely proper to Old Hsu – in many cases the law made one answerable for the crimes of one's neighbours. Had he been a lawyer he would have known it did not apply here. For the wickedness laid against Dr Shih pre-dated the accused man's residence at Apricot Corner Court.

As it was, Old Hsu enthusiastically ushered the crowd of supporters outside, just as the judge directed. Cao waited, all the while trying to catch Shih's eye. For the first time the accused wore a hopeful expression, yet kept his forehead low.

When the courtroom was almost empty and Old Hsu's allies had gone, His Honour turned to the constables: 'All Dr Shih's neighbours display a shameful, rebellious spirit. Their presence implies a criticism of the Son of Heaven's benevolent rule. Therefore all residents of Apricot Corner Court shall suffer collective punishment. Five strokes of the bamboo for each of them!'

A stunned silence greeted these words. Widow Mu cried out in fear and half-rose. Then she dragged her daughter, Lan Tien, forward.

'Your Honour,' pleaded Widow Mu. 'We are not all to blame! It is Old Hsu! He threatened to hurt me and my daughter if we did not come here. It was him, sir, not us! I beg you!'

His Honour's frown deepened.

'Is this true?' he demanded.

Old Hsu shook his head contemptuously.

'Your Excellency!' wailed Widow Mu, beside herself with fear. 'He holds traitorous views, sir! He claims the Mongols are our brothers, or could be!'

Now His Honour leaned forward.

'Do you?' he asked, quietly.

'All men have the potential to be brothers,' declared Old Hsu, while his sons desperately tried to hush him.

'Constables, take hold of this outrageous fellow,' ordered His Honour.

The fan-maker gasped as his arms were seized, but did not struggle.

'I sentence him to five extra strokes! He shall receive what the woman and her daughter are spared.'

But Old Hsu seemed uncowed: 'This is not just!' he declared.

Now His Honour flushed with rage.

'Very well, fifteen strokes!'

'Why do you keep looking to that doctor in fine silks for his approval?' jeered Old Hsu. 'Who is judge here? Him or you?'

'I sentence you to twenty strokes!' roared His Honour.

'Is this proof you possess the Mandate of Heaven?'

'Thirty strokes! Constable, let the sentence be carried out at once!'

Again the courtroom was silent except for Widow Mu's sobs. Old Hsu was approaching his seventh decade. So many blows were likely to have only one effect. The constables muttered among themselves, none eager to take the lead. At last, the youngest was chosen by his fellows. He swished the thick bamboo to test it.

Two constables tore Old Hsu's shirt so that his spindly spine was revealed. One could see his ribs pressing against papery skin. Cao glanced in horror at His Honour. Perhaps he regretted his angry judgement, for sweat had appeared on the fleshy forehead beneath the brim of his purple hat. But to alter his sentence now would entail loss of dignity. His Honour swallowed, moistening a dry throat.

'Proceed!' he said.

Even Dr Du Mau demurred.

'You Honour!' he broke in. 'This brings us no nearer to punishing Dr Yun Shih! May I beg that the old man wait his turn!'

'Proceed!'

Yet His Honour was not to be granted the last word. Old Hsu unexpectedly called out: 'One day the Great Society will sweep away all corruption! Men will live as brothers, whether you like it or not, and wise judges shall dispense justice freely!'

After such an outburst the bamboo-wielding constable had little option but to lay on with a will. A lack of zeal might suggest agreement with the crazy old man.

The first blow fell on Old Hsu's shoulders and he collapsed. Another hit him sharply across the spine, making a cracking noise. It was strange to hear an old man shriek so loudly. The third struck low down, at the base of the spine. With each blow, the young constable gained more confidence, as though beating an old man who resembled his grandfather was quite customary. He bent his knee stylishly and acquired a rhythm. After the fifteenth blow, Dr Du Mau cleared his throat.

'Your Honour,' he said. 'As an experienced practitioner, I must advise you that the constable is beating a corpse.'

The judge rose awkwardly, pushing back his high chair painted with images of King Chu Jiang. He glanced nervously at the crowd outside. People were peering in through the paper-curtained windows near the entrance.

Cao felt too weak to even lift her head. Her heart beat as though it would burst, yet the rhythm in her head was of the bamboo stick rising and falling. Old Hsu's sacrifice appalled her. She was afraid her own actions had caused his death. A gasping sob rose in her throat, yet she was too shocked to weep.

Cao could hear voices being raised. Certainly a riot was possible when Old Hsu's fate became known. At once she understood that Wang Ting-bo would hardly be pleased with His Honour for provoking a disturbance. The last thing the authorities needed in siege-time was public disunity. This hearing, after all, involved a relative of the Twin Cities' beloved hero, Captain Xiao. In a flash, Cao doubted whether Wang Ting-bo even knew of Shih's imprisonment.

'We will adjourn,' announced His Honour. 'Carry away the old man at once. Those gathered outside must disperse. Summon the Captain of the Guard so he may supervise it.'

Now it was Dr Du Mau's turn to grow angry.

'The verdict on Dr Shih is urgent!' he declared.

His Honour glared back.

'We shall deliver our final verdict on Dr Shih in a month's time. This hearing is over.'

His Honour hurried out and the lowly people pressed their foreheads to the ground. Dr Du Mau followed after him, as did Chung, quickly rising to his feet so that he would not be left alone with his former master and neighbours.

Cao watched the gaolers drag her husband away by his manacled hands. He seemed about to call out to her. Before he could speak, the door leading to the Prefectural prison closed with a bang.

Perhaps His Honour believed no trial would be necessary in a month's time, given the conditions Shih endured in gaol. Perhaps his soul would already be kneeling in another court – before the Infernal Judges of Hell.

憺

fourteen

'Disorder is the twin
of order.
Fear is the twin
of courage.
Weakness is the twin
of strength.

On dreadful ground,
hasten somewhere safer.
On death ground,
fight. . .'

From *The Art of War* by Sun-tzu

竹子

The Yangtze, Eastern China. Summer, 1267

The Winged Relief Fleet floated on the mighty Yangtze. An Immortal, flying across Heaven, could have counted two hundred craft bobbing like water dragons on the silver ribbon below.

But dragons have wings to carry them across the Eight

Directions. These ships possessed oars and stiff bamboo sails, paddlewheels driven by the hopes of a generation. Winged dragons are free to choose any roost. These ships shared one route – whether to glory or destruction no one could say.

Guang sat in the prow of an eight-oared barge, accompanying his patron, Wang Bai, to a vital ceremony. Their desperate attempt to re-provision the Twin Cities depended on securing Heaven's favour through a properly conducted rite. The light craft passed between merchant junks so laden with supplies they rode low in the water. Sailors and soldiers watched the progress of Wang Bai's barge from high rails and painted forecastles, noting the Wang clan's standard of three yellow chrysanthemums. A pair of shrieking gulls fought over scraps thrown from a war junk. When the oars dipped they released a clean river smell and trails of bubbles.

Guang noticed these small things. He remembered a poem by his illustrious ancestor where a river clearly represented love. Tender feelings seemed weakness in days like these, and no less precious for that. He glanced with brooding eyes at Wang Bai who was staring straight ahead, long-nailed hands hidden in trailing sleeves. Ever since the secret message to Mah-Chu in the capital, his patron had avoided private conversation. Sometimes he caught Wang Bai examining him in a calculating way.

Soon they reached the flagship of the fleet, a huge floating castle, three stories high. It was armed with a dozen catapults and devices for flaming naphtha, giant crossbows and a crew hundreds strong. An Imperial standard flew bravely from the topmost deck. Now Prefect Wang Bai deigned to look at Guang.

'I would advise you,' he said, quietly. 'Do exactly as I do, however unconventional my actions may seem.' He hesitated, then added: 'Let it never be said that the Wang clan does not reward its followers.'

Guang frowned at these strange words but followed Wang Bai up a wooden ladder to the topmost deck of the floating castle. A number of high officials had gathered, accompanied by magicians and soothsayers from the Imperial Bureau of Divination. To the side, wearing a mild smile, stood a slight, elderly figure in unpretentious robes. Guang recognised him as the new Supreme Pacification Commissioner for Nancheng Province, appointed to oversee Wang Ting-bo.

Wang Bai directed a look of barely-concealed scorn at the placid old man. Then his features smoothed.

The rites commenced with loud chanting and the banging of gongs to scare away hostile spirits. A white banner with *shen* painted upon it fluttered from a mast, indicating the cardinal point of the ceremony. A white goat was sacrificed on an altar with nine sides and nine arrows were fired west. Magicians read the shapes of clouds, muttering among themselves. Finally, the admiral of the fleet proceeded from the lower decks in white robes.

Guang blinked at the sight and could not help smiling, despite the importance of the occasion. For Admiral Qi-Qi made an incongruous figure in splendid silks. He had been commanded to lead the Relief Fleet up the Yangtze and Han River, an appointment of excellent wisdom, for no one knew the confused waterways leading to the Twin Cities better.

Yet when Admiral Qi-Qi took out the leaf-shaped ritual knife to behead a white cock upon the altar, his long robe caught on a splinter in the deck and he stumbled. Everyone gasped in horror. Guang, who stood nearby, lunged forward to steady him. He also momentarily lost his balance, though he kept the admiral upright.

The latter went quite pale. Well he might. Such a slip was a message from Heaven.

After the ceremony, Guang and Qi-Qi found time to draw apart from the others. The magicians and officials were drinking Five Blessings Wine to toast the Son of Heaven. The two soldiers met each other's eyes candidly.

'I slipped,' said Admiral Qi-Qi.

His face was still pale. It was noticeable that the soothsayers drew away from him when he came near, lest he infect them with bad luck.

'It was nothing!' declared Guang.

'Ah,' said Qi-Qi sorrowfully. 'You are kind. I fear there are some who will rejoice that Heaven sent so clear an indication of my ruin.'

He glanced over at the Excellent Wang Bai, who stood near the altar, listening attentively to everything the new Supreme Pacification Commissioner said. Guang would have liked to deny his patron was capable of such feelings, but he was an honest man, so he said: 'In steadying you, I slipped a little, too. We share the same fate and will deny it together!'

Zheng Qi-Qi smiled.

'You're a good sort, Yun Guang,' said the admiral. 'And you have grown in stature since the siege began. One day you will no longer need the Wang clan. . .'

He was interrupted by Wang Bai approaching the new Pacification Commissioner, to offer a perfunctory bow.

'Sir,' he drawled. 'Which is to be your honoured flagship?'

The old official smiled toothily.

'I did intend to use this fine vessel,' he said, indicating the floating castle on which the rites had been conducted. 'But Admiral Qi-Qi has advised me to join him on his own craft. It is a great secret, seemingly. For the Mongols will believe I am here, when really I am there.'

Wang Bai nodded.

'I see, Your Excellency,' he said, then withdrew.

Later, on board their paddle-wheel destroyer, Guang observed Wang Bai whispering to a merchant dressed in grey silks who had been allowed on board by special permission. The merchant hurried off and took a rowing boat back to Jiankung. Guang turned away, wondering what such a conference might mean. Wang Bai, like many scholars and aristocrats, was fastidious about shunning the *shang*, or merchant classes. Except, of course, for the sake of profit.

'Commander!' called a sharp voice. Guang turned to meet

the glint of his patron's bright eyes. 'If you had not tried to steady that fool Zheng Qi-Qi you would not have stumbled. As it is, Heaven has infected you with his misfortune. Therefore, keep your distance from him. I believe he will never return to Nancheng.'

Guang bowed obediently. Yet his heart revolted against Wang Bai's prudence.

竹子

A week later, the Ineffable Winged Relief Fleet reached the confluence of the Yangtze and Han rivers. They had been treated like heroes in town after town on the way. Every ship in the fleet wore crowns of wilting flowers. Some places they passed hired orchestras to play martial themes on the shore. Others sent out gifts of food and drink, as well as lucky banners petitioning Heaven to reward its Chosen Son, for none of the local officials dared appear disloyal. Always there had been flowers plaited to form fortunate characters or loaded in baskets woven from reeds.

Guang observed such outbursts of revelry with mixed feelings. So obvious was the Relief Fleet's progress that surprise was impossible. He knew from past experience the Mongols were capable of deadly preparations. Another part of him wished that these people, so willing to feast and toast in opposition to the great Khan, would take up halberds and crossbows instead. He confided this doubt to Chen Song.

'One could arm the peasants and merchants as you suggest,' said his friend. 'But they would mill around in confusion. His Imperial Majesty lacks advisers capable of mobilising the people's zeal!'

He had rarely seen his friend so earnest. Guang felt a deep confusion, one he dared not speak aloud. And so, he did not reply.

The meeting place of the Han and Yangtze rivers was a water country of wide lakes and flooded rice fields. Despite its strategic importance only a small fortress stood there. It was assumed the Mongols would never manage to advance beyond the Twin Cities. Guang watched flocks of white seabirds on sandbank islands, envying their freedom. Compared to the vast, ever flowing waters on which they floated, the Ineffable Winged Relief Fleet seemed insignificant. So intense were his feelings that he did not notice the Excellent Wang Bai's approach.

'Yun Guang,' said Wang Bai, softly. 'I am glad to find you without your shadow.'

'Chen Song is inspecting one of the other ships in the flotilla, sir,' said Guang. 'At my instructions.'

Wang Bai looked at him sharply.

'I believe you to be an intelligent man. Indeed, one who will prove useful to my family when all the threads of these days have unravelled. Is my faith misplaced?'

'I do not understand, sir,' said Guang. 'You must be more plain.'

Wang Bai smiled sadly.

'We all become things we never expected,' he said. 'So it is from early childhood. One cannot deny the common fate. But I will speak plainly, as you ask. At dawn I must leave this fleet and travel overland back to Nancheng. I advise you to join me. I fear the Ineffable Winged Relief Fleet will never reach the Twin Cities. It has another destiny.'

Guang shook his head in wonder.

'Does the new Supreme Pacification Commissioner know of your decision?' he asked.

'No, and nor shall he, until I have gone. I take it I may rely on your discretion?'

Guang nodded reluctantly. Wang Bai's action might be called desertion, even cowardice. He could not comprehend his noble patron's motives.

'So you will accompany me?' asked Wang Bai.

'Sir,' said Guang, unable to meet his patron's eye. 'I cannot do as you suggest. It is not. . .'

He meant to say 'loyal' – to comrades and friends, to the Son of Heaven himself. But he did not wish to diminish Wang Bai's face. Yet for the first time he considered his patron as someone new – the vile word *coward* hovered at the corners of his mind. Wang Bai sighed.

'I suspected you would choose what you have chosen. Are you not Captain Xiao, after all?'

Guang stiffened and Wang Bai smiled mirthlessly.

'I do not mock you!' he said. 'Indeed, I envy your noble simplicity. Goodbye, Captain Xiao.'

To Guang's surprise, Wang Bai ruefully nodded his head. It was a small movement. Not a proper bow. Yet it spoke more than ten thousand characters.

Guang slept as usual beneath the stars, covered by a single quilt. When he awoke, dawn mists filled the river. He found that Wang Bai had left the paddle-destroyer with a small escort of his closest servants, leaving the Wang family banners at the prow and stern. Guang chose to let them remain. After all, one might as well die beneath the flag of a Wang as a Son of Heaven.

Paddle wheels churned and oars rose. The Winged Relief Fleet entered the gauntlet of the Han River, advancing towards the Twin Cities. Guang watched for traces of his patron on the shore. The land was a vast confusion of villages, lakes, paddy fields, low hills and terraces. Peasants were specks. Wang Bai had vanished altogether.

竹子

'You should report his defection!' insisted Chen Song.

'That is too harsh a word,' replied Guang. 'And unjust.'

Chen Song shook his head.

'He has abandoned his duty!'

'How so? His mission was to advise the court of our plight. No stipulation was made of returning to the Twin Cities by ship, rather than overland. He can hardly be called a traitor for that. And he is not yet under the new Supreme Pacification Commissioners' jurisdiction, which does not come into force until we reach Nancheng.'

'An unpleasant word might be used,' muttered Chen Song. 'One fatal to his honour.'

To this Guang had no reply.

'Thankfully the new Supreme Pacification Commissioner is made of sterner stuff,' continued Chen Song. 'Of course the Wang clan hopes he will never arrive in Nancheng. Their authority in the province will be greatly damaged when Wang Ting-bo is no longer in charge.'

'No doubt,' said Guang.

He nodded courteously to his friend and departed to inspect the readiness of the marines and catapults. It was nearly midnight. They had travelled up the Han River for three days and were within another day's sailing of Nancheng.

Early that evening, as dusk released clouds of mosquitoes, Admiral Qi-Qi called a meeting of commanders on his flagship. No one remarked upon Wang Bai's absence. After all, he was a civilian rather than military official and so might view a conference of war as beneath his dignity. Certainly the new Pacification Commissioner did not stoop to attend.

'Meticulous timing is necessary to prise apart the jaws clamped round the Twin Cities,' declared Admiral Qi-Qi. 'Once the Relief Fleet has burst through General A-ku can gnash his teeth in rage.'

He ordered that they must arrive at sunset, when the Mongol artillery and crossbowmen would be hampered by poor visibility. Qi-Qi then unrolled a map, showing the twin fortresses constructed by General A-ku on either side of the river, a few *li* downstream from the Twin Cities. 'These are their fangs,' he said. 'Yet if we are swift, their catapults will only sink a few vessels. The rest of us will assuredly reach our destination.'

The other commanders were silent as he concluded. Perhaps they wondered if their own ships would perish. More fearful than drowning was the prospect of capture; the inevitable march north to a lifetime of dishonour and drudgery in a mine, never to see one's parents or ancestral shrine again. Suicide was obviously preferable.

At last Guang spoke up: 'The enemy have assembled a fleet of their own. I believe they will be deployed against us where the river is broadest. Our vessels are heavy and theirs are light craft, easily rammed and sunk. Hence they will seek to harry us like wolves running round a herd of deer.'

'That is quite certain, though their navy is small,' replied Admiral Qi-Qi. 'I advise a good night's sleep. If Heaven favours us, we shall drink the ritual wine of happiness in Nancheng tomorrow evening!'

No one mentioned that Heaven had showed little favour when the Admiral's robe snagged on a splinter.

Guang usually slept fitfully before battle. Many around him found no sleep at all. Low conversations and the creak of footfalls on deck carried across the still water. A bamboo flute uttered mournful trills like a grieving nightingale.

His paddle-wheel destroyer had been positioned in the vanguard of the fleet, for it was large and well-armed. When he glanced back from the raised stern he saw a tangle of black shapes silhouetted by the east: raised oars and masts; wooden turrets floating on blocks of shadow; lines of red and blue lanterns like fire-flies.

Tens of thousands manned these ships – sailors and soldiers, merchants and craftsmen. The new Supreme Pacification Commissioner was accompanied by scores of handpicked officials, ready to replace laggards and incompetents in Wang Ting-bo's administration.

Tomorrow all this weight of wood and metal and human flesh must be propelled through a rain of hostile missiles. If the Relief Fleet ground to a halt, they would be lost. If they became entangled with the Mongol river fleet, they would be lost. If the enemy had somehow managed to obstruct the river, ship upon ship would pile up stern to prow – and they would be lost.

Yet Guang did not consider these things. His thoughts flew up the dark river to Nancheng and, once there, entered Water Basin Ward and Apricot Corner Court. There he brooded, wondering whether the people he loved most in this illusory world would weep if he perished. Father would barely notice. As for Shih and Cao, he knew their hearts well enough to foresee both their grief and, in time, acceptance of his loss.

There was another who should not have entered his thoughts. When he closed his eyes Lu Ying's lovely face filled the scroll of his mind, unrolling through the brief moments they had shared together, nearly all awkward yet, somehow, significant. But that was nonsense! How would she behave if his body was found face down in the cold river? Would she show even a moment's distress?

Guang sighed. He lay down on the deck, protected from the dawn dew by his coarse quilt. The thought of her was merely a longing for a new life. One he had never believed possible.

When he awoke, the flying dragon paddle-wheel destroyer was in motion. True to Admiral Qi-Qi's command they laboured upstream all day, slowed only by the merchant junks' heavy cargoes.

Sixteen hours later, the light was thickening in a way peculiar to magnificent summer evenings, when blues darken and high clouds lose their reflected sheen. The fleet advanced, silent except for the creak of oars and bamboo sails, the low beat of drums, the constant plashing of paddle wheels.

Everything was ready for battle on Guang's ship. Bombs of various kinds were stowed and hidden from fire arrows. Quivers of crossbow bolts stood beside ropes and grappling irons. Buckets of mud had been strategically placed to choke fires. Chen Song, ever filial, conducted a rite to deter river-demons, involving red earth and yellow powder. It seemed every vessel in the fleet was deploying magic. Strange coloured smokes rose and the river was littered with strips of paper on which spells had been inscribed.

Thirty *li* south of the Twin Cities they encountered the first signs of the enemy. Horsemen rode along the shore where it was not too muddy, monitoring their progress and galloping off in relays to inform General A-ku. A few sailors bellowed insults. Some loosed crossbow bolts until ordered not to waste arrows. Every shaft would be needed soon enough.

At a bend in the river, the stream narrowed to a mere two *li* in width. At last the Mongols commenced their assault. A dozen large catapults had been erected behind a bamboo palisade, assisted by a battalion of archers. As the Relief Fleet crept past, the air filled with arrows and bombs trailing smoke. A ram-vessel alongside Guang's own was struck by a thunder-clap bomb and set ablaze. For a moment he flinched, aware they could not slow to help the stricken boat.

Admiral Qi-Qi ordered his ships to reply in kind and, miraculously, the Mongol forces were soon faring worse. One by one their catapults were set on fire. As they sailed past, Chen Song ducked to avoid a flight of arrows.

'Here we are forced near to the shore,' he said. 'Why do they not deploy more artillery?'

Guang shared the same doubt, yet answered airily: 'Because General A-ku has built two splendid forts which he hopes will crush our spirits like two bricks gelding a horse!'

Chen Song laughed and loosed an arrow of his own. By now the Mongol horsemen on the shore were numerous. As dusk fell, a few lit flaming torches. It seemed every clump of reeds or copse on the bank concealed archers vying to test their skill. Arrows whistled past Guang's head as he stood boldly by the helmsman, who crouched under cover beside his rudder. Such a display of fearlessness had a purpose. Guang longed to conjure a name from his men – and soon enough, he earned his reward: 'Captain Xiao! See how Captain Xiao scorns their arrows!'

But the danger was real enough and he ordered the troops to stay low.

Now the river widened considerably as they approached the Twin Cities. Twilight was deepening. Clouds drifted in the night breeze. To the west, in the direction of Nancheng, the sky bore a red tint as though the Twin Cities were ablaze.

Admiral Qi-Qi ordered the deployment of blue lanterns. At this signal, the Ineffable Winged Relief Fleet slowly took up a rectangular formation. The merchant junks and supply vessels were surrounded by four walls of attack ships. Guang's paddle-wheel destroyer had been assigned a forward corner of the rectangle – a most honourable station because especially dangerous.

When the manoeuvring ceased, the fleet drifted silently in the current, awaiting the signal to commence the final thrust. In this pause, Guang descended below decks. A hundred tired sailors lolled near their treadmills. The hold of the ship stank of sweat and lamp oil, as well as rancid bilge water. A few feeble lamps glimmered in the darkness, catching the white sheen of anxious eyes.

'Sergeant,' he ordered, loudly. 'Ensure wine is passed among these men!'

For a strange moment he recollected the wineskin that had been passed to Li Tse in the fog of the Mongol camp. How the artillery officer had been captured and tortured until broken. He shook the memory away – it seemed an omen.

Back on deck there was no time for doubt. The last ship had closed the defensive walls of the rectangle and Admiral Zheng Qi-Qi ordered a signal rocket into the star-lit sky. It exploded with a silver flash.

'Advance!' bellowed Guang.

His shout was matched by a thousand other voices. The Ineffable Winged Relief Fleet slowly gained momentum, each captain keeping a close eye on his neighbours' positions until the foremost ships traversed a wide bend in the river flanked by low, bamboo-clad hills.

'Beyond this bend we shall glimpse the Twin Cities,' said Chen Song.

He had to shout, his voice drowned out by enthusiastic drumming and the rumbling splash of the paddle wheels. As they rounded the river-bend Guang examined the terrain ahead.

General A-ku's forts stood on either shore like a parody of Fouzhou and Nancheng. Many torches and braziers illuminated them at night. But this did not explain the fiery glow the Relief Fleet must pass through to reach the Twin Cities. Hundreds of fires had been lit along the shore. The night stank of burning wood and damp straw. Sparks and wisps of curling hay rose towards the stars.

Every catapult and huge siege crossbow A-ku possessed had been moved to the area round the river forts – an incalculable labour, and one that required prior warning of the exact timing of the fleet's approach. Guang met Chen Song's startled gaze. Both shared the same thought: treachery had woven this noose. Then he seized Chen Song's arm.

'All buckets must be filled to extinguish fires,' he ordered. 'All crossbowmen must loose at will.'

Chen Song's armoured figure clattered away. By now they were drawing parallel to the first, upright silhouettes of the Mongol catapults. The fires on the shore illuminated the Relief Fleet clearly and a loud, ululating cheer reached them from the enemy lines. Guang's impulsive gorge rose.

'Loose! Loose!' he roared.

Their volleys of crossbow bolts and lime-bombs were handfuls of sticks thrown at a waterfall. For the sky filled with clouds of flaming arrows. Thunderclap bombs streamed down from heaven like meteors. Some bounced and exploded on the water, spreading clouds of arsenic and thick smoke. Others, iron-cased, detonated with huge, echoing reports, scattering shards of metal and stone. One bomb landed on the front section of Guang's ship, exploding with a roar that killed half-a-dozen men and shattered two whirling tiger catapults. The wounded lay on the splintered planking of the deck, gashed by bomb casings. Guang stumbled through smoke to the injured. Screams filled the air. He found Chen Song already there, bellowing for help.

'The hatch!' shouted Guang. 'We must take them below!'

He reached down to ease a wounded man to his feet and slipped in the pools of blood on the deck. So the warning from Heaven was coming true! Guang picked himself up, a wild, reckless expression on his handsome face.

'I defy you,' he muttered, though only Heaven could hear him.

With unexpected tenderness, he scooped up a wounded soldier whose arm had been almost torn off by a shard of iron and carried him into the hold of the ship. At the bottom of the steps, willing hands took the man. Guang felt something drip on his head through the broken planking of the deck and glanced up. A droplet landed on his lips. It took a moment to recognise the iron taste.

Back on deck he surveyed the fleet, or what was visible of it in the darkness and smoke of the battlefield. Several ships were sinking or on fire. From one, amidst a roaring swirl of flames, he saw armoured men leaping into the river. Elsewhere a small craft had been struck by a boulder. It floundered in the water like a stricken whale. Guang watched in horror as the huge mass of Admiral Qi-Qi's flagship ploughed into the little boat, sinking both vessel and crew, who were crushed by the whirling paddlewheels.

Yet Qi-Qi's ship was itself constantly struck by missiles. The Mongol commanders seemed to know it contained not only the Admiral, but the Son of Heaven's new representative in Nancheng Province. As a commander of artillery, Guang recognised a clear pattern to the missiles falling around Qi-Qi's ship. Whole teams of catapults on the shore were trained on the secret flagship.

The Emperor's standard fluttered, stiff as a bamboo sail; the entire fleet advanced upstream. Now they drew close to the forts on either side of the river. From the battlements, siege crossbows poured a steady stream of giant bolts tipped with flaming gourds onto the fleet. A small war junk behind Guang's took a hit from a thunderclap bomb, tearing open its decks. Yet the ship struggled forward. They had no other choice – the shore meant death or worse. There was no turning back.

At last the Relief Fleet passed through the snapping jaws of A-ku's fortresses and artillery. It was said by survivors that the decks of many ships were ankle-deep with blood. Yet only a few sank from the relentless bombardment. Those that survived found themselves entering an ever-widening stretch of river, more like a long lake, with only a few *li* to traverse before reaching the safety of the Twin Cities.

Guang felt his heart lift at the sight of the city walls and towers. There was Fouzhou across the water from Nancheng! Gallant Fouzhou! And surely that distant line of fireflies on the river, joining the two cities, was the Floating Bridge's lamps. He noticed a yellow alarm rocket rising from Qi-Qi's flagship, followed by another.

'Halt!' Guang screamed at the helmsman. 'Halt, but maintain the formation.'

For creeping across the water, barely lit by dim lanterns, were lines of low shapes. Their shadowy approach suggested a desire to win the advantage of surprise. It was the Mongol river fleet, deploying in two phalanxes to block their way. All this had been anticipated. Yet no one had expected so many. When Guang left the Twin Cities a few months earlier, only dozens of hostile craft were afloat. Now hundreds filled the river.

竹子

'How are there so many?' asked Guang, in wonder. 'It is not possible. And how did they get past the Floating Bridge?'

'I suspect the answer is simple,' replied his friend. 'Those boats were constructed upstream and carried overland round the Twin Cities, thereby avoiding the barrier of the Floating Bridge. And see! Though their craft are numerous, all are small war barges, easy enough to carry. We may thank traitors for that.'

Guang thought of Wang Bai when Chen Song spoke of an overland route.

'One may not blame traitors for everything,' he said, sullenly.

'Let us hope you are right,' said Chen Song.

No time remained for further speculation. A blue signal rocket rose from Admiral Qi-Qi's paddle destroyer. Once again the exhausted Relief Fleet advanced. A mere six *li* and they would reach the Water Gate of Morning Radiance! Six *li* and they would be safe!

Perhaps this prospect goaded them on, for they gathered speed quickly. Meanwhile the horde of Mongol attack ships, manned by Chinese conscripts and turncoats from the North, rushed towards them. Guang at once discerned their tactics, as did the resourceful Admiral Qi-Qi.

'Close the gaps between ships!' he bellowed.

Flags waved from the crow's nest to reinforce his orders. Few could see them in the smoke and darkness. And there was no time. In a moment nimble Mongol war barges were riding between the larger vessels, trying like wolves to find the weak merchant junks at the heart of the Relief Fleet. Crossbow bolts and catapult-hurled bombs flew. Jets of naphtha fell upon several enemy ships so that they blazed fiercely. A new scent joined the reek of burning powder and smoke choking the Han River: that of roasting meat.

Yet a dozen war barges waited to take the place of every one the Relief Fleet sank. The progress of the larger ships slowed to a wallowing halt. Guang watched in horror as twenty of the small craft swarmed round Admiral Qi-Qi's stricken paddle destroyer. It was as though, like the artillery earlier, they knew the ship's importance. No sacrifice seemed too great to destroy the yellow ship. Naphtha grenades were being hurled from every side. Soon the river was a nightmare of flames.

'No!' cried Guang.

Too late. Admiral Zheng Qi-Qi, one arm protecting the terrified Supreme Pacification Commissioner, went down, punctured by crossbow bolts. Then the yellow flagship was engulfed in fire and Guang turned away, too sickened to watch.

Elsewhere the Mongol war barges were suffering. The survivors fled back towards their fellows, forming a mass of confused boats between the Ineffable Winged Relief Fleet and the safety of Nancheng. Guang slowly raised his eyes and looked around. With the loss of its great leader, the fleet seemed to falter. They were trapped. A hundred war barges lay ahead; behind lay the gauntlet of A-ku's catapults.

All his life Guang had longed for glory. Yet when his shining hour came there seemed no nobility to it. Barely even a choice. If valour may be called a skill he had exercised it many times – strutting on the battlements of Swallow Gate while boulders fell around him, sneaking behind Mongol lines. These preparations amounted to one thing: that he should not care whether he grew old.

'Chen Song!' barked Commander Yun Guang. 'I assume temporary command of the Fleet. Order our own ship to the front of the formation.'

His lieutenant lost no time in doing so. Guang felt his blood quicken as they left the protective rectangle of the fleet. Now all eyes could see his craft. The light from Qi-Qi's burning flagship spread across the water.

This was not enough. Guang took up a flaming torch and stood on the high stern of his paddle-wheel destroyer. He shouted to a nearby ship: 'Commander Yun Guang orders all craft to rush the enemy, and not cease until their prows touch the jetties of Nancheng! Captain Xiao orders a complete advance!'

For a moment there was silence. Then his command was shouted from deck to deck. With it came cheering, incoherent at first, then the familiar name: *Captain Xiao! Captain Xiao!* At this he could barely restrain himself.

'Forward!' he bellowed. 'May we be reborn as tigers not sheep!'

The paddle-wheels creaked and turned. Almost immediately he outstripped the front lines of the Relief Fleet's rectangle, a lone, reckless craft. But his was by no means the fastest vessel in the fleet. Soon others had drawn alongside, equally wild in their desire to meet the enemy.

Now it was the Mongol's turn to waver. The failure of their initial attack had daunted them. Scores of the war barges fled to the shore before the onslaught of the Relief Fleet. Quite as many held their station. Naphtha bombs arched from ship to ship, along with missiles of every kind. Those who had run out of better weapons hurled curses and strips of shattered planking. Within the space of a few minutes hundreds of families on both sides were given reason to grieve for long years.

Yet one by one the ships of the Relief Fleet reached the safety of the Twin Cities' high stone ramparts. Commander Yun Guang's was among the first to arrive at the Gate of the Vermilion Sparrow, where the Floating Bridge linked Nancheng and Fouzhou.

Jubilation greeted the bump of its prow on the stone jetty. Men hugged each other, tears on their grizzly cheeks. A most splendid thing! Their beloved Captain Xiao had won through yet again. How noble was his demeanour, like a fearless tiger! A dragon of the Empire! If only, many onlookers thought privately, Wang Ting-bo and the Son of Heaven's ministers were like him. Then the Mongols would be banished soon enough and their Great Khan driven back to his barbarous palace in the wastelands.

Slowly the frantic cheers died away. A long silence was followed by muttering. For on the deck of the ship lay a familiar figure, clad in a suit of armour well-known to the defenders of Nancheng. His armour was torn open at the chest. His face caked with blood and soot. A stubby crossbow bolt protruded from Commander Yun Guang's left shoulder.

Another hero well-known to the onlookers, Captain Xiao's

dogged lieutenant, Chen Song, knelt beside the fallen man. Then a question passed from mouth to mouth. *Is Captain Xiao dead? Is he wounded or dead?*

He did not twitch when the crossbow bolt was gently pulled loose and blood welled over his lamellar armour. Perhaps that spurt indicated his heart was still beating. A doctor might have answered that question at once. As if by good luck, Dr Du Tun-i, returning from his uncle's house in Fouzhou to the North Medical Relief Bureau, was among the bystanders. He hesitated, then stepped forward to offer assistance, a strange, wilful look on his young face.

竹子

Shih had been moved to this tiny cell a day after the trial. The Chief Warder had appeared and personally led him away from the main prison block with its chains and diseased stench.

'I never knew you had a wealthy friend,' the Chief Warder said, more affably than Shih had believed possible. 'Aren't you Captain Xiao's brother? Perhaps that explains it.'

Shih's cracked lips had attempted a ghastly smile. His brother's superiority and influence, once vexing, seemed the most desirable thing in the world – anything to escape the Prefectural prison. Yet it seemed he had escaped without any assistance from Guang, who was far away. The Chief Warder winked when Shih asked the name of his benefactor, saying he should thank 'a pearl, sir, a real pearl!'

Dr Shih found himself in a narrow cell, four feet wide, yet tall enough for him to stand upright. It possessed a single window, heavily barred. Through that window came light and air, proof of day and night. Then vegetables and rice arrived. At first Shih examined the food suspiciously. Did His Honour or Dr Du Mau mean to poison him? But his nostrils urged the wholesomeness of the meal. Quite as miraculously it was followed by other meals, equally nourishing, each and every day. The Chief Warder regularly opened his cell door to examine him, as one might a pot-bellied sow fattened for market. Always he grunted the same question: 'You well?' When Shih nodded so did his captor, and the door slammed.

At dusk he was allowed to exercise by the outer walls of the Prefectural enclosure. There he would listen for stray sounds from the city. No visitors were allowed and no messages reached him from Apricot Corner Court. Often Shih slumped against the wall as darkness gathered, longing for someone whose loyalty and love were quite proven – and no longer taken for granted.

On the evening of the Winged Relief Fleet's arrival in Nancheng, Shih lay on the floor of his cell, listening to the muffled echoes of distant explosions through the brick wall. He understood from the noise that an intense battle was devouring itself. Quite unexpectedly he sensed Guang's presence out there amidst the thudding reports.

Hours after midnight, Shih was woken by a great ringing of gongs and bells. He remained by the door, staring into darkness. Slowly night crept towards dawn, painting a feeble rectangle of light round the doorframe. He heard the tramp of feet marching at the double. They seemed to pause for a while at the prison gates. Then boots trotted toward his cell and halted outside. He detected the Chief Warder's voice murmuring deferentially. Dr Shih shrank back, certain His Honour had brought forward the trial date. When the cell door swung open a soldier in full armour was revealed.

Shih stared at him in half-recognition. Could this be Guang's friend, Chen Song? If so his splendid armour had been torn, its silver tassels burned away. A long gash on his cheek wept a discharge of watery blood.

To Shih's amazement, Chen Song bowed. It was the first respect he had been shown since his arrest.

'Dr Yun Shih,' said Chen Song. 'Very sorry to see you in this place!'

'I am accused of a serious crime,' said Dr Shih. 'Have you heard?'

Chen Song nodded.

'I bring good news,' he said. 'His Excellency Wang Ting-bo has authorised the abandonment of all charges. On a single condition. You must follow my instructions without argument for the next few hours.'

'What are these instructions?'

'First you must accompany me.'

Shih hesitated. He sensed Guang lay at the heart of this mysterious offer.

'Is my brother safe?'

Chen Song looked around, checking whether they were overheard. Warders were nearby, kneeling in respectful positions.

'You must accompany me,' repeated the soldier. 'I can say no more.'

A carriage drawn by three horses waited at the prison gates and Shih's sense of wonder grew. It was one of those used by Wang Ting-bo himself.

Though Chen Song urged him inside, Shih held back, remembering the last time he had entered a carriage. He looked around. They were at the summit of Peacock Hill, one of the highest vantage points in the city. From here he could see the river below, full of ships. The Ineffable Winged Relief Fleet was feverishly unloading its cargo, stripping the vessels of anything remotely useful to the Twin Cities. Although Shih could not know it, nearly all the merchant junks and warships had survived the battle.

When Shih gazed upstream, north of the Floating Bridge toward lands occupied by the Great Khan, he breathed in sharply.

'Is *that* what I believe it to be?' he asked.

'It is.' The scholar-soldier sounded unutterably weary. 'The enemy have gathered a large river fleet and mean to destroy the Floating Bridge from upstream. If they succeed the Twin Cities must perish.'

'Where is my brother?'

'There is more,' said Chen Song, pointing at Swallow Gate. Shih sought out the Mongol encampments and shrank back in surprise. Tens of thousands of warriors were spreading out like a black stain. Between their regiments stood huge wooden bridges on wheels, wide enough, when joined together, to cross the ninety-foot moats around the city. Behind the mobile bridge were scores of cloud ladders and siege towers.

'How is this?'

Despite his tiredness, Chen Song smiled sadly.

'The enemy anticipated our every move. First, they expected to destroy the Relief Fleet. However, in that they were unsuccessful. Nevertheless, while we are in mourning and confusion, they will attack by land and water – seizing both the Floating Bridge and our ramparts. General A-ku has deployed every single man in his army.'

Chen Song's grip on Shih's arm unconsciously tightened as they stared from Peacock Hill at the advancing horde.

'Can they be stopped?' asked the poor doctor, out of his depth.

'Perhaps,' said Chen Song. 'That is why I have come to collect you. You see, our forces down by the river have lost the will to fight. Not only is Admiral Qi-Qi dead, but an ugly rumour circulates that Captain Xiao has also perished. That all hope is lost.'

Shih gasped. Guang lost! He could not imagine Guang taken away. So strong and brave! He could not accept it.

'You are a liar!' he cried .

'Exactly!' nodded Chen Song. 'Exactly! Captain Xiao cannot perish, today of all days. Climb into the carriage, I implore you. We have little time.'

They set off with a jolt. So frantic was the pace that Shih was thrown around inside. He could hear the canter of Chen Song's horse alongside. Now they were passing through the market place, deserted except for huddles of hungry peasants in makeshift tents. Parting the curtain, he recognised a large tea-house and knew they were near the Gate of the Vermilion Sparrow, leading to the Floating Bridge.

Chen Song led the carriage into a small courtyard filled with shadow. The place was deserted, apart from a few guardsmen with tense expressions and a high official wearing the turquoise robes of the Third Grade.

As Shih emerged, Chen Song threw a blanket over his head and led him into an echoing building. A door slammed behind them. The blanket was twitched away.

At first Shih wondered if Guang's corpse had been laid out on a long, low table. But no, it was his suit of armour and helmet. The armour was torn across the chest and blood-stained. Then Shih understood.

'Ah,' he sighed, glimpsing he was alone again in this world. Utterly alone except for Cao. 'Ah.'

Tears began to well in the corners of his eyes. Chen Song nodded stiffly.

'The entire fleet reacts as you do,' he said, 'especially the defenders of the Floating Bridge. They believe resistance is futile without Admiral Qi-Qi and Captain Xiao. Some have even cast down their weapons. But see! Does not that armour fit you exactly?'

Shih's bowed head did not rise. Indeed he rocked a little in his distress.

'I will answer my own question for you,' said Chen Song, doggedly. 'It fits you exactly.'

Shih lifted his head in astonishment but Chen Song's look was implacable.

Half an hour later the doors were flung open and a procession trooped into the street. At its head marched Commander Yun Guang, carrying an extravagantly tasselled halberd, his face half hidden by a visored helmet. Chen Song followed a little behind. As they approached the Gate of the Vermilion Sparrow they met a group of fleeing men. The retreating soldiers stopped in their tracks at the sight of Captain Xiao in his blood-stained armour and exchanged fearful glances. One by one, they fell to their knees. The familiar spell was whispered *Captain Xiao! He's come back. He wants to fight them!*

The Mongol river fleet was manoeuvring into an attack formation upstream from the Floating Bridge. Ordinarily, such a frontal assault would have been suicidal. In addition to a man-made island constructed in the middle of the river, topped by a high tower, hundreds of iron-tipped stakes were embedded in the mud to halt attacking ships. But these defences meant nothing without determined men to hold the ground.

Confusion was everywhere. News of the vast army outside Swallow Gate had thrown many into despair. The soldiers wavered, debating in groups or slipping quietly towards Nancheng and the possibility of a hiding place if the city fell. Then the floorboards of the Floating Bridge resounded with heavy footfalls.

Some peered in disbelief, unwilling to trust their own eyes. Could one who had been carried out feet first recover so quickly? Of course it could be so! His features were well known. How proudly he walked beside his companion, the Honourable Chen Song!

When Captain Xiao marched down the wooden planks of the Floating Bridge in his mauled armour, nearly every man present took it as a reproach to their faltering courage.

At the man-made island he addressed a gathering of officers, Chen Song whispering in his ear. Certainly it was Captain Xiao's voice that spoke, though less harshly than usual. It seemed a clear sign of his unshaken confidence. Meanwhile the Mongol fleet drew closer.

'They cannot defeat us if we hold firm!' he cried.

There was a pause.

'They are fools!' shouted Commander Yun Guang, after more murmuring from his lieutenant. 'Their ships shall be trapped on our lines of iron-tipped stakes! Burn them with naphtha and maintain a wall of crossbowmen! All we need do is stand firm!'

Now the assembled officers grasped a course of action. Crates were hurried along the bridge from the Gate of the Vermilion Sparrow. As the enemy ships entered range, the air filled with crossbow bolts and fire arrows. Meanwhile Captain Xiao had climbed the tower for a better view and was hurriedly conferring with Chen Song. When he had finished, Commander Yun Guang raised his tasselled halberd and strolled from the tower to join his men on the Floating Bridge.

'A thousand years!' he cried.

That fervent hope flew from mouth to mouth.

A thousand years! A thousand years!

憎

fifteen

'Terrible to be born a wretched woman!
What on earth is so forlorn?
Nurtured without true affection,
For her family a temporary burden.
On the board of marriage a pawn,
In shuttered rooms she sits hidden,
All contact with her family forsaken,
Her husband's love as distant as the sun,
Yet she follows his moods as leaves do the sun!
What misdeeds in a former existence
Condemn one to rebirth as a wretched woman?'

Fu Xuan

竹子

Water Gate of Morning Radiance, Nancheng. Autumn, 1267

The sky no longer drifted with rain and other signs of autumn arrived. Day by day darkness settled earlier. Birds gathered on the river and chill winds whistled down from Mount Wadung.

Just such a breeze tugged at the baggy clothes of three women working a narrow strip of land between the stone ramparts of Nancheng and the River Han. They made an unlikely collection. One could not call them family – none bore the slightest resemblance to one another. An observer on the ramparts might not even have detected a joint purpose between them. Two of the women worked with a will while the third's movements were slow and resentful. At last they paused and surveyed a large tangle of coarse-smelling weeds surrounded by boggy ground.

'Are we to reap all *that*?' asked a supercilious voice.

The voice belonged to Lu Ying; and Madam Cao struggled hard to conceal her irritation, for she could not ignore the extent of her obligation to the former concubine.

After Dr Shih's trial, Old Hsu's funeral had been a noisy affair. Apricot Corner Court filled with wailing and the sound passed as a rumour through Water Basin Ward to other districts of the city. Few who heard the tale sympathised with the authorities. Madam Cao had wept as freely as Old Hsu's relatives, her grief barbed with guilt that he had died defending Shih's honour; she knew that the crack of the bamboo club on the old man's spine would echo in her dreams until the day she died.

However, there had been one mourner in Apricot Corner Court who took Madam Cao by surprise. Lu Ying made no secret of her remorse at not petitioning Wang Ting-bo on Dr Shih's behalf: 'If I had done as you suggested, who knows whether that funny old man would still be alive!' she had cried, biting her plump lips. 'I am a selfish creature, Madam Cao, not like you or your kind husband.' But it also became apparent that when it came to the ways of Peacock Hill, she was a practical one. Not content with a mere petition (which Lu Ying doubted would even reach the Pacification Commissioner's eyes) she disappeared to her room and returned with a lacquer box decorated with fortunate symbols. When she opened it Cao had gasped. On a silken tray lay two small black pearls no larger than the tip of a lady's little finger. Their flawless, dusky surfaces glowed in the sunlight.

'Take one to the Chief Gaoler,' said Lu Ying. 'Tell him that if Dr Shih is still alive and healthy when he comes to trial in a month's time, he shall receive its companion.'

Cao shook her head, overwhelmed: 'How can we repay you for this?'

For a moment Lu Ying grew thoughtful: 'There are ways. I am tired of being helpless. Teach me where everything is kept so I may make myself tea and food. And if you should tell Captain Xiao what I have done. . . I would also be grateful.'

Cao glanced sharply at Lu Ying for some explanation of this strange request. But the former concubine's features were bland.

The question of Widow Mu remained. She could hardly live next door to the Hsu clan, when her hasty, hysterical testimony had cost Old Hsu his life. Yet where else were she and her children to go? Those ineligible for state rations starved on the streets, and to lose eligibility one need only lose one's home and become a vagrant or offend a minor official.

Cao wondered what Dr Shih would have done to help Widow Mu, if anything. It was his nature to strive for reconciliation. In the end the decision was made for her. She crossed Apricot Corner Court to knock on Widow Mu's door and found it wide open. Her old friend had fled without a word. Cao stood forlornly for a while, remembering their closeness, then became aware of someone behind her: Lord Yun, uncharacteristically out of his chamber. The old man looked round the empty rooms suspiciously. Cao bowed in the proper manner but he did not notice her existence.

'Not here,' he muttered. 'I'll make her. . . Oh, yes! Obedient. . . Ha!'

His voice trailed away. There was something repulsive about his ravings. A moist, fetid wind had stirred the leaves of the apricot tree. Cao could hear sobbing from within Old Hsu's house. Then she led Lord Yun back inside and mixed him a dose of medicine which he had gulped like a thirsty child, sighing with relief.

*

Which was why, as the remaining women of Apricot Corner Court reaped herbs by the riverbank, Madam Cao tried hard not to show her irritation in case she inconvenienced Lu Ying. No one could deny that without her generous bribe of the black pearl, Shih would have perished in the Prefectural gaol.

'There is little point in digging and sowing in the spring, if one does not intend to harvest in autumn,' she said, soothingly.

The third woman, Old Hsu's Widow, grunted then stared across the wide waters at the Mongol forts upstream. Since her husband's death she had fallen into a taciturn grief. Her mourning was not of the wailing kind that neighbours call virtuous. It manifested itself through an absence – Hsu's Wife had always been a matron of great humour, especially at her husband's expense, and now the wells of her laughter were dry.

'We've only filled one wheelbarrow,' she said. 'And that's with bletilla tubers. Dr Shih still needs the mugwort and ginseng.'

The Pacification Commissioner's former concubine was not so easily deterred.

'It is not the work itself,' she said. 'It is just that I am needed by one in great pain!'

Madam Cao noticed how the girl's hand crept to her girdle for a costly silk fan that no longer hung there. Instead, Lu Ying fanned herself daintily with her broad, conical hat. Her glossy mound of black hair caught the sun like spun silk.

'He is a gentleman used to sacrifices,' said Cao. 'We may be sure he does not feel neglected. Besides, when we left him, he was in a deep sleep.'

Lu Ying sighed and picked up her scythe. They waded through the marshy ground, releasing peaty, ripe smells. Midges buzzed round them. Because of her bound feet, Lu Ying used a hoe to keep balance.

Cao glanced back at the ramparts. Half a dozen soldiers were watching from on high, joking among themselves. No need to guess the object of their interest. Even in shapeless peasant clothes, Lu Ying's figure and movements attracted attention. Cao felt invisible in comparison.

Up to their ankles in mud, they swept at the plants with their scythes, building piles of pungent stalks. Easy work compared to the bletilla tubers. Those had required patient loosening of the soil before a sharp, decisive tug. Neither Cao nor her unwanted guest had ever learned such skills. The long, long siege was changing them and most other respectable folk in drastic ways. Nearly all Lu Ying's wealth had gone on costly food, despite Wang Ting-bo's extra rations, for she passed all she received straight to Madam Cao. Many notable families were parting with precious heirlooms to fill their bowls. Everyone was gaunt, their clothes threadbare. Few maintained a worthy face. Once fine ladies could be seen toiling like landless peasants to grow a few edible shoots. As for Cao, all her fortune lay in the man she relied upon.

By noon the last of the herbs were loaded onto the waiting wheelbarrows.

'Now I really must return to Apricot Corner Court,' said Lu Ying. 'If nothing else, your Honoured Father cannot bear a late meal.'

Madam Cao had to agree with that.

'Very well,' she said. 'If you and Madam Hsu will push the wheelbarrows of herbs home, I will take care of the tools. Now I must seek out Dr Shih and ask what is to be done with our harvest.'

The three women trudged through the Water Gate of Morning Radiance. Lu Ying and Old Hsu's Wife launched their load in the direction of Apricot Corner Court, leaving Madam Cao at a crossroad. Her destination had been unthinkable only a few months before.

竹子

The triumph of the Ineffable Winged Relief Fleet lay in its cargo. Supplies and goods had been packed into every conceivable space in the ships – provisions worth twenty thousand Mongol lives.

General A-ku realised this. He knew the siege must now endure for at least another year. His army's heroism had drowned in the wide moats surrounding Nancheng and Fouzhou. Without new tactics, the campaign might drag on for decades. Meanwhile his best troops and horses succumbed to strange illnesses in the damp air. It was a climate of endless disappointment.

Yet the siege lines were maintained. Although Mongol horsemen marauded around the Twin Cities the blockade remained porous, messages from the Imperial court winning through. Another new Pacification Commissioner was sent to replace the affable gentleman who had perished with Admiral Qi-Qi, but was seized by the Mongols when using a previously secure route into the Twin Cities. So Wang Ting-bo remained supreme arbiter of all civil and military affairs in Nancheng Province. He made great efforts to reward those who had ever proved useful to the Wang clan, and that included a certain doctor.

At the North Medical Relief Bureau, Madam Cao found Mung Po performing a rite before a cheap woodcut print of the Yellow Emperor. Snakes of incense rose. The Chief of the North Medical Relief Bureau watched closely, along with his Assistant. They had just concluded a hopeless application of the moxa and needed divine favour to pull the patient through. Madam Cao nodded politely to both men, but especially the Bureau Chief. The Assistant glanced nervously at his superior, evidently concerned the ritual had been ruined.

'Mung Po, leave off that for now!' commanded the Chief. 'Start the rites again when there are no females present.'

'I have come to tell you all the herbs have been gathered,' said Madam Cao.

'You have worked too hard!' said the Chief, in a voice of quiet concern. 'Go home and rest. The other ladies must be exhausted, too.'

The Assistant Supervisor readily concurred with the opinion of his Chief.

'Perhaps Mung Po could escort Madam Cao home?' he suggested, diffidently.

'That will not be necessary, Dr Du Tun-i,' replied Shih. 'I shall return with Madam Cao to Apricot Corner Court.'

Then he turned to the new Assistant Supervisor. 'Please ensure all the patients are examined before their next meal.'

Dr Du Tun-i nodded and the Chief of the North Medical Relief Bureau left with his wife. Dr Shih's plain, homespun blue robes were stained with spilt medicine and blood; Madam Cao's clothes were still muddy. Yet their demeanours possessed a dignity and inner peace lost to them for many months.

Dr Shih's restoration as Bureau Chief had occurred several weeks earlier. Pacification Commissioner Wang Ting-bo ordered it as a reward for Shih's impersonation of Captain Xiao, on condition the promotion was accomplished discreetly. His Excellency did not wish it known that the city's saviour had in fact been a humble doctor on trial for unfilial behaviour. The people needed heroes in the midst of their suffering, as simple food requires salt.

The high official who communicated the good news to Dr Shih had added: 'Dr Du Mau and other influential members of the Physicians Guild are unhappy that you have been given back your old position. I believe one Dr Du Tun-i is the current Bureau Chief? No doubt a relative of Dr Du Mau?'

'Indeed he is,' replied Shih.

'He shall be dismissed at once,' said the official, airily.

Shih had hesitated. The young man had saved his brother's life by staunching Guang's wounds on the dockside at Nancheng. Because of this he could not welcome Dr Du Tun-i's complete demotion.

'Perhaps, sir,' he said. 'He may be retained as my assistant at an appropriate salary?'

The official had looked surprised, then yawned.

'As you wish. His Excellency is minded to grant any reasonable request. Personally, I advise you to get rid of the fellow. He'll only cause you trouble later.'

Yet Dr Shih had got his way, however disregardful of future trouble.

Madam Cao considered these changes as they walked through Water Basin Ward. Shih stared straight ahead, apparently lost in thought. Since his release from the Prefectural gaol he often seemed distant, even cold. Cao believed he had not fully returned from that dreadful place; a great part of his spirit, perhaps the best part, still languished in chains.

'Husband,' she said, timidly. 'You walk so fast! I can barely keep up.'

He slowed and frowned.

'I am sorry,' he said. 'My life is all hurry – and yet I travel in circles! Forgive me.'

'You are tired, that is all,' she said. 'You work too hard.'

Shih glanced at her keenly.

'I am grateful for your help at the Relief Bureau,' he said. 'It reminds me of when we first married. Ah, what happy times those were! We were with each other from dawn until dark.'

'I remember,' she said, softly.

Cao's eye fell upon a tea-stall near their home. For a moment the couple exchanged looks of surprise. The stall had been closed for over a year, a victim of the long hostilities. Today its banners were out, a little faded perhaps, as were the paper and bamboo umbrellas on poles bearing the characters *Eternal Refreshment*. It had been a favourite haunt when they first came to Nancheng and could afford no better entertainment.

'Husband,' she said. 'Let us take tea at Mao's stall, like we used to do!'

Dr Shih hesitated.

'What of Guang?' he asked.

'His usual nurse takes care of him very diligently.'

At this his face darkened. She wondered at his exact feelings.

'It would please me so much to take tea,' she said, without a trace of wheedling, though her eyes combined reproach and entreaty.

'Then the matter is settled,' he said. 'Besides, Mao needs at least one customer.'

Yet the stallholder turned out to be a stranger who had bought the business from Mao in exchange for millet rations. As for tea, he had only a few leaves. He explained that he merely wished to try out the banners and umbrellas for when peace returned.

'I beg you to sit for a while,' he continued. 'You shall be my first honoured customers! I shall return with boiling water.'

Cao and Shih waited while he rushed to a neighbouring courtyard, kettle in hand. It was a situation to provoke a smile, then laughter.

'I hope you are not thirsty,' said Shih, discreetly reaching out his arm so that their sleeves touched. 'We may be waiting until the siege ends.'

She blushed at this immodest public display but did not remove her arm.

'It's pleasant enough here,' he said, looking round.

Indeed it was. The chill wind from Mount Wadung had shifted. North Canal Street glowed softly in the autumn sunshine. A few people passed but Water Basin Ward, normally full of bustle, was unusually peaceful. The stall overlooked North Canal, its motionless waters covered by a delightful carpet of lily pads.

Cao looked into her husband's lined face. He was watching the progress of a colourful moth over the lilies. At once she thought of Lu Ying and grew uncomfortable.

'I saw Widow Mu yesterday,' she said. 'She was near Ping's Floating Oriole Hall. I saw no sign of her daughter, Lan Tien, the poor girl. Or her son.'

'It is no longer Ping's house,' said Shih quietly, as though recollecting something too unpleasant to discuss. 'He died in the same prison I walked away from. Dearest Cao, how can that be? Why does one man live and another die?'

'I do not know,' said Cao. 'No one knows.'

They sat in silence for a moment. There was still no sign of the stallholder.

'I wonder how Widow Mu feeds her family now,' said Cao. 'It seems hard the children should suffer.'

Shih pressed his arm more warmly against her own.

'We cannot help them,' he said. 'We have too little to share. In any case, we dare not. It would dishonour Old Hsu's spirit and offend his relatives.'

'You are right,' sighed Cao, relishing his touch. It seemed so long since she had been touched with affection. Warmth flowed through her whole body and she forgot her sympathy for Widow Mu. His touch emboldened her to probe: 'Have you noticed how Guang gains in strength so quickly?' she said. 'I'm sure we may thank his nurse.'

Dr Shih grew thoughtful again. His arm, though still apparently resting against Madam Cao's, imperceptibly moved away.

The stallholder returned in triumph with a full kettle and found two troubled faces awaiting eternal refreshment. Even after a golden brew of dried lily flowers and jasmine, saved for such a propitious occasion, they merely nodded when he refused their offer of payment – so that he wondered if his first customers were lucky after all.

竹子

After washing in a basin of cold water and scrubbing with a liquid soap of rose leaves, Lu Ying sat in her room to apply make-up. What little she possessed was poor stuff: a face powder of crushed chalk and, for the eyes, a dark pigment of ground charcoal. Yet her face had gained a natural colour from unaccustomed exercise. And unlike many of the neighbouring courtyards, at least no one in the Yun household starved.

Of course this was Wang Ting-bo's doing. One of several

signs of gratitude he showered on the patient recovering in Apricot Corner Court. Two burly guardsmen had even been posted at the front gate in case A-ku's spies attempted an assassination. Yet Lu Ying wondered if he possessed other motives for his generosity; motives connected to herself that he wished to keep from his ever-vigilant First Wife.

Lu Ying's room was next door to Guang's bedchamber. Because the walls were made of paper and strips of bamboo she heard nearly everything that transpired in there. The patient's days passed in fitful rest: sometimes groaning and occasionally snoring, but usually in a state of feverish half-sleep. When he cried out in his sleep a troubled spirit was revealed.

Her toilet complete, Lu Ying sat for a while and rested. She was tired after her labours outside the Water Gate of Morning Radiance. Her thoughts, usually darting like restless fish, were sluggish. Closing her eyes she recalled the last few weeks as a succession of flurried feelings, for she habitually reasoned through her emotions.

The terrible battle following the arrival of the Ineffable Winged Relief Fleet had affected more than just those bearing weapons. Wives and children, aging parents, all had waited fearfully for the outcome. Lu Ying grew more afraid with each explosion and cry of alarm. Finally, she convinced herself the city must fall, that all pretty girls would be rounded up and enslaved as concubines. Images of the Emperor's own concubines, marched across freezing steppes set her heart racing. It would not happen to her. She would drown herself first.

Lu Ying had remembered the Moon Goddess staring up from the waters of the canal when she was first banished to Apricot Corner Court. That had been a message. She understood it now. If the city fell, she must step through the watery doorway shown by the Goddess. She must weigh herself down with her few remaining silks and precious things, until the dark waters of the canal closed over her head. Perhaps she would be reborn as one of the Moon Goddess's eternal handmaidens.

Of course, it had not come to that. The Mongols had been driven back. Yet Lu Ying felt proud of her willingness to destroy herself rather than risk dishonour.

A day or so after the victory, Dr Shih had been released from the Prefectural gaol, surprisingly unchanged by his ordeal except for a terrible sadness round the eyes. Gratitude towards her for securing his safety in prison made him bow exceptionally low; indeed, Lu Ying had feared Madam Cao might find fresh cause for jealousy.

Of course, Shih had not returned alone. Captain Xiao had insisted, as soon as he woke from unconsciousness, on being carried to Apricot Corner Court in a litter so he might die among his own family. After that, Shih tended his brother's wounds day and night; often she heard his soothing voice as Guang moaned with pain. Yet Lu Ying detected a hidden reserve between the two brothers, for all their apparent closeness, and wondered how to explain it.

That had been a month ago. Lu Ying had watched the cortege of four guardsmen carry Guang to a chamber next to her own. At that time the city was awash with wounded. Processions of wheelbarrows carried them to temporary hospitals through the constant rain. Although Dr Shih stayed beside his brother's bedside, he was desperately needed at the North Medical Relief Bureau, and would hurry there whenever Guang fell into a deep slumber, so that he barely found time to rest at all. Then Madam Cao would replace him at the wounded man's side, tending both Guang and her Honoured Father-in-law.

It soon became obvious Lord Yun had once again retreated into madness. He spent days staring at his bowl of circling minnows – anything larger having been eaten – sometimes with a cunning expression, but more often murmuring spells. At such times, Lu Ying overheard him muttering the name 'Bayke' over and over.

All in all, they were a joyless household.

One afternoon she found Madam Cao pacing round the

shuttered shop. It had been eighteen hours since Dr Shih last slept.

'Madam Cao,' she said, brightly. 'May I prepare tea?'

Lu Ying was excessively proud of her new tea-making skills.

'No, no,' said Madam Cao, dabbing her eyes.

'I beg you to sit down,' said Lu Ying.

'How can I rest?' demanded Cao. 'I am so worried! Heaven knows what miseries Dr Shih suffered in prison! His essential breaths are horribly unbalanced. He told me his *yin* and *yang* devour one another like wolves! Yet he works and works – and never listens when I beg him to rest.'

'His is a noble labour,' offered Lu Ying. As the phrase sounded wise and impressive, she added: 'A very noble labour.'

'If it kills him, how noble will he look then?'

The tears rising in Madam Cao burst forth, like seeds from a swollen pod. Several planted themselves in Lu Ying's heart.

'If only I could go to the Relief Bureau and help him!' sniffed Madam Cao. 'I could at least ensure he eats properly. But Brother-in-law and Lord Yun's meals can hardly be entrusted to a stranger.'

The former concubine watched Cao's plain face – positively ugly when distressed – and wondered how she could ever have compared this kind, sad lady to Wang Ting-bo's shrewish wife.

'Perhaps,' she offered. 'Perhaps – if you will trust me with so important a duty, perhaps I might undertake those tasks? Then you could join your husband at the Relief Bureau.'

Madam Cao had looked at her doubtfully.

'How will you cook? Though the Governor provides rice and vegetables for Captain Xiao, one must still know how to prepare them.'

'That is simple,' said Lu Ying. 'Old Hsu's Wife can cook all the meals in return for a small share.'

'What of the medicines? Dr Shih is insistent they should be administered at fortunate times of day. That is why he rushes back and forth between Apricot Corner Court and the Relief Bureau!'

'Also simple,' said Lu Ying. 'You shall write a list of the times and I shall learn it by heart. When the monks beat the hour on their drums, I shall hear and know what to do. Really, the matter is quite simple.'

Still Cao had hesitated.

'I must ask Dr Shih.'

When she did so he reluctantly agreed. Henceforth, Cao went to the North Medical Relief Bureau to assist him, along with a dozen other nurses. Twice a day he returned to Apricot Corner Court, taking his brother's pulse and sniffing his breath. As he detected no cause for alarm, recovery was allowed to find its own pace. He nodded gratefully at Lu Ying for her help, and she was pleased to be appreciated for something other than her usual attractions.

Those attractions had a predictable effect on Lord Yun. As soon as he realised Cao and Shih were away from the house, he offered many gallant attentions. Lu Ying realised she must win a decisive victory over him or endure a siege as tenacious as that maintained by A-ku's horde.

At first she had no idea how to repulse the old man. It would show the utmost disrespect to Dr Shih, as her host, to offer rudeness. Then again Lord Yun was insensitive to subtlety.

One day she was measuring out Yun Guang's medicine in the shuttered shop when she became aware of an acrid smell. Turning quickly, she found Lord Yun directly behind her, watching with bright, intense eyes.

'Sir!' she exclaimed, to hide her confusion. 'It is unseemly to approach a lady in this. . . and stand so close.'

He laughed hoarsely. Lu Ying detected the odour of cheap brandy on his breath. Somehow, despite the siege, he had gained access to strong wine!

'You are no lady, my dear,' he said. 'I know exactly what you are. Come to my chamber. I have something to show you.'

For a moment Lu Ying wavered. She found it hard to refuse

the command of a venerable gentleman. All her life she had been taught to obey those senior to one's self. Besides, there was something about Lord Yun, a force she could not explain... Yet her spirit revolted against conceding to his request. In a flash of inspiration she said quite scornfully: 'I do not believe Bayke would allow that!'

Lu Ying barely understood what she meant but the effect was immediate. Lord Yun's looming face shrank back. His fierce gaze was replaced by hurried blinking. Even his handsome mouth, a moment before curving at the corners in a complacent smile, trembled a little.

'What do you know of Bayke?' he hissed. 'Is he here?'

'I know he will be displeased,' she said.

Now he was staring quite through her, his breath quickening.

'You are his spy!' he cried. 'You are Bayke's whore!'

Lu Ying did not flinch at the vile name. She had been called far worse. Now Lord Yun was backing away.

'I shall have restitution,' he muttered. Realising she had overheard his secret thoughts, he added hurriedly: 'Tell Bayke...' Suddenly he grew confused as though the fantasy so real to him a moment before was losing its hold. 'Tell him...'

Then he had gone. Afterwards he avoided Lu Ying except for dark, malevolent glances.

竹子

Water Basin Ward had soaked up many refugees from the surrounding countryside, including hundreds of the Dong minority, well known for their ululating choirs, and a great many lived in tenements around the Water Basin. Dong choirs often broke the silence of autumn nights.

So it was, one early evening when Cao and Shih were engaged at the North Medical Relief Bureau, Lu Ying entered Guang's chamber on shuffling feet and paused, her eyes drawn to the open window. Several Dong women were singing an ancient tune entitled 'Youth Is Passing' while they washed clothes. She met Guang's gaze as they both listened. Then both remembered themselves and bowed.

'Commander Yun Guang must rest,' chided Lu Ying, enjoying the ambiguity of their mutual positions. Was she not Dr Shih's assistant? Almost an apprentice! Yun Guang settled back on his earthenware pillow.

'I would sooner talk. I have many questions.'

Lu Ying silently poured out his medicine. The choir outside began to sing an amorous tune, accompanied by a gay flute.

'Commander Yun Guang can hardly think himself unique in that,' she said.

'Perhaps Miss Lu Ying would condescend to sit in the room for a while?'

It was hard to oppose what she desired. Yet she said: 'Why?'

His eyes found her face. He shrugged.

'For news. And company. I am bored lying here day after day.'

'Am I to be a little entertainment?' she asked.

'No, no, I do not mean that. . . But my brother is so seldom here! How am I to discover what happens in the world? He has abandoned me.'

'Your brother is at the North Medical Relief Bureau,' said Lu Ying.

A rift between two brothers who were mirror images of each other seemed an affront to nature – and anyone who contributed to it would surely face punishment.

'I do not reproach Shih,' said Guang, quickly, as though reading her thought. 'I merely refer to my own feelings.'

Again Lu Ying did not know how to respond. She felt her body tightening in unexpected places.

'All face difficulties,' she murmured.

Then she met his eye. There was a watchful, nervous expression on his high cheek-boned face. 'You are not the only person who lacks company,' she added.

Yun Guang nodded stiffly and the movement made his eyes narrow with pain.

'Tell me,' he said. 'How is it you look after me?'

Lu Ying placed her hands in her lap but was silent.

'Why are you suddenly shy?' he asked. 'Do I offend you? I cannot believe you are afraid of me.'

Again she lifted her eyes until they met his own. Just as deliberately she lowered them.

'No,' she said. 'Only, I fear indecorous behaviour and what it might become. It brought me here, you will recollect.'

She left, bowing politely – as surely one should to a noble Captain Xiao. A trace of her perfume lingered in the room.

The next day Yun Guang was apologetic.

'Lady Lu Ying must forgive me,' he said. 'If I offended her yesterday it is entirely my fault.'

He began to cough up specks of blood. She leaned forward in concern. He waved her back and at last smiled.

'I still lack company,' he said.

Lu Ying felt herself blush.

'Then perhaps I shall engage Commander Yun Guang in conversation.'

'It would be welcome.'

They sat in an embarrassed silence for a long while.

'If you speak, I cannot help but hear,' she said.

'What if *you* were to talk?' said Guang. 'My own voice wearies me. I'd sooner listen to you. Tell me, who is undertaking my duties? Who has replaced me?'

Lu Ying comprehended his fear exactly.

'One who is loyal to you,' she said. 'Chen Song has been temporarily appointed as Commander of Artillery.'

'Ah, Chen Song. That is good.'

Yet she could tell he was considering the news from many perspectives.

'Do you know,' he said. 'I had a strange thought as I sailed into Nancheng at the head of the Relief Fleet. Indeed, a moment before the thunderclap bomb tore open my chest, I thought something entirely new. For me, at least.'

She waited expectantly.

'But I am being tedious,' he said.

'No, I do not think so.'

'Then I shall tell you.'

Yet he merely picked at the blanket, his large brown eyes downcast. Lu Ying noticed sweat on his forehead and that he was feverish.

'I would be happy to listen,' she said, quietly.

'Then I will share my thought. Our ship was damaged in a dozen places. The decks were sticky with blood. I myself had taken a crossbow bolt in the shoulder yet dare not show pain, in case my men lost heart.'

'You are brave,' she murmured.

'No, it was not bravery. To be brave one must overcome fear. But I did not fear anything. Do you know why? I truly did not care what happened to me.' He cleared his throat. 'A wise friend once told me that about myself. He understood me better than anyone.'

'You must not alarm yourself,' she murmured.

'Just before that thunderclap bomb exploded, I did not care what would happen to me,' he repeated. 'Who would miss me, after all? No one! Even my twin brother – oh, he has grievances you cannot imagine, Miss Lu Ying! Justified grievances, let me say, placed between us by one who should have taught us to be friends, one who betrayed. . . but never mind that.'

His feverish face grew thoughtful again.

'Everyone knows a man's body belongs to his parents and ancestors, for they granted him life. Yet I did not care what happened to my own body, so long as it was not too painful. Even then there are ways of using pain. Or some kinds of pain.'

They both looked up, startled by a harsh laugh from Lord Yun's chamber. Was the old man listening? Recently his madness had grown intense and inward-looking, so that his only reply to civil questions or remarks was a dark glower. Certainly he had shown little interest in Guang since his arrival, other than to ask fearfully whether his son was also a prisoner of Bayke.

'I, too, have a thought,' said Lu Ying.

He nodded and she noticed tears in his eyes.

'When Father sold me to Wang Ting-bo,' she said. 'And left me along with a dozen similar girls, I watched him push a handcart of precious things down Peacock Hill. Then I realised he had already forgotten me. All Father cared about was packed in lacquered boxes on that handcart. Afterwards, part of me ceased to care what happened. Yet I always prayed my family would visit or send word.'

'Did they?'

'They never came. Years later I was told they had all drowned in a sudden flood. I was quite alone in this world until my next birth. And I half wished to hasten it, just in case I was reborn as someone happier.'

Lu Ying bit her lip. She had never said so much about her family. And to a stranger! An unforgivable weakness. Yet Yun Guang did not seem offended.

'When I was young,' he said, 'I always longed to be a famous poet like my Great-grandfather Yun Cai. Think of it! All the explosions he caused were in people's hearts. If I may say so, Miss Lu Ying, I'm sure you have caused a few such in your time.'

He coughed, and she thought it best to let him rest.

Another day. After Guang had taken his medicine they were talking humorously when both became aware of a watcher in the doorway. Dr Shih stood silently, looking between Lu Ying and Guang. She had no idea how long he had been there. His expression mingled doubt and exhaustion. A fleck of dried blood stained his cheek. He blinked irritably.

'I hope you do not tire my brother,' said Dr Shih.

Lu Ying could not help feeling ashamed.

'We were. . . I mean, I was reminding Commander Yun Guang of certain droll characters in the Pacification Commissioner's establishment. . .'

Her voice trailed. Dr Shih's face, normally affable, hardened.

'Oh, really,' protested Guang. 'It can do me no harm to smile now and then! Is that not so, Youngest Brother?'

Dr Shih flashed him a scornful look.

'I am glad you have leisure to smile, *Eldest Brother*.'

He laid such strange emphasis on the name that Lu Ying looked up in alarm. Guang also flushed. Whether because of anger or distress she could not say.

'Continue to enjoy your reminiscences of the noble folk on Peacock Hill,' said Dr Shih. 'Only do not laugh too hard. It might re-open your wound.'

He left with a slight bow and Lu Ying followed soon after. She sat uncomfortably in her room for a long while. Could Dr Shih really be jealous of her conversation with Guang? One might think so. She paled at the thought of his assumptions about her. That she was trying to seduce the Hero of Swallow Gate. That she was perfidious and ungrateful. That she was, as Lord Yun had suggested, a mere whore.

The next afternoon, when Cao returned briefly from the North Medical Relief Bureau, Lu Ying hurried to greet her.

'Madam! May I speak with you?'

Cao looked almost as exhausted as her husband. The stream of wounded had only abated a little. She leaned on the wooden counter of the shop and waited politely.

'Madam!' repeated Lu Ying. 'Dr Shih believes I tire his brother through foolish talk and frivolous gossip. In short, that I am a bad influence.'

Cao's eyebrows lifted a little.

'He did mention something to that effect,' she said

'Oh.' Lu Ying pursed her lips, her eyes blinking rapidly. 'Well then, I shall cease to deliver Commander Yun Guang's food and medicine as from today.'

'Dr Shih seemed to think that would be a good idea,' said Cao, smiling slightly. 'But I told him, little harm comes from the conversation of a cultured lady. Especially one who has behaved with such decorum since joining our household.'

Now Lu Ying looked up.

'How did Dr Shih reply?'

'Merely by repeating that his brother needs rest. And there we left it. As you can imagine, we are reluctant for strangers to witness Lord Yun's. . . bad days. Unfortunate gossip would diminish us all.'

This turn of events was unexpected. Lu Ying felt oddly elated, as though redeemed in some unspoken way.

竹子

Chen Song arrived at Apricot Corner Court on a fine horse, accompanied by an escort flying gaudy pennants – trappings that had once belonged to Captain Xiao. The latter gentleman was in no state to witness this theft of fortune. As usual he was in bed. His mood was surprisingly light-hearted. The terrible gash across his chest had drained away old poisons, just as a boil empties when lanced. He did not feel jealous of Chen Song's success. In fact, his pleasure at seeing him was unreserved.

Lu Ying divined this as she sat on her divan, listening quite shamelessly to their conversation through a crack in the wall, a habit she had acquired in Wang Ting-bo's harem.

'You have been tardy in your visits,' said Guang reproachfully, after their initial enthusiasm at being reunited had subsided.

'You should know why better than anyone,' came Chen Song's muffled reply. 'My life is no longer my own. Please resume your duties soon, then I can reclaim myself!'

Guang started coughing and Lu Ying frowned. She hoped this wonderful friend of his would not weary him with his clever jokes and asides.

'Tell me,' said Guang. 'What is the news from Peacock Hill?'

At that name Lu Ying strained after every word.

'Ah, it might be simply expressed,' replied Chen Song. 'The Wang clan hang onto power by their little fingers and at the same time extend their influence constantly. It seems nearly every appointee to public office is a Wang, or somehow connected to their family. I do not like it.'

'Why?' said Guang. 'As long as they are capable.'

'It is our tradition to appoint men to public office through the Imperial examinations! Did you not have to pass a test to become a commissioned officer? They go beyond themselves.'

A significant silence followed. Lu Ying could tell both were thinking.

'If you put it that way,' said Guang. 'It doesn't seem right, but His Excellency is a good man and loyal to the Son of Heaven.'

'So far,' conceded Chen Song. 'So far.'

'Why do you say that?'

Even through the wall, Chen Song's sigh was audible.

'There is talk,' he said, reluctantly. 'I have met with General Zheng Shun and other commanders more loyal to His Imperial Highness than to Wang Ting-bo. Some believe messages pass between Peacock Hill and General A-ku.'

'That is a vile slander!'

Lu Ying half rose in alarm. Guang's passion surely threatened his health!

'I hope so,' replied Chen Song. 'There is more. It pains me to say this, Guang, but your patron, Wang Bai, receives strange visitors.'

'No doubt he has spies within the city,' said Guang. 'There will be an explanation tending towards his honour, we may depend on it.'

Once more they were silent. Lu Ying wished she could reproach Chen Song for causing a nuisance. She understood less than half of what he meant except that it was unwise to trust the Wang family – and she could have told Guang that herself.

'Consider this,' said Chen Song. 'How was it that when a replacement Pacification Commissioner was despatched from the court, he fell straight into Mongol hands? Yet other messengers pass with ease into the city.'

'One may blame misfortune,' said Guang.

'*Good* fortune for Wang Ting-bo and his family,' said Chen Song.

'It proves nothing,' countered Guang.

'What of the fact that the enemy so pointedly aimed their missiles at the ship carrying Wang Ting-bo's first replacement? As if they knew of his presence. We both noticed it.'

Lu Ying waited for Guang's response. When it came, his voice was sombre.

'I refuse to believe that so great and noble a man would stoop so low. As for his nephew, Wang Bai, I have every reason to feel gratitude. My promotion came through him. I am in his debt. Just as I am in yours. Rest assured, the Wang clan have proved their loyalty to His Imperial Majesty a thousand times.'

Chen Song laughed.

'It is the next time I fear! But Guang, you are not indebted to anyone. The obligation lies in the opposite direction, both in Wang Bai's case and my own. Too much modesty is a kind of blindness, at which point it ceases to be a virtue.'

'You are a harsh judge.'

'A clear headed one, I hope.'

Lu Ying's ears pricked up. Was that the sound of liquid being poured? Loud, contented slurping?

'My brother would not approve of this medicine,' said Guang. 'Too much heat, too much *yang*.'

'Heat is good! Ah, I miss those evenings when the tables were covered with blank paper and the ink was mixed! When the wine and moonlight inspired us to verse! Then we lived as men should.'

'My own poems were lamentable,' said Guang, honestly. 'You are the fully-examined scholar here. I am just a soldier.'

'Your great-grandfather was a poet to rival Li Po himself!'

Her attention wandered as the two friends drank and joked. She might have ceased listening altogether, had not her own name jolted her.

'What of the beautiful Lady Lu Ying?' asked Chen Song.

'Are you captivated, as our wise Pacification Commissioner once was?'

'My body is so broken that the slightest ardour would be my last,' joked Guang.

She blushed and leaned forward, eager to hear more.

'Is it true your brother has not taken her as his concubine?'

Now Guang sounded serious.

'Dr Shih has not. Believe me, it is a delicate matter.'

'Then he is generous to provide her with food in times like these,' said Chen Song. 'Especially as she was forced upon him against his will. I have heard she is a vain, foolish creature. But generosity comes naturally to your family.'

'You flatter us. Wang Ting-bo sends her ample supplies of food.'

Chen Song cleared his throat.

'Perhaps your brother will be freed of his burden soon,' he said. 'I have heard rumours that Wang Ting-bo is on the point of sending his First Wife to stay with relatives in the capital. Maybe he will summon back his former concubine.'

'Perhaps.'

Lu Ying felt sure Guang's voice was uncomfortable.

'Well, we shall see,' said Chen Song. 'It is of little importance. Get better soon, Guang, so you can resume your former position. You are missed, my friend.'

He left as the third hour was beaten on the ward drum. The sound echoed from the Water Basin right up North Canal Street. Lu Ying's heart fluttered at Chen Song's news. Could her recall to Peacock Hill be imminent? She should be glad! So very glad! Yet, somehow, the prospect touched her with loss and disappointment.

Two months after Guang's arrival in Apricot Corner Court, he stood in the centre of his bedchamber. Tall like all the Yun clan, he over-shadowed Lu Ying. Yet his mastery was an illusion, for this broad-chested man leaned on her as an old dotard depends on his stick. If she let him go he would topple.

'Another step?'

Her voice was coaxing. She sensed the flutter in his heart. That he who had defied every Mongol weapon was afraid to lose his dignity. This aroused her pity but she said: 'Commander Yun Guang could perhaps reach that chair by the wall?'

It was the seat she normally used when conversing with him, a decorous distance from the bed. Leaning heavily on her arm he lurched to the high-backed chair and lowered himself slowly, struggling all the while for air.

'My chest,' he gasped. 'Not my legs. My chest.'

Several days later the exercise had been repeated many times and he could walk across the room with the assistance of a stick. Lu Ying watched and clapped her hands to frighten off demons or invisible fox-fairies.

'How glad I am!'

Then she faltered, embarrassed to have shown so much enthusiasm. He hobbled back to his bed and settled under the covers. Autumn was becoming winter, cold and dry. In the mornings patterns of frost lay across the glazed paper windows. Lu Ying sometimes wrote the only characters she knew well in the layer of white crystals – those of her name.

'I am surprised the Mongols have not resumed their assaults,' he said. 'Chen Song believes they are waiting for something. But what? What?'

Wrapped in a heavy brocade shawl against the cold, Lu Ying took her usual seat.

'I am no wise general,' she said.

'Of course, forgive me.'

'But I am quite as stern as the Infernal Judges themselves in one regard!'

'What is that?'

She tried to maintain her pose of varnished good humour. Sincerity shone through the corner-glances of her eyes. She lowered her gaze to the floor.

'You will be better soon,' she said. 'Each day your strength doubles. Yet I fear that when you return. . .' She gestured at the city outside, visible as a thousand straight wooden lines and towers against a pale sky. 'When you return to the ramparts, I am afraid you will not care what happens to you.'

Guang looked up with deep-set, brooding eyes.

'Miss Lu Ying, first tell me. Do you care what happens to *you*? Once you told me you did not.'

He had trapped her so easily. Her heart was a moth enclosed in his hand.

'There was a time when I did not,' she said, cautiously.

'What has changed your view?'

His voice was insistent.

'Oh, I cannot say. Do not ask me.'

'I do ask.'

She felt herself redden.

'Perhaps I feel things that make me more alive,' she said, reluctantly. 'And when one feels alive, one fears to lose life.'

He nodded. Then Guang shook his head in a gesture of wonder.

'Thank you,' he said.

'For what?'

'Do you really not know?'

Now Lu Ying buried her slender hands in broad sleeves. Oh, he was provoking! At least Wang Ting-bo had been simple to manage. One merely listened and occasionally joked about those who offended him. Nothing more was required. With Guang came a necessity for something alien to Peacock Hill. She had no name for it, other than sincerity.

'You thank me for delivering your medicine and meals at the times prescribed by Dr Shih,' she said.

'You are wrong. There's more to it than that!'

Her tongue felt thick. Her throat dry. Lu Ying detected a foolish trembling in her limbs.

'I do not understand,' she said.

'I believe you do. Perhaps you choose not to understand. No doubt you expect to be recalled as His Excellency's concubine at any time. After all, what is a poor soldier like me compared to a Pacification Commissioner? I believe you know exactly why I thanked you.'

His look grew hard, so that for an uncomfortable moment he resembled Lord Yun. Then it softened and he sighed.

'I wish to thank you for helping me to glimpse the future again,' he said, smiling gently. 'That is all. I have learned to face the past over these last few months. How sick I am of war! How tired of everything I once thought glorious. Do you know how I calm my spirits when I think of resuming my commission? I close my eyes and imagine Wei Valley, as it was, before Bayke came. Then I daydream and hear the cries of the gibbons at dawn and dusk. I walk down Wei Valley with Shih at my side, fishing poles in our hands. How we joke and laugh! You see, the past can be quite resolved if one daydreams. . . As though mistakes and unkindness had never been.'

His voice trailed. A look of sorrow aged his handsome face. He turned his head on the pillow toward the blank wooden wall.

'I have said too much,' he muttered, falling into a troubled sleep.

But for Lu Ying he had not said enough. Or not the thing she had begun to secretly desire. She rose and sat beside him on the bed, stroking his long black hair. Slowly Guang's eyes ceased to flutter and he snored softly. Lu Ying maintained her position as dusk entered the room. Finally, she leaned forward and touched his forehead with a brush of her lips. Guang murmured anxiously in his sleep.

竹子

Even in siege-time the Feast of Lanterns could not be neglected. People flowed through the streets as the first moon of the New Year rose above Mount Wadung, greeting neighbours or simply waving lanterns attached to bamboo sticks. An Immortal peering down from the Jade Emperor's Cloud Terrace would have seen a hundred thousand fireflies or winking stars dotting the streets and ramparts of the Twin Cities. Had that same Immortal looked beyond the city, he would have spied as many fireflies in the Mongol encampments, and perhaps wondered in what way besieger and besieged differed, for both created light.

Before the Mongols arrived all respectable folk would have been decorously drunk by midnight. Now, only the very wealthy or those with influential relatives had the means to blink up at the full moon with a spinning head.

Lu Ying attended the Yun family party in a gown of night-blue silk. It was her plainest, chosen not to shame Madam Cao's simple wardrobe. Still she looked exquisite; more beguiling for a little modesty.

Because the night was mild they sat round the apricot tree, which Guang had festooned with paper lanterns. The sound of drums and flutes floated through the night air. Many of Old Hsu's relatives were on the other side of the courtyard, having a celebration of their own, their first sign of public happiness since his death. All the people of Apricot Corner Court used the communal cooking fire to prepare what little grain and vegetables they had gathered to greet the promise of spring.

At first Lu Ying felt uncomfortable in such humble company, though a quantity of wine provided by friends of Captain Xiao to speed his recovery, warmed everyone's spirits. In that small taste of oblivion they fared better than many a grieving heart in Water Basin Ward.

So Lu Ying tipsily followed Shih and his brother's passionate conversation about the Great Khan's ambitions. Their faces, always peculiarly similar, seemed more alike than ever in the red glow of the flickering fire. She was surprised by the intensity of their debate. The brothers seemed to assume contradictory positions almost by habit, circling each other like watchful cocks. As often before, she sensed some unspoken resentment between them and – without troubling herself too deeply – thought it a shame. Their argument was all about Imperial policy, nothing real or close to a person's heart. Lu Ying caught Madam Cao's eye.

The older woman leaned forward conspiratorially, her glance bright from unaccustomed draughts of wine.

'It reminds me of when Guang and Shih were first re-united after their long separation,' she whispered. 'Before you knew them.'

'I wish I had,' said Lu Ying, quickly raising her wine-bowl to cover her confusion, for she had revealed too much. Madam Cao nodded.

'Actually, when they were arguing then, they were just as dull as they are now.'

The two women shared a secret smile concealed by hands.

Shih soon left for his bed, too exhausted by his labours at the Relief Bureau to pass up an opportunity for sleep, even at Festival-time. As a dutiful wife, Cao followed, though Lu Ying suspected she was enjoying their midnight conversation.

Once they had gone, Lu Ying realised she was alone with Guang and that even the noisy Hsu clan had gone inside. A fat, smiling moon floated above Apricot Corner Court. She was used to Guang's company after tending him through his long weakness, but tonight she felt his presence as a kind of restlessness. She said nothing, and waited for him to speak.

Guang seemed fascinated by the embers of the fire.

'Lady Lu Ying,' he said, at last. 'Are you cold?'

'My shawl is quite thick,' she replied.

He resumed his examination of the glowing ashes, then said, 'Lady Lu Ying, will you allow me to ask an impudent question?'

'That depends on the extent of its impudence,' she said, pleased by the cleverness of her reply. And indeed he smiled, though she detected he was uneasy.

'Quite so. Then my question is this: has His Excellency Wang Ting-bo approached you to. . . in any way one might construe?' he fell silent. 'But perhaps I pry where I should not.'

'You do not pry,' she murmured.

'Very well, I shall be blunt. Has His Excellency sent word that he wishes you to regain your former position?'

Now both were looking into each other's eyes in a disturbingly frank way, the hasty beat of her heart uncomfortable and longed-for.

'He has not,' she said. 'But there have been hints! Do you not recall the letter you read out to me? I hardly understand it, except as a hint.'

'I remember it well,' he said.

Guang sat back on the gnarled bench beside the apricot tree.

'Hints are not certainties,' she offered.

'Of course. They are possibilities, nothing more.'

When Guang rose his expression touched her with foreboding.

'Soon I must return to my duties on the ramparts,' he said. 'Because of your attentions – and Shih's, of course, and Sister-in-law's – my strength is almost what it once was. I wish to thank you.'

He bowed stiffly.

'If we were free,' he said, quietly. 'To choose as one might wish. . . but you are bound to another, a great and noble gentleman, one whose generosity feeds my dearest relatives. I must consider their welfare before my own. You appear startled! Forgive me for adding to your confusion. You, too, must always choose what is best for you.'

Before she could reply, Yun Guang left her alone beneath the branches of the apricot tree and the waxy, shining moon.

The next morning he resumed his busy office as Commander of Artillery in a ceremony witnessed by hundreds of guardsmen and Wang Ting-bo himself. So pressing were his duties that, as in the days before his wound, he scarcely found time to visit Apricot Corner Court. Lu Ying believed he was avoiding her; and while she approved his prudence, found it oddly disconcerting.

竹子

Madam Cao could not deceive herself: Lord Yun's bad days were more frequent. They swept through Apricot Corner

Court, touching all its inhabitants. The old man had taken to railing at Fan-maker Hsu's family, threatening eviction if they did not pay a greater share of their harvest. Perhaps he believed their fans had magically become baskets of rice. Certainly he was obsessed by the thought of hoarding food – or what it might buy during a desperate siege. Although Dr Shih assured his neighbours no eviction would take place, Lord Yun created ill-feeling where none had existed before.

Bad days were when an invisible demon called Bayke stalked every room and peered in through shuttered windows. Bayke's eyes glowed like coals and his bushy eyebrows smouldered. Bad days were when Lord Yun's only comfort was his fishbowl full of friendly demons. A feeble comfort. The fish-demons could only hold off Bayke, never vanquish him. Whenever Dr Shih heard that Bayke was back, he hurried home from the North Medical Relief Bureau and administered a potent dose. After that Lord Yun slept fitfully, plagued by evil dreams.

Not all days were bad. Cao dreaded the good ones most of all. They started predictably. Lord Yun would bellow for his breakfast and when it came, find fault with every morsel. If Cao brought it, he might fling down the bowl, wasting precious food. However, if Lu Ying delivered the meal, shuffling daintily, he would pretend it was a banquet, insisting she stay until he had finished every mouthful. Cao sometimes listened at the door, but he said little. Lu Ying later told her that Lord Yun never took his eyes off her, even while dipping chopsticks or dabbing his mouth with a napkin.

Cao and Dr Shih were too busy at the Relief Bureau to maintain a constant guard. On several occasions quantities of food sent by Wang Ting-bo to nourish his former concubine went missing. Afterwards Lord Yun would be found drunk on the coarsest of home-brewed spirits imaginable. Then his railing lost all decency. He taunted Shih and Cao with their childlessness, accusing his son of lacking a man's natural *yang*. As for Cao's womb, it was a shrivelled dried out plum, an ugly, malodorous bladder. Or worse. These insults struck deep. It had long been a fear of hers that their lack of children stemmed from a cursed womb; that her own father had punished her unfilial conduct with barren organs.

Then low spirits would settle like a freezing river fog on Madam Cao. For she could not deceive herself: her failure to produce a child had put the treasure of Shih's love in question. One could hardly reproach any man for wishing to fulfil his duty. That meant the production of heirs, so the ancestral rites would be maintained forever. Yet she had failed. Her womb, as Lord Yun said, was a shrivelled, dried-out plum.

Often his drunken tirades ended in a threat to order his son's divorce, leading to rumours in neighbouring courtyards. Those keen to defend a parent's rights supported Lord Yun out of strict principle. Some even averted their eyes as Cao hurried through Water Basin Ward.

Most odious of all were his demands that Lu Ying should become his concubine, given his son's evident impotence. At such times Cao noticed a terrible intensity in her beloved, patient Shih's face that frightened her. He would increase the amount of Lord Yun's medicine until the old man grew stiff and could only speak with difficulty.

It was several months since Dr Shih last attended a private patient, all his energies being directed to the Relief Bureau. In between, he had endured imprisonment and trial, the near loss of his brother. Now, as he packed his old medicine bag, Cao watched him intently, aware the summons he had received concerned a family to whom they were forever indebted, for the extensive Xue clan had formed a large part of the sympathetic crowd at Shih's trial.

'I shall have something warm for you on your return,' she said.

Shih paused.

'You could come with me, if you like,' he suggested, tentatively. 'I would be grateful for your help in holding the patient.'

Within moments Cao had found stout wooden-soled shoes and a thick cloak of hemp.

'Do I look like an apprentice?' she asked.

'Do not remind me of apprentices,' said Shih. 'Thankfully you do not resemble one at all!'

They stepped out of their shop door into a murky river-fog. The houses they passed wore tendrils of mist and the fog seemed to close around them like malicious, swirling gossip.

Cao threaded an arm through her husband's as they walked through the deserted streets. The curfew bells were ringing early today. But Dr Shih carried an official passport, stamped by the Prefecture, and so did not fear the Watch.

Their destination was Xue Alley, a narrow, twisting street full of dark corners. Most of the buildings were two or more storeys high and seemed to disappear upwards into the fog. Laughter escaped through open windows; anxious mothers called in naughty children who were defying the curfew. It was suppertime in Xue Alley and steam rose from communal cooking pans, though such poor folk had little enough to broil or steam.

Shih led his wife to a rickety door and knocked. They were answered almost at once. Over a dozen people of all ages filled a small room opening directly onto the street, sat on the floor around a central fire-pot. The assembled family looked up in surprise as Shih entered. Instantly Carpenter Xue was on his feet.

'Dr Shih!' he cried. 'I was quite sure you would call tonight, though my wife said you would be too busy for humble people like ourselves. "Be silent, woman!" I told her. "You do not understand Dr Shih as I do!" I beg you and Madam Cao to eat with us. Eat, sir! Eat, Madam! We have plenty.'

They could hardly refuse, though Cao noticed the bowls Xue offered were only large enough to maintain the carpenter's face. After Shih had scooped up a single mouthful with the chopsticks he carried in a pouch at his belt, he belched with satisfaction and set the bowl aside.

'Forgive me!' he said. 'Your stew is so rich that I am quite replete. No, I can eat no more! Do not press me, I beg you.'

'Nor can I,' added Madam Cao, hastily, though she had tasted none of it.

Carpenter Xue pretended to be sorrowful. Nevertheless he indicated to a daughter that the bowls should be collected from his guests; and the contents were promptly poured straight back into the family pot.

'Let me repay you for that banquet by examining the infant you sent word about,' said Shih. 'My wife will hold her.'

Dr Shih conducted his usual readings of pulse, breath and colour while Cao held the wriggling child on her lap. She was face to face with all she had never possessed. Familiar emotions gushed through her – tenderness and a kind of breathless pain. Such a bonny child! Yet the girl's complexion was mottled by rashes. Her brown eyes fixed themselves on Cao's face. After Shih had reassured the child's mother that the malady was not severe, he promised an ointment would be ready by noon tomorrow. Carpenter Xue bowed them out, a fixed smile on his shrewd face.

'I suspect old Xue was testing out the extent of my obligation to him,' muttered Shih, as they walked away. 'The baby was in no danger, though one would have thought from his summons it was about to die.'

The early evening fog was thinning as they reached North Canal Street. Stars shone in a clear winter sky and wisps of cloud floated through heaven. Suddenly Cao laughed.

'Why do I feel so light?' she asked.

Shih smiled.

'I'd sooner feel light because of a flask of wine,' he said.

'Husband, take my arm. I cannot give you wine but, well, I shall say no more.'

They walked back to Apricot Corner Court and the medicine shop full of jars. Most had been emptied over the course of the siege. Yet just as a bankrupt preserves at least one precious object from the wreck of his fortune, Cao had held back a quantity of a certain infusion tasting of lamb's fat and pepper, mingled with a coarse, everyday root especially revered by Daoist hermits seeking visions.

Madam Cao sat her husband down and boiled water on a small stove. While the fire caught, they eyed each other wordlessly. Cao's mind was full of the evening they had just shared.

'You seem happy,' said Shih.

'Is that so strange?'

'Nowadays, perhaps,' he said. 'I am glad.'

'Are you happy?' she asked.

Shih stretched out his long legs and shrugged.

'We spend so little time together, that I cannot help but be happy tonight. But Cao, there is something important I have meant to say for a long time.'

She waited. Behind him wisps of steam began to rise from the kettle.

'Cao, we have been uneasy together ever since I cured His Excellency's son. Ever since Lu Ying joined our household. How foolish it all seems now.'

'We need to look at each other more often,' she said, firmly. 'Then we will remember who we are.'

She bit her lip in confusion. Would he think she was foolish?

'I'm looking,' he said.

'Are you thirsty?' she asked.

She poured the water and, as the leaves suffused, a complex smell filled the shop, blending earth and plant and animal aromas. Cao remembered an ancient drinking game.

'If I pour you a bowl you must sing me a song,' she said.

He took the cup and drained it in one. For a minute he stared into space then began to sing tunelessly, but with feeling:

A handsome gentleman
Waited at the gate:
How very sad I did not accompany him!
For him I wear my unlined skirt,
My skirt of brightest silk.

Oh, sir, gracious lord,
Give me a place in your coach!

Cao, who had been sipping steadily while he sang, sighed then giggled.

'You sing like an actor!' she exclaimed.

Her husband smiled shyly.

'Cao, you have no idea how I acted when they transformed me into Captain Xiao!'

Although Shih had told her this tale, she still did not quite believe it. As ever, he read her mood exactly.

'You cannot imagine that I, humble Dr Shih, became Captain Xiao! But if you had a voice murmuring in your ear and punishment cells at your back, even *you* could become Captain Xiao!'

Cao blushed, glad Guang could not hear their conversation, for it might be viewed as disrespectful.

An hour later both were intoxicated to the point where almost anything seemed hilarious, especially anything disrespectful. Fired by a strange enthusiasm Shih mimicked several officials who had visited the Relief Bureau. Gradually their drunken laughter subsided, first into chuckling, then silence.

'Painted puppets, that's all,' said Shih. 'No one is spared a part. Must ours be unhappy? My dear love, why must we be unhappy? I can see no good reason at all!'

Cao leaned forward. She reached out and twined her fingers round his hand.

'If you pour me a bowl I must sing you a song,' she said. 'I've learned an old one, far older than yours, all about planting.' And she sang:

Chop, chop, we clear the elms
And pile branches on the bank,
He neither sows nor reaps!
How has our lord five-hundred sheaves?

He neither traps nor shoots!
How do badger pelts adorn his courtyards?
Those lords, those handsome lords,
Need not work for a bowl of food.

'What has that to do with anything?' he asked, when she had finished, clasping her hand tightly.

'What is a *handsome gentleman* and his coach to do with me?' she asked, in a coy manner she had once observed Lu Ying using when talking to Guang.

Their eyes were glassy.

'Make more of that tea and I'll show you!' he cried. Then Dr Shih blushed. 'Am I too loud?' he whispered. 'Perhaps I inconvenience the neighbours.'

'Not at all!' replied Cao, pretending to shout.

Another pot later, followed by a prolonged embrace on the counter of Dr Shih's shop, he led her into the dark central corridor. Lu Ying heard them creep along the wooden floor with all the subtlety of water buffalo, their arms laden with quilts and blankets.

They giggled immodestly as they mounted the ladder to the tower room, *shhhing* each other every few steps. A faint thudding noise vibrated throughout the house for a long time, just as when Dr Shih mixed medicine by the light of a full moon because the Goddess Cheng-e's light grants the whole world good fortune. So it was for them.

Cao stared out of the window at stars above Nancheng and listened to her husband's breathing as he slept. A wisp of cloud blew across the moon. For a moment cloud and moon entwined. Then the cloud floated beyond the frame of the window and Cao fell into a deep, contented sleep beneath the quilts, her bare arm resting on Shih's chest, aware that her husband's surname meant 'cloud'.

竹子

While Cao slept in her husband's arms, Lord Yun's door quietly opened. A thin pre-dawn glow lit the central corridor of the house. He crept towards the kitchen and the grain bins with their heavy porcelain lids. In his hand was a small hemp sack.

The house was silent except for the mournful sound of wind in the eaves. The old man pushed open the kitchen door and peered inside. All the shadows belonged to inanimate things. He lifted the lids of the grain bins one by one. For a moment he muttered to himself, looking round suspiciously. At last he found a few handfuls of rice, representing the family breakfast and scooped them into his hemp sack. Some grains fell to the floor but he did not worry. Household deer would soon devour them, for the rats were starving. Those foolish enough to get caught found themselves roasted on spits.

Lord Yun retreated the way he had come. Instead of returning to his chamber, he unbarred a wooden door at the back of the house that gave straight onto a narrow footpath beside the canal. Across the water stood Ping's Floating Oriole House, dark and strangely forlorn at this hour. Lord Yun walked to a humped bridge over which North Canal Street passed.

At first there was no one to be seen. Then he stepped forward haughtily. A thin shape rose from the darkness and knelt before him in the gloom. He did not deign to look down, but affected a yawn. When at last his eyes lowered, they were narrow and cold. The kneeling figure rose timidly and bobbed towards him. Lord Yun made a guttural noise at the back of his throat, as one might when summoning a dog or a horse with a hard journey ahead of it. Widow Mu's daughter, Lan Tien, at last drew close. Her wide eyes fastened on the little bag of grain he held out temptingly, then she glanced aside into the black waters of the canal.

憺

sixteen

'Fouzhou was far smaller than Nancheng when I was young, though many notable prefects sought to increase its size. Always they were thwarted by the city's watery setting, especially the marsh known as Liu's Pond. The Fouzhou of my youth was an old-fashioned kind of town. Indeed, many of the ancient ward walls and gates remained from the Tang Dynasty. We had three uncles in Fouzhou and I always found them as stiff and formal as their city. . .'

From *Sundry Recollections Of My Youth* by Du Fan

竹子

The Ramparts, Fouzhou. Autumn, 1268

The party of gentlemen on the battlements gazed at the Mongol siege lines. Winter was long forgotten, replaced by summer rains then an unseasonably hot early autumn. The enemy could be seen creating temporary camps well beyond the range of Fouzhou's scant supply of artillery. Pacification Commissioner Wang Ting-bo sat stiffly on a portable throne decorated with ivory chrysanthemums that accompanied him everywhere.

'Gentlemen! Gather round!' he ordered.

The small crowd of commanders and high officials obliged. A few of the more ambitious sank to their knees before His

Excellency. Guang hesitated, then caught General Zheng Shun's sharp glance and remained upright.

'Gentlemen!' continued Wang Ting-bo. 'I have summoned you to Fouzhou for a reason. I am sure many of you are surprised.'

This was true. Fouzhou on the northern bank of the great Han River had attracted few assaults due to its location amidst marshes and a lattice of canals. Instead the Mongols had concentrated on the foremost of the Twin Cities, Nancheng, lured by its importance as Gateway to the South.

'My reason is this,' said Wang Ting-bo. 'As all know, the continuing drought aids our attackers. Fouzhou has been rendered vulnerable by the drying of its moats and marshes. Even Liu's Pond has dried out. Yet magic and other rites have so far failed to conjure rain.'

'Fouzhou's ramparts remain strong, sir!' broke in General Zheng Shun. 'As is our resolve!'

Zheng Shun had grown more sullen since the loss of his cousin, Admiral Qi-Qi, but no less fiery in his determination to resist the enemy. Wang Ting-bo's eyes narrowed at this interruption.

'Perhaps so,' replied Prefect Wang Bai, on his uncle's behalf. 'But what of those mountain-tower monsters over there? What are *they*?'

All turned in the direction of Wang Bai's pointing finger. Certainly the enemy was busy. Four catapults of an unimaginable height had almost been erected. Observers on the ramparts reported trains of wagons bearing timber and huge stone balls. Most baffling of all, was the novel design of these catapults.

'Perhaps Yun Guang can explain,' said General Zheng Shun. 'After all, sir, he understands artillery better than any.'

Guang bowed to acknowledge the compliment. His wound and slow recovery had altered more than his appearance. Not only had he gained weight but his former restless intensity had softened. Some remarked that he no longer defied death by exposing himself to Mongol missiles, as though it was a game or way of taunting General A-ku. Most applauded his new-found caution – losing Captain Xiao was unthinkable. He had become a talisman to the Twin Cities, ever defiant, ever returning from death to fight on.

'Your Excellency, I am puzzled,' said Guang. 'There are no ropes for men to drag. How is a missile to be discharged? The missiles themselves are inordinately heavy – no catapult ever devised can fling stones of such weight and size. Finally, they stand beyond all conceivable range. Perhaps they intend to move the devices forward when they use them. But, if so, why are the wooden supports buried in the ground?'

Guang caught Wang Bai watching him closely, a mocking look on his face. Unexpectedly, he remembered another such look, on another man's face.

'Your Excellency,' he added, earnestly. 'Two years ago I entered the Mongol encampment and took a prisoner, whom we interrogated.'

'Ah, that wretch!' broke in General Zheng Shun. 'A traitor to his ancestors, a man of Han kneeling to barbarians!'

'His name was Li Tse,' said Guang. 'He mentioned a great city far to the west. Quagdad, I believe he called it. He said terrible engines brought down its stone walls so that the whole city was put to the sword.'

'A likely tale!' scoffed Zheng Shun.

Wang Ting-bo cleared his throat: 'They are constructing four more mountain-tower catapults outside Nancheng. I can see them from my terrace when I take morning tea.'

Zheng Shun stepped forward, bowing with uncustomary respect so that Guang knew at once he was after something.

'Sir! There is a more urgent threat,' said the General of Land Forces. 'Tens of thousands of their best troops have been ferried across the river to surround Fouzhou. We may be sure they plan a grand assault. I beg that we transfer three regiments from Nancheng to Fouzhou without delay!'

'Your Excellency,' added Guang. 'We should transfer catapults and siege crossbows at the same time.'

A glance passed between the Pacification Commissioner and his nephew, Wang Bai. The latter said hurriedly: 'No! They mean to trick us. If we weaken Nancheng we may be sure they will attack there.'

'How?' asked Zheng Shun, mockingly. 'When all their best troops are on this side of the river?'

Before anyone could say more Wang Ting-bo rose from his portable throne, indicating an end to the discussion.

'We shall maintain our current dispositions,' he said. 'Let us wait until the enemy's intentions are clear. My thanks, gentlemen, and a good day to you all!'

With that the Pacification Commissioner left the Gate of Revealed Splendour, accompanied by a flock of officials, including many members of the Wang clan. Four sweating servants carried his ivory throne on their shoulders. At last only Chen Song and Guang remained on the battlements.

'I plan to walk back to Nancheng rather than ride,' said Chen Song. 'Will you accompany me?'

'A pleasant suggestion.'

Though Guang suspected his friend had unpleasant topics of conversation in mind.

Nearly nine months had passed since Cao and Shih grew intoxicated and lay together in the tower room of Apricot Corner Court, their bodies washed by moonlight.

As he tramped the streets of Fouzhou, Chen Song by his side, Guang's thoughts drifted to Cao's delicate condition. A small escort followed, leading their horses. Fouzhou was far smaller than Nancheng, and older. Many of its wards retained the severe walls and forbidden places of Tang Dynasty despots, whereas merchants and pleasure-sellers had colonised every available corner of Nancheng. People on the south bank described Fouzhou folk as dull and dour. Their northern neighbours replied that Nancheng folk were flighty and frivolous. Wise heads maintained that to have *yin* one must have *yang*.

'His Excellency should follow Zheng Shun's suggestion

without delay,' complained Chen Song. 'The garrison here is too small to repulse a full assault, especially if the walls are breached. Now that the marshes are dry, even the deepest moats may be waded by a tall man with his head above water.'

Guang gave no sign that he heard. His thoughts lingered in Apricot Corner Court. By chance he had blundered into the medicine shop on the day Cao acknowledged her pregnancy to Shih. They were embracing beside the counter. A bucket of pungent plants stood by their feet and Guang had recognised it as the mugwort Sister-in-law had sowed and harvested by the Water Gate of Morning Radiance. He had expected them to spring apart at his entrance, yet to his surprise Shih clasped Cao tighter.

'Is all well?' Guang had demanded. 'Father? Is he. . . ?'

There were tears on both their cheeks.

'No,' said Shih. 'No.'

'Then what is it?'

Cao appeared to be trembling.

'What is it Sister-in-law?' asked Guang. 'If anyone has dishonoured you, let him beware!'

Both Shih and Cao had laughed joyfully as he watched in incomprehension.

'It is not that,' said Cao, dabbing her eyes. 'Oh, you must tell him, Shih!'

And so he had. That Cao's pregnancy was quite certain. After all these years the apricot stones buried in the spare room of their house had put forth blossom.

As Guang walked through Fouzhou with Chen Song, he realised her time was drawing close. And if Cao's delicate condition resulted in a male heir, a crisis would inevitably arise. After all, Honoured Father surely could not last much longer. Although strong for a man of his age, he was still venerable. When he passed away the Lordship of Wei Valley must, like a noble hat, find a new head. Never mind that the title was empty, that Bayke ruled their ancestral lands. Guang still fervently believed what had been stolen would one day be reclaimed, and there lay his dilemma.

When he jokingly referred to Shih as Youngest Brother both twins grew confused. Neither could meet the other's eye. Sometimes Guang came close to mentioning Shih's banishment as a child but his courage always faltered. Afterwards he berated himself. How could there be reconciliation when the past was unresolved? Without truth, how could there be restoration?

For months after his recovery these questions troubled him, yet paradoxically Shih became a closer companion than even Chen Song. Often when he returned from the ramparts to Apricot Corner Court, the two brothers talked until late into the night. Still the dilemma of who was the true Eldest Son lay between them.

Chen Song's voice broke into his thoughts. They had just reached the Floating Bridge linking Fouzhou to Nancheng.

'What amazes me, my dear Guang, is the ineptitude of His Imperial Majesty's advisers! Why was no fresh attempt made to raise the siege this summer? And now it is autumn, a season favourable to the enemy. It is as though the Chancellor has decided we can only defend, never attack. Unless we take the fight to them, we shall never recover our lost lands. And then to decide that Wang Ting-bo should remain Pacification Commissioner despite failed attempts to replace him! I call that a questionable decision.'

Guang nodded as though in complete agreement. His thoughts remained in Apricot Corner Court. Of course, Cao's pregnancy preoccupied his brother so that even his work at the Relief Bureau suffered. Yet no one could have anticipated Lu Ying becoming a prop to Madam Cao, their rivalry forgotten. She had even taken up the duty of serving Lord Yun's meals. Guang sometimes met her emerging from Father's room with an empty dish and a vexed flush on her pretty face; and he honoured her for sparing Cao from Lord Yun's malicious mumblings about cuckoos and true fathers. Lu Ying once confided to Guang that on his bad days Lord Yun believed Khan Bayke to be the unborn child's demon-father.

Rarely Lu Ying visited Guang's room to bring cordials and other refreshments. Then they talked in a free manner, as when she had been his nurse. In all other respects the lady maintained a strict decorum he found provoking – as, no doubt, she fully intended.

'Really, Guang!' said Chen Song. 'I swear that I have been speaking to myself since we left Jasper Gate!'

Only then did Guang realise they were half way across the Floating Bridge. He turned and looked back at Fouzhou. The strange catapults were clearly visible. Huge scaffolds with which General A-ku hoped to strangle the Twin Cities.

'What are those things?' he muttered.

'I do not know.'

'Do you think Nancheng could hold out if Fouzhou fell?' Guang asked quietly, in case their escort overheard.

'If the Pacification Commissioner does not transfer troops there right away, we may find out,' replied Chen Song.

竹子

It was Lu Ying's suggestion to visit the pleasure gardens beside the Pavilion of Pure Distance. At first Madam Cao refused. For months no rain had fallen, making the streets close and dusty. The level of the Han River sunk alarmingly, transforming it into a wide maze of shingle strips and deep, treacherous channels. The skies behind Mount Wadung remained cloudless.

Heat filled Apricot Corner Court even at night. The only breezes were stray gusts carrying grit and dust through open windows. Unpleasant enough weather for anyone – but as Cao sat on the shady bench beneath the apricot tree, irritably wafting herself with one of Old Hsu's largest fans, she touched her swollen belly and moaned. Surely no woman was supposed to grow so large! The heat made her swell like a gourd.

There seemed no end to the movements inside her womb.

Sometimes Cao wondered if she had conceived a frog with powerful back legs or a bird constantly fluttering its wings. Then she felt afraid of such thoughts in case demons made them come true. Everyone knew a pregnant woman must guard her thoughts.

Cao had been scrupulous in other ways: eating light-coloured food whenever possible so Baby would be fair-skinned; sleeping with knives under the bed to deter sneaking fox-fairies. Neither would she sit on crooked mats or look at clashing colours except accidentally and then it made her worry all day. Despite such precautions Cao often felt disheartened.

Old Hsu's Widow assured her Baby's movements were normal and very suggestive of *yang*. The midwife commissioned by Shih concurred. Only a boy, she said, possessed such vigour, for girls are naturally meek from the moment of conception. Cao did not like the midwife. She had always hoped Widow Mu might perform that service, in the days when they were close friends.

Of course there were many other anxieties. What if the child turned out to be a girl? After all the years of waiting, a mere girl! She was sure her kindly Shih would love the infant, whatever its worth in the world. Or she trusted he would. Most of all Cao dreaded losing the child. Nine months of nagging fear until her head ached constantly! Yet she dared not mention it to a living soul, in case naming what she dreaded made it happen.

Cao looked up as Lu Ying emerged from the house with two parasols and a small lacquered box. She came over to Madam Cao and sat beside her on the bench. Flies buzzed around them. It was early evening but the sun still beat fiercely.

'Just think, in a fortnight the child is due!' observed Lu Ying, brightly. 'How quickly the days pass.'

'If Midwife Tui-Lo's calculations are correct,' cautioned Cao.

'And Dr Shih's,' added Lu Ying.

'Indeed.'

'So you see,' said Lu Ying. 'There is little time left for us to visit the Pavilion of Pure Distance before your confinement.'

Cao flapped her hands. The benefits of trailing through baking streets to sacrifice to the Buddha seemed outweighed by the discomfort of getting there.

'Here is an offering of old jewellery,' said Lu Ying, holding out the box.

Now Cao sat up anxiously. She knew her honoured guest's precious jewellery was being traded piece by piece for bags of fourth grade rice, more husk than grain, to supplement the family's rations.

'You are too kind!' she said.

'Not at all.'

Lu Ying smiled.

'I have gone so far as to hire two sedan chairs. And before you ask, Dr Shih has indicated his agreement with my plan. It was his idea that it should be a surprise.'

'Then it seems I must go,' said Cao.

Half an hour later they arrived at the Pavilion of Pure Distance. Most of the city's pleasure gardens had been turned into vegetable plots. Not so this one. It adjoined a notable shrine and contained a large rock shaped like an arch. Its many ornamental ponds were said to cleanse misfortune. Prudent women of all classes came here to purchase favour at the Pavilion then pass under the stone arch, praying to Lord Buddha for a painless childbirth.

At the shrine Cao grew tearful and might have shown a disreputable face had not Lu Ying guided her into the evening sunshine. There she composed herself, hidden by her friend's parasol.

'You cannot imagine,' she sniffed, 'the anxiety I feel.'

'True,' said Lu Ying, wistfully. 'But Madam Cao, dry your eyes, for we must pass beneath the lucky arch! Why come here without that?'

The two women entered the area of ornamental ponds, a maze of paths shaded by moon-gates and tasteful stands of bamboo. They turned a corner and Lu Ying went rigid. Painful fingers found Cao's arm. For coming towards them, shuffling on lotus feet, was a group of fine ladies six or seven strong. Despite the heat they wore exquisite silk gowns. Their silver-chased headdresses stood a foot high. Each lady fluttered a silken fan to ward off insects. Two sturdy servants armed with clubs followed at a distance, along with a crowd of maids.

'We must turn back!' hissed Lu Ying. 'It is Wang Ting-bo's First Wife! I should never have come here!'

It was too late to escape. Cao pulled Lu Ying to the side of the path and both women bowed respectfully. Their best hope was to be deemed unworthy of notice, but the great lady recognised Lu Ying at once. And though her emotions were hidden behind thick layers of white cosmetics, her small, alert eyes did not leave the former concubine for a moment. Cao guessed what she saw – a rival reduced to miserable poverty, unable even to afford make-up. Then she bristled inwardly on Lu Ying's behalf.

At first it seemed the great lady would pass without comment. When level with Lu Ying she halted, forcing her companions to do likewise. A maid carrying a broad parasol to shade her mistress bobbed uncertainly.

'Ah, Lu Ying!' said First Wife. 'I barely recognised you. How changed you are!'

The younger woman said nothing, her eyes fixed on the gravel path.

'I'm sure my husband would not care to recognise you at all!' declared First Wife, pleasantly. At this, her companions tittered. 'Who is your companion? Are you her maid?' When Lu Ying did not reply, she clapped her hands sharply. 'I instructed you to speak!'

Now Lu Ying lifted her eyes.

'May I present Madam Cao,' she said. 'Dr Yun Shih's honoured wife.'

First Wife seemed surprised and said: 'So Dr Shih's wife

swells with his child while his concubine's stomach is flat as a shield! I see that nothing changes.'

Again the ladies were amused. Lu Ying glanced darkly from face to face. Most were former companions. The click and flutter of their fans was constant. One by one they fell silent.

'Madam, Miss Lu Ying is not my husband's concubine,' said Madam Cao, pointedly. 'And never has been.'

The Pacification Commissioner's wife smiled thinly.

'I am glad, for your sake,' she said. 'Dr Shih is a man I respect. He saved my Little Tortoise when all the world had consigned him to the tomb.'

Madam Cao bowed gratefully.

'He often does good.'

'Unlike that slut beside you!' exclaimed First Wife with a sudden fury, quite unbecoming in a lady of quality. 'I warn you, never trust a fox-fairy!'

Cao recoiled in surprise. She composed herself and tilted her head, as though puzzled. Lu Ying trembled beside her. When Cao answered it was in an agreeable manner.

'Miss Lu Ying is our Honoured Guest. She brings good fortune to our house.'

Now Wang Ting-bo's First Wife was at a loss for words and Madam Cao pressed home her advantage.

'Madam,' she said. 'Miss Lu Ying's behaviour has been very proper indeed.'

The Pacification Commissioner's wife sniffed contemptuously, seeking a suitable reply, but she had already said enough to start a hundred whispers on Peacock Hill. She clapped to indicate her party should proceed and the ladies soon shuffled away and turned a corner.

'Let us find a bench,' murmured Cao. 'I feel faint.'

They fanned themselves in silence, occupied by different thoughts. Slowly the flush of mortification drained from Lu Ying's face until she managed a smile.

'You are fierce for someone with such a quiet demeanour,' she said. 'I'm sure First Wife was quite afraid of you.'

'Never mind her, where is this lucky arch?' asked Cao. 'My belly is so huge that I need a corresponding amount of good fortune.'

As twilight gathered, Lu Ying helped her friend rise and the two women found the auspicious stone. Both murmured prayers, one to the Buddha, the other to the Moon Goddess Cheng-e. Really it was more an expression of gratitude than a prayer, for having a friend willing to speak out bravely on one's behalf.

That evening Madam Cao received word from Shih he must spend the night at the Relief Bureau. Yun Guang was also away, patrolling the ramparts of Fouzhou, for the Mongols were testing the defences over there with a night sortie.

Cao sometimes felt uneasy when the men were absent. Water Basin Ward had grown more lawless as hunger taught desperation. But Old Hsu's burly son lived just across the courtyard; at the first sign of trouble, help was close. Besides, Apricot Corner Court possessed stout doors and windows. She had no cause to feel troubled. Yet the foreboding would not pass. Cao sat on her bed, propped up by rolls of cloth and sweated in the breathless air.

Everyone seemed to be going a little crazy in the drought. She had witnessed neighbours shoving each other on North Canal Street, their shrill voices disturbing the peace of the ward. An unusual number of crying babies broke the night's stillness. Cao wondered if her own child would wail so piercingly. She was hungry for it. She stroked her stomach, seeking the reassurance of a kick or movement. Whoever waited in there, boy or girl, chose not to oblige. Cao sighed, then grew alert.

A door was opening in the corridor. It could only be Lu Ying or Lord Yun, unless Shih had returned. From the soft, shuffling footfall she divined it was Lu Ying. Instead of stepping into the courtyard for a little air as Cao expected, her guest climbed the ladder to the tower room. Cao could not blame her. The breezes were cooler up there.

She settled once more and dozed until another noise disturbed her. Again, a door. From the long, stealthy creak it belonged to Lord Yun's chamber and Cao felt uneasy. What could he want at such an hour? She listened closely, expecting him to sneak into the kitchen in yet another attempt to steal grain. Everyone in the household knew that he traded it for home-brewed spirits with the new owner of Ping's Floating Oriole House. As a result, all their stores of food were hidden.

Tonight the old man did not sneak past Cao's door towards the kitchen. He took the opposite direction. His feet could be heard scraping on the stair-ladder to the tower room and Cao grew alarmed. It would be most improper for him to come upon Lu Ying sleeping up there. No doubt he would poke his head through the trapdoor and see the girl, then retreat. She listened for the sound of his footsteps, climbing back down the stairs. It did not come. Now Cao sat up on the bed.

She could hear a scuffling noise through the floorboards of the tower room above her head. A loud, insistent: 'No! Please! No!'

Lu Ying's voice! Straightaway Cao was upright and hurrying down the dark corridor to the stair-ladder. The scraping feet like dancers on a wooden floor were louder now, as were Lu Ying's frightened moans and a chuckle belonging to Lord Yun.

For Cao the effort of climbing the stairs was huge. Not so much the strain of her arm muscles on the rail as what she feared to find. When her head poked through the trapdoor Cao blinked, adjusting her vision to the starlight. She cried out in alarm. Lord Yun stood over Lu Ying. The girl had been pushed to her knees. He was panting heavily.

'Be quiet, stupid girl!' he hissed. 'I mean you no harm!'

A smell of rank spirits filled the room. His handsome, noble features were twisted, desperate. His drunken eyes were without focus. He held her slender wrists in a desperate grip. As Cao watched he thrust out a hand and grasped Lu Ying's shoulder to hold her still. Whether deliberately or by accident the nightgown tore at the front so that her jade mountains were revealed.

'No!' Cao's voice was a loud sob. 'Father-in-law!'

Her vision faded in on itself. Went black. Suddenly she was sliding down the stairs. A strange, calm inner voice told her she had fainted. . . The floor sped upwards and she landed with a crump, legs folding beneath her. Then the calm voice urged, *Your baby, Cao! Your baby!* She gasped and howled at the realisation her thighs were sticky with warm blood.

竹子

Dr Shih could hear sounds of fighting across the river. Word had reached the Relief Bureau hours earlier that the Mongols were attempting a night attack on Fouzhou.

He stood in the street, a bowl of tea warming his hands. Mung Po, his orderly, crouched against the wall meditating. Both glanced up sharply at the sound of voices drawing nearer. Soon a procession of three wagons pulled by dozens of peasants came into view. They rumbled along at a brisk trot. Inside the wagons, wounded soldiers groaned or cried. Some stared sightlessly, their eyes wide, overcome by the bumpy journey across the Floating Bridge to Nancheng.

It took a moment for Dr Shih to recognise the youth leading the wagons. Mung Po followed his gaze and instinctively reached for a bamboo club he kept by the door. The plump, sweating figure drew nearer. He wore the robes and hat of an apprentice physician. A servant ran beside him, carrying a pale lantern.

Mung Po glanced at his Bureau Chief's rigid expression and stepped forward to block the intruder's way. Meanwhile, half a dozen other orderlies led by Dr Du Tun-i rushed from the Relief Bureau to transfer the wounded men to makeshift cots. During this frantic activity Mung Po and Dr Shih remained on the street.

'Shall I, sir?' asked Mung Po.

His question was no figure of speech. The club was half-raised. Dr Shih did not reply. The young man before him stood uncomfortably, head lowered. Perspiration on his brow glinted in the languid torchlight.

'Why are you here?' asked Dr Shih, though he already guessed the reason.

'My master. . . I mean, Dr Du Mau sent me here. With a message.'

'I see.'

But having come so far Chung seemed reluctant to deliver it. He glanced fearfully at his former master's face then looked away.

'Dr Du Mau wished me to say, sir,' he said. 'There are too many wounded for the relief bureaus in Fouzhou, but that if you find. . . that is, if you discover. . .'

He fell silent with embarrassment.

'Quickly!' commanded Mung Po.

'If you find,' continued Chung, rushing on. 'Any wounded are beyond your skill, you have Dr Du Mau's permission to consult. . .' Chung coughed before adding: 'Me.'

Dr Shih and Mung Po listened incredulously.

'A memorable message!' said Dr Shih, laughing coldly. 'Please assure Dr Du Mau we are grateful.'

He was about to re-enter the Relief Bureau in disgust when he realised Chung had followed, his head bobbing. Mung Po growled and raised the club, but Dr Shih waved him back.

'Is there more?' he asked. Then a mocking sneer, quite out of character, made his face ugly. 'I should have warned Dr Du Mau how easily you forget messages. Or anything at all for that matter – unless you can use it to cause mischief.'

Tears glistened round Chung's eyes.

'I have another message, sir,' he said. 'For Madam Cao. Tell her I am sorry.' Dr Shih raised his eyebrows ironically. Quite unexpectedly Chung fell to his knees. 'And you, too, sir! I am sorry how it all ended.'

'Worthless apologies!' declared Shih. 'I do not accept them. No doubt you dislike your new master's strict ways.'

Mung Po grunted approvingly and shook his fist over the kneeling young man.

'Get away!' he advised. 'Those who slip by accident into North Canal sometimes never climb out.'

Yet Chung stayed kneeling on the street.

Dr Shih's bitter heart remembered the Prefectural prison, the hellish indignities he had suffered and Old Hsu's cruel death. Finally he realised who Du Mau hoped to punish by sending Chung here to be humiliated. Against his will he felt righteous anger soften. Perhaps he saw the little boy who had once knelt before him, a frightened, weak-willed little boy. As every drought is followed by rain the natural pattern of Shih's sentiments asserted themselves.

'I will tell Madam Cao you are contrite,' he said, more gently. 'Go now, Chung.'

His former apprentice rose and hurried towards the Floating Bridge and his new life in Fouzhou. Tears pricked Shih's own eyes as he turned to help Dr Du Tun-i supervise the unloading of the wounded.

'You should have let me use my club,' muttered Mung Po.

An hour later another sweating messenger arrived at the North Medical Relief Bureau. It was Old Hsu's Son. He had run all the way from Apricot Corner Court, defying the curfew and the soldiers hurrying to reinforce the Floating Bridge. On the way he heard rumours that the Mongols had surprised Fouzhou's inadequate garrison. Only the resolve of General Zheng Shun and Captain Xiao prevented the ramparts from being overwhelmed.

Mung Po led him straight to Dr Shih who was using the needles to lessen the agony of a man wounded by an arrow in his kidneys. The orderly whispered in Dr Shih's ear. His eyes widened and he almost dropped the needle he was about to place in the soldier's groin. With an effort, he composed himself and completed the patient cycle of testing pulse and twisting the needle. At last he looked up and closed the man's staring eyes. 'Place him with the others,' he said. 'I must return home at once.'

Dr Shih rushed into the night, Old Hsu's Son talking excitedly beside him. The first signs of dawn were showing as they reached Apricot Corner Court. Shih found Old Hsu's extended family whispering around the apricot tree. Its fruit were shrivelled by the long drought. They fell silent as he entered his house.

Shih paused in the kitchen and his nose wrinkled. Incense of a kind associated with cleansing and desperate prayer was being burned. Then he heard a long, keening wail followed by the murmur of reassuring female voices. Shih followed the sound to his own bedchamber where he found Lu Ying and Old Hsu's Widow beside the bed. Cao lay on her back, towels stained dark by blood beneath her.

He hurried to his wife's side and gently took her wrist. After reading her pulse, he noted her colour and sniffed for indications of putrefying matter. Then he turned to Old Hsu's Wife.

'What of her waters?' he whispered.

The old lady shook her head.

'Cao, do not distress yourself!' he urged. 'All will be well. I will prepare medicine to halt your loss of blood. I shall return in a moment.'

His wife clutched his hand.

'Do not go! Do not leave me!'

'Old Hsu's Widow is here. I promise it is just for a moment. No longer!'

He rose, indicating to Lu Ying with a twist of his head that she should accompany him to the shop.

'What happened?' he asked, hastily mixing an infusion of the same dried herbs harvested by the women outside the Water Gate of Morning Radiance. At first Lu Ying would not speak. 'Something happened! I must know the truth if I am to help her.'

Lu Ying sobbed as she told the tale of Lord Yun's unseemly behaviour and Cao's fall down the stairs. How the bleeding followed immediately. By this time the medicine was ready.

Shih returned to their bedchamber. It took a struggle to transform his look of frozen rage into a confident, reassuring smile, as though his wife merely had a mild fever and he had prepared a simple draught. He helped her sit up.

'Drink this,' he said. 'I shall apply massage in a moment.'

For half an hour he massaged places correlating to the womb and conducive to sleep. Every so often he indicated to Old Hsu's Widow that the towels should be changed. At last the flow of blood slowed. Cao fell into a restless doze then a profound sleep.

Shih sat beside her for a while, looking at her swollen belly. At last he whispered to Old Hsu's Widow: 'Tell me if she wakes or the bleeding changes in any way.' The grim look was back in his eyes. Again he indicated to Lu Ying she should follow him from the room.

'Where is Lord Yun?' he demanded, once the door was shut.

Lu Ying shook her head.

'I do not know.'

'I will find him.'

Shih strode into his father's chamber. It stank in subtle, pervasive ways. Of unopened windows and chamber pots. Of endless days and nights spent waiting for Bayke – and chewing the bitter roots of a thousand imagined insults and wrongs. Shih looked down contemptuously at the bowl of fishes, his father's familiars. He kicked it so savagely the earthenware broke in two. Water rushed over the floor and tiny grey fish flapped helplessly.

'Dr Shih!' cried Lu Ying, who had followed him. 'You will frighten Madam Cao!'

He thrust her aside and climbed the ladder-stairs to the tower room. The shutters were closed and at first he could not see clearly. At last he spied a figure on a low stool in the shadows, apparently meditating.

'Bayke has sent you!' Lord Yun's drawl was forced. 'I knew he would.'

Shih walked over to the shutters, throwing them open one by one, until light filled the wide room. Lord Yun blinked at the sudden brightness of morning and covered his eyes. Dr Shih stared at the old man in wonder, as though seeing him for the first time. Could this man really be his Honoured Father? Or Guang's? Perhaps Lord Yun sensed his repulsion and wished to defy it, for a look of icy contempt crossed his face.

'My wife is bleeding downstairs,' said Shih. 'She is carrying the heir our ancestors crave. Do you feel no shame?'

Lord Yun looked puzzled.

'She is not carrying your child,' he said. 'You are impotent as a eunuch. In any case, you are not my son.'

Abruptly, the old man grew agitated.

'Guang is my son! I have no son but Guang! Do not come near me!'

But Shih did step closer.

'If anything happens to my wife or unborn child. . .' His threat dangled. He became aware that Lu Ying had climbed into the room after him.

'Come away, Dr Shih!' she urged. 'I am sure Lord Yun wished only to stop me from calling out. Oh, I have never seen you like this! Please, come away and sit with your wife!'

Dr Shih did not seem to hear. He turned back to Father and took yet another step closer, his fists bunched.

'You have ruined half my life,' he said. 'If my wife bleeds to death or my child. . .' He could not finish the thought, too dreadful to be spoken aloud. Perhaps he feared demons would hear the violent promptings of his soul.

'Get away, you devil!' screeched Lord Yun, shrinking back in his chair. 'Guang! Save me!'

'Be quiet, you will frighten Cao!'

'Get away!'

Shih's arm, as though controlled by something outside himself, swung back in preparation for a slap. A blow that would have cost his life, for striking a parent was a capital crime. He was saved by a parade ground bellow from the stairs.

'You will *not*!'

Shih went limp. Guang, still dressed for battle, climbed into the room. His armour, repaired many times, showed fresh signs of damage. His helmet had taken a dint and a lotus-shaped bruise disfigured one cheek. Now Lord Yun crowed with delight.

'You see! I have summoned my real son. He always comes when I need him! Guang, punish this devil! Throw him down the stairs!'

Yet Guang had taken Shih's arm. His brother was sobbing painfully.

'You saw!' continued Lord Yun. 'He meant to hit me! I told you he was not my real son. All those years ago, I told you. Throw him down the stairs, Guang!'

The soldier seemed near the point of exhaustion. He stepped over to the table Shih used for the preparation of medicines and sat down heavily. Then he removed sword and scabbard from his belt, casting them onto the wooden boards with a loud clatter. Dagger and gauntlets followed.

'Father,' he said, finally. 'Enough.' His voice was calm.

'Yes!' urged Lord Yun. 'Do as I command. That is a true son's duty.'

'Father,' said Guang. 'You know quite well you have two sons. The Eldest you repudiated because. . . Oh, I cannot say why! I dare not, Father, for I suspect it diminishes all your honour! As for the Youngest – *me* – you gave him a fine hat that has never fitted his head.'

Guang's eyes did not shift from the old man's face.

'Do not betray me like the others!' gasped Lord Yun.

'Oh, Father! If you do not admit right now that you have two sons, I shall walk from this room and tell all the honourable men of my acquaintance that I am to be called Youngest Son from now on.'

'You would not dare!'

Guang laughed.

'You would not throw away the title to Wei Valley!' continued Lord Yun. 'You would not!'

'That title is nothing now. In any case, I renounce whatever false claim I once had to it.'

The old man's confidence drained. His face was very red. He seemed to have trouble breathing and began to scrabble at his left arm as though in pain.

'I admit there were two,' he whispered. 'Two identical husks of rice!'

'Who was the eldest husk, Father?' asked Guang.

'Why, you! You are my chosen heir!'

Guang turned to Shih, who had stood throughout this debate with a lowered head. Then he glanced back at Lord Yun: 'No, Father, I am *not* the eldest husk.'

Lord Yun's breathing was heavier. Sweat appeared on his forehead. He began to pull more fiercely at his stiffening arm. Now Shih stirred, examining the old man's complexion with alarm.

'Father is not well,' he murmured. 'Perhaps if I took his pulse? Something is not right.'

Guang waved him aside angrily

'In front of witnesses, I declare that Dr Yun Shih is the rightful heir to Wei Valley!'

'I am a good man.' moaned Lord Yun.

A deep silence followed. Time became a doorway through which the Yun clan's fortunes must step one way or the other. Guang went over to the window and looked down on the people gathered in Apricot Corner Court. Their upturned faces stared in surprise at the warrior leaning out of the window towards them. There was little doubt they had heard every word of the preceding conversation.

'Let all our neighbours know!' he roared. 'A mistake has been made!' Then he laughed oddly. 'Caused by bad astrologers. Yun Shih is Eldest Son and I am Little Brother! Pass the message that Captain Xiao honours Dr Yun Shih as Eldest Brother!'

Guang pulled back his head and said almost hysterically: 'It cannot be unsaid now! I am free of that lie!'

His triumph faltered. Lord Yun had fallen from the chair and was in Shih's arms. The old man gazed glassily into space.

'He has had these fits before,' muttered Shih. 'Sometimes if he has taken too much medicine by mistake. . . We shall carry him to bed.'

Several burly men were needed to achieve this. Then, before the magnitude of Guang's declaration could strike Shih, he was summoned to attend Cao.

It was late afternoon when he emerged and stepped into his father's room. The smashed bowl still lay on the floor, surrounded by dead demon-fishes. Lord Yun lay on his back, blinking at the ceiling.

Old Hsu's Widow popped her head into the corridor: 'Madam Cao's flood has come early,' she whispered. 'Dr Shih, fetch the midwife. Fetch her at once.'

Then hooves were striking the baked earth of the street. There was a hasty knock on the door and a messenger called out for Commander Yun Guang to arm himself.

竹子

Captain Xiao had often derided the Mongol artillery's best efforts – but he was cowering now. Every few minutes the enormous catapults facing the Gate of Revealed Splendour in Fouzhou gracefully released their missiles. Enormous stone boulders curved up and just as remorselessly span down towards the ramparts. They seldom missed their target. The artillerymen summoned from the West by their Great Khan had found the range now. Their weapons appalled the city's defenders. Many believed they were operated by demons.

No catapult in the Empire's long history had possessed the power to destroy city walls. These monsters, with their vast height and system of weights, unleashed the careless strength of gods.

Guang watched from a high temple pavilion within the ramparts and thought the hundreds swarming round the machines were human enough. The problem was reaching them. The Mongols could only be attacked by the largest of the defenders' siege crossbows and these remained across the river in Nancheng at the Pacification Commissioner's express command.

A stout figure climbed up the spiral stairs to join Guang. It was Chen Song, who had dashed across the Floating Bridge and Fouzhou to get here. As they watched, another huge missile curved towards the Gate of Revealed Splendour, the principal entry-point into Fouzhou. Down, down it fell, striking the centre of the fortifications with an echoing crash. Clouds of dust and masonry rose. There was a loud sound of tearing wood, creaking stone. The centre of the Gate slowly collapsed in on itself, raising yet more dust.

'A few more like that and the Gate will be rubble,' said Guang. 'And see! Tens of thousands of infantry are waiting for a chance to assault.'

Chen Song followed his gaze. Phalanxes of Mongols on foot, General A-ku's most fearless, lined up patiently around scores of cloud ladders and mobile towers.

'Are regiments from Nancheng making their way here?' asked Guang. 'We must have reinforcements now.'

The expression on Chen Song's face answered that question. Both men had fought against the Mongol night attack the previous evening. The fall of Fouzhou had come surprisingly near. Not only did the enemy know the most unprotected sections of the ramparts, but the same problem of reinforcements forced the defenders to show desperate resolve. At last General Zheng Shun had disobeyed the Pacification Commissioner's orders, appearing with five thousand soldiers from Nancheng. The Mongols withdrew, allowing the exhausted defenders of Fouzhou a respite. Some whispered the Wang clan were exchanging messages with General A-ku in anticipation of defeat – and hastening it in exchange for favourable terms.

By now the dust was beginning to settle around the battered Gate of Revealed Splendour. Screams from the wounded contended with shouts of encouragement. Swarms of brave soldiers could be seen placing thick chains across breaches in the walls. Behind them, others attempted hasty repairs with buckets of stone and earth.

Unworthy thoughts whispered in Guang's mind: *So long as those I love do not perish, let Fouzhou fall. Let the Son of Heaven be humbled, rather than lose those dear to me.* Traitor's thoughts. Coward's thoughts. He felt glad Chen Song was no Immortal capable of eavesdropping a man's fears.

'It cannot be long before they attack,' said Chen Song. 'The Gate of Revealed Splendour is not the only part of the ramparts they have damaged. That corner tower to the south has almost entirely collapsed.'

'The Jade Emperor has abandoned us,' muttered Guang. 'Let it just rain as it should! Heaven itself conspires against us. As though His Highness is no longer Heaven's Son, as though the Mandate of Heaven has been withdrawn.'

Chen Song stepped back in horror. A look of haughty disdain crossed his features.

'I take it you are unwell,' he said, stiffly. 'I advise you to leave such nonsense to your patron, Wang Bai, and those like him. I am going to join General Zheng Shun in the lanes below.'

He departed with a clatter of boots. Guang was left alone, shame-faced at his weakness. What had gripped him? To talk like a fearful woman, to question what is eternal! Then Guang sensed the problem – as one might a question of baffling complexity, too hard to even attempt – love was threatening to confound itself, if that was what he truly felt. By loving a woman, he risked losing the resolve needed to protect her. And hundreds of thousands like her throughout the Empire.

More boulders landed on the Gate of Revealed Splendour. Dust rose like a pillar of smoke. Drums could be heard, signalling the Mongol attack.

What was he doing up here, watching instead of fighting! He

could see Chen Song hurrying up the street to join the battalions General Zheng Shun had marshalled, ready for a desperate counter-attack. Yet assisting Zheng Shun did not seem dangerous enough to atone for his moment of cowardice. Was he not Captain Xiao? Even if, thanks to Wang Ting-bo's folly, they lacked sufficient men, he would take a last stand on the Gate of Revealed Splendour and hold the Mongols back by himself until reinforcements arrived from Nancheng!

Two hours later Guang stood with Chen Song in Fouzhou's great central market square, deep in the city. Once merchants had thronged here, selling goods from every circuit of the Empire. Now the square was bare, the trestle tables long ago used for firewood and siege defences.

Guang was grey with dust, darkened by crimson patches of blood – not his own this time. Chen Song had also seen close action. His ornate halberd was broken and he carried only sword and bow.

'Where is the relief column?' asked Chen Song. 'If they come soon we might yet drive them back and out of the city.'

'What of Zheng Shun?' asked Guang. 'When did you last see him?'

'Surrounded on all sides, but still fighting.'

The two officers had rallied a few hundred men. It was Guang's idea to use the open market square as a killing ground. Chen Song, however, was all for retreating to the Floating Bridge.

'If Fouzhou falls,' he urged. 'We must prevent the enemy from crossing to Nancheng.'

A madness had gripped Guang since their conversation in the tower. No risk seemed great enough. No casualties were significant – as long as the Mongols were matched corpse for corpse.

'We have archers and crossbowmen,' said Guang. 'Let us tempt them to charge us across the square.'

'These men would serve our cause better on the ramparts

of Nancheng than in their graves,' replied Chen Song.

'We must delay the enemy until reinforcements come!'

'There are no reinforcements! All that matters now is securing the Floating Bridge.'

Their debate was cut short by a company of Mongol cavalry cantering into the square. Guang and Chen Song began to loose the remaining arrows in their quivers and all around them crossbows clicked as they discharged. Dozens of rocket-arrows were lit, whooshing at the enemy, throwing their horses into panic. The square filled with confused shouts and neighing. For a moment the Mongols seemed about to charge, then they retreated and found their way blocked by a column of their own infantry, mercenaries from North China serving the Great Khan.

The air filled with arrows until the sight of so many enemies brought Guang to his senses.

'Back!' he shouted. 'While they are in disarray! Every man to the Floating Bridge! Maintain order! Close the ranks!'

A terrible retreat followed. Weighed down by their officers' armour they made slow progress. At one crossroads they encountered a melee between Mongol cavalry and a company of Guards. When the latter realised Captain Xiao had joined them, they regained courage and drove back the horsemen.

Smoke and the reek of burning were beginning to thicken. To the North, where the enemy first gained entry into the city, screams could be heard – women, perhaps children, it was hard to be certain amidst the uproar. One thing was sure: many tens of thousands lived in Fouzhou.

'The Floating Bridge!' urged Chen Song. 'We must secure the Bridge!'

'It's not far, sir,' called out a sergeant beside them. 'I know the quickest way.'

They hurried after the man down a narrow alley at the rear of a Daoist temple. Suddenly they were on the wharf-side where a large crowd of soldiers and townspeople waited to gain passage to the Floating Bridge. Hundreds streamed across it to Nancheng, a headlong, terrified mass of every age and degree. All distinctions perished in the desire for safety. Inevitably, many were trampled. As Guang watched, he saw a young woman holding a baby forced by the crowd into the river. She splashed helplessly for a while, struggling to keep her child above water then vanished.

'We must regain order!' he bellowed. 'Close the ranks! Force a way through!'

He led their company of men slowly into the crowd, shoving and beating to create a path. Those paralysed by fear were brutally thrown to one side or trampled by the advancing Guards. At last Guang reached Jasper Gate, where the Floating Bridge connected to the shore. Its defenders had already fled back to Nancheng, apart from a single officer, who struggled to control the flow of refugees. Guang ordered his men onto the battlements and, above all, to prepare for the closure of Jasper Gate.

'Chen Song,' he said. 'It is clear Fouzhou is lost. We must destroy the Floating Bridge. To do this we must seal Jasper Gate, otherwise it will be impossible to stop the fleeing people.'

Chen Song looked at him in revulsion.

'There are thousands waiting to cross!' he cried. 'We cannot abandon them! Such a decision lies with the Pacification Commissioner.'

'If we do not act now the Mongols will be the ones crossing to Nancheng!'

Did he think of protecting Shih and Cao? Of Lu Ying awaiting his return to Apricot Corner Court? Later he could never be sure. Still the refugees streamed onto the wooden planks, so that the timbers shook and vibrated dangerously. At last enough of Guang's men were in position, ready with axes to sever the thick hemp ropes binding the pontoon bridge together.

Guang stood by the entrance to Jasper Gate, urging the refugees onwards with his sword. He could not bring himself to close the gates until the last possible moment. Above all he longed for General Zheng Shun to appear, so he might relinquish command to the more senior man. Finally he heard the sounds he had been dreading. Wails and the clash of weapons. Cries of panic. The Mongols were attacking the rear of the retreating column.

Instantly the shuffling crowd shoved forward, desperate to gain the safety of the Bridge and Nancheng. Moans and cries filled the air. Guang realised with horror that if he did not dam the flow of refugees soon, they would lose their chance to destroy the Bridge. 'Close the gates!' he roared.

'There are still thousands on the wharf-side!' protested Chen Song.

Several arrows struck the battlements of Jasper Gate. Mongol archers had climbed nearby tall buildings and were firing into the crowd from rooftops and windows. Their intention was obvious. To goad the people into a fatal panic as one might a herd of deer.

'We must close the gates *now*!' repeated Guang.

Aided by Chen Song, dozens of sweating Guardsmen struggled to push the double gates, inch by inch, until finally they met with a bang and the vast bolts went home. Guang and the soldiers were left in the dark tunnel of the gatehouse, leading to the river and dragon-decorated entrance arch of the Floating Bridge. Terrible cries of despair reached them from the area outside Jasper Gate. They could hear the drumming of fists and feet kicking on the brassbound doors. It took little imagination to picture the tangle of limbs and bodies and bundles on the other side. Many of those on the wharf jumped into the river sooner than endure the crush. Meanwhile Mongol horsemen were harassing the crowd on all sides.

'Cut the ropes!' ordered Guang. 'Cut loose the Floating Bridge.'

People were swimming towards the pontoons. Some crawled onto gravel banks and cried out for help. But there was no one to save them except themselves.

Guang saw General Zheng Shun gallop onto the wharf-side

with a dozen men. They halted, surveying the chaos. At once Guang prepared to order the reopening of Jasper Gate. To do so would allow thousands to spill onto the Bridge. Yet he knew Zheng Shun would not thank him for risking the safety of Nancheng. Nor would he do the same if their positions were reversed.

Chen Song led the cutting of the ropes with axes and saws. Finally the first section of the pontoon bridge broke free and was set alight. It floated downstream, trailing flames and smoke. Another soon followed. As each portion of the bridge drifted away, Guang's men retreated closer to Nancheng. More smoke was billowing from Fouzhou. A thousand voices screamed or begged, protesting at the absurd fate that had bred them for peace and civility then abandoned them to barbarity.

Guang realised he was shaking. Helpless tears were on his cheeks. Had he closed Jasper Gate too early? Perhaps he could have saved more. But already the Mongols had seized the gatehouse and were firing arrows at the Guards as they struggled to cut the ropes and set fire to the Bridge, section by section.

Finally, they had dismantled enough. They reached the island-fortress in the centre of the river and Guang ordered a halt to the destruction. He and Chen Song wearily climbed to the spot where Dr Shih had pretended to be Captain Xiao. For a long while they watched people being hunted like panic-stricken animals on the wharf-side of Fouzhou. They seemed small and far away. Amidst the billowing smoke one could hardly distinguish friend from enemy, butcher from victim, as night descended.

'One need not die to witness hell,' said Chen Song, at last.

竹子

Dr Shih helped Cao from their bedchamber to the shop. Here she was installed in an armchair padded with clean cloths and turned north to flatter her *yin*, so that the unseasonably hot weather might be offset. Dr Shih had prepared spells painted on coloured paper and, while his wife's pain grew, he pinned them to doors and windows. That way fox-fairies could not enter the birth-chamber and steal the child's soul.

Lu Ying found herself ignored. Yet she did not like to return to her room in case Lord Yun recovered consciousness. She took a seat in the corner and attempted to lift everyone's spirits by smiling sweetly at the joyful event of Madam Cao's confinement. The lady in question did not notice. Indeed she clutched her swollen womb as though it contained burning stones.

'Do not be afraid,' said her husband, soothingly. 'Madam Midwife is boiling scented water and will join us soon. Do not distress yourself, dearest Cao.'

Tears streaked Madam Cao's face.

'I will fail you!' she sobbed. 'After all our waiting. . .'

She faltered, silenced by a wave of pain. Lu Ying rose from her corner.

'Perhaps a little something?' she whispered to Dr Shih, making a drinking motion. He blinked stupidly for a moment.

'Of course! I have prepared a great quantity. Miss Lu Ying, if you could be so good as to serve Madam Cao whenever she asks?'

So Lu Ying was assigned a useful role and felt rather proud, as though her small suggestion had quite solved the problem of childbirth. However, Cao still moaned, even after several deep sips of Dr Shih's medicine, an unappetising green brew that left specks of herb on Cao's upper lip. Lu Ying took a gulp herself when no one was looking and felt remarkably serene afterwards.

The midwife returned with a large pitcher of hot water and a tray bearing covered bowls of rice. Shih waited patiently, holding his wife's wrist, while Madam Midwife drifted over to the window and listened. Lu Ying also went over.

'My daughter married a tile-maker from Fouzhou and moved across the water,' explained the midwife. 'I heard those devils,' (she spat on the floor to banish any present) 'tried to sneak into Fouzhou last night.'

'Then you need not worry,' said Lu Ying. 'Captain Xiao himself informed me that the barbarians were driven back.'

Lu Ying renewed her smile but the midwife seemed far from reassured.

As if to confirm her fears a messenger arrived from Dr Du Tun-i, begging Dr Shih's assistance at the North Medical Relief Bureau. He whispered to the man, a soldier wearing the uniform of the Militia, then returned to the birthing-chair with a troubled expression. He sat beside his wife who had grown comfortable as the herbal draught took effect, even a little dazed.

'I have received an urgent summons from the Relief Bureau. Fouzhou is once again under attack. There are countless wounded.'

Lu Ying noticed the midwife's look of alarm.

'You must go,' said Madam Cao, reading her husband's mind. 'It is your duty. I feel quite at ease now.'

'No,' he said. 'The pain may return soon and far worse. You will need me then.'

'Madam Midwife and Lu Ying are here to help,' said Cao. 'And you are only a few minutes away when we must call you.'

Shih was on his feet by this time, pacing restlessly.

'Then I shall go. Just for an hour. I know Dr Du Tun-i would not summon me without good reason. Send word as soon as your labour begins in earnest. I shall fly back like a swallow.'

Afternoon advanced into dusk and still Cao's labour held back. A messenger arrived from her husband but all the midwife could say was that she would summon him when the time came. Lu Ying remained in her corner seat, watching with great interest as the midwife murmured and counted the intervals between Madam Cao's 'lucky earthquakes', as she called her contractions. Exactly what she meant was a mystery to Lu Ying, but she did not wish to show ignorance.

The room was close and dark. At Cao's insistence Lu Ying opened the doors leading to Apricot Corner Court so that a breeze of sorts sluggishly explored the house. While doing so, Lu Ying decided to clear her head and wandered to the gatehouse of the courtyard. Here she met Old Hsu's Widow, accompanied by her eldest son. He carried a roll of bedding and the urn containing her dead husband's ashes and charred bones. All bowed solemnly.

'Is Madam Cao at ease?' asked Old Hsu's Widow.

They had earlier sent gifts of food and a lucky fan bearing the character for 'son'.

'Exceedingly,' said Lu Ying, though she had no idea whether it went well or not. Yet it was always best to maintain a good face. 'You are going away?'

'To my sister's house. Such terrible news! Still one should not believe rumours – unless they float face up in the canal.'

Inexplicable fears woke in Lu Ying at these words. The old lady had merely used a common expression. But it made her think of something bad, something she had often dreamed or imagined. It seemed a terrible omen. She became aware of people hurrying through the twilit streets and realised that, for the first time in years, the curfew was being utterly ignored.

'What rumours?' she asked. 'What is happening?'

'Do you not know?' asked Old Hsu's Son. 'Miss Lu Ying, the barbarians have entered Fouzhou! Some say it has already fallen.'

Lu Ying shrank back against the wooden statues of *Men* and *Shen* protecting Apricot Corner Court.

'What of Captain Xiao?' she asked, in a faint voice.

He shook his head.

'I do not know.'

They hurried into the dusk and Lu Ying re-entered the house. An unpleasant aroma assailed her nostrils as she crossed the central corridor. It came from Lord Yun's room. Reluctantly, she crept to his open doorway. Now the cause of the smell was clear. The old man lay on his back, staring at the ceiling and occasionally twitching, as though struggling to move. In his distress he had soiled himself. The aroma, worsened by a long day's heat, made Lu Ying gag and she hastily closed the door. Someone should be informed of Lord Yun's condition. One could not leave him lying in his own filth. Yet who would clean him up, if not herself? She shrank from such a prospect. The best thing was to pretend she had never seen his disgraceful state. Then he would not feel embarrassed when he was himself again. Assured she was doing the proper thing, Lu Ying sought out Madam Cao.

She arrived to an unwelcome sight. Madam Midwife had gathered her bags and stood at the open door of the shop, conversing with a short, swarthy man. Cao remained in the birth-chair, groaning softly to herself.

'What is happening?' demanded Lu Ying. 'By opening that door you have broken the spells Dr Shih pinned there!'

The midwife was unconcerned.

'This is my nephew,' she said. 'I must go with him. The city is about to fall.'

'You cannot leave us here!' spluttered Lu Ying. 'I order you!'

The midwife's face contorted with dislike: 'I do not take orders from *you*! Where is your former master now?'

With that she had gone, not even closing the street door. Lu Ying was left alone with Madam Cao, who was gripping the arms of her chair in a way that surely denoted an imminent birth. Panic gripped Lu Ying. As a girl, it was true, she often nursed her baby sisters, but Mother never allowed her near during the births. She had no idea what was required. In desperation, Lu Ying found the jug of medicine entrusted to her by Dr Shih and persuaded Cao to take a little – then had another large nip herself.

For a moment she hovered anxiously. Madam Cao doubled in pain. All her clothes were damp with sweat. Was that blood as well, seeping onto the towels? Lu Ying tried to recall how one should act. Perhaps one should do nothing at all. Then again, why else did one employ doctors and midwives? They must do *something*. This thought led to another. Of course! She must locate a midwife until Dr Shih arrived home to take care of everything. That shouldn't be so hard. Water Basin Ward teemed with children. Someone must have helped during all those births.

'I shall return very soon,' she assured Madam Cao. 'Trust me! I shall be very soon.'

'Do not leave me!' wailed Cao, but Lu Ying had no choice – for both their sakes.

She hurried through Apricot Corner Court onto North Canal Street and looked around. All the stragglers and hurrying people had gone, hiding in whatever holes they could find. Night unfurled banners of stars hidden by day. The Moon Goddess, almost full, shone fat and languid above the wooden rooftops of Nancheng. From the direction of the river – and Fouzhou – Lu Ying saw a distant glow and shadowy, winding columns of smoke.

As her eyes accustomed themselves to the gloom she became aware of three crouching figures around a willow beside North Canal. A woman had one arm round a teenage girl and the other around a small boy of ten or so. Then Lu Ying recognised them. For a moment she hesitated. Although Widow Mu was said to be a midwife, she was also the woman who had betrayed Old Hsu before the magistrate. Fortunately, Old Hsu's widow was hiding at her sister's house in a neighbouring ward.

Lu Ying shuffled across the dusty street on dainty slippers.

Three pairs of eyes watched her approach. The boy rose, fists balled defiantly, and she struggled to remember his name.

'Little Melon,' she said, in a moment of inspiration. 'I must speak with your mother.'

The boy stepped aside and she nodded politely to Widow Mu, who remained on the ground hugging her daughter. The girl's looks had deteriorated since her family's ejection from Apricot Corner Court. There was a wild, almost disturbed quality in her doe-like eyes.

'Widow Mu,' Lu Ying began. 'This is a fortunate meeting for us both.'

A distant cry of pain reached them from Dr Shih's shop.

'Madam Cao is giving birth,' said Widow Mu. 'We watched the midwife leave. That is why you wish to speak to me.'

Now Lu Ying was on safer ground.

'Of course! And to offer you a generous payment for your services.'

She looked at the gaunt, emaciated figures of Little Melon and Lan Tien. Then her voice went hard, as it had in the old days when blackmailing servants to spy on her behalf: 'Act as Madam Cao's midwife until Dr Shih returns and your children will eat. Otherwise they will continue to starve. And another thing, I have no doubt Captain Xiao will punish you severely if you leave Madam Cao to suffer. As will I!'

Another forlorn cry from Apricot Corner Court made Lu Ying lean forward: 'Choose now, you wretched woman! Not that you have a choice. And for goodness sake, wash before you present yourself to Madam Cao!'

Widow Mu bowed fearfully. It took a struggle for Lu Ying to re-construct a serene expression. Finally, she gave up. Really, it had been too trying a day. Snapping impatient fingers, she ushered Widow Mu towards Dr Shih's shop.

As the birth progressed, Lu Ying found it increasingly distasteful and decided to stand outside, away from the noise and smells.

She had dispatched Little Melon to Dr Shih, urging him to return at once. As for Lan Tien, the strange girl refused to even enter Apricot Corner Court. She had seemed a good candidate for solving the unbearable aroma emanating from Lord Yun's room, but when assigned the task began to weep, evidently afraid. So Lu Ying reluctantly allowed her to accompany her brother.

She stood in the dark courtyard. The moon rose high now. Lu Ying felt her gaze drawn upwards. How the Moon Goddess smiled at their small concerns! Lu Ying understood exactly, for once she had imagined that when Wang Ting-bo named her as his new First Wife she would smile, just so, at the little people scurrying round the foot of Peacock Hill. A painful memory. That desire, once so deeply felt, mocked what she had become. Even the aspiration had been faulty.

For a moment Lu Ying wondered if she should hurry back inside Dr Shih's shop and learn as much as she could about giving birth. Lu Ying froze. A man had pushed open the wooden gates of the courtyard. She recognised him and stepped forward:

'Master Hsu!' she called. 'What is the news from the city?'

Old Hsu's Son shook his head in distress.

'Fouzhou is no more. Only the river lies between us and the enemy.'

She was left alone in the courtyard while he moved from room to room in his small house, gathering the few valuables they owned. It seemed tactful to conceal Widow Mu's return to Apricot Corner Court in the honourable role of Madam Midwife.

Lu Ying listened to Cao's cries seeping into the night from Dr Shih's shop. For a moment she remembered Lord Yun lying in his own incontinence. Where was Dr Shih! Over half an hour had passed since her messengers left to fetch him.

She shivered and stared up at the moon once more. How gay the goddess looked. One might think she was smiling. A sad, pitying kind of smile, it was true. One might almost think the moonbeams were roads to the Jade Emperor's Cloud Terrace. Abruptly, Lu Ying's thoughts were dragged back to earth.

If the Mongols stormed the city, how hungry they would be! Two years of frustration and terrible losses would fan their revenge. It would not take long to parade every pretty girl in the streets, to establish a slave market. Everyone had heard about their cruelty. Worse things existed than death. One might suffer as Madam Cao did now, only not to bear a handsome child of the House of Yun whose ancestor was the great poet

Yun Cai, but a hideous bastard impregnated through. . . she must not think of it.

Lu Ying realised she was shaking and hugged herself. Tears stung her soft cheeks. Sooner join the Moon Goddess than that! Sooner drown herself in North Canal and float like a beautiful lily pad, its flower forever open to the moon.

竹子

Dr Shih tried to keep pace with his colleague. The young man's walk was more like a run. Moonlight cast a silver sheen across the Water Basin, as they followed the canal to the Water Gate of Morning Radiance.

'Dr Du Tun-i!' called out Shih. 'Our duty lies back at the Bureau. Besides. . .'

He did not explain his 'besides' – that messages from Apricot Corner Court could hardly reach him if he was scampering through the streets of Water Basin Ward on a mission of doubtful benefit to anyone. However, Dr Du Tun-i was defiant.

'I must see if the rumours are true. Please accompany me, Dr Shih. You are my father when I am in Nancheng,'

'Very well,' sighed Shih. 'But we may leave our posts only for a few minutes.'

Dr Du Tun-i was already climbing the steep stairs leading to the ramparts above the Water Gate of Morning Radiance. At the top a sergeant of the Militia blocked their way, the same man who had given Madam Cao permission to grow herbs on the riverbank. A dozen other soldiers were staring north.

'Dr Shih, go back!' urged the man. 'You should not see this. Go back, sir.'

Dr Du Tun-i pushed past the man to the stone battlements. There he went very still. Shih joined him and laid a hand on his shoulder.

From the high Water Gate one could clearly see Fouzhou across the moonlit river. It was a night of unusual beauty. The Han River glowed eerily like polished jade. The wrecks of sunken ships exposed by the drought cast strange shadows. There was a gentle, constant murmur from the current.

Then one's eye found the wharf-side of Fouzhou where a mound was being raised. Gangs of slaves, supervised by Mongols on foot and horse, were dragging wagons and handcarts to the small hill, their labours illuminated by huge bonfires. Sparks rose and drifted into the cloudless sky. Whenever a cart reached the mound, slaves emptied its contents, spurred on by clubs and whips.

Still the mound grew higher. Wails and screams from Fouzhou drifted through the calm summer night. It seemed the rumours were true. General A-ku was making good his promise to put every living thing to the sword, including household animals. Shih swirled with nausea and terror. Despite the many, many deaths he had witnessed since becoming a doctor's apprentice this was a different kind of dying. How many thousands were on the mound? It rose almost to the height of the battlements of Jasper Gate. How many corpses did that take?

'Come away,' Shih urged Dr Du Tun-i.

'What if my family are dragged out!' sobbed the young man. 'Mother and Little Sister. . . I have heard A-ku has pledged to search every room in every house.'

He broke down. Dr Shih took the young man's arm and led him down the steps. His own spirit felt a racing panic, a revulsion against men and what they will do to each other, for the sake of self-preservation, or ambition, or fear, or honour, or greed. He heard himself speaking as though someone else was using his voice: 'I am sure your family are well hidden. We shall make an offering to Huang Ti Nei's image. The Yellow Emperor will surely listen.'

They walked back to the North Medical Relief Bureau. At the entrance Shih recognised two figures crouching in the dusty street. He was too dazed by what he had seen to remember his grievances against their mother, so he ushered Mung Po over to help Dr Du Tun-i and blinked down at the children.

'Little Melon? Lan Tien? Why are you here?'

The boy shot his sister an angry look, then grovelled at Shih's feet. It distressed him to see the boy so wretchedly thin. As for Lan Tien, there was something odd about the girl, suggestive of madness rather than physical infirmity.

'Forgive us!' blurted out the boy. 'I would have come sooner but *she* would not let me.'

Lan Tien scrabbled at her brother's arm to silence him and Shih bent down beside them.

'Children, have you been sent with a message?'

Then Little Melon rushed it out: how Lady Lu Ying had sent him to say that Madam Cao needed his help; that her labour was difficult and the midwife had deserted them. How Lan Tien had forced him not to come because she was afraid of being sent to Lord Yun. How, in the end, Little Melon had decided to defy his sister and had run here as fast as he could.

Shih flinched at Lord Yun's name. He did not care to think how near he had come to striking Father. A memory of the Tower Room and the old man's avid observations suggested the reason for Lan Tien's fear.

'When was this? How long ago?'

Lan Tien buried her head in her hands but Little Melon said stoutly: 'I counted two hour bells, sir.'

Dr Shih rose, eyeing the children angrily. That delay might cost him either his wife or unborn child. And yet again his father's mischief was the cause.

'Mung Po!' he bellowed. 'Mung Po!'

竹子

Cao could barely glimpse the room for pain. When not screwed tight, her eyes swam with tears. Shadows swirled in the lamp and candlelight. Never had she imagined such pain – every inner place, every entrance and exit of her body, all burned and shrieked as though connected by scalding rivers or fiery chains. And then, unexpectedly, the pain receded a little, enough for her to gasp a lungful of precious air. When her vision cleared she could see Widow Mu's anxious face and hear her voice: 'Roll the boulder, Madam Cao!' she intoned. 'Clasp and roll it! Good! How well you are doing. Soon we shall see your son!'

Cao laughed hysterically at such a prospect. Mu had repeated the word 'soon' so many times over the last hour.

'Where is Shih?' she wailed, abruptly recalling his absence. 'Why has he not come?'

Indeed a summons had been sent to the Relief Bureau at least an hour ago, carried by Little Melon and Lan Tien. As the next lucky earthquake gathered force, billowing out to shake her exhausted body, Cao suddenly cried out: 'I hate him! He is still chasing that whore! Oh! *Oh!*'

Widow Mu squeezed her hand, while peering beneath the sheet she had placed over the arms of the birthing chair. Suddenly her eyes opened wide.

'Clasp the stone!' she cried. 'Madam Cao! Clasp the stone! His head! Madam Cao, his head!'

Certainly more blood and fluid than before was dripping from the wooden chair to the earthen floor. As if through a haze of sound Cao distinctly heard screams of alarm on North Canal Street. They seemed to belong to another world, far away from this hot, dark well. Yet she could feel the child emerging, moment by moment, finger-breadth by finger.

'Squeeze!' cried Mu excitedly. 'Now breathe! Breathe deeper, *deep*! Like this *aaaah*!'

Another lucky earthquake made Madam Cao moan out a stream of curses at her faithless husband.

'His shoulders!' cried Mu. 'Here he comes!'

Then, preceded by a flow of blood and mucus, the baby slid into the midwife's waiting hands.

Cao closed her eyes and tried to breathe. It would end now. All that mattered was that it would end. Why then did her pain feel no less than before? Another wave was mounting, burning through her lower body.

When she opened her eyes again, Cao found Widow Mu

diligently swaddling the baby in a hemp blanket, a guarded expression on her face. Then Cao knew the child must be stillborn. A wail began to form and her chest heaved, but Widow Mu was slapping the baby's feet and, miraculously, like a bud opening out in a single moment, the child wailed and Madam Cao's incipient cry of despair turned into a sob of joy.

If it had not been for the continuing pain she might have collapsed back in relief, staring in wonder at the baby's streaked, contorted face as it howled, features so long anticipated and dreamed about. Still she held back from reaching out for the child that had caused so much agony.

'Healthy!' declared Widow Mu. 'I've never seen one stronger!'

Cao suspected something hidden in Mu's manner.

'Is he?' she said. 'Is he *whole*?'

Mu shrugged apologetically.

'He's a she,' she admitted, softly. 'But quite, quite whole.'

'Aieee!'

Cao's scream tore through Apricot Corner Court. Widow Mu clasped the child to her breast in alarm.

'Do not despair!' she said. 'Think, Madam Cao, how great a blessing a daughter can be!'

Then she fell silent, puzzled by the way Cao writhed on the birthing chair. At last a look of comprehension spread across her face.

'Madam Cao,' she said, shaking her by the arm, 'are the lucky earthquakes continuing?'

Now Mu was feeling and squeezing Cao's stomach, all the while examining her closely. She looked up and laughed.

'Him a doctor, too!' she exclaimed. 'And he didn't even know!'

Oh! Oh! Help me! Oh! Madam Cao's protestations filled the medicine shop. Again and again Widow Mu intoned: 'Clasp the boulder! Squeeze the stone!'

For long minutes nothing emerged, either still or alive. Now

Mu's voice grew more insistent and Cao saw through her clouds of pain that the midwife was afraid.

'Breathe!' she urged. 'And *squeeze*!'

The change, when it came, was sudden.

'Coming!' cried out Mu. 'One more time! Nearly here!'

Cao felt herself tear open, her whole lower body tear open, so she was undone, forever emptied. Her breath panted quicker than her heart. She felt herself fading, flowing away. How often had Shih reported such things in a solemn voice about other women. Women she had envied for the gift they left on this earth, whatever its cost. Amidst her agony came snatches of clarity. Widow Mu crowing, 'A boy, Madam Cao, a boy this time!' And her chest heaved with laughter that fled towards stupor, the numb, retreating blackness from which all the ten thousand creatures come and go, life after life, and to which each returns, forever and ever, when Nothingness is attained.

懵

seventeen

> 'The Song Dynasty may well be inept at ruling their domains, but Linan will not capitulate without terrible losses on all sides. To lust after life and fear death is merely natural. When the Men of the South choose death over life, it is simply because they do not believe our promises to spare and reward those who surrender to us. We should therefore repeat our pledge to favour all who renounce their loyalty to the Song. . .'
>
> From *Secret Memorandum to the Great Khan* by Yao Shu, a Chinese adviser to Khubilai Khan

竹子

Peacock Hill, Nancheng. Autumn, 1268

It was a bright morning on Peacock Hill. The pleasure gardens constructed by ancient kings danced with colour and shadow. Charms of finches twittered from branch to branch. Gardeners cast fearful glances towards the river as they went about their duties, the sharper-eyed among them observing the new hillock that continued to grow, day by day, on the wharf-side of Fouzhou.

Guang sat in the gardens beside a moon-gate, awaiting a bell of summons. He wore his splendid uniform and waist-badges of office. His head was bowed, as though pressed earthward by care. So still did he sit that the finches lost their fear and pecked the gravel path near his feet. His eyes were half-closed, gazing inwards.

Shih and Dr Du Tun-i were not the only ones to witness the corpse-mound's construction. Guang and Chen Song had watched from the Gate Of The Vermilion Sparrow. Even now wagons were discharging their burdens and hurrying off for a fresh load. It had surprised him he should tremble and stutter when answering Chen Song's questions. How absurd! Had he not braved worse sights than this? Captain Xiao did not quiver like a frightened boy!

But Guang was weary of Captain Xiao. He could not avoid the knowledge that he alone had ordered the closure of Jasper Gate and demolished the Floating Bridge, trapping tens of thousands in Fouzhou. Loyal Chen Song assured him that otherwise Nancheng would have fallen, the slaughter fifty times worse. Yet Guang could not reason away the piles of dead, or the screams – pitiful, keening voices – or the grief visible everywhere. Mongol resolve was implacable and now their attention was rapidly returning to Nancheng.

A bell rang from the Old Palace. The Pacification Commissioner had ordered Guang to attend an audience where future strategy would be decided. In the past, such a prospect would have filled him with enthusiasm.

He rose from the bench and the finches scattered in alarm. They perched on nearby branches and watched him go with bright, unblinking eyes.

Over thirty of the Province's most senior military and civil officials conversed quietly. Chen Song joined Guang near the front. With the death of General Zheng Shun and other officers over the last few days they had gained in seniority.

'An interesting choice of room for our meeting,' murmured the scholar-soldier.

Wang Ting-bo had again summoned them to the Hall of Obedient Rectitude, once the audience chamber of a petty king.

'Behold!' added Chen Song, drily. 'Even the thrones are back.'

Two huge new chairs of lacquered wood, marble and ivory, had been placed on a freshly constructed dais. The two men wandered over to examine the carvings. The significance of river-dragons entwined around chrysanthemums was obvious.

A gong echoed and a grand procession entered the audience chamber. Lesser officials carrying ink and paper led the way, followed by fan-bearers. Finally came the Pacification Commissioner himself in full uniform. At his side walked his nephew, Prefect Wang Bai.

All the company bowed. Some fell to their knees in grovelling homage – as though Wang Ting-bo's right to rule had grown, rather than been diminished, by the appalling loss of Fouzhou and its entire population. Guang felt listless and subdued as the Pacification Commissioner and Prefect settled on their new thrones.

'Gentlemen!' said Wang Ting-bo. 'Powers beyond our control have heaped disaster upon us. Despite our brave strategy and our unflagging resolve, Fouzhou has been overwhelmed as is a beach by the tide!'

The only sounds came from the click of the fan-wafting servants. Guang recollected the reinforcements that never came and wondered how inevitable A-ku's victory had been. Perhaps Wang Ting-bo comprehended the feebleness of his explanation for he repeated: 'Like a beach swept by the tide!'

No one spoke. The Pacification Commissioner nodded to his nephew who surveyed the waiting men imperiously.

'For three hundred years,' said Wang Bai, 'the Royal House have ruled our Empire. Think how we have benefited! For three hundred years the Mandate of Heaven has ensured their rule – despite, it is true, the unfortunate loss of half our ancestral lands due to extravagance and folly, as well as the ignoble purchase of peace through tribute – but let us not speak of those things. Endless errors have laid bare the bosom of our Empire, but I say again, let us not mention them. Now we must ask ourselves, what is to be done? Now we must answer those who say the Mandate of Heaven no longer belongs to our Holy Ruler, due to lascivious greed, incompetence and waste! We must answer them, as best we can. We must find ways of answering such voices. Or conclude – a dreadful thought! – they are right.'

All listened in amazement to this speech. Guang was not sure he understood Wang Bai exactly. Was he criticising the Emperor or calling for the utmost loyalty? Others shared his confusion. A few watched the Pacification Commissioner carefully, waiting for his next words.

'Our duty, gentlemen,' said Wang Ting-bo, 'is to ensure Nancheng does not suffer the same fate as its sister city.'

All could agree with that.

'But how, Your Excellency?' called out an old man.

'Ah!' said Wang Ting-bo, raising his finger for emphasis. 'The sounds of woeful lament echo through our province! We must act with resolve and wisdom to soothe the people's wounds.'

They waited for more but none was forthcoming. Now Guang longed for the presence of lost leaders. General Zheng Shun and Admiral Qi-Qi would have known what to do. They would have suggested a strategy involving the least risk and utmost honour.

'Grave days!' broke in Wang Bai. 'Grave, grave days! Even now, some in the city suggest that the Great Khan has received the Mandate of Heaven. They argue it cannot be treachery to bow to Heaven's will. I say to you all, gentlemen. Urgently find an answer to such arguments in your own hearts.'

Wang Bai settled back, his habitually suave demeanour flushed and eager. It seemed the discussion might be over, for Wang Ting-bo began to rise. Suddenly Chen Song was on his feet.

'Your Excellency,' he said. 'Forgive my stupidity! I thought we were here to organise our defence. How is it to be conducted, sir?'

Guang resisted an urge to drag Chen Song back to a sitting

position – for his friend was risking a great man's enmity. Of course, Zheng Shun would have pressed Wang Ting-bo for a practical response, but then he had been a general of great standing, a hero of the Empire. As the most senior surviving officer it now fell to Guang, not Chen Song, to ask that question – but his mind was strangely blank.

The Pacification Commissioner peered at Chen Song as though at a troublesome child.

'Our defence is to be conducted with unfailing courage and the broadest sense of duty,' he replied.

A dark cloud settled on Chen Song's face.

'Your Excellency,' he said. 'Nancheng is still strong. We must learn from the fall of Fouzhou. I believe that breaches in the walls caused by their new weapons need not dismay us. Unlike Fouzhou, we still possess wide moats. Our artillery and crossbows could cause hideous casualties should they seek to attack. Moreover, our army numbers tens of thousands. Our granaries retain enough for a year of short rations. We need not despair! Or question the Mandate of Heaven.'

Murmurs of agreement spread among the assembled officials and officers. All had more than just homes and possessions to lose. Honour, once compromised, is a cracked mirror. It will distort the reflection of an entire man's life.

'Your Excellency,' continued Chen Song. 'We must form companies of skilled men to repair breaches in the ramparts caused by their new catapults. We must set up appropriate stores of materials at key points along the walls. Flying columns of the bravest and best could be stationed to rush like angry tigers wherever they are needed. . .'

'Enough!' called out Wang Bai. 'You go beyond yourself! Gentlemen, return to your duties and await His Excellency's decrees.'

Again Wang Ting-bo's procession formed up. As they left Wang Bai shot Chen Song a venomous glance.

Once they had gone, the latter muttered to Guang.

'*Decrees?* Since when does a Pacification Commissioner

formulate decrees? That is a royal prerogative.' He grew thoughtful. 'Unless, of course, one aspires to the plenipotentiary powers granted by the Great Khan to his Provincial Governors. . .'

Guang was not listening. A small crowd had gathered round him, applauding his decisive actions on the Floating Bridge. Others, especially those with strong Fouzhou connections, muttered at the loss of so many.

'A most disappointing audience,' grumbled Chen Song as they strode down Peacock Hill. 'You appear in a hurry, Guang! Where on earth are you going?'

'To a happier audience than the one we have just attended. I beg you to join me. There are those I would like you to see. One especially. . . though that is another matter.'

竹子

Cao's father once told her in his most serious voice, reciting something learned by rote at the Imperial Medical Academy: 'Noble are the rites. They fulfil what is desired.' She was sure his voice had been solemn – perhaps it had been humorous. Father had been a man of considerable forbearance, or *ren*. Given the rift with his Honoured Parents, the loss of a dear wife and blatant attempts by unloving brothers to seize his considerable property as he lay dying, he had needed *ren* in abundance.

Right now, so did she, as all those around her conspired to bring an avalanche of misfortune on the family. Shih was quite determined they should advance the bathing rites normally practised on the third day after a birth because of the desperate state of the siege. But how could a bungled rite please the ancestors or fulfil what is desired? As she was forbidden to leave her bed, it was hard to mount an effective resistance to his plans.

'Will it not be unlucky?' she asked, for the twentieth time 'We dare not risk such a thing.'

'Then I fear we shall lack Guang's presence in the rite,' he had explained. 'Guang expects to take his place on the ramparts as soon as the Mongols begin their next assault. That could be at any time.'

'Why must you keep mentioning them?' she asked.

Cao hugged the bundles sleeping on her chest, then sighed: 'I only want what is best.'

'I am sure of one thing,' he said. 'I have never seen the sense of waiting three days for the first wash. It is an unclean practice.'

So it had been decided.

Noon lit the corners of Apricot Corner Court as Cao plumped her pillows and was helped into her best bed-gown by Lu Ying. Such an attention naturally pleased Madam Cao – once it had seemed certain the concubine would lie where she did, cradling their family's future.

When Cao was presentable, Lu Ying retrieved the babies from their cots, a dreamy expression on her flawless face, as though she was imagining her own children if Heaven proved kind. It amazed Cao how adroit Lu Ying was at handling babies, considering she was useless at almost everything else.

One by one the infants were fed at Cao's breast while Widow Mu hovered, urging her not to grow dispirited if their gums took time to clamp.

Widow Mu's continued presence in Apricot Corner Court stemmed from a notable bargain brokered by Dr Shih. Old Hsu's clan had every reason to detest the dumpling seller, yet if Widow Mu had not acted as midwife, Cao's labour would surely have ended in tragedy, for the delivery of twins is a formidable matter. Dr Shih was also aware that if he drove her back into the streets, she and her children would starve.

A middle way occurred to him – one that required a remarkable quantity of *ren* on all sides. That Widow Mu's son should be indentured without pay for seven years as Old Hsu's Son's apprentice. As for Widow Mu and Lan Tien, they would re-occupy their former quarters until peace returned. Then they must find a living elsewhere.

Cao considered the dangers of her husband's actions as she guided one warm mouth after another to her nipples. Old Hsu's family would hardly treat Little Melon well, especially with so little food to go round. Though Widow Mu seemed grateful now, Cao knew her well enough to suspect the condition was unlikely to be permanent.

At last the children suckled peacefully, both appearing content. Cao had feared she would need to favour the boy at the girl's expense. 'Plenty for everyone,' Widow Mu remarked smugly, as though her own breasts' abundance were in question. Sweeps of joy and pride crossed the clogged places of Madam Cao's spirit. Happy tears filled her brown eyes and her arms tightened round the sleepy babes.

Under Shih's direction, candles and lanterns were lit to form a magic trail from Apricot Corner Court to the bedchamber where Cao lay in state. Such meagre refreshments as they could afford in siege-time were laid out in the medicine shop for their guests.

The men gathered outside, talking of Fouzhou's bloody end and the Mongols' next assault. Meanwhile Lu Ying and Widow Mu squabbled over whether to heat the babies' bathwater with locust branches or artemisia leaves. Cao waited patiently, cradling her babies, who ignored the debate, gorged on milk. Finally, Lu Ying gained ascendancy for only she could afford to place a string of *cash* and a strip of red silk round the tub.

As was often the case, Widow Mu soon recovered her dignity. In her position as Honoured Madam Midwife it was customary for her to lead the bed ceremony. She sat on the covers where Cao lolled, then scattered a straw sieve, mirror, rusty key, onion, comb and an ancient bronze weight stamped with a cloud seal, all round the bedclothes. Incense offered to the god and goddess of the bed burned nearby.

Naturally, the boy must bathe first, then Little Sister. Widow

Mu remarked that the girl would surely benefit from drinking her brother's dirty bath water. However, it was not long before he soiled the bath in a copious manner. All the women grew alarmed. Did it denote bad luck? Perhaps it showed he disapproved of Little Sister.

'I suggest we tell no one,' whispered Lu Ying.

'I'll tip the water out of the window when no one's looking,' said Widow Mu.

Finally the room was prepared. Madam Cao appeared as a dowager Empress in her bower, babies in swaddling cradled in her arms, the bathwater pure as a mountain stream. A bowl and spoon were set up beside the tub, supervised by Lu Ying. All was ready and Widow Mu meekly entered Apricot Corner Court. The assembled guests regarded her silently. Old Hsu's relations barely suppressed their hostility. But to disgrace the rite would disgrace themselves and break their bargain concerning Little Melon's cost-free apprenticeship. So they quietly joined the queue into Dr Shih's house.

First came the father himself. He carried slices of apricot, cut from the courtyard tree. Without removing his eyes from his wife he dropped the fruit into the bathtub, along with a coloured egg carved from wood – a real egg was too precious to waste in hungry Nancheng. Then he scattered a spoonful of cold water into the bath, along with all the silver coins he still possessed from healing Wang Ting-bo's heir.

For a moment Shih hesitated. Madam Cao met his eyes, happy and triumphant, yet somehow uneasy, as though all this unexpected good fortune might be plucked away. Then he smiled and impulsively kissed his wife's hand. Lu Ying fluttered her fan at the intimacy of this gesture, while Madam Cao flushed crimson.

Next came Commander Yun Guang. He was covered from head to knee in lamellar armour, though he left his weapons at the door. He seemed more aware of Lu Ying, who was standing modestly by the bathtub, than the two infants. Yet Guang reached out for the sleepy boy and Cao worried at his roughness as he held him up to the window, laughing to his brother: 'Note the brow on this little fellow! Loaded with thought! Evidently he takes after you.'

He passed the boy back, quite ignoring the baby girl except for a curious glance. That, thought Cao, is to be the way of it forever.

After all the other guests had gone and Shih was allowed to sit beside her, they looked up, startled by their bedchamber door rattling. Shih rose to open it.

Lord Yun clutched the lintel, leaning heavily on a stick. His hands were shaking and a little drool dribbled from his mouth. It was the first time he had fully recovered consciousness since his fit, three days earlier. Since then Shih had washed him and spooned rice gruel into his mouth, while Lord Yun struggled to speak a single coherent word.

'Father! You should not be out of bed.'

The old man peered across the room, his eyes fixed on the babies. Instinctively, Cao hugged them closer to her chest. Lord Yun blinked furiously. Half his face had permanently frozen, not a muscle moving, but the remaining half retained expression. He tried to speak and a strange sucking noise came forth, followed by a hiss. A look of great confusion crossed the wreck of his handsome face. He glanced from Shih to the babies.

'They are your grandson and granddaughter,' said Shih, softly. 'Do you wish to bless them, Father?'

For a moment Lord Yun hesitated, blinking with his good eye. Cao wondered how much of his wit was paralysed. Whether his feelings still possessed full movement. The old man seemed to nod. Perhaps he was merely shaking.

'Now that Guang has renounced the title of Firstborn,' added Shih, defiantly, 'my son is my heir, just as I am Eldest Son and heir to your title.'

Cao wished he had not mentioned this. It surprised her Shih should be so heartless. The effect on Lord Yun was immediate. The little softness in his gaze was replaced by pride, angry hauteur. The half-paralysed mouth twisted and he managed a contemptuous snort. After a fierce effort of crab-like shuffling, he turned his back on the children.

Shih helped Lord Yun from the room, a strange smile in the corners of his mouth, and Cao's eyes pricked with tears. Both for the son who had never known a father's affection and the lonely old man who seemed incapable of earning any love at all, except through duty.

竹子

There were few quiet moments at the North Medical Relief Bureau. Even at night the enemy contrived ways of injuring the city's defenders – their huge new catapults were constantly busy, lobbing boulders and thunderclap bombs, many stolen from the captured arsenal of Fouzhou. Fire arrows flew over the walls day and night, so that special squads patrolled Water Basin Ward, extinguishing blazes with sand and wet hemp cloths.

Still, no direct assault on the ramparts had been attmpted since Fouzhou's fall. The explanation had nothing to do with clemency. General A-ku was ferrying his full army across the river, including more of the giant catapults, so they might choke Nancheng to death.

The lull allowed Dr Shih and his assistants to bandage up those who had survived the previous battles and send some back for more. It also enabled death, a constant lodger in the Relief Bureau, to claim more chosen sons.

Orderly Mung Po entered the small office where Dr Shih was taking a rest and nodded a greeting. Master and servant had relaxed their manners over the course of the long siege. Mung Po held a bowl of tea and dish of cold rice mixed with specks of dried, grey meat of the kind known as 'miraculous mushroom' because no one cared to name its source.

'This was delivered from the ward canteen,' said Mung Po, apologetically. 'It tastes fresher than yesterday's.'

Shih grunted and took the bowl of tea instead.

'Why not visit your wife and son for a while?' asked Mung Po.

'I cannot leave until Dr Du Tun-i's spirits recover a little. You know that.'

Dr Du Tun-i lay on a cot in an adjoining room, lost to grief. Since the sight of the corpse-mound there had been little work from him. However hard Shih urged him to recollect courage and duty, Du Tun-i turned away with hopeless eyes.

'Well, it is a hard thing to lose one's entire family,' conceded Mung Po. 'Although the loss of his uncle is scarcely to be regretted.'

'If they did indeed perish,' said Shih, aware Du Tun-i might overhear. 'Which I doubt.'

Mung Po left him to his supper. Though he took no pleasure in the meal, Dr Shih swallowed every last grain of rice and shred of meat. Then he closed his eyes and relaxed to aid digestion. A body starved of regular food must take care. Thoughts of Lord Yun flitted. The old man stayed on his bed except to fulfil necessary actions, and even then he had to be held upright. It was a sad decline. Half his face remained immobile. The other seemed alert as ever. Sometimes Shih wondered if the drugs he had used to quieten the old man's awkwardness had poisoned him. There was no knowing. Some questions are better left unasked.

Dr Shih's tired mind drifted far from the North Medical Relief Bureau and he fell into a dream until he was a boy again, back in Wei Valley, Guang running alongside him up the steps of Three-Step-House. How swiftly they floated! Hand-in-hand up the steps! Birds sang all around and the plum trees were decked with white blossom. At the topmost house two women waited, their arms held open to catch the rushing boys: Mother and Aunt Qin. How young they looked, always young! Shih buried his head in Aunt Qin's silken dress and looked at Guang. Their eyes met without shadow. Then a darkness fell across the boys and both flinched. Someone tall and broad leaned over them. But Shih's fear evaporated as quickly as it had come, like breath clouding a mirror, for it was Father. Dear Father! The boys bowed respectfully to the smiling, handsome man, then reached up for his embrace. All along Wei Valley the trees murmured in the wind like surf and the sky was peony blue, all the way to Incense Burner Peak, and Shih felt happiness fill the dome of Heaven . . .

He sat up with a jolt. Dusk had deepened in the room. Something had woken him. A noise. Voices outside. Shih rose and hurried into the street. A small crowd had gathered, pointing excitedly at a pair of pagodas belonging to a Daoist monastery. The towers were a landmark in the city. They stood a *li* behind Swallow Gate on a man-made mound said to have been constructed by a Buddhist angel.

'They've hit South Bell Tower!' cried a man in the crowd.

It was true, a stone from one of A-ku's infernal catapults had smashed into the pagoda, so that it leaned dangerously. To the dismay of thousands who watched, the building collapsed, storey by storey, falling across its sister tower. Then the second pagoda toppled more suddenly than the first. The crowd went silent. The significance of such an omen, given Fouzhou's fate, could hardly be plainer.

Shih noticed a rider cantering towards them, followed by a small escort of cavalry. Many in the crowd fell to their knees. For the people's faith in Captain Xiao had grown as the siege grew more desperate. Guang leaned down from the saddle.

'We must talk earnestly,' he said. 'And in a private place.'

His expression filled Shih with alarm.

There was nowhere without eavesdroppers in the Relief Bureau, so Guang used his influence to clear a section of the battlements near the Water Gate of Morning Radiance. Only swifts nesting in cracks in the stone walls or frogs singing to one another on the muddy riverbank might overhear them.

The two brothers leaned against the parapet and stared at the waters below. The moon, full only yesterday, had already begun to wane. Both averted their eyes from the corpses rotting on the wharf-side of Fouzhou. Guang hurriedly turned so he faced Nancheng. His gaze crept over the rooftops to the Prefectural buildings on Peacock Hill. He met Shih's troubled look.

'You are wondering why I have deserted my post at such a time,' he said.

Shih waited until a sudden thought made him start: 'Cao is safe? The children?'

'Oh, yes,' said Guang. 'I stopped at Apricot Corner Court earlier, hoping to find you. All are well. Except for Father, of course. He is never well. Never has been from the moment I found him living in his own filth at Whale Rock Monastery. That seems a long time ago.'

Neither felt comfortable around the topic of Father. If Shih feared his medicine had hastened the old man's paralysis, Guang had every reason to imagine his public denunciation in the tower room had brought about Lord Yun's fit of apoplexy.

'I came to tell you something,' he said. 'A most unbelievable thing has occurred. This morning General A-ku came on foot to Swallow Gate, accompanied by an interpreter and a flag of truce. He requested to speak with Wang Ting-bo. Of course, you can imagine how seldom our Pacification Commissioner treads the ramparts these days. Yet he was persuaded to speak with A-ku by his nephew, for Wang Bai is forever whispering in his uncle's ear.'

'I thought Wang Bai was your patron,' said Shih.

Now Guang looked confused.

'I would be nothing without him! Yet one may admire the fox for its cunning without liking it.'

'What was A-ku's message?'

'I heard it quite clearly. He shouted up that Wang Ting-bo had maintained the Twin Cities like an island in a raging torrent. That the Great Khan himself admired dogged loyalty. He said there was no hope of relief, not even the birds dare risk the nets surrounding Nancheng. But he said that if Wang

Ting-bo surrenders, he will be given an honourable position. That all he need do is bow to the Great Khan as the new Yuan Emperor, as the bearer of Heaven's Mandate, and the entire city shall be spared. Lastly, for he could clearly read Wang Ting-bo's thoughts, he assured him that he would not be killed.'

'I cannot believe A-ku is so foolish,' said Shih. 'Wang Ting-bo is no traitor.'

'You must listen,' said Guang. 'Wang Bai took his uncle to one side and murmured urgently. When he had finished Wang Ting-bo seemed shaken. He told A-ku that he would only consider his proposal if he received the firmest of assurances.'

'He said *that*?'

'My heart was in my mouth, Shih! Wang Bai evidently saw my distress for he took me to one side and ordered me not to cause a panic among the men. He urged me to think of Fouzhou. How averting massacre was our highest duty.'

'At the cost of honour?' asked Shih. 'Of loyalty to our Holy Ruler? Of *xiao* itself?'

His brother flinched at the word.

'Four times General A-ku repeated his offer. At last he took out an arrow and snapped it across his knee to show that if he broke his word a terrible misfortune would afflict his bloodline. Then Wang Ting-bo believed him, for the Mongol deserter we use as an interpreter stated such an oath was unbreakable.'

All along the ramparts lamps were being lit, as they had each dusk since the siege began. Strings of dwindling fireflies appeared round Swallow Gate in the distance.

'Have we suffered for two long years, just for this?' asked Shih, dully.

'Nothing is settled yet,' said Guang. 'Except that Wang Ting-bo will give his reply before noon tomorrow.'

'I cannot believe our situation is so bad!'

'It is possible we could fight on,' said Guang. 'Our only hope lies in a relief army sent by the Court. But after two years, where is it?'

Shih shook his head.

'They tried to reach us,' he said. 'The Mongols drove them back.'

'Perhaps Wang Bai is right,' said Guang. 'Perhaps we must consider those who are helpless now.'

He hesitated, then laid his gauntleted hand on Shih's arm

'There are other things I wish to say. You know General A-ku has sworn to take Captain Xiao's head, don't you? If the city surrenders, he will fulfil that oath.'

'You must flee the city!' hissed Shih, looking round for listeners. 'Find a way out.'

'Then A-ku's vengeance would fall on you and Cao. I cannot allow that. And there is something else. When I visited Apricot Corner Court, I spoke to Lu Ying.' He grew tongue-tied for a moment. 'I spoke to Lu Ying,' repeated Guang. 'And she told me how she feared the Mongols, that she would be marched north as a disgraced whore by some barbarian. She was tearful, Shih! I cannot explain how it made me feel. I promised to ensure her safety, even at the sacrifice of my own life.'

'I understand,' said Shih. 'There are unspoken understandings between you. You both hope what is hidden now will become open when peace returns.'

Guang blinked at his brother.

'You are not angry? After all, one might say she was given to you.'

'Such a lady gives herself or is a slave,' said Shih. 'I am glad there is an understanding between you.'

Then a most absurd thing happened, one that would stay with the brothers and bind them together through a hundred calamities. It was customary for Youngest to pay homage to Eldest, but Guang did not fall to his knees as was proper. He clasped Shih to his armoured chest so tightly the object of his affection could hardly breathe.

'You are wise, Eldest Brother!' cried Guang, tears running down his cheeks. 'And full of forbearance!'

'Please let me go,' whispered Shih. 'Or I shall need medical help myself.'

When the twins returned to the Relief Bureau they found a messenger waiting. Commander Yun Guang's escort sprang to attention. All secretly marvelled at how alike the brothers were – their walk, the tones of their voices and features. Yet how different, too, one dressed for war, the other wearing a doctor's hat with its long earflaps. One scarred across the cheeks, the other soft-faced, except for deep thought lines. Each man complemented the other.

The messenger stepped forward: 'Sir, Captain Chen Song begs you to meet him at your pavilion on Peacock Hill. He says he will wait as long as he can.'

Guang turned to Shih, aware all his men were listening.

'I may not call at Apricot Corner Court again. You know why. Say what is proper to Sister-in-law and Father. And think of me fondly.'

'You will call there again! You must!'

'I fear it is out of my hands,' said Guang.

He summoned his horse and with a brief salute to Shih, rode into the moonlit evening of the siege.

竹子

As Guang rode east towards Swallow Gate he passed groups of men talking anxiously. The curfew – previously enforced by harsh lashes of the bamboo – was in disarray. Even the City Watch kept to their barracks and guard posts. Rumours of Wang Ting-bo's conversation with General A-ku were everywhere. All knew of his promise to give the enemy an answer by noon tomorrow. Many disbelieved General A-ku's assurances. Not after Fouzhou and the dozens of other towns laid waste in Nancheng Province. Those spared a slit throat would be enslaved, it was said, especially women of charm. Then beauty would cease to be desirable and ugliness the most prized attribute for a wife or daughter.

Thousand of survivors from Fouzhou had set up camps on open ground throughout the city. They made a pitiful sight. Guang and his escort trotted past one such huddle at the base of a high ward wall. Most of the wretches ignored him, but one stared avidly. For a moment Guang did not recognise the young man. He slowed his horse to make sure. Yes, it was Chung! It seemed Shih's former apprentice had survived the wreck of Dr Du Mau's fortune.

Guang contemptuously twitched his reins and rode on. Black doubts crowded his soul. Of the tens of thousands who perished, Heaven had selected this idle, disloyal youth for a long life! Guang was inclined to gallop back and achieve what the Mongols had failed. Oh, the world was bad! Why had he not seen it before? Virtue was of no account. Luck and cunning decided all men's destinies. How many sacrifices might be called worthless – worse, folly or vanity? One might strut with a puffed-out chest and call one's self – what? Hero? Loyal servant of Heaven's Son? Even Captain Xiao! The fact remained that noble General Zheng Shun and Admiral Qi-Qi were dead, while cowards prospered like dogs licking a new master's hand – or foxes feeding in new dens.

Perhaps these same doubts grew in Pacification Commissioner Wang Ting-bo's mind as the hours stole towards dawn. Guang suspected they had long dwelt in Wang Bai's breast.

He arrived at Peacock Hill to find two Guards companies taking up position, having been withdrawn from the ramparts. Regular troops from the East rather than natives of Nancheng, they stood fully armed with crossbows and fire-lances. Guang greeted the Captain at the gatehouse and reined in his horse. The man recognised him and bowed low.

'Is the city calm, sir?' asked the Captain, anxiously.

'People are afraid,' replied Guang. 'Why are you here, Captain? Why have you left the ramparts? General A-ku may be tricking us.'

The officer shot Guang a meaningful look.

'We are here to suppress disorder, sir. The Excellent Wang Bai gave the order in his capacity as Prefect. He said the matter falls within his jurisdiction because it involves traitors.'

Guang refrained from asking who the traitors were: the Son of Heaven's supporters or the Wang clan? This same confusion divided everyone on Peacock Hill. He cantered through the gate to his pavilion. It was a while since he had slept here. Apricot Corner Court's attractions were far warmer.

Inside the courtyard he was surprised to find a huddle of armed men in travelling clothes. He recognised one as the ruthless Fukkien who had helped him penetrate the Mongol camp at the start of the siege. How simple everything had seemed then! One fought and lived or died. No choice had been necessary beyond that.

Dismounting hastily, Guang entered the reception hall where a single candle burned. Beside it, wearing the same plain, practical clothes as the men outside, sat Chen Song. Night moths circled and shadows danced on the walls from the candlelight. When Chen Song turned, his face was gaunt and troubled. The two friends faced each other and solemnly bowed.

'I see you have found some wine,' said Guang.

Chen Song nodded.

'There is a second cup.'

They sat together and sipped. The wine was excellent, though old-fashioned in style and perhaps too long in the jar.

'Where did you get this?' asked Guang.

'In the capital. At a merchant's shop within sight of our Holy Ruler's palace. I thought such a proximity would make it lucky. I hoped we would share it in celebration on the day our enemy lifted the siege.'

Guang sipped more cautiously.

'One can hardly celebrate that tonight,' he said.

'So you have heard?' asked Chen Song.

'Only what all know. That His Excellency debates how to preserve the city. That he must reply by noon.'

Chen Song's laugh was harsh.

'Preserve the city? Or preserve the Wang clan? I suspect we all know which takes precedence in his deliberations.'

Guang did not show any sign of knowing.

'I must tell you,' said Chen Song. 'Your faith in that gentleman has been misplaced. As you are aware, I have kept up my contacts with His Imperial Majesty's agents in the city. They came to me tonight and reported that Wang Ting-bo has already decided his response to the Mongol offer.'

Guang leaned forward eagerly, as though the question was open to doubt. Yet in his heart he knew the answer before Chen Song spoke.

'At noon tomorrow, the Great Khan will gain many new servants. We are betrayed, Guang! Heaven's rightful Son is betrayed! Once Nancheng falls they will advance to the Yangtze and rake the soft belly of our Empire with their claws! The number of dead will make Fouzhou or even the loss of Nancheng seem nothing.'

'Do not speak so loud,' hissed Guang. 'I do not trust my servants. All were here when Wang Bai granted me this temporary residence.'

With a steady hand, Chen Song poured out the last of his expensive wine. They raised their bowls and sipped.

'You see, dearest Guang, each of us must choose. Whether to follow the Pacification Commissioner in his treachery or find another way.'

'What other way can there be? Except destroying one's self?'

'That would certainly be a noble end,' conceded Chen Song. 'I am sure many will embrace it. We are more fortunate. No doubt you recognised our friends outside, waiting in the courtyard?'

'I did.'

'Then you know they can be trusted.'

Chen Song leaned forward, his voice an urgent whisper.

'Come with us, Guang. The Fukkien knows a secret way out of the city. By dawn we shall stand beyond the Mongol siege-lines. In any case, the enemy are feasting in General A-ku's camp tonight. Their grip loosens as their complacency grows.'

Guang swirled what little of Chen Song's wine remained in his bowl. Then he set it down gently on the lacquered table.

'I cannot,' he said, unable to meet his friend's eye.

Chen Song sat back in surprise.

'Do you not trust my judgement?' he asked. 'We have food, weapons, strings of *cash*, a reliable guide. Within a few weeks we shall be in the capital.'

'I cannot,' repeated Guang.

This statement earned a disbelieving laugh.

'Why ever not?'

'I must stay to protect Shih and Cao, and Father. There is another I must protect, Chen Song. I promised that no harm would befall her.'

'Come now!' Chen Song spoke like one who refuses to fall for a joke. 'You could never be happy as a traitor. It would destroy all you have won. Let us not speak nonsense!'

Guang clenched his fists, then bolted down the last of the wine.

'I cannot,' he repeated. 'Though I long to join you with all my heart. You know A-ku has sworn an oath that he will take Captain Xiao's head. If I flee, surely that punishment will fall on my family. And those I love.'

Now Chen Song's demeanour was stiff and angry.

'Has your beloved Wang Bai been whispering to you?' he sneered. 'Perhaps he has promised a high position when the Wang clan are like kings, ruling Nancheng Province on the Great Khan's behalf.'

'No, he has said nothing. We have not even talked.'

For a moment Chen Song seemed about to say more. Then he shrank back in his chair.

'I do not believe that we can meet as enemies. Is that

possible, Guang? Would you surrender our whole civilization to the barbarians, in order to preserve your family?'

Eyes fixed in shame on the floor provided Chen Song's answer.

'I see,' said Chen Song. His voice was steady as he asked: 'I take it you will not betray our intention to escape the city?'

Now it was Guang's turn to look up angrily.

'Of course not,' added Chen Song, hurriedly. 'Forgive me.'

He rose, smiling sadly at Guang.

'If you see me in your crossbow's sights,' he said, 'aim a little to the side. For our friendship's sake.'

He left and low voices could be heard outside. There followed a long, unbroken silence. Guang leaned forward, head in his hands. Then he choked back sobs rising from his heart so violently they injured all he was, or might have become.

竹子

Lu Ying woke with a start. She had barely slept all night, troubled by a hundred contending fears, until at dawn she sank into a deep, dreamless sleep. Now the sunlight entering through the curtain-cracks told her morning was well-advanced. Elsewhere in the house Madam Cao could be heard cooing as she fed one of the babies. Otherwise Apricot Corner Court was unusually silent.

Lu Ying rose and had almost finished dressing when a loud stranger's voice in the medicine shop made her pause. Dr Shih answered the man, his exact words indistinct. Soon there came a knock on her chamber door.

'Lu Ying,' said Shih. 'You have a visitor. And,' he added more quietly, 'a very important one if his own estimation of himself is to be trusted.'

Lu Ying nodded, touched by foreboding.

'Is this visitor from Peacock Hill?'

Dr Shih nodded.

'Would you like me to sit with you while he delivers his message?'

'No, no. Thank you.'

He nodded.

'Then I shall see if Cao needs my help with First Son and Daughter.'

Lu Ying found the messenger taking his ease in the most comfortable chair available. At the sight of her he rose and bowed slightly, his red-rimmed eyes looking her up and down until she grew uneasy. No doubt he had heard tales of the concubine who bewitched His Excellency and was banished for it.

'Lady Lu Ying,' he said, in a nasal voice. 'I come from the Pacification Commissioner on a delicate matter. His Excellency sends the following message: *Come without delay to the concubines' quarters at the rear of the Palace and you shall be given protection. Come by noon at the latest.*'

The man waited, observing her reaction. He seemed fascinated by her jade green eyes.

'Is that all?' she asked. 'No letter? No. . . other message?'

The man shook his head.

Her heart beat quickly. So it had come at last! The summons she had anticipated for more than two long years! Through changing seasons and countless miserable hours in her bed-chamber crammed with boxes – many of which stood empty because she had sold her store of precious things, item by item, to help her new friends. Now Wang Ting-bo was summoning her for a reason, because he knew the city would not be safe after the noon bell sounded.

Yet Lu Ying understood the manners of Peacock Hill well enough to fear such a summons. So brusque a message told its own story. This was no honourable invitation to resume her former station; Wang Ting-bo merely offered his protection in return for the lowest form of concubinage a girl could merit. The quarters at the rear of the palace were reserved for women who had grown ugly or worthless. They lived there in poverty and isolation, unless ordered to toil as drudges for First Wife.

'Well then,' said the servant. 'I have a handcart outside. You may take a few items that might please His Excellency. I shall take good care of them for you.'

Lu Ying shrank back. Handcarts reminded her of the last glimpse she had of her father after he sold her, pushing one laden with silk and valuables down Peacock Hill.

'You must not just stand there!' said the man, impatiently. 'I am in charge of your quarters, so you'd do well to oblige me.'

The way he smiled suggested how. And Lu Ying might have obeyed Wang Ting-bo, had not two tall men emerged from the central corridor of the house. At once she cried out with relief. For Guang stood beside Shih, wearing his burnished armour and weapons, having entered through the courtyard door a few moments earlier. His handsome face was haggard and pale, as though he too had failed to sleep.

'There has been a message from the Pacification Commissioner!' she cried.

It took only a few moments to relay it to them, while the servant bobbed obsequiously, awed by the presence of Captain Xiao. At last Guang noticed him and glanced significantly at the door. When the man did not take the hint, Guang frowned.

'Out,' he said, quietly. 'And do not return until summoned.'

The servant hurriedly obliged, leaving Lu Ying alone with the two brothers.

'This is unexpected,' began Dr Shih, cautiously. 'I take it His Excellency's summons is agreeable to your wishes?'

The look of mortification on her face answered his question, and he said: 'Rest assured you will always be welcome here, Lu Ying, whatever happens! I have not forgotten the black pearl you sacrificed when I was in prison. Or how you secured Widow Mu's services as midwife when Cao was slipping fast. We will never forget those things.'

Guang cleared his throat, so that Lu Ying knew something of significance was coming. 'Eldest Brother,' he said, solemnly. 'May I beg that you allow me to speak alone with your Honoured Guest, Lady Lu Ying? If you think it is not proper to leave us alone together, of course. . .'

Shih blinked in surprise, stopping him with a bemused smile.

'How very polite you are, Guang!' he said. 'I can hardly forbid what has already happened a thousand times before.'

With that he left the medicine shop, closing the door behind him. Lu Ying and Guang stood awkwardly for some moments. Then he turned to her, his face colouring.

'All you longed for has at last occurred,' he said. 'I congratulate you.'

There was no bitterness in his tone, only resignation.

'Has it?' she asked. 'I was not aware.'

'Wang Ting-bo is offering his protection,' he said. 'In times like these – and on this day in particular, when the safety of the city teeters on a cliff-edge – it would be foolish to refuse such an offer. If the Mongols enter the city, they shall have an eye out for beautiful ladies such as yourself. Ladies who are the greatest prize a man might imagine.'

She did not react to his compliment, but felt her breath quicken, as it so often did in his presence.

'I always was foolish,' she said.

Now he met her frank gaze. But still she could not say more. Oh, it was for him to speak now! To say what no man had ever said to her!

'I understand your feelings,' he said.

Yet still he hesitated. Lu Ying cast around for ways to encourage him. Abruptly, he laid the helmet in his hands on the shop counter and cast his studded gauntlets beside it.

'If I truly loved you,' he said. 'I would urge you to accept Wang Ting-bo's protection. But it seems I do not love you.'

Her hand rose to her mouth. Tears began to fill the corners of her eyes.

'For I wish to make quite a different suggestion,' he said, 'one that puts you, me, perhaps even Shih and Cao and the children at risk of a great man's displeasure. Nevertheless, I will make that suggestion.'

Lu Ying was watching him, silently longing for him to continue.

'You will think I do not honour you because I cannot employ

a matchmaker, as is proper,' he said. 'But there is no time for that, and in any case your parents are dead. And no doubt you will wonder that I do not consult astrologers or send you a list of my property on little red cards as gentlemen of fashion do, or provide you with three gold ornaments as is also proper, or do such proper things.'

Still she waited, her head bowed in a way she hoped would denote future submissiveness, however improper his behaviour.

'Despite all these objections,' he said, 'I will still make my honourable offer, certain you will find me impudent. Perhaps you will be angry I say such things to you, on the very day His Excellency offers you protection. In any case, Lu Ying, I ask you to be my First Wife. And I swear there shall never be a concubine to rival you as long as you live.'

Lu Ying looked up. Her small gasp for air became an intake of joy.

'I do not find you impudent,' she said, hurriedly. 'How can you think it? And I am so very far from angry.'

Then in contradiction to all propriety she took two steps towards him.

'I have never found you impudent,' she repeated. 'Only a little backward when reading a lady's desires.'

There was no need for words after that. The servant from Peacock Hill waiting outside rattled his handcart impatiently but dared not disobey Captain Xiao. Lord Yun could be heard moaning like a simpleton down the corridor, eager for soothing numbness, as Shih brought a fresh draught of his special medicine. The babies decided to cry in unison, competing who would be loudest. Through it all Lu Ying and Guang maintained their embrace. The strength of his arms and chest rendered her correspondingly weak. When they drew apart his armour was wet with her joyful tears.

'It is rumoured Wang Ting-bo has chosen to join the Great Khan,' she whispered. 'Will you go with him?'

Now Guang's face lost the happiness it had found a moment before.

'You would despise me, for I would be a traitor.'

Before she could state her opinion, which was by no means the one he assigned to her, the ward bell began to toll the hour. Suddenly Guang grew stiff.

'Noon!' he said. 'I am awaited at Peacock Hill to lead the Honour Guard to Sparrow Gate. Lu Ying, promise you will hide here! Do not venture out, whatever happens. Await word that I am safe. I shall send it within a few hours at most. A few hours at the very most. And dress as plainly as you are able, so your beauty is concealed. Will you obey me in this, as your future husband?'

'Yes!' she cried. 'Always! But Guang, what if you do not send word?'

He took her hand.

'Then the worst will have happened. If that is the case, do not be sentimental. Seek Wang Ting-bo's protection and keep me as a secret in your heart.'

'No,' she whispered. 'Never will I go back to that man!'

'I shall send word, my love,' he promised, gently lifting her chin with his hand so she met his gaze. 'Whatever I do shall be for the benefit of my family. And you are a Yun now.'

Lu Ying nodded tearfully. A wave of reassurance made her giddy. A *Yun*! He had said it quite clearly. No longer would she be without family or clan, no longer invisible. Once more the ward bell rang out. After a single backward glance, he hurried to the horse waiting in Apricot Corner Court and galloped furiously in the direction of Peacock Hill.

When Guang had been gone a decent interval, Wang Ting-bo's messenger popped his head into the medicine shop. Lu Ying looked up from silent tears of joy and noticed the hand-cart waiting behind him. It seemed a most odious, contemptible object.

'Tell His Excellency I decline his offer,' she said, haughtily. 'Tell him I am under the honourable protection of Commander Yun Guang. Tell him I will never require his protection, or even his notice, ever again. Tell His Excellency *that*!'

Lu Ying closed the door in the servant's astonished face. Then she stood, shaking and hugging herself, as the handcart rattled back in the direction of Peacock Hill.

竹子

An hour before noon hundreds gathered before the Prefectural buildings, once the palace of a petty king. To look at the procession one might think the king had returned. Wang Ting-bo's palanquin was so laden with costly jade gifts that a dozen men were required to lift it. Behind came a lesser palanquin, but still splendid, carrying Wang Bai; then dozens of sedan chairs heavy with officials of the highest rank, mainly members of the Wang clan.

At the head of the column rode fifty cavalry in gaudy uniforms, weapons burnished, freshly-washed pennants on every lance. Yet this fine body of men lacked a commander. Wang Bai poked an impatient head out of his palanquin at the delay.

At last, riding his familiar dappled grey horse, came Commander Yun Guang to lead the escort. His face was unnaturally stiff. Like many present he seemed to have difficulty looking people in the face. Still, he took up his position, armour gleaming, and sent a messenger to ask Wang Ting-bo whether they should proceed to Swallow Gate.

The line of cavalry and palanquins advanced through the gatehouse of Peacock Hill. As they rode, Guang tried not to notice the sullen crowds lining their way. A few called out his name hopefully as though Captain Xiao might still save them from disgrace. Others muttered fearfully. One man, wearing the tattered uniform of General Zheng Shun's volunteer militia shouted out in a sardonic voice: 'Captain Xiao! Oh, Captain Xiao!'

Then some of the people laughed and Guang reddened. Yet many knew General A-ku wanted Captain Xiao's life and wondered how he could ride so calmly to his own execution.

More than any argument the Pacification Commissioner might devise, this sacrifice, so characteristic of Captain Xiao, made people believe surrender was necessary to save the city.

A tang of smoke caught Guang's nostrils and he looked round in alarm, fearing a loyalist ambush. Plumes were rising from a prosperous ward near Peacock Hill where most of the Son of Heaven's officials occupied mansions and pleasure gardens. An officer riding beside him whispered that a dozen officials still loyal to the Emperor had chosen to destroy themselves sooner than be dishonoured. Their families were joining them in suicide pacts, sometimes to the third generation, by taking poison or burning themselves in their pavilions.

'You have said enough!' barked Guang. The officer shrank back in surprise.

Finally they reached Swallow Gate, after passing the floating corpses of women who had drowned themselves in South Canal rather than be violated by the Mongols.

Swallow Gate was the scene of Captain Xiao's triumphs. Here he had earned the respect of friend and enemy alike. The procession halted in the street leading up to the long tunnel of iron-bound gates. Guang climbed with leaden feet to the topmost battlements where all could see him. The soldiers on duty bowed, their fear obvious. He looked down and saw a handkerchief flutter from Wang Bai's palanquin. Still he hesitated. When he tried to speak the command came out as a cough. Then Guang filled his lungs. Staring forward, he bellowed: 'Open the gates for His Excellency!'

He stood stiffly, his eyes narrowed, as the iron-bound doors of Nancheng swung open, one by one, until the way lay clear. Wang Ting-bo and Wang Bai's palanquins were carried into the killing ground beyond the moats. For a moment Guang contemplated ordering the closure of the gates and seizing control of the city so they might defend themselves a while longer.

General A-ku rode over, alone except for an interpreter carrying a large, flat rectangle covered by silk cloth. General A-ku bowed half as low as Wang Ting-bo, then gestured at the flat rectangle. At his command the servant removed its silk covering. Even from a distance Guang recognised it as a portrait. Wang Ting-bo and Wang Bai exchanged confused glances. They fell to their knees before the picture, banging their heads on soil stained with the blood of thousands. General A-ku watched, a hand on his hip, half-approving, half amused.

It was a measure of A-ku's confidence that he accepted Wang Ting-bo's invitation to a banquet on Peacock Hill while his army was still entering the city. Accompanied by only a hundred officers and men, he rode through the streets, looking round curiously, followed by Wang Ting-bo's jogging palanquin.

On Peacock Hill musicians played flutes and the *pi-pa*, while drums, gongs and cymbals kept time. The great banqueting hall, formerly reserved for the Twin Cities' notables, had been filled with tables and stools – so many that the Mongols were outnumbered by pieces of furniture. At first they sat down suspiciously. Then, after hoarded wine had been served and the earnestness of their welcome became apparent, hands crept away from sword-hilts to clasp delicate bowls.

Guang watched from the side while the feast advanced. Either he had been forgotten or his arrest would follow later. Perhaps he should flee while he could, sidle to the door, find a horse, ride into the city; there were places to hide, loyalists to offer shelter. But he knew the first place they would search was Apricot Corner Court.

He glanced up at the high table where Wang Bai and Wang Ting-bo sat beside the Mongol general. A-ku was around Guang's age but appeared older, a squat, swarthy man, his skin tanned by fierce steppe winds. The painting of the Great Khan had been propped behind A-ku's chair like the image of a god. After eating and commenting on each dish through an interpreter, General A-ku spoke to Wang Ting-bo; the former Pacification Commissioner bowed solemnly and scanned the great hall until he located Guang, who was leaning against a frieze depicting noble ancestors at a moon-gazing party. Wang Ting-bo waved him over to the high table, a stern expression on his face. Clearly no support could be expected from that quarter.

Commander Yun Guang bowed low before the assembled notables then drew himself to his full height. A-ku would want a swift revenge for the indignities Captain Xiao had visited on him, yet Guang suspected he might wait until the Mongol army had taken full possession of the city before ordering executions. All that mattered to Guang was fulfilling his plan – or desperate hope – to save Apricot Corner Court.

Silence spread from the nearby tables as Mongol commanders who had lost hundreds to Captain Xiao's artillery examined their enemy curiously. At last General A-ku spoke through an interpreter.

'I swore that I would behead you after we captured this city,' said A-ku. 'You killed two of my cousins through your catapults. Both were dear companions of my childhood.'

Guang looked up expectantly. When his chance came he must seize it, nothing more was left to him.

'But I promised Wang Ting-bo that the entire city would be spared,' said A-ku through his interpreter. 'Are you part of the city? Does one oath cancel out another?'

The great hall waited in silence.

'Wise general,' said Guang. 'My family are part of the city. By the terms of your oath every one of them must be spared. As an honourable man I hold you to that. As for me, I do not care what happens, so long as you fulfil your oath to spare the city and therefore my family, I ask no more.'

When the interpreter had translated these words, General A-ku guffawed and his officers followed suit.

'Your request is granted, your family will be spared. As for you, why should I break my previous oath?'

Guang's heart raced. His mind moved slowly. He could think of no good reason.

'Glorious General!' broke in a smooth voice. It was Wang Bai speaking through the interpreter and A-ku glanced at him in surprise. 'Your Excellency,' continued Wang Bai. 'Forgive my interruption, but if Yun Guang submitted to the Great Khan he would no longer be your opponent. In a sense, he would have died and been reborn. Then Your Excellency might choose to forget your oath.'

The courage of such an outburst did not escape Guang – or Wang Ting-bo, who motioned anxiously to his nephew that he should be silent.

General A-ku took a moment to consider Wang Bai's meaning. He drank more wine and summoned the portrait of Khubilai Khan. Deftly the servants held it up. Guang stared at the portly figure in the painting. The Khan of all the Mongols and a hundred nations possessed a strong nose and narrow eyes; his ears were large, denoting great character. He looked no different from any foreign merchant one might meet in the market: a fat, plausible merchant. Guang slowly lowered himself to his knees and bent forward, pressing his forehead against the polished wooden floor. Three times he abased himself, as was customary, then he awaited General A-ku's verdict.

Two muscular hands came together. A loud clap echoed round the room. Guang glanced up to find the general looking down at him and speaking to the interpreter in their ugly tongue: 'My enemy Yun Guang has passed away,' said the interpreter. 'The glorious A-ku need not pursue his oath, for it is already fulfilled.'

Then one of the Mongol officers rose, knocking aside his wine bowl. He glared with red-rimmed eyes across the room at the accused. For a moment Guang did not recognise him. When he did, his hand reached for a sword he was no longer allowed to carry. Khan Bayke spoke and the interpreter continued to translate: 'General!' called out the man, in a harsh voice. 'You might be able to renounce your oath with honour but I cannot forget mine. I demand justice! I demand the head of the man who murdered my eldest son.'

Silence in the hall. Guang did not take his eyes from Khan Bayke's face. He had often dreamt of meeting him, but never like this. Always it had been in battle, an equal fight between two fully armed men to decide two families' honour. Sometimes, in his dreams, Bayke's head had been severed from its neck with a single blow, sometimes it had been his own. Then Guang's dream would assume the garish intensity of nightmare – Bayke's men sacking Apricot Corner Court, dragging out Cao and Shih, dispatching Lord Yun after he had abased himself shamelessly; and, finally, as one saves the tastiest morsel for last, Lu Ying. Those had been the shadows of fear. Now he faced a man of bone and sinew quite prepared to make them real.

'General A-ku is wise,' continued Bayke. 'But I appeal to the *yasa*. This man has robbed me. Everyone knows how my son was taken from me.'

Many of the officers murmured their agreement, yet more were silent, showing neither approval nor disapproval. Among this last group was General A-ku. He glanced over at Guang then addressed his followers: 'The *yasa* states that the injured party must lead the captured one to justice at once or there can be no punishment. Bayke's son was taken from him years ago.'

The interpreter's voice grew excited as he translated Bayke's reply for the benefit of Wang Ting-bo and the accused.

'But it was no fair fight between warriors, Wise General! He killed my son while he was naked and sporting with his whore.'

Now A-ku's cold eyes fixed on Guang.

'Is this true?'

'I interrupted his pleasure, Great General,' he said. 'Then he went for me. I had no choice but to kill him.' Another recollection of those terrible moments outside his ancestors' tomb came to him. 'General, two armed servants of Khan Bayke immediately attacked me after Bayke's son was dead. One I killed, but the other I blinded and allowed to live. Had I been intent on murdering all that belonged to Bayke, surely I would have killed the blind one, too?'

His argument provoked further muttering amongst the officers. It was the kind of nicety the more learned among them enjoyed. Khan Bayke flushed.

'How these swamp people can talk!' he declared, contemptuously. 'If they could fight half as well, their Empire would be secure! But Great A-ku, I have more to say. Has not the Great Khan himself decreed that the Chinese are to be ranked as the very lowest of creatures known as men? Why then is the law used to protect this one?'

Those Mongol officers sympathetic to Bayke banged the table, cracking delicate porcelain bowls. Even A-ku hesitated, examining Guang's face for marks of guilt.

Then all heads turned as a calm, refined voice addressed the interpreter: Wang Bai again, his expression thoughtful.

'Commander Yun Guang is a difficult case!' he declared. 'The people in the city call him Captain Xiao on account of his filial piety. His orders led to the death of hundreds of the Great Khan's servants.' Wang Bai gestured expressively. 'All in honest battle.'

Now he had the full attention of the room; Bayke seemed about to shout him down until A-ku glared for silence.

'Every father of the thousands he caused to die are just like Khan Bayke,' continued Wang Bai. 'They, too, want revenge!'

Guang listened as the interpreter relayed this speech. All that mattered to him was that A-ku kept his promise and spared Apricot Corner Court. The Mongol general, however, was regarding Wang Bai with genuine respect, not because of his arguments, but because he had the courage to state them.

'Your point?' he asked. 'Be brief.'

'My point, Mighty General,' said Wang Bai, 'is this. If Yun Guang is to be judged a murderer, let him be killed. But the effect on every Chinese who hears about his fate will be immeasurable. They will see only that Captain Xiao was promised his life if he surrendered – then he was executed.

After that, who will dare to surrender to the Great Khan? One might as well die fighting.'

A-ku sat back in his chair. He waved for more wine and drank it slowly. No one spoke. At last his bowl was drained and he set it on the lacquered table with a light rap. His eyes sought out Khan Bayke.

'I understand your desire for vengeance, that you cannot feel complete without it, but these are new times, complicated times. This is my final judgement concerning Yun Guang, who has already taken up too much of my attention. All his former crimes are to be forgotten, as are those of the other soldiers who fought gallantly against us and surrendered willingly today.'

One by one the assembled commanders saw the prudence of such clemency and grunted their approval. How else could the Great Khan conquer this vast land, teeming with people and cities?

Guang's expression showed no trace of triumph; he had been spared death to endure a lifetime of dishonour and defeat. Meanwhile Wang Bai gestured impatiently that he should withdraw and the feast resumed, the Mongols talking loudly among themselves. Bayke and two of his sons left soon after A-ku's judgement, their boots echoing on the wooden floor.

Scents of roasting meat filled the air as laden platters were carried in by a procession of servants. Where Wang Ting-bo had found such delicacies, Guang could not imagine. The aroma made his mouth water and, having been spared death, his appetite returned.

One of the Mongol officers rose and ceremoniously invited him to join his companions. It was hard to refuse without causing offence, so he shared the meat put before them and drank the wine. No one at the table spoke Chinese. Wine brought the illusion of good cheer and fellowship as the Mongol officers emptied bowl after bowl.

An hour passed in this way. Although Guang longed to return to Apricot Corner Court and tell Lu Ying of their deliverance he was too ashamed. So he drank and joked, mispronouncing the Mongol word for *wine* to the great amusement of his new companions.

By now Chen Song would be looking back at the distant ramparts of Nancheng from beyond the siege lines, his honour intact. Waves of exhaustion and disgrace swept Guang's soul. How could he face Shih or Cao or Lu Ying with any semblance of pride? General A-ku was right, Commander Yun Guang had passed away, Captain Xiao had passed away, leaving a wretch who grinned and shared wine with those who put the people of Fouzhou to death – man, woman, child, regardless of age or innocence. It was a long, long feast for Guang.

竹子

Twilight was approaching when Guang finally entered Water Basin Ward, escorted through the curfew by a detachment of Mongols led by the drunken officer who had befriended him. He could not return to his old pavilion on Peacock Hill because it had already been seized by one of A-ku's commanders.

Before he left the banqueting hall, Wang Bai had sent for him and whispered that he would receive a worthy commission as soon as the Mongols advanced east. In the meantime, he should keep out of sight in Apricot Corner Court. Wang Bai waved impatiently when Guang tried to thank him for speaking on his behalf. 'Be cautious,' he said. 'For the sake of your family, if no one else. All we need do is keep them pacified until they leave.'

Guang parted with his escort some way from Apricot Corner Court. He did not want them to know where his family lived, though that was no secret in the city.

Glancing round, he patted his horse, amazed he had been allowed to keep it when they stripped his armour and weapons. There had been few signs of looting on the ride to Water Basin Ward and none of massacre apart from the self-inflicted kind. An eerie silence shrouded the city. He passed shuttered windows, aware their occupants were cowering inside, speaking only through whispers in case they attracted the attention of Mongol patrols fanning out across Nancheng.

Guang sensed Lu Ying was waiting for him, also afraid. What he might say to justify his defection was unclear. Perhaps it would be enough for her, for everyone, that Wang Ting-bo had led the capitulation. Perhaps he would suffer no loss of honour after all. Were they not merely reacting to circumstances, as a bird swoops to avoid a tree or mountain? He had done everything to preserve his family, even at the cost of his future peace. But Guang suspected the sacrifice would not be enough, would never be enough.

He was so absorbed in these thoughts that the clip-clop of hooves behind him remained unnoticed until quite close. Then Guang glanced back and comprehended the depth of his folly. For although General A-ku could not be seen to condone Captain Xiao's execution in public, he could let him perish in the streets without witnesses.

Khan Bayke was trotting towards him with three companions. Two were clearly his sons, the third an armed retainer.

Guang swung his leg over the saddle of his horse, intending to gallop away from his enemies. Every movement seemed agonisingly slow. His feet were in the stirrups, raised to spur the horse forwards. Simultaneously the horse dipped and quivered in shock. Two arrows had pierced it: one near the buttocks, the other in its neck. Guang saw the earth rush towards him as he was thrown and somehow found his footing, so that he stumbled away from the screaming animal. This saved his life.

When he glanced up, Khan Bayke and his sons were cantering forward with fixed expressions, putting their bows away and drawing curved swords. The fact that they loosed no more arrows told Guang what to expect – they wished to take him alive for a little fun.

He fled down the nearest alleyway. Hoof-thuds drove him on, hunting whoops usually reserved for deer. Guang realised that the twisting alley was taking him towards the Water Basin. Two and three storey tenements rose on either side, their doors giving onto the street. Although he did not know it, he was approaching the warren of Xue Alley.

Suddenly a canal blocked his route; the only way across was a worn rope footbridge and Guang gasped with relief for Bayke could take the horses no further. He scurried over the bridge just as his pursuers arrived at the other side. An arrow flew past his ear, then he turned a twisting corner, another shaft quivering in a lintel behind him.

Guang found himself descending a slope towards a parallel canal full of small boats of the kind used to carry passengers through the water-roads of the city.

He paused, assessing his position. He was in Xue Alley without a single weapon, pursued by four men armed from boot to plumed helmet. Yet he was sure Bayke would leave one to mind the horses. That left three warriors.

He had been taught at the Western Military Academy that the ground where simple survival calls for a perilous fight, where we perish without a desperate fight, is Dying Ground. When he reached the canal, Guang realised he had entered Dying Ground. Bayke would not expect him to turn here. And indeed, where did he have to turn? Certainly he could never lead his enemies back to Apricot Corner Court.

So Yun Guang paused at the bank of the canal and looked round. He noted the boats and remembered the adage: 'Water assists an attack mightily.' Then he seized a long bamboo pole used for propelling boats and awaited his enemies. As he stood there, striving to regulate his breaths, several curtains in the densely packed houses around him stirred. Faces peered out, whispering to those within.

Soon enough Khan Bayke and his two sons turned the corner at a jog, their swords drawn; Guang noticed at once they had left their bows with the horses, and for the first time he felt a flicker of hope. They halted at the sight of Yun Guang, bamboo staff in both hands as though it was a noble halberd instead of a peasant's excuse for a weapon.

Khan Bayke laughed and said something to his sons, who obediently stepped forward.

Guang levelled the bamboo like a spear poised between the two young warriors. He was deliberately near the bank of the canal, several flat-bottomed boats directly beneath him. Then he stepped back, even closer to the edge.

Bayke's sons glanced at each other and advanced, confident of overwhelming so lightly armed an opponent. Guang's own expression was taunting. Yet he stepped back again, so that he teetered on the canal bank. Conscious of their father's approval, they rushed forward, each eager to claim the honour of avenging their brother. Swords swung and passed through empty air for Guang had jumped down into the flat-bottomed boat floating on the canal.

Now Bayke's sons leaned over the water, swords in hand. Guang, however, thrust up his bamboo pole so that it snagged on one of the Mongol's chest armour and, with one swift movement, toppled him. For a moment the young man flailed in mid-air. Then he fell with a bellow into the canal. He had every reason to cry out. A man in full armour could not hope to swim long. Most Mongols, accustomed to the dry steppe-lands, could not swim at all.

Guang ignored the splashing figure as his brother swung a savage sword blow at his head. Bamboo parried metal. One bounced off the other. Yet the bamboo was splintered, its force broken. Guang knew the next blow would surely finish him. He jumped into an adjoining moored boat, then another, and climbed onto the opposite side of the canal.

A narrow footbridge lay between him and his enemies. The Mongol in the water was only being saved from drowning by his brother, who had found another long pole. It was clear neither could swim.

Guang waited on the opposite bank while Bayke examined him, no doubt wishing he had brought his bow. The footbridge was his sole route of access to the man he had sworn to kill, the murderer of his eldest boy. For a moment Bayke watched one son drag the other out of the canal. Baring his teeth in a grin, he walked with complete confidence across the footbridge, aware a sword against a splintered bamboo pole usually yields one victor.

Then something unanticipated occurred. Doorways in Xue Alley flew open and a dozen men led by Carpenter Xue charged out, rushing over to the Mongol brothers. They were in no position to defend themselves, for their swords had been set aside while escaping the water. A moment later both had been seized and were once again floundering in the canal. This time they were lucky, managing to cling to the side of a boat out of reach of their attackers. One of Carpenter Xue's brood reached down and picked up an abandoned sword.

Bayke paused on the footbridge. Believing his sons were in no immediate danger, or perhaps maddened into indifference by his desire for revenge, he charged at Guang with a terrible cry, sword raised.

Against such an attack Guang could only give way, raising the bamboo staff to deflect Bayke's blow. It splintered into two pieces. Aware he was hopelessly out matched, Guang lunged to the side as Bayke launched another fierce downward slash.

Then he heard a cry: 'Captain Xiao! Take this!'

Guang dodged to avoid a stroke and glimpsed a curved shape land at his feet. He snatched up the sword just in time to parry a blow aimed at his head, then another. Despite the fury of his resistance it was apparent the Mongol officer was the stronger fighter: blow after blow fell on Gunag's sword and he found himself always on the defensive.

At last Khan Bayke stepped back, panting. On the other side of the canal a dozen Xues had found long poles and were threatening to push his two sons deeper into the water. Guang waited, his sword raised to fend off Bayke's next attack, but it never came; the Mongol turned unexpectedly, desperate to cut a way through to his drowning sons. In that moment, as he placed his foot on the bridge, his back was exposed and Guang darted forward, stabbing Khan Bayke near the base of his spine, finding a gap in the armour, pushing the sword in deep so that blood welled across the blade. Then Guang twisted the sword, gasping and cursing, worrying it back and forth. Finally, he released the hilt, slippery with blood, and shoved Bayke into the canal, grunting triumphantly; a loud splash followed; for a moment the water frothed, then the armoured man vanished from sight.

Guang hurried over to the jubilant members of the Xue clan, who had finally finished off their enemies.

'There is another one holding their horses at the entrance to Xue Alley,' he said. 'Send a boy with a message from Bayke to lure him here. I shall do the rest. And we must hide these bodies or they will bury our entire families alive – after they have flayed us to the bone.'

But all three Mongol warriors had already sunk to the bottom of the canal. It seemed no further concealment was necessary.

竹子

Of course she was used to waiting. Who among the ladies had waited so hard as she? Lu Ying sat on her worn divan and listened to sounds of panic drifting through the open window: a woman wailed in a neighbouring courtyard; shouting broke out across the canal in Ping's Floating Oriole House. She peeped out, expecting Mongol warriors to flood through Water Basin Ward like a swarm of giant rats, but it was only a pair of drunkards, quarrelling to satisfy some petty grievance. Her bamboo curtain fell with a rattle and she sat very still, struggling to compose herself.

Lu Ying rose and paced the room. The ward bell chimed noon. Now Wang Ting-bo would be surrendering the city to the enemy. She could barely believe him capable of treason, yet the proof was everywhere. How General A-ku had promised to preserve his life and noble position, how the city would be spared fire and sword. No one believed that last part, of course, when a hill of corpses rotted across the river in Fouzhou. Soon the Mongols would ride through the streets and it would begin. Everyone knew they liked to mingle a little pleasure with their grim work. Lu Ying shivered at the thought, hugging her chest.

Perhaps she should join Madam Cao and Dr Shih, who were hiding in one of the back rooms with their babies, waiting for the storm to pass. A little company might lift her spirits. And she would have gone except that something she could not express held her back, maybe even their kindness. Her nerves were too raw and jagged for kindness – Dr Shih's soothing voice was likely to make her scream. No, it would be best to wait in her room for Guang; surely he would come soon.

Noon shadows and bars of light shifted across wall and floor. How long since the last bell? An hour? Perhaps more. Time enough for Guang to send word that he was safe, that he had found the means to protect her as he had promised.

That was a foolish thought. How could he preserve her when Swallow Gate was thrown open? No one in the city could call themselves safe, except for Wang Ting-bo and his clan. Oh, they were safe! The Wangs of this world were always safe. Words sung long ago, it seemed, filled her memory and she hummed softly to sooth her fears:

Chop, chop, we clear the elms
And pile branches on the bank.
He neither sows nor reaps!
How has our lord five-hundred sheaves?
He neither traps nor shoots!
How do badger pelts adorn his courtyards?
Those lords, those handsome lords,
Need not work for a bowl of food.

Lu Ying realised her hands were trembling and squeezed them tight. Her chest had grown constricted, she could hardly breathe.

Another hour bell rang out. More sounds of panic in the streets. Lu Ying stepped into Apricot Corner Court and heard a rumour from Widow Mu that high officials were throwing themselves into wells rather than surrender. It seemed the hysteria was spreading; a whole house of singing girls had linked arms and drowned themselves in East Canal. Little wonder Lu Ying was glad to escape back to her room, yet even here she could see confirmation of Mu's words: people running for shelter, treasured possessions clutched to their chests; smoke rising from the better districts of town. It was true, all true, the end had surely come.

Despite the numbness of terror, Lu Ying understood that more than the lives of a few high officials were ending today. She struggled to make sense of her idea. The victory of the Mongols would bring something to a close. . . she could not explain it. . . a frivolity, perhaps, a world where duty did not impede the round of pleasure for long. Indeed, where elegant pleasures were a kind of duty. How gay the streets had looked at festival time! Instead, there would be grim-faced warriors and harsh ways, curfews and slave-markets. It was not hard to explain their loss. Lu Ying knew all she had lived for was passing like youth or summer, unless Guang somehow restored her future.

Yet where was he? Why did he not come? It was too cruel of him not to come. Had they not exchanged promises? Perhaps he had forgotten them already. Men were fickle, one dared not trust them yet could not help it. Wang Ting-bo had forgotten her soon enough, the instant she disappointed him. Maybe Guang had decided she was a disappointment, too.

By the third bell Lu Ying's despair was absolute. He had abandoned her, as Wang Ting-bo had before him. Then her hand flew to her mouth. Why had she not seen it before? Captain Xiao would never surrender or turn his coat like a Wang! He had chosen to perish rather than sell his honour. Whether by his own hand or the enemy's, he had chosen death.

Her body shook with sobs, until at last she subsided and a cold, troubled expression smoothed her face. She went over to a maple chest and took out a long, heavy silk and brocade dress of deepest blue. She was quite calm now. Of course, the Moon Goddess had taught her what she must do. Really, it was quite simple. Quite simple to leave her plain clothes in a pile and hurriedly dress in the finest silks left to her. Simple to put on all her remaining jewellery, her jade amulets and gold hairpins, to apply her make-up so the Moon Goddess would clap her hands in admiration of her beauty when she came before her.

A distant scream made her start. They had penetrated Water Basin Ward. She had little time.

Lu Ying would have liked to say farewell to Cao and Shih, to their tiny babies, and to Apricot Corner Court itself where she had deserved no welcome at all, yet earned kindness in some miraculous way. She would have liked to say farewell to her memories, especially those of nursing Guang, but there was no time left.

She walked gracefully on her lotus feet as she had been taught, a most delightful, elegant walk, to the back door of the house. It opened easily and she found herself on the narrow path separating Apricot Corner Court from the canal. There Lu Ying gasped, for a woman was floating face down in the water, a woman in plain clothes, not the precious silks Lu Ying wore to advance from one life to the next. It was a sign, a warning not to falter. So she stepped forward, once, twice, and no one called out as the dark waters rushed to embrace her. Soon the sack of precious things tied to her girdle, ornaments and jades, a favourite bronze statuette of a court beauty, dragged Lu Ying to a place where sorrow, pain, joy, might begin again with her next incarnation; or perhaps to a silent emptiness, where passion faded forever.

竹子

Guang knocked on the gatehouse door and called out Shih's name. At last it opened a crack and he was ushered inside by Old Hsu's Son.

'How did you get through the curfew?' he whispered. 'Their soldiers are everywhere.'

'I was lucky,' said Guang, furtively. 'And the Mongols have been well-behaved so far. General A-ku has promised death for any of his men who loot or rape. He does not wish to deter other cities from surrendering.'

'Ah,' said Old Hsu's Son. 'I did not know.'

Then the fan-maker grew solemn.

'You must see Dr Shih, sir! A most terrible event! It is best that Dr Shih explains.'

The kitchen door of his brother's house was not barred. Guang found that the central corridor of the house was wet when he stepped inside and that water formed a trail to Dr Shih's medicine shop.

'Shih!' he called. 'Lu Ying! Cao!'

No one replied. He heard quiet sobbing from Cao's bed-chamber. Still he advanced toward the shop. Pushing open the door, he called out again: 'Lu Ying! Cao!'

Then Guang recoiled, instinctively reaching for a sword he no longer possessed, as though it might defend him from what he saw.

A single candle lit the woman in heavy silk clothes. Her hair, once an elegant black coil shining with beauty, was disordered. Pools of water spread from her limbs. She lay on several low tables pushed together, a slender hand dangling to the floor. Her delicate fingers were pale and still.

Shih sat by the counter, dark shadows round his eyes.

'Do not look!' he said, rising in alarm. 'Who let you in?'

But Guang stared, his jaws clamped until a lack of air forced him to gulp. His out-breath was an involuntary cry of disbelief. No tears relieved his pain. He could not stop staring at the curves of her cheek, her lips and sightless eyes.

'She took her own life,' said Shih. 'Do not look!'

'No!' cried Guang. 'No! Why did she not wait for me to return? Why did she not trust me?'

Still the relief of tears would not come to Captain Xiao. He glanced round angrily, willing to fight and kill anyone to prevent this, but there was nothing left to kill, no one to fight. No one except himself and all he had once aspired to become. In his heart's deep core he knew Heaven had punished him for his betrayal.

Then a steady arm was round his shoulders, leading him away from the shop to the central corridor, and at that moment the babies began to cry, first one, then the other, howling until Apricot Corner Court filled with hungry voices. Shih clasped his brother's arm and murmured words of consolation Guang barely comprehended. Cao's voice could also be heard trying to hush the children. Eventually they settled and the house reverted to the profundities of darkness and silence.

憺

Epilogue

Treading the Green

竹子

Apricot Corner Court, Nancheng. Spring, 1282

The Celebration of the New Wine drew the province's new rulers to Nancheng. They rode in parties a hundred strong: illiterate warriors granted the rule of large, complex districts by the Great Khan, wearing gaudy holiday silks over battle-scuffed armour, their women and children jolting along in wagons dragged by sweating oxen; slaves followed with boxes and sacks on their backs, tending flocks of sheep and goats destined for the spit.

Many of the towns and villages they rode through appeared deserted. The people were hiding until their new masters had passed. The nomadic Mongols regarded closed doors and curtained windows – indeed any building at all – with suspicion. They sensed hidden emotions and memories; resentments vigorous as bamboo.

Dr Shih watched just such a cavalcade head down North Canal Street in the direction of Peacock Hill and a great *kuriltai* of the local Mongol lords. He let the paper curtain fall softly. Shuffling feet disturbed him from his thoughts and Cao entered the medicine shop, her eyebrows raised in silent enquiry. He shook his head.

'I hope he has not got into trouble,' she said. 'Or annoyed an official. You know how stubborn he can be.'

Dr Shih smiled slightly.

'I do,' he said. 'Tell the boys to stand guard with *Shen* and *Men*. They shall warn us when he arrives.'

An hour later a cry went up: 'He's here, Father! Come quickly! He is here!'

Shih hurried from the medicine shop into the courtyard, just in time to see a single traveller instructing a porter where to lay his bags. For a moment Shih paused, oblivious to the children or even Cao bowing by his side. His entire attention was fixed on the leathery, scarred face of the traveller. Their eyes met – eyes an identical shade of brown. Fourteen years apart could never erode that.

The traveller glanced at the line of children Cao was busily instructing to kneel. They stared up at him in wonder. The stranger seemed to recollect something and a small, sad smile played across his mouth. Advancing a few steps he knelt awkwardly, wincing from an old wound in his side. A dozen family members and dependents watched as he bowed low before Dr Shih to offer the proper respect.

'Eldest Brother,' he said, solemnly. 'I present myself to you.'

A stifled sob from Cao broke the silence. Shih strode forward and knelt in the dusty courtyard beside his double.

'Oh, Guang!' he cried, rocking on his heels. 'Guang, how thin you are! What have they done to you?'

They laughed and wiped tears. Then, still kneeling, they embraced. At last both rose to find a tray of wine being offered by Shih's eldest daughter. Through lowered eyes she examined the uncle so often mentioned by strangers and neighbours when whispering about the old days. *Captain Xiao* who everyone thought had perished in the Great Khan's armies as a warning to all.

*

Nearly fourteen years had passed since Guang last slept in Apricot Corner Court. As the first shadows of evening gathered the two brothers sat beside the apricot tree to fill lost years with stories. Shih started with his news. How Lord Yun had died quite suddenly six months after the Mongols occupied Nancheng. How more children had arrived after the twins, three in rapid succession until five ran or toddled round the courtyard. How Shih had discovered Ibn Rashid's son starving in the streets and indentured him as his apprentice. Above all, how their prosperity had neither diminished nor grown despite the Great Khan's tax farmers stripping Nancheng bare each autumn.

Then it was Guang's turn. He alternated between reluctant speech and defiance. Shih learned that he had been forced to serve in General A-ku's artillery companies in battles against the former dynasty. Finally they invaded a distant land across the sea called Nippon. Heaven's judgement in that campaign had been merciless: 'My ship escaped only by a miracle. The typhoon drowned a hundred thousand men around me,' Guang said, staring into his tea bowl as though recollecting the terrible, boiling waves. 'We managed to struggle westwards, our ship damaged in a dozen places. When my feet touched ground again it was far from the Middle Kingdom in a place called Koryo. It took me two years to return to civilised districts. A friend of mine in Suchow had kept safe what little wealth I had garnered in the Mongols' service and let me winter with him. I was too sick from old wounds and fever to travel further so I sent a message to you. At last I recovered enough to join a merchant's junk heading up the Yangtze. A most pleasant journey! After so long away I have learned that nothing in our homeland is unworthy of notice.'

Shih stifled a hundred questions.

'Apricot Corner Court is your home from now on,' he said, firmly. 'A permanent room has been prepared for you. Without your sacrifice we would not be here at all.'

He fell silent. Guang had turned away to conceal tears. They ran down gaunt cheeks criss-crossed by tiny scars. 'I did not know you had guessed the choice I made all those years ago,' he said, in a thick voice. 'I thought of you and Cao constantly, and hoped you remembered me.'

'We did,' said Shih. 'We always will.'

They sat in silence watching swallows and swifts flit through the twilight. The blessed peak of Mount Wadung loomed over the city, its summit capped by snow.

'Is your service with them over?' asked Shih.

'They believe I am dead, that I perished with the invasion fleet on the coast of Nippon. At least, I think so. Even if I am discovered, I cannot fight again. I would sooner take my own life.'

Shih watched his brother carefully.

'Tomorrow is the Celebration of the New Wine,' he said. 'Let us start the rites early.'

The spring air was mild. They sat beneath the apricot tree, celebrating flask after flask while the children crept from the house and began to play in the courtyard, quietly at first, then competing to attract Honoured Uncle's approval.

Cao served a procession of small dishes popular in Nancheng: pickled salad, omelette with meat sauce, double-cooked pork, poached kidneys with hot sauce. Whatever the brothers left was shared among the children and servants. For tonight, at least, there was more than any could eat. No one stepped outside Apricot Corner Court, for the curfew was strict and the punishments severe.

Despite a heavy head Guang rose at dawn and wandered through grey streets until he reached Swallow Gate. For a moment he hesitated, staring at battlements he had once paced in a commander's heavy armour, jade badges of rank adorning his girdle, a tasselled sword swinging at his side. Guang closed his eyes to suppress emotions long held at bay, then climbed stiffly onto the ramparts.

A few poorly armed North Chinese conscripts stood guard, all too young to remember the man with iron-grey hair who leant on an embrasure and gazed west, lost to his own thoughts.

Those thoughts danced like midges over a river – images of faces long dead, others perhaps still living. Faces containing skulls that had swirled with dreams and desires and hatred and love ephemeral as blossom-time. He blinked. For a moment the ground before Swallow Gate filled with ghostly phalanxes of warriors, hazy entrenchments and wooden palisades. A gigantic tower on wheels full of flag-fluttering men toppled until it sank into the earth, disappearing as suns are swallowed by horizons.

Guang shook his head, feeling his chest and breath tighten. When he looked out again the vision had faded. The only traces of the Mongol camp were paddy fields sculpted by resourceful farmers from trenches and embankments. No doubt their ploughing turned up countless bones. Yet the spring crop was already stretching hungry leaves to the sun and swaying in time to the wind like a crowd of slender dancers.

Guang leant on the parapet for a long while, his head bowed as though meditating. The North Chinese conscripts talked excitedly of that afternoon's parade to the Prefecture, for it appeared they had been granted leave to celebrate the New Wine. Eventually he noticed a figure watching from a distant tower and felt a shock of recognition. The silhouette was familiar, yet he could not be sure. Guang shielded his eyes because the rising sun lay between them; when he could see clearly again the watcher had vanished.

He glanced round nervously. Had he been recognised as Captain Xiao? But that was foolish. Already he had heard that name muttered as he passed. No, he would not hide, whatever punishments came his way. He had returned here precisely to test the consequences of being visible – to stop running from danger to danger.

*

'Are you sure this is wise?' asked Shih.

'I would like to see the procession,' said Guang. 'Any reminder of civilized customs is a cordial after years in barbarous places.'

Shih could understand that.

'Very well,' he said. 'But Cao and the children shall remain in Apricot Corner Court. They can watch from the window of the tower room. This is the first year the Governor has agreed to the traditional parade. If there is rowdiness the authorities may over-react.'

'It shall be just you and I,' said Guang.

'We will certainly attract attention,' warned Shih. 'We were always noticeable.'

'Let people look,' said Guang. 'The Yun clan does not skulk from anyone.'

Doubts stirred even as he boasted. What if someone openly accused him of being a turncoat, a traitor? Never mind that hundreds of thousands had chosen the same road. The very name *Captain Xiao* weighed upon his spirits like a prisoner's heavy wooden yoke.

'We need not hide,' he said more softly. 'Brother, I think I shall sleep for a few hours before the parade.'

Shih, who understood more than he ever showed, ordered his children to be silent while Honoured Uncle gathered his strength. Then he went on a circuit of patients with Ibn Rashid's son, now a serious young man and very promising doctor. Up in the tower room Dr Shih's other assistant, Mung Po, prepared herbs and infusions.

The former monk was a fixed resident in Apricot Corner Court. When the Mongols seized Nancheng the North Medical Relief Bureau abruptly closed its doors and Mung Po found himself without a livelihood. After that it had seemed quite natural for him to join Dr Shih's household, sharing a small room with the apprentice.

It was early afternoon when Guang emerged from his chamber.

He seemed refreshed and wore his best clothes in honour of the coming rites. Shih had also donned silks for the occasion.

The two brothers entered North Canal Street from Shih's medicine shop, stepping into a noisy crowd that craned and jostled to watch the procession. At its head were a dozen bright banners of red, yellow and green, each as long as ten men lying end to end. Representatives of various guilds carried the banners suspended from high poles. Then came hundreds of prostitutes and courtesans, divided into four classes. One might tell each lady's price by her clothes and ornaments.

'You can tell Nancheng's governor is Chinese,' muttered Guang. 'A Mongol would never allow us to congregate together in this way.'

'I have heard the Governor of Suchow does not even allow people to pray together in public,' whispered Shih.

'Best not to speak of it.'

It would have been impossible to hear even if Shih had spoken. Drummers and musicians made a noise to startle Heaven itself, escorting burly porters who bore huge jars of rice wine. After the customary procession of actors dressed as Immortals came the representatives of the guilds: pet fish sellers and breeders of dwarf trees, jewellers following their Guild Chief, Fu Sha, and fishermen, hunters, butchers, tailors, carpenters, sellers of sweet food, purveyors of bitter sauces – and noble representatives of the doctor's guild. Guang laid a hand on his brother's arm as these latter gentlemen passed, led by Dr Fung, Among the twenty doctors who accompanied him was a fat, amiable fellow.

'I see Chung prospers,' remarked Guang, quietly. Those who knew him well might have detected a veiled threat in his tone. Shih grunted something incomprehensible in reply.

But soon Chung had passed, replaced by members of the fan-maker's guild, including Old Hsu's Son who waved cheerily at Dr Shih. His flushed cheeks indicated he had been celebrating the New Wine for some time.

Finally, groups of little boys and girls carried five-stringed lutes, staring round as though unsure whether to be amazed, proud or terrified. Shih glanced up at the tower room of Apricot Corner Court where the bobbing heads and shoulders of his own children watched enviously. Many respectable parents did not share his scruples about allowing their children to join the parade. Perhaps he was too wary, Cao certainly thought so.

It was traditional for men on horseback to bring up the rear of the procession. However the new laws forbade Chinese from owning horses. Many in the crowd laughed to see how a few wits evaded the prohibitions by riding paper horses pasted onto bamboo sticks. Ripples of applause rolled up and down North Canal Street. The hundreds of Mongol cavalry assigned to ride at the rear of the parade seemed oblivious to the joke. Their grins made it clear they believed the applause was intended for themselves. Once the armed men had passed Guang turned to his brother.

'Shall we follow?'

'Is that wise? You know. . .'

Shih was silenced by an upraised hand.

'Eldest Brother,' said Guang. 'The children are watching us. How will we tell them what happens if we lack the courage to take part?'

Such a reproof left Shih little choice but to shrug and laugh hollowly. He bought frothing green wine from Mao's Refreshment Stall and the two revellers swigged, passing the flask between them as they followed the crowd towards Peacock Hill.

Many stared curiously at the twins and Guang grew tense, feeling himself besieged by a thousand eyes. Yet Dr Shih brightened as the wine seeped through his soul. The old pride took hold at walking beside his noble brother, for Guang was still a handsome man – despite his wounds, the years had brought distinction to his looks rather than frailty – still a notable man, the very image of a fine warrior.

'Brother,' said Shih. 'You will be surprised by the changes on Peacock Hill.'

'How so?'

'The last fourteen years have sadly aged our governor. Many of the families who once provided our province's officials, including the Wang clan, have been replaced by foreigners.'

Guang wondered why Shih avoided the use of Wang Ting-bo's name. But nearly all freedoms had perished with the last dynasty. The crowd pressed around them and might conceal a hundred spies.

'His Excellency prospers?' he asked.

'In his office, but not in his health,' said Shih, adding in an undertone: 'His wife rules him now, so I hear.'

'What of his heir, the boy you saved?'

'He lives and is now a young man. They say he is destined to succeed his father.'

Guang considered this for a moment.

'What of my old patron, Wang Bai?'

They were interrupted by a surge of people spilling out of Jasper Ward, drums pounding and flutes trilling hysterically. When the crowd was flowing again Shih said quietly: 'His Excellency's nephew no longer resides in Nancheng. He has been appointed head of the Bureau for the Stimulation of Agriculture and dwells in Da-Du beside the Imperial City.'

'Only beside? Not within?'

'He is Chinese,' muttered Shih.

'Ah.'

This news unsettled Guang. He could never hate Wang Bai, who had spoken out on his behalf during the trial before General A-ku.

He was granted little time to consider the past. The crowd pushed on toward Peacock Hill until it reached a great square before the gates of the former prefecture, now Governor Wang Ting-bo's palace. Here lay the inn where Guang had once stood on a balcony, hailed as Captain Xiao. He glanced furtively at his brother, afraid he might remember. But Shih, along with the rest of the crowd, was studying the gatehouse at the foot of Peacock Hill.

Dozens of soldiers and high officials thronged the battlements, staring impassively at the sea of faces below. An orchestra played the ancient melody *Dew At Sunset*, a regal, stately march, and Governor Wang Ting-bo appeared before the crowd, leaning on an ivory stick. Guang craned for a better view of his lost patron.

Though far away in time he pictured His Excellency's features just as they had been, noble and dignified, before the years of compromise. Perhaps fear had betrayed Wang Ting-bo – or simple greed for more power. Confusion agitated the waves of Guang's soul. How he had loved that old man leaning on his stick! How he had craved the slightest sign of respect and notice from him! He had risked every sinew of his young body for just that. But when Guang had needed him during A-ku's trial, that same noble Wang Ting-bo refused to speak up for him. And so disillusion takes root, spreading out ugly creepers.

Now it was Shih's turn to lay a reassuring hand on his brother's arm. He leaned forward and whispered in Guang's ear: 'It is said the Great Khan only keeps him in office so he can point to at least one Chinese governor. Wang Ting-bo barely remembers his own name unless his wife reminds him of it. He will not recollect you.'

The frail man on the tower raised a silver bowl and drank, vanishing as soon as the rite of the New Wine was over. Officials threw down handfuls of *cash* coins and banknotes from their high vantage point. Only the poorest fought for them. The new emperor's addiction to printing paper money to finance his conquests had debased an already fragile currency. Many were sullen as the paper rectangles fluttered down like a mockery of blossom.

'Well, it is over,' said Guang.

They were leaving the square along with thousands of others.

'For another year, at least,' said Shih. 'Such ceremonies always return.'

By now they had grown used to passers-by staring and whispering the name *Captain Xiao* or *Dr Yun Shih*. If Guang was to remain in Nancheng it must become something they either relished or ignored. Neither seemed likely.

'We should return home and celebrate the festival with hot dishes,' said Shih. 'After all the Cold Food Festival begins tomorrow.'

'Let me buy some . . .' Guang's offer trailed. He halted in surprise. They were passing one of the numerous portable theatres erected all over the city by competing troupes of actors.

'What is it?' asked Shih, still hazy from green wine.

He frowned. Guang was staring at the stage with a strange intensity. An actor's voice boomed out across the crowd: 'I am Chang Xi! Sent through all corners of the Empire on my great master's orders to find a girl, a truly virtuous and beautiful girl, who appeared to the Emperor in a dream. See, here is her picture! Has anyone seen her?'

Guang seemed transfixed by the figure on the stage.

'What is it?' repeated Shih. 'Do you want to see the play?'

Again, no reply. Guang's lips silently followed Chang Xi's lament at the corruption and greed in the land, how all were unmindful of their filial duty. Evidently he had heard this speech so many times he knew it by heart. Finally he turned to Shih with a troubled expression.

'Yes,' he said. 'I remember now what I meant to say. I shall buy a chicken for Cao to pluck.'

The actor's voice followed them as they left the square: 'How can I find such a girl? Impossible! *Impossible!*'

竹子

Guang did very well in Apricot Corner Court. His nephews and nieces flagrantly adored him, and they were not alone. Festival presents appeared outside the gatehouse – vegetables arranged into plum blossom shapes, a basket of coloured eggs. It seemed his brief hour as Captain Xiao had never faded from many people's hearts. Yet Guang dared not welcome such attention. Enthusiasm at his reappearance could easily become its opposite or, worse, provoke the authorities. Guang took care to hide his face from passing Mongols, mindful a relative of Bayke or a former comrade might recognise him.

When her duties allowed, Cao joined her brother-in-law beneath the apricot tree and they talked of small things. These mundane conversations – gossip about neighbours and the cost of millet, reminiscences of curious incidents – were inexpressibly sweet after so many years of war. Despite their long separation, she was still very dear, second only to Shih in his affections, unless he included ghosts and lost friends. Yet he could not help noticing that the children, while scarcely dimming Sister-in-law's spark and humour, were exhausting creatures. Gaining everything she had ever wanted surely cost a price. Her face, too, had aged more than was justified by fourteen years, but then she had always been plain. Yet she was evidently contented in ways he could scarcely imagine, and so could not envy.

He waited three days before seeking out the actors. As dragon boats raced up and down the Han River and traditional tugs of war between the young men of Fouzhou and Nancheng took place, he strolled into the city. The streets were deserted. Sensible folk occupied themselves with frivolity and betting on the races – including a contingent of Mongols who found their new vassals' effeminate ways oddly enticing.

As was customary during the Cold Food Festival, all fires in the city had been extinguished with the exception of the invaders' encampment on Peacock Hill. Aromas of wood smoke and roasting meat drifted in the spring air from Wang Ting-bo's residence, along with the noise of almost continual feasting. The Governor spared no expense in entertaining his guests, using revenue intended for the restoration of Fouzhou.

When Guang reached the market square he hesitated. What

exactly did he hope to gain by hunting ghosts? All his dreams had fallen from the stem and dwindled to dust. Only the greatest Immortals or sorcerers could restore green to dead leaves.

The square was deserted except for a few refreshment stalls and fortune-tellers reluctant to surrender their pitches. After all, those watching the races were sure to return. For this reason he was not surprised to see activity near the theatre that had fascinated him a few days before. Two labourers were hanging a huge banner from long bamboo poles. A stout, middle-aged man directed them from the empty stage. He fell silent as Guang approached.

They stood without speaking for a long while, each reluctant to be the one who first averted his eyes. Both had aged in different ways: Guang's face bore the evidence of many fights, but the man on the stage had suffered a different kind of harm. Swollen blood vessels on his nose told stories of reckless debauch; eyes ringed by shadow suggested bitter, uneasy nights.

Guang made a stiff bow. An offensively blank demeanour was all the return his courtesy received. Finally Chen Song's shoulders relaxed and he jumped down, bowing as Guang had – only with a trace of mockery.

Small birds fluttered and cheeped round the empty market square. The sky was soft and oddly blue, almost too blue to be natural, the kind of flawless spring sky the young assume will always come their way – because the future stretching out before them is endless and there is plenty of time to become whatever they wish, to mend the world's faults.

At last Chen Song's feelings bubbled over: 'Need I be afraid of your presence here?' he demanded. 'You who enlisted in the Great Khan's armies? Captain Xiao who *enlisted* with the enemy! I wept when I heard it, Yun Guang, I wept. But perhaps you no longer go by your old name. Perhaps you have adopted one of *their* names!"

Guang blinked at this absurd accusation, then adopted a haughty expression.

'I was given little choice but to enlist.'

'We all had a choice!'

'My own determined the safety, no, the very existence of my entire family!' Guang bit back angry words. 'I did not come here to justify myself to you.'

Then he realised that was exactly why he had come.

'I came here,' he said. 'Solely to see if you prospered and to offer any assistance within my power. To honour. . . our former friendship.'

Chen Song smiled thinly at Guang's strained dignity. There was something earnest and boyish and absurd about it, especially from so weathered a man.

'I do not need your assistance,' he said. 'But if you like I shall consider myself suitably honoured.'

'Good!' grunted Guang. 'That was my intention.'

They watched the twittering birds squabble over grain and scraps left over from the previous day's festival market. Chen Song's expression softened.

'Do you remember the crowd hailing you as Captain Xiao when you stood on that inn balcony over there?' he asked. 'I often think of those days. They were the best of my life.'

A hollow space in Guang's throat made him swallow hard. He laughed uneasily and Chen Song shot him a quick glance.

'A few days ago I recognised you at dawn on the battlements of Swallow Gate,' he said. 'I suspect we both went there for the same reason – to remember and mourn a little.'

Guang nodded.

'Anyway, after that I followed you back to Apricot Corner Court. There I discovered a most astounding and delightful thing. Your honoured sister-in-law's barrenness has become a stand of green, green bamboo! Who could have predicted so many sons and daughters! Yet when I made enquiries at a nearby tea stall the owner confirmed the children are your nephews and nieces.'

'There are five,' said Guang, proudly. 'Each is healthy and pleasant in its own way.'

'So I noticed.' Chen Song paused, looking at his former friend carefully, before adding: 'While I stood at that tea stall I had a strange thought. You might almost call those children your own. If you had not served the Great Khan not a single one of them would exist. Then I despised myself for allowing my anger to weaken. Sometimes anger is all that keeps me going.'

Guang bowed his head in recognition of such feelings. 'I have grown tired of anger,' he replied. 'The war has been over so long, Chen Song! And we lost! We *lost*. Now we must retrieve what we can from defeat. I want to live again, while I still may.'

'You sound like that old fool Wang Ting-bo or the countless others who justify disloyalty to the former dynasty!'

Guang looked round nervously to see if they were overheard, but the labourers had withdrawn and could be heard hammering and laughing at the back of the stage.

'Perhaps,' he said. 'Yet you are not fighting, Chen Song, as you could be. Loyalists to the old dynasty still hold out in the jungles of the south. Why not join them?'

'It is true, I could do that,' admitted Chen Song.

'Unless,' said Guang, pursuing a sudden thought. 'You have returned to acting in order to accomplish the same. . . secret mission as when I first met you.'

Chen Song laughed hollowly.

'You enquire whether I am a spy! If only that were so. There is no one left to spy for, Guang, that is the problem. No higher cause, just waking and eating and sleeping until the next day comes. I write and perform vulgar plays to fill a bowl with rice.'

'Is no other way possible?'

'You will be aware that, as a scholar, I am forbidden from holding office,' said Chen Song. 'According to the new emperor's laws I rank lower than a prostitute! So I write plays to suit the popular taste and chant mournful poems in secret.'

'I see,' said Guang.

Chen Song examined his old friend. 'Perhaps I could do a little spying on your behalf,' he said.

'Please explain.'

'I am planning to take my travelling show all the way to Chunming Province. When I get there I could ask how things fare in Wei Valley. The fee I ask for this service is sharing a dozen fiery bowls when I return. As we used to, all those years ago.'

'You are serious?'

'Why not? So long as we don't come to blows, of course. I'm quite flabby, you'd be sure to win.'

'Chen Song,' said Guang with great solemnity. 'When we parted, you asked me to aim a little to the side if I saw you in my crossbow's sights. I always checked if you were facing me.'

'I'm glad,' said Chen Song, dryly. 'And also glad we were never put to the test.'

Distant shouting reached them from the river. The dragon boat races were reaching a climax. Soon the streets would fill again and another performance must begin. Chen Song bowed in farewell and went round the stage to find out what the labourers were doing to his banner. Guang departed for Apricot Corner Court with a lighter step than he had known in a long while, unaware his old friend's sad gaze followed him until he vanished behind a high wall.

竹子

Spring winds stirred green buds and ruffled the downy feathers of chicks in their nests. The young felt it keenly, glancing slyly at one another. Roads were dusty and crops in the fields hardened their seeds.

The evening before the ceremony of *Treading the Green*, Guang produced a handful of sulphur matches he had bought at the market. It was traditional in Nancheng to await the sounding of one's ward bell before re-lighting household fires after the Cold Food Festival. Guang had enlisted his nephews and nieces in a way Cao found worrying, as did Shih, though he pretended amusement.

The bell tolled out the eighth watch and Guang ordered his eldest nephew to ignite a sulphur match. To everyone's surprise it flared almost at once. When the flame was dancing like a golden ear of corn, Guang allowed each child to kindle a taper and scamper to appointed stations round the courtyard. At his command they lit trails of black powder. Fizzing, flaring, white-hot snakes sped across the soil culminating in a series of loud thunder cracks and bangs that echoed into neighbouring courtyards. The youngest children were so excited they capered on the spot while Cao reproved their rowdiness. Uncle Guang chuckled at his brother's alarmed expression and went off to purchase yet more green wine from Mao's Refreshment Stall before the curfew drained the streets of life.

Ten thousand roosters greeted daybreak in the backyards and courts of Nancheng. For once the people were ahead of dawn. Old, young, men and women of every class and trade were up early, woken by an excitement reminiscent of childhood, that time when nothing is wholly familiar or taken for granted. And *Treading the Green* was never without consequence: bungling the rites might displease influential ancestors and bring unthinkable consequences.

Shih was mindful of this as he dressed in the quarter-light before dawn. Cao snored in the bed beside him, her face at peace. She had grown stout since the children came, though their demands were enough to make anyone gaunt. Yet she rarely complained. He knew unspoken fears often besieged her – illness or accident sweeping away a precious life, losses too painful to be imagined. And sometimes he shared her anxious thoughts.

But now Guang had returned he felt nothing could go very wrong for their family. What had been broken was again whole. Shih wondered at their good fortune. A jealous, grasping desire occasionally made him scheme to keep Guang within Apricot Corner Court forever. Yet such feelings never lasted long. Was he to become Guang's jailor as once he had been regarded by Father and poor Lu Ying?

Recollecting her brought Shih to the heart of his dilemma. For he questioned the propriety of Guang's intentions with regard to the dead lady. How would the ancestors regard her presence among them? Great-grandfather Yun Cai would surely greet her tolerantly. His faithful love for the singing girl Su Lin was still a matter of popular legend on account of his verses. Shih was less sure of the other ancestors. Grandfather had been notably stern when it came to unorthodox conduct. As for Father. . . well, he hardly counted. When Shih imagined the ancestors gathered together, Father was always relegated to a corner where he sat in silence like a naughty, wilful child who has behaved very, very badly. That image fanned bright a glow of satisfaction until he recalled certain harsh words and questionable medicines forced down the old man's throat – moments when he had behaved almost as badly as Father.

Treading the Green offered a chance to tame poison dragons and Shih was far too practical a man to let that chance pass. Yet now Guang threatened disharmony with his absurd demands – and all the while Shih knew he could deny his brother nothing.

'Are you unwell?' asked a sleepy voice.

He turned to see Cao propped on one elbow, looking up at him. The light piercing through gaps in the paper curtain left half his face in shadow. He did not reply but glanced at the floor.

'You are still troubled by Guang's plan,' she said.

'On a day when the dead draw near, who can help painful feelings?' he asked.

She reached out and took his hand.

'They are always near,' she said. 'You may be sure they want us to be happy. Even Lord Yun desires that now.'

'How do you know?'

'Because we are the only future they have left. If we pass away their memory dies with us. Such things are well known.'

The hissing, staccato bangs of firecrackers startled them.

Shih ran a weary hand across his eyes. No need to say who had provided the children with fireworks.

'Guang will make arsonists of them,' he muttered, hurrying into the courtyard. 'If he does not bankrupt us first by buying so much wine!'

Five penitent faces listened with downcast eyes as he admonished them for disturbing the neighbours' peace. But after he had gone the children simply found a different game to play.

Two hours later the entire family – including Mung Po and Ibn Rashid's Son – left Apricot Corner Court. Mung Po pushed a wheelbarrow laden with jars of wine and picnic food. It was the same wheelbarrow Shih and Cao had borrowed after her father's death, repaired many times and as sturdy as ever.

Led by the two brothers they proceeded up North Canal Street. The whole city was streaming beyond the walls, sick of confinement and eager to tread the green of fresh spring grass, to listen with wonder to mating birds. However, the Yun clan followed an unconventional route. Instead of joining countless thousands heading for the fields surrounding the city they turned into Xue Alley and soon arrived at the Water Gate of Morning Radiance.

A guard waved them through and they emerged onto a narrow strip of land between the ramparts and the River Han – the same place where Cao and Lu Ying had planted healing herbs. A little further downstream lay the rotting jetty where Shih had once recollected his enforced exile from Three-Step-House.

The base of a high, rectangular tower stood to one side; on the other spread endless *li* of water, twisting currents of shade and glitter, sinuous threads flowing all the way across the Middle Kingdom to swell rolling seas. For all its wild beauty – haunt of herons and wildflower, furze and butterfly – the strip of land was a strange place to tread the green. Indeed, the Yun clan had it quite to themselves.

Guang looked round while Mung Po and Ibn Rashid's Son unloaded sticks to build a fire for boiling water.

'When you told me we would be picnicking just outside the ramparts I did not anticipate *this*!' he said.

Shih coughed apologetically.

'When Father died the Mongols had just imposed new taxes on land purchase. I could not afford a plot of the best land, so I placed his gravestone here.'

'I see.'

'It occurred to me Father would like to be near water because he loved his fishes.'

'Perhaps.'

'Evidently you believe I was at fault!' whispered Shih, aware the children might overhear. 'But when Father died we were going hungry! My income dwindled along with everyone else's, especially after the Relief Bureau closed. It was the best I could do!'

Or a final act of revenge against the old man, thought Guang. Yet he remained silent. What saddened him was that he had heard his nephews speaking disrespectfully about their own grandfather. He could not doubt who had taught them such attitudes.

'We must make the best of it,' said Guang. 'When the time comes we shall restore Father's tablet to the ancestral shrine above Three-Step-House.'

Shih laughed.

'Do you still believe that time will come?'

'Yes! And your sons must be taught to believe it! And *their* sons. Until what was lost has been restored.'

Guang's voice echoed off the ramparts to the flowing river.

'I'm sure you are right,' said Shih.

They swept Lord Yun's gravestone at the foot of the ramparts, burning incense and offering food. As they did so, all were relieved to see other clans arriving to honour dead relatives who had been buried beside the city walls. Yet the newcomers were a decidedly cheap crowd and Dr Shih – aware his ancestors were watching – was inclined to forbid his children from playing with their offspring. But Cao whispered in his ear and he relented. Though their clothes marked them out as superior, the Yun children were soon throwing sticks into the river and digging muddy canals alongside the sons and daughters of mere artisans.

Guang took Shih to one side. He had rapidly drunk half a flask of special 'thrice-blessed' wine (the blessing had come from a sorcerer selling lucky spells in the market) and appeared agitated.

'I would like to do it now, Eldest Brother,' he said.

Shih blinked at this formal title; Guang had rarely used it since his return.

'As you wish.' Shih took his brother's arm. 'Do you have the contract?' he whispered.

A neatly rolled document appeared from Guang's girdle.

'Did you write it yourself?' asked Shih.

'No, I hired a scribe.'

'Ah. That is always more. . .' Shih struggled for the word. 'Yes, *proper*.'

The two stood uncertainly, watching the children throw handfuls of mud at each other. Cao and Mung Po rushed forward and the air filled with blame and declarations of innocence.

'Let's do it while they're busy,' said Shih. 'We need no other witnesses.'

They advanced across the thick grass to Father's grave tablet, bowing as they went. Guang had already cleared the earth in preparation. Now he laid down a plain stone tablet bearing the characters for Lu Ying and naming her: *First Wife of Yun Guang*. A carving of an oriole, so crude one might easily have mistaken it for a crow or gull, had been attempted by the mason. Even that had strained Guang's purse.

Once the tablet rested in the earth, Shih realised his brother had begun to sob and glanced round to see if the children had noticed. Guang's was a painful, gasping way of crying; sorrow dragged out by cruel hooks. Shih placed an arm on his brother's shoulder. Throughout these tears Cao's querulous voice continued to nag the children, threatening that Big Eyes Yang would punish them with his terrible voice.

'Burn the marriage contract now,' urged Shih. 'And remember to smile or her ghost will think you are not a happy groom.'

As though in a dream, Guang took the smouldering stick Shih fetched from the fire and lit the contract above Lu Ying's new grave tablet. The flames spread along its length. He held it until his fingers were scorched then dropped the ashes onto the carved stone.

'So you are now a widower,' said Shih. 'Lu Ying will clap with delight at the honour you show her.'

But Guang's thoughts were in another time, so he did not reply. He glanced up at the blue sky and noticed an oriole skimming over the river. Golden wing feathers and a scarlet beak flashed in the sun. Then the bird landed with a light flutter on the battlements above them and, to his surprise, began a sweet, clear song of trilling notes, all the while dipping and raising its head, peering this way and that. Guang stared up, his lips parted. For half Lu Ying's name meant oriole.

More tears gathered but he held them back. Shih was right, she must not see him weeping on their wedding day! Yet he longed to become a bird like her, to rise with her above the broad lands.

Still her song flowed as she crouched on the scarred stone of the fortifications. At last she fluttered golden wings one last time and flew upwards. Up, up until those she had known and loved were specks on a strip of land beside the flowing river.

Guang imagined that when she was truly high the Twin Cities themselves would diminish: Nancheng with its maze of streets and canals, its towers and decaying palace on Peacock Hill; Fouzhou where thousands toiled each day to rebuild what had been destroyed.

The oriole flew toward the sun rising over Mount Wadung and there he lost sight of her, blinded by white beams. He turned to tell Shih what had happened but found him gone. His brother had joined Cao in teaching the children how to identify and gather useful herbs – though it was quite obvious his real intention was to divert them from ruining their holiday clothes.

Guang shielded his eyes against the sun's brightness and stared up at Mount Wadung. She must be far away by now. But he sensed the meaning of the song she had trilled on the battlements – or possible meanings, so many were plausible. Perhaps she meant to tell him that forbearance outlasts all empires; that all are granted little and much, or. . . oh, he hardly knew what. Instead her lovely face filled his mind and he remembered her laughter and dignity as he lay wounded in Apricot Corner Court, the pleasing music of her voice. Her fragrance as she leant over him to straighten his pillow, and her sadness. Even when gay, she had retained a secret core of sadness.

In his very human ignorance he bowed to her grave tablet and wandered over to join his brother and sister-in-law. While Shih's pedantic voice explained to the children how the 'hidden rabbit root' benefits one's *qi*, not to mention *yang*, Guang drank the remaining half of his 'thrice-blessed' wine and watched the Han River wink a million silver eyes like fitful stars.

Author's Note

As with the first volume of this trilogy, *Taming Poison Dragons*, all characters and places are fictional apart from the Imperial capital, Linan, now known as Hangchow. However, military historians will detect echoes of the epic siege of Xianyang in the geography and fate of Nancheng. They might also scratch their heads over the dates. If so, I would advise them to waste no more time. My chief concern in terms of accuracy is not chronology, but a convincing depiction of human nature while not succumbing to anachronisms. If readers find that faulty, the fault is mine. Mankind's institutions, customs, culture and attitudes vary endlessly over the millennia, but I believe our essential humanity is more prone to continuity than change.

A note on gunpowder, invented by the Chinese in the 9th Century. Many might find the Song Dynasty's gunpowder weapons scarcely believable, yet none are fictional: fire lance, thunderclap bomb (we might use the word 'shrapnel'), rocket-propelled arrows. . . all were deployed to deadly effect. As were fleets of paddle-wheel warships.

Recently it has become popular to present history from the Mongol perspective in fiction. And why not – as long as one does not minimise the dreadful sufferings of those they slaughtered and the civilizations they permanently erased. They were not the first to believe destiny had granted them a right to conquer and rule the world. Sadly, they are not the last.

The third instalment of my trilogy, *The Mandate of Heaven*, will explore the Yun clan's continuing story in Mongol-occupied China.

Acknowledgements

Thanks to everyone at Gregory and Company, especially Stephanie Glencross whose incisive editorial advice smoothed my way. Thanks again to those people generous enough to read and comment on early drafts of the novel: Richard Murgatroyd; my parents, Dori and Jim Murgatroyd; Alex Quigley (who deserves special thanks for some very useful suggestions); and, last but not least, Bob Horne. Thanks also to Craig Smith for his illuminating thoughts on the writer's craft. Gratitude and appreciation, as ever, to my wife Ruth for her tireless support and inspiration. Finally, many thanks to Ed Handyside for his sharp editorial eye and for making this book possible.